A Conversation with the Mann

also by John Ridley

Everybody Smokes in Hell

Love Is a Racket

Stray Dogs

A Conversation
with the Mann

a novel

John Ridley

WARNER BOOKS

An AOL Time Warner Company

Warner Books, Inc., 1271 Avenue of the Americas, New York, NY 10020

Visit our Web site at www.twbookmark.com.

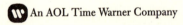 An AOL Time Warner Company

Printed in the United States of America

First Printing: June 2002

10 9 8 7 6 5 4 3 2 1

Library of Congress Cataloging-in-Publication Data

Ridley, John, 1965-
    A conversation with the Mann / John Ridley.
      p. cm.
    ISBN 0-446-52836-6
    1. African American comedians—Fiction. 2. Harlem (New York, N.Y.)—Fiction.
3. Civil rights movements—Fiction. 4. African American men—Fiction. 5. Comedians—
Fiction. 6. Racism—Fiction. I. Title.

    PS3568.I3598 C66 2002
    813'.54—dc21
                                                      2001052605

I
II
III
IV JER V

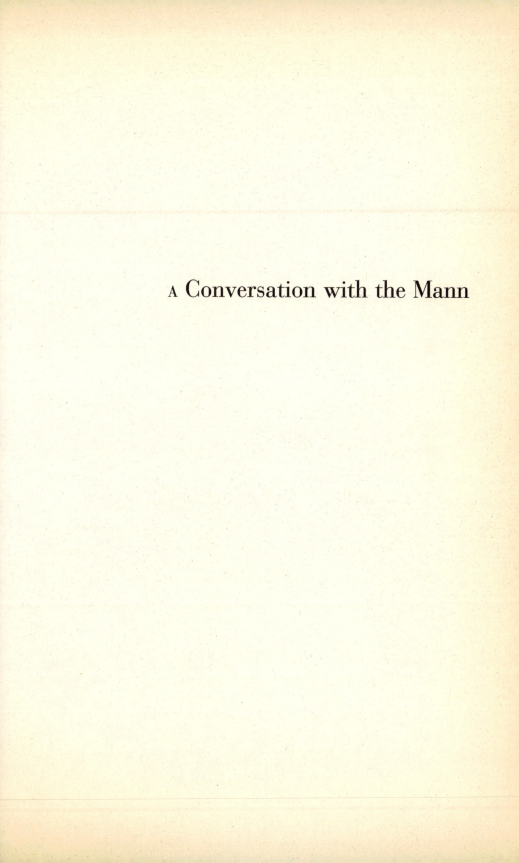

A Conversation with the Mann

Introduction

The Green Kitchen was where I first met Jackie Mann. The Green Kitchen was on Manhattan's Upper East Side. The Green Kitchen was a little restaurant/diner kind of place where me and the boys—Sweeny, Richie, Raider, God bless him—used to chow down after doing sets at The Strip, Catch, and Stand Up, among very few other comedy clubs we were limited to working. That is, if you call hanging out till two A.M. hoping to go on for the six people left in the audience working. But that's what we did, hang out, because the two A.M. slot was when all the hotshot club bookers—who used to be bartenders before the comedy boom in the eighties turned their saloons into comedy spots and made them hotshot club bookers— would swing young comics like us. Of course, the eighties ended, and so did the comedy boom, and most of the clubs closed and the hotshot club bookers went back to being bartenders. But that's not the story I'm trying to tell.

I'm trying to tell the story of how I met Jackie Mann at the Green Kitchen, where us wannabe comics used to chow down. It was a good hangout. After a hard night of fifteen minutes of joke telling, there was much griping to be done and many road stories to be swapped. One morning, post-griping and swapping, when the boys were ready to head home, I took our collected money to the counter to pay the bill. Standing there was an old black guy who mumbled at me: "Gimme a dollar. I don't have enough to pay for my fries," or something close to that. The man didn't look shabby or indigent. He just looked like a guy who'd left home a little short and was asking to get covered for a buck. But he'd said what he said sharp and matter-of-fact. He said it like I owed him a dollar. He said it in a way that made me think the entire world owed him a little something.

I gave him two dollars.

I got no thank-you from him. He said, instead, that he had seen me around a few times and wondered what I was doing at the Green Kitchen so late at night, and I told him I was a comedian and he laughed a little and said "Yeah?" and I said "Yeah" and he said "You know, I used to be a comic."

I didn't know that, not even knowing who this old black guy was.

He told me his name was Jackie Mann and I told him—young and cocky like I used to be—my name, and that he should remember my name because one day my name was going to be real well known. One day I was going to be very famous.

Jackie laughed again. *At* me. And then he told me that I shouldn't get any ideas about being a star, because that's all they would most likely ever be.

This time I did the laughing. Who was this guy to tell me I wasn't going to be famous? All of us, me and the boys—Sweeny and Richie and Raider, God bless him—were going to be big.

Didn't much work out that way. Sweeny went on to write gags for talk shows, Richie kept plugging away in the club scene in New York. Raider . . . God bless him. But that's not the story I'm trying to tell.

I'm trying to tell the story of how, after I met Jackie Mann, I couldn't quite get him out of my head. I don't know why. I had never heard of him, and that right there should've made him very forgettable. I was a comic and I knew comics and I don't just mean the big guys with the sitcoms or the bigger guys with the movie deals. Pigmeat Markham, Olsen and Johnson, Ernie Kovacs, Godfrey Cambridge, George Kirby. Famous or not, black or white, I knew my history, and if I didn't know anything about Jackie Mann, then Jackie Mann wasn't worth the energy it took to speak his name.

Still . . .

The way he laughed at me, said to forget about having big dreams, it made me think he knew what he was talking about.

There was a comedienne who hung out with me and the boys whose father used to work in television back in the golden age. I asked her to ask her dad if he had ever heard of Jackie Mann.

She asked him.

Boy, had he heard of Jackie Mann. He remembered, pretty clearly, the stories that I would come to know real well: Jackie's days doing shows at the Copa and Ciro's, mixing company with the likes of Sinatra, Dino, and Damone. His on again, off again, up/down relationship with his girl Tammi, the surprise wedding, the thing with the Fran Clark show. And, of course, the Sullivan show.

I feel embarrassed now, listing events and incidents that, remembered and familiar to many, were once unknown to me. I feel ashamed that a guy like me, a guy who thought he knew a thing or two about the history of both comedy and his people, was so completely ignorant.

I chose to be ignorant no more.

I went back to the Green Kitchen a few times before happening across Jackie again, and asked him—begged him—to share his memories with me.

Thankfully, he did.

And over many plates of french fries Jackie told me tales of a long-gone era with a verve and lingo that made every moment fresh and vivid. Putting Jackie's story on record—a story of time and place and history—has taken well more than a decade. It waited as I went from New York to Los Angeles, from stand-up to television and screenwriting to finally—thankfully—publishing. Fortunately, like a fine wine, Jackie's is a story that has only gotten better with age.

And that is the story I'm trying to tell.

John Ridley
March 28, 2002
Hollywood, California

L et me tell you:
You stop. You can't go on. Can't say another word. The clapping roadblocks you; the sound of the flesh of a thousand hands beating against each other. Men's hands—manicured, most likely, and pinky-ring-decorated. Women's hands—most likely jeweled on five or six or seven out of ten fingers; rings that match bracelets that match necklaces that match earrings. Most likely. You don't know. Not for sure. To all that you're blinded: the gems, the bouffants and pompadours, the sharkskin suits and the satin dresses; you're blinded to the high style of the times. The arc light spotting you cuts your vision and knocks down the people and all their finery to a silhouetted mass—a living ink blot—that jukes and jives and howls as a single thing.

Let me tell you:

It's better that way. Better they should be unreal and unintimidating, and that you are ultrareal, illuminated. Glowing. Three feet taller on the stage where you stand over the tables where they sit. Sight gone, all you're left with is the taste—yeah, the taste—and smell of the people; the smoke belched train-style from Fatimas and Chesterfields, chewably thick and unavoidably swallowed, but overpowered by twenty varieties of perfumes that run the scale of stink from Chanel to Woolworth's. You're left with the sound of the thousand hands and the whistles and the roaring voices with the occasional call that comes after a joke: "That's true. That's funny 'cause it's true." And all that keeps you from saying another word. You can't go on.

So, let me tell you:

I didn't go on. I stopped and I stood and waited for that ink blot to finish cracking up. I stood and I waited and I soaked up its applause and affection. I waited, and the waiting took time. The time the waiting took made the second show in the Copa Room at the Sands hotel and casino in Las Vegas, Nevada, run long. Like an unbreakable law of nature, the second rule of casinos was that the entertainment shows never ran long. The first rule was that you let the customer drink for free. Drink for free, eat for free, lodge for free . . . Generally you kept 'em happy so that you could keep 'em at the tables, where the odds are so stacked against them it's nothing but easy to separate money from their well-liquored, well-fed fingers. But for the casino to get their dough the customer had to be at the tables, and they couldn't be at the tables when they were in the show room laughing it up, swinging to some crooner, or otherwise engaged in non-gambling. The management, the boys from New York and Chicago and Miami—a balancing act of strong-armed Italians and slick-minded Jews—who quietly, very quietly, ran the casinos, didn't much care for their customers to be non-gambling. They hadn't traveled from city to desert to open a chain of hospitality suites. So rule number two: The entertainment shows never ran long. Hardly ever. The first day of October 1959 was an exception; twenty-four hours that were particular otherwise only in their insignificance: The Russians were behaving themselves. The Donna Reed show was new to TV. It'd only been a bunch of months since Barbie's first date with America. Freshly fifty-stated America. Other than that it was just another Ike-is-president Castro-is-evil Elvis-is-God day. Except, the second show in the Copa Room at the Sands hotel and casino in Las Vegas, Nevada, did the unthinkable and ran long, and it ran long because of me, and I wasn't worried in the least about upsetting the Italians or the

Jews. I was the opening act for Mr. Danny Thomas. The opener of any show got exactly six and a half minutes to warm up the audience for exactly forty-three and a half minutes of headline, straight-from-Hollywood, star-powered entertainment before they were herded back out to the casino for another complimentary mugging. But on that night, same as a lot of nights, I'd killed. I hadn't just done well; I'd slain the crowd, left that ink blot flopping in the aisles. I had to stand and wait for the people to drain themselves of laughs and claps.

Some headliners don't dig an opener going over big. You get rolling and they'll have you yanked two and a third into your six and a half. The show is about them and only them, and don't even try to give them something to follow. But Danny Thomas wasn't Charlie Small-time. Danny Thomas was the spit-taking star of the number four Nielsen-rated show on television. Danny Thomas could follow whatever I put out and take it higher. He tossed me the signal to stretch, to do an extra couple of minutes. An extra couple of minutes that would make the long show run even longer. So what? The management wasn't so Guido they didn't know an audience *that* good-time high translated into a bunch of crazy bets once they got back to the tables.

So let me do some extra bits.

Keep that customer happy.

I finally wrapped and Danny hit the stage, bringing me back out for a few bows. As he launched into a trademarked "Danny Boy"—the backing band big and brassy—and rode the crowd into his own special groove, I took up a spot at the back of the room, got perspective, and started questioning myself: How did I get here? A black kid from Harlem working the finest club in the glitziest city in the world, opening up for one of the biggest acts in entertainment. After only a handful of years of really making a break in show business, and there was almost nothing I didn't have. There was almost nothing I couldn't do.

Nothing, except walk out the doors of the Copa Room and into the casino itself.

It was 1959, and the only difference between Las Vegas, Nevada, and Birmingham, Alabama, was that down South they posted signs telling a black man where he couldn't go and what he couldn't do: WHITES ONLY, COLOREDS NOT ALLOWED. In Vegas you had to figure that out on your own. You figured it out quick-style. Stay off the Strip, stay in Westside. Stay the hell away from *their* casinos. Didn't matter how well you did in the show room, didn't matter how much the audience laughed or clapped or how many bows you took, *out there* it was still 1959, and *out there* blacks weren't welcome. Not to stay overnight. Not to eat. Not to gamble.

More than anything in the world I wanted to gamble.

Not for the jazz of laying a bet, or the sake of wagering money. What I wanted was to stand at a table with all those people—suited men, ladies in their best dresses—living high and living fast and living Cocktail Society. I wanted to see them do a Red Sea–part as I made my way to the roulette wheel and listened to all their starstruck bits: "Great job tonight, Jackie." "Heck of a show, Jackie. Don't know when I cracked up as much." "Would you mind saying hello to the Mrs., Jackie? She's such a big fan of yours. It would mean so much." I wanted them to fawn and gush and throw me their love same as they threw it at me when I was performing, when I was standing three feet above them.

I wanted them to accept me.

Accept me? They couldn't even see me. I got paid nearly a grand a week, I got pulled back up onstage to do more time by the biggest stars alive, I got standing O's . . . And when it was all over I got sent out the back door.

You know what went out the back?

Trash went out the back. Stinking garbage and rotting food and black comics got sent straight to the alley, never mind how well they'd just done in the show room.

Danny Thomas had the audience swinging. He had to swing them hard to keep them from thinking back and recalling a bit I'd done and murmuring about me. I was that good.

I felt warm. I felt vain. I felt a shot of pride, and it made me high.

And then I did it. No back-and-forth debate with myself, no working my way to a decision. I just did it. I just pushed open the doors and walked out of the Copa Room and into the casino.

Loud as the casino was with all the pinging of slot machines and the mucking of chips, with crisp new money being crackled across the green felt, I swear the second I took step one onto the floor the place went morgue silent and twice as cold. I could hear every whisper. I could *hear* every look. Some of the looks said: Isn't that Jackie Mann? A few said: I didn't know this joint was progressive. Most of the looks said and said quite clearly: What the hell is a nigger doing in here?

And all that big-star bravado I'd carried with me melted from their hot stares and quiet contempt. I got the shakes. I got the sweats. I could feel a sheen of it collecting across my forehead. I remembered those pictures of the Little Rock kids, the ones who'd integrated the high school. I remembered the Jesus-don't-lynch-me fear sopped up in their race memory that seeped from the cracks in all that stoic jazz they put on. I knew that's how I must have looked just then: Jackie Mann, Negro agitator for gambling rights.

But I kept on. Doing my best high-class bits, I swaggered Peter Lawford–style for the roulette wheel, my eyes on the prize. A hundred-dollar bill came up out of my pocket. Let them all see. Let them see how big Jackie Mann plays. I just hoped they couldn't see the sweat stain that Ben Franklin's face had soaked up from my palm.

So close to the table . . .

That's when I got stopped. Blocking my path, one of the casino housemen—horned into a suit that didn't begin to cover his heft—planted himself between me and the roulette wheel.

"No" was all he said. That plain. That simple. That harsh. Not "I'm sorry, Mr. Mann" or "You know the rules, Mr. Mann" or at least "Hey, Charlie, beat it before you find out what hot water is." He just said no like I was some dog he had to scold for soiling his favorite afghan.

Everywhere else in the casino the stares got louder, they encouraged the chucker to do something about the uppity colored who'd wandered into their playground.

I tried to peek around the guy. If I couldn't gamble, at least let me see the table up close. At least let me get tossed from the floor having accomplished that much. Or that little. I couldn't hardly see anything. The goon was not an easy cat to look around.

He said to me again, "no," then cracked the knuckles of his right fist, weeded with black hair, in the clutch of his left hand. The sound was the same as rocks getting crunched. This one got paid to deal with trouble. Trouble was what he was hoping I'd give him. Hell, trouble or no, he was ready to throw me a beat down just for practice—one more in a string of abuses I'd been taking the whole of my life.

Defeat crawled over me. Humiliation crawled with it.

From behind: a hand on my shoulder.

Swell, I thought. The houseman's got pals. A beating was about to come at me from all sides, front and back, panoramic and in Vista-Vision.

Except . . . The houseman's eyes went wide and his lips started to jump around. A lyrical voice behind me said to the heavy, told him: "It's okay. Charlie here's with me."

First off I thought it was Jack Entratter, the hey-boy who fronted the Sands for its out-of-town owners, who'd stepped in to square things for me. But as I looked, I saw the hand on my shoulder was dark-skinned. Dark-skinned to the point it made me look octoroon. The sight of it was a sock that knocked me over to Queer Street.

What black man, what black man in Las Vegas in 1959 could put that kind of fear into a roughneck on the casino payroll?

I turned and I saw. I turned and I looked into the eyes, the one good eye, of Mr. Sammy Davis, Jr.

In America, in the late 1930s:

The average annual income for a white male was right around three thousand dollars. A black male earned about half that.

One in eight white men couldn't find work. For black men it was one in four.

On average a white man could expect to live sixty-one years. A black man, ten years fewer.

Per year, just about sixteen blacks were killed by lynching— hung or burned or beaten to death.

Officially.

That is the world I came into.

Early On

I don't think you can imagine the loneliness of a child born different. Not physically different, not handicapped, not deformed or marked. A child born different in a way you can't describe or recognize, but that's just as real as the kid with a bad leg or mangled hand—always the outcast, always the one standing in a corner, ghostlike, watching the rest of the world parade by. It's as if there's something about him, some odd and un-normal thing inside him, invisible but clearly advertising he's not the same as everyone else. The response from everyone else being laughs and ridicule because they don't know what to do with a kid born different except to mock it. And that feeling of not belonging, of lonely isolation in a world of people and the knowing that you will never ever be like them and will never ever be accepted by anyone . . . It's a feeling that lasts a lifetime. It's a scar that never fades.

I WAS BORN IN HARLEM. More than that, the specifics, the exact where and when of the event, are lost to me. By the time I was old enough to want to know those things about me I had no one to ask. My pop, Kenneth Mann, and I didn't talk much. My mother, Anna, I couldn't talk to at all. What I can say for certain is the fondest memory I have of my childhood is the day I was able to leave it all behind me.

I was an only child. The only child my mother would have, and the only child my father would want, and to say "want" is an assumption, as he often made my desirability questionable. My father was a big man, over six feet and carrying nearly two hundred pounds, and is best described as a combination of angry and pathetic. His anger was easy to understand. He was a black man, and being a black man in the early parts of the twentieth century would be enough to give the mildest of men some rage. He was a poor man, too. Even in the North, the industrial, progressive North, finding a steady, good-paying job was a trick he never got down to habit. My father took whatever work he could: a shoe shine, a bathroom attendant, a janitor in the subway system. A newsboy. A grown man, six feet plus, working as a newsie. "Don't Look" jobs, I heard my father call them. The people you serve don't look at you while you clean their shoes, pass them a towel to dry their hands. Just do your work, make change for their crisp new fives and tens, and give them a "Thanks yuh, suh" when you're done. To them you don't exist. You don't matter. I said before: Pop's anger I could understand.

What I couldn't understand was him being so pitiful. It had to do with, I guess, his accident. About as far back as I can remember my pop had been debilitated. At one point he had worked in construction. Not as any kind of skilled laborer or tradesman. Blacks didn't much get the education needed for that kind of work, and if they did they just plain didn't get that kind of work. So my father, like a lot of other black fathers, was a human pack-mule: lifting lumber, carrying bricks. Doing whatever kind of labor was too much or too hard or too far beneath the whites. One day, on the job, he'd injured himself, his back or hip lifting or hauling or doing whatever. I'm not exactly sure how. I'm not exactly sure how badly. He walked fine, without much of a limp I could see. Had no problem with stairs or heavy loads that I could tell. But he was hurt. So he'd say. He was hurt enough to stop working and start on the dole. Start, and never quit. Why should he? To his way of thinking, why should he slave; why shine shoes or shill newspapers when he could be handed money? Why try when not trying paid the same? With nothing else to do, he passed the hours with booze, and pretty soon, when a liquor buzz couldn't last him the day, he graduated to grass and pills. Pop became an equal-opportunity abuser. He would drink anything too thin to eat. He would smoke anything you could roll. In a tight spot, glue in a bag would do just fine. His highs expressed themselves with their own personalities. The speed high that kept him jittery and dancing, eager to get somewhere even though he had nowhere to be. His booze high was a sullen low that put heat to the anger he carried. It recognized no one, came at whoever crossed it with swinging fists looking to pay back the whole world for all the no-good it'd handed him. And there was the weed high that kept Pop laughing when there was nothing to laugh at. Didn't matter. Pop would make up things to laugh about, act a clown and laugh at himself if he had to. He would make noises, do big, broad pantomimes of people who lived in the building. Put on a whole little crazy act. Watching him was no different from watching a program on television. Better than that. A TV show didn't chase you around the apartment, tickle you to the ground when it caught you. A TV show didn't take you, lift you in the air, smile at you with a grin that was almost coonish but full of love, and tell you: "You my boy, Jackie. That's my boy." And me and Mom would laugh along and play along, and bad as things were, even though we were laughing at a man lifted on dope, for a while Pop could make us forget the troubles we lived with. If I had to pick, without a doubt that was my favorite high. Thing of it was, the pop I left when I went to school in the morning was never the same one I returned to at night. That made going home real frightening, every step of the walk asking: Is there a hug waiting for me, or a slap? A story that won't end, or a whupping that'll go on and on? Sometimes I'd be too scared to climb the stairs to the apartment. Long after the other kids had gone home for dinner and there was no one to play with, I'd sit on the stoop of our building and try to listen through all the other noises that fought each other in the city. If I could hear laughing from our apartment, I'd go up. If I heard screaming, crashing dishes . . . Well, it got so I taught myself to sit on the stoop well into night when I had to.

But no matter the high, Pop was high. Always. The drink and drugs made him useless, and being useless—a father that was no good for his family—that's what made him pathetic. That left caring for the family, what the three of us had that passed for a family, to my mother.

My mother was beautiful. I remember that most about her. She was a very dark-skinned lady, from the Caribbean, or at least her family was. She had soft features and was a little plump, which made her face more round than angular. Her hair had no kink. It was wavy and near shoulder-length, what back then got called "good hair." In my memory, my mother was without blemish.

What else I remember is Mom worked hard to give us what Pop's aid couldn't: decent food and wearable clothes. Our home, our apartment—a couple of rooms off three flights of stairs—was what you would call a "make-do" home. We made do with bread when there was no meat to stick between the slices. We made do with watery soup when there was no bread. We made do with the occasional rat because they ate the cockroaches that infected every dark corner. In the winters we were always cold, but we never froze. We were always hungry, but we never starved. Somehow, because of Mom, we always made do.

Mom was a domestic. Domestic was polite for maid. She was a cleaning woman for the white folks on the East Side and the Upper West Side, any side of town she could find a floor that needed to be scrubbed, a toilet that could use some polishing. Mom worked a lot. Work was easy for her to find. People liked her. She was honest. She was, I remember, cheerful. She would wake up mornings early and fix me breakfast, doing little extras like cutting strawberries and leaving them for me to put on my cereal, then go out into the dark before dawn to ride a subway to the first of four, five apartments or houses she would clean that day. She would come home again, late, tired, but not so tired that she couldn't make me a meal, wash me, then put me to bed. And every night after my mother turned out the light I would feel a butterfly kiss on my forehead. Then I would hear her voice in the dark whispering to me: "You're a special one, Jackie Mann. Don't let nobody ever tell you otherwise."

Special, she would say. Different, I would think.

After that Mom would leave, but through the door, before I fell asleep, I could hear her humming or whistling a tune. I could hear her laughing at something funny that must have come across her mind.

Sometimes I could hear her arguing with my pop. More than sometimes. Truth is, he did most of the arguing—about how we were broke because Mom didn't work hard enough, or about how no matter everything else she had to do she didn't keep our apartment straight enough, or about how she hadn't come home with his nightly bottle of booze soon enough. But with all that I never recall once hearing Mom cry with despair or sigh with the weight of the day that would only get added to tomorrow. I never heard her complain when my father would stumble in at all hours from a late-night binge, breath so strong it filled the apartment with a gin perfume, and pass out on the bed or the couch or, if his aim was off, the middle of the floor. Despite her life, my mother was without gripe. All I ever remember hearing from my mother were gentle songs she sang to herself late into the night.

───

MY HARLEM WAS NOT IN RENAISSANCE. My Harlem, the Harlem I grew up in, was no longer a colony of black culture—no longer home to Hughes and Barthe, Ellington and Webb—but had declined into a ghetto for the colored. Colored is what we were. Not yet Negro or black and a long way from being African American. In the day we were colored. At best. Mostly we were *them,* and *those people* when we weren't just plain old niggers. And while we had things better than blacks down South—easy on the Jim Crow, light on lynchings—being black in Harlem came with its own troubles.

The Depression had hurt everyone. Everyone was looking for a way to earn money. Out-of-work whites started taking menial jobs they'd previously thought worthy only of blacks. Blacks were left with no jobs at all. But still they kept coming to Harlem, blacks from other parts of New York. Southern blacks and Jamaican blacks and blacks from the West Indies. They crammed into tenement buildings and row housing, jammed themselves into apartments that were divided, then subdivided again, all in the belief that living in the black capital of the world would give them opportunities they wouldn't have anywhere else. They believed wrong. Harlem became one block after another of folks who couldn't get work enough to keep food on the table.

Mornings would find a string of humanity—weary-looking men, mothers with children, most in the po' folk's uniform of secondhand clothes worn threadbare—on a corner of 131st Street, stretched a block or more, waiting to rub a hand over the trunk of the Tree of Hope. The tree was just a tree, nothing special about it except that people believed with a blind desperation in a myth that had grown with the wood: that it had the power to bring good luck. The luck being whoever touched it would find a job. Any job. I don't know if I realized it then, or just felt it later: How sad it was to see so many black people, their belief in themselves so worn away, their only faith was superstition.

Into the decay, mix poor housing, poor facilities, poor schools and education. Add the heat of summer, and you've cooked yourself up a riot. It's what happens when you treat humans like animals and keep them in a twenty-by-twenty-block cage. Riots are what happen when you take away a person's status, when the only voice you leave them is the self-expression of violence. Twice in my era Harlem burned. Once in 1934 after a white store-owner beat a black teenager for shoplifting maybe a nickel's worth of goods. The second came in 1943 when a white cop shot a black serviceman who'd come to the aid of a drunk woman. A drunk white woman. Didn't matter it was a northern city—New York City. A black man who mixed with a white woman could usually count on nothing better than a bullet for his trouble.

But Harlem, even in decline, had its own flavor. For most living there it never occurred to live anywhere else. Each street and building spilled with life. From any given fire escape came the sound of a young man working his sax or horn, while down below, girls would double-Dutch to his riffs. There was all manner of food cooking night and day: Jamaican food, Caribbean food, West Indian food. Soul food. The whole of Harlem was an open-air kitchen, and the smells would find their way into every inch of every block. Fire hydrants were for hot days, and parked cars were for dodging snowballs in winter. And beyond Harlem was New York City. New York City, with parks and trains and skyscraper canyons, was like a whole wide world unto itself. The world belonged to me and Li'l Mo, Li'l Mo being my best friend. Don't recall how we got to be friends. He lived in the building next to mine, but so did about a hundred other kids.

Other kids didn't get along with me.

Other kids didn't like me.

Other kids thought I was different.

Mo was and always would be short for his age. He was plump, but in years would burn off enough fat to pass for stocky. He had very dark skin, and sitting in the middle of his otherwise large, round head were very narrow eyelids. So narrow you'd think, from looking at him, his eyes were no good for seeing. Sometimes he would stand outside of five-and-dimes pretending to be blind just to get free candy. He got a lot of free candy. The other peculiar thing about Li'l Mo was his ears. They weren't all crinkled and curved like most people's. They were a solid mass of flesh, looking like a mold someone had filled with hot wax but forgot to scrape clean. A kid had teased Mo about his ears one time. Mo beat the boy silly. He got sent out of school for two weeks for that, but no one ever said anything about Li'l Mo's ears again.

Maybe because, same as me, he knew what it was like to be different, me and Mo took to each other. Together we took to the streets: The subway was an all-day roller coaster to be ridden from the Bronx to Brooklyn and back again. Central Park was always good to roam, a big Cracker Jack box with a daily surprise. It's where Mo and I saw our first naked woman, a lady bum, dirt caked, breasts stretched balloons, taking a bath in the lake. She was scaly and hideous. Even from a distance you could smell her stink. But same as with a carnival freak, as she washed, not me or Li'l Mo could peel our eyes from her. We stared long and hard. The peep show ended when a couple of beat pounders splashed out into the lake to get the woman. She gave them a good wrestling, but they finally got her out of the water. Me and Mo hooted the cops as they hauled our introduction to womanhood away.

There was an evening I came home from running the streets with Mo. We'd been playing for I don't know how long when we headed back to the apartment building where I lived. Outside on the stoop were a lot of people standing around and carrying on. I didn't think anything of it. New York, Harlem, a stoop was a social club where everything from Plessy vs. Ferguson to Bebop versus Traditional got discussed. I didn't think much, either, when all them people looked at me coming, then looked away, not wanting to catch my eye. They shuffled from my path, all quiet and nervous, as I walked into the lobby. By then an ill feeling was walking with me. I was a child, but old enough to know that when adults got quiet and nervous, there was always some badness around.

I was not hardly ready for the badness waiting for me.

At the bottom of the stairs that led to our apartment, sprawled among groceries that had spilled back down from the first landing with her, was my mother. Dead. Climbing the stairs to fix dinner, or wash clothes, or just do whatever it took to make it through another night before the next long day, her heart gave out. Quit, as if it had suddenly decided the hard and thankless life my mother lived wasn't worth the effort it took to pump her blood. So it let her off the hook. It let her die.

Alone.

I wasn't around. I'd been off playing when maybe I could've been home helping out, doing chores, doing something to lessen my mother's burden.

My father wasn't around. He'd been out lessening his own burden with liquor.

I stood for what seemed like a day short of forever, staring at my mother heaped right where she was. All those people around, and no one bothered to cover her or move her. No one came to take me away and lie to me about how everything was going to be all right and how my mother had just gone on to a better place.

I guess that part wouldn't have been a lie. Not by much.

But all those people, they did nothing. They just viewed the scene in confused quiet—an audience come to see a show, but disappointed with what they got for their money.

In time Grandma Mae, who wasn't my grandma or anyone's grandma but just a nice old lady from up the block who everybody loved and everybody called Grandma, came and took me to her apartment. She gave me some moo juice to drink and told me it was all right to cry if I wanted.

So I cried.

Eventually Grandma Mae took me back to my apartment building. Mama's body was gone. So were the groceries that had spilled to the floor with her. We climbed the stairs, passing the landing that had ended my mother's life, and went inside.

Eventually my pop came home, his breath filling the space with its usual stink of booze. Grandma Mae told him what had happened to Mom.

He stood where he was for a second, looking shocked. Then he said: "Goddamn it. You know how much them caskets cost?"

WITH THE PASSING OF MOM life changed. Changed more than just me missing her every minute of every hour. Pop may have been the only adult in the house, but Mom being gone made him no more of a parent. Opposite of that, he became less of one. With the guilt he carried, that I hoped to God he carried, without Mom around to mellow him, or maybe just because he was free to live any way he wanted, Pop applied himself to being an addict of the lowest order, trading his many highs for one. The angry, sullen one. It's only variation: Either he was awake and in a mood to hit something, or plain passed out. If ever he was in no condition to work, to provide, he only got more that way. Relief bought *his* basic needs: drinking money to pay for his benders, rent money to pay for a roof to pass out under. Food money, clothes money, money for any other thing *we* needed to get by had to come from somewhere else.

Somewhere else was me.

And very instantly my days of being a kid—running the streets, playing—were over. Not even in my teens and I was working whatever job I could find for whatever money I could make. Mostly it was piece work, sympathy work: shop owners who knew my mom was dead and my pop was dead drunk and let me do what I could around their stores—washing dishes, washing windows, scrubbing floors. Between trying to go to school and whatever time I had on weekends, if there was something to be cleaned, brushed, swept, or polished, my little black hands were having at it. At too young an age I learned what labor was. Hard labor. I got an education in what it was like to come home every night, fingers cramped in the shape of a scrub brush and a hot ache in my stooped back.

At the end of the first week of what felt like a month of slaving, I counted the money I'd earned. I counted the nickels and the pennies, the two quarters I'd been given. Three dollars in total. Not even. All together it was something near thirty cents short of that. One week. How many hours? Three dollars. Not even.

I started to cry. I cried for myself and my youth that was gone. I cried for my mother, for the life I now knew—knew by experience—she'd lived; empty work muled through from morning deep into night. I cried for my future—in sudden, sharp focus—of me being no better, no different than a poor dumb animal that labored only for the sake of living to labor another day.

When I got done crying, I took my almost three dollars and put it in a jar that got hidden in a drawer. I put myself to bed and slept. I got up to work again.

Eventually I found steady work with Sergeant Kolawole, who ran a reclamation shop. A junk dealer is what he was. He'd find busted fans and radios and clocks, fix them up, sell them again. In an area where buying things new was strictly a luxury, Sergeant Kolawole did himself a good business. But the straight-from-the-garbage scrap made his shop filthy. Cleaning it was hard work. Harder was sitting through the sergeant's stories. According to him, he had been a resistance fighter in Ethiopia and had been forced to flee to America just ahead of the Italian army. That was basically the tale. The details were always changing, and never interesting. But the sergeant paid good, so I listened like I cared.

When I wasn't odd-jobbing it, I was in school. School being no more pleasure than work. Besides being whipped from scraping and scrubbing, besides falling behind because I didn't have any time to study—no one at home to help me study—I was very quickly becoming the target of every wise-cracking kid there was. With the little money we had, the little I made and the little my father didn't drink or shoot or sniff away, there wasn't much for new clothes or shoes. As raggedy as most every other Harlem kid might have been, with my too-short pants and ventilated shirts I looked as if I'd just made a break from the poor farm. Kids aren't kids until they've got someone to pick on—the fat kid or the kid with glasses. Now they had a new one: po' boy Jackie.

I was an easy target.

I was different.

I got hit with every sharp remark there was: "Just come in from the cotton fields, Jackie?" "Jackie, don't you know Lincoln done freed the slaves?" "You ain't foolin' us, Jackie. You ain't colored; you just dirty." Bad as all that was, worse was when, time to time, some of the kids would give me pennies and tell me to polish up their shoes or fetch them something like I was their nigger. That hurt the most—getting treated like a nobody. It made me angry they didn't respect me, didn't care how hard I had to work to provide for me and my father. But hurt as I was, angry as I was, I wasn't so much of either that I didn't take their pennies. The shame, the humiliation I felt, was my own. But so was their money. Every little bit helped.

I saved up what I didn't spend, always making very sure I had enough money to go out and buy my father a high if he was too strung out to do the job himself. In Harlem, highs were easy to come by. Everywhere else in the city the police might've been cracking down on pushers and addicts, but across 125th Street it was just coloreds getting lifted. Coloreds robbing coloreds to get lifted. Coloreds killing coloreds because they were lifted. So what? Coloreds? Let 'em bleed.

Not that there's any right age for it, but I was far too young to be buying liquor and such. I brought that up to my father once, the fact that a kid had no business running down to a corner or dark alley and copping dope. He smacked me in the head so hard it made my ear bleed. We never discussed my age and his drugs again.

Sundays were good days, about the only decent time clinging to the skeleton of my childhood. Sundays were when I used to go to Grandma Mae's for dinner. I would make the walk of a couple of blocks around five o'clock in the evening, my father not much caring if I was going to see her or going to play on the third rail of the IRT line. Not caring so long as I'd remembered to leave him a bottle of booze or a bag of grass.

More than a block from Mae's and already you could smell her cooking: glazed ham, apple fritters, bread fresh made and hot. The aromas alone would have just about floated you to her door if you didn't know the way. Sometimes it would be only me and Mae for dinner. Most times she would invite others from the neighborhood. Maybe a single mother who didn't have much to feed her kid. Maybe a widower who would otherwise be sitting alone, again, eating some of whatever out of a can. So on and so forth like that. If there was a soul in the neighborhood who was in need, Mae was there to provide.

While Mae finished making dinner I would do chores for her around the apartment; clean or scrub whatever needed it. If she had a leg loose on a chair I'd nail it, a rusty hinge would get oiled. All the other work I did during the week was just warm-up for the kind of muscle I'd put into what Grandma Mae needed done. Everyone else, no matter how well meaning, just gave me money in exchange for my labor. Mae gave me love.

Dinner conversation stretched for hours, Mae with endless stories about life as a girl growing up in Indiana. It was, it seemed, never very good and always very hard, but often filled with little pleasures: picking fresh apples from a tree while walking to school.

Having an open field for a church because the local congregation couldn't afford building wood or the nails to hold it together. Learning to cook everything from corn bread to collard greens alongside her mother and grandmother. That was a pleasure I could taste with every forkful of what was sitting on my plate.

And as long as the stories seemed to go on, they stopped promptly at five minutes to eight o'clock. It was right then that bowls of ice cream were handed out and chairs were gathered around Mae's Philco. At two minutes to eight the television was turned on, giving it plenty of time to warm up, and at eight o'clock it happened. For us, for almost everyone in America, *Toast of the Town* was on.

Ed Sullivan was on the air.

Satellite television, cable television, before all that there was only regular television. And on television there were only three networks. And on those networks there was only one Ed Sullivan. From some seventy city blocks and a universe away, from Studio 50 on Seventh Avenue and Fifty-third Street came a flood of glamour and spectacle, song and dance. For one hour me and Mae, whoever else might be with us, whoever else was watching all over the country, would sit and stare trance-style while Ed held forth with the biggest actors from Hollywood and Broadway, the best singers and musicians, variety acts from all over the globe—countries I'd never even heard of before.

And comedians.

From as early as I can remember, I loved most watching the comedians. There was something about them, about what they did: one person standing out on that stage, alone—no orchestra backing them, no magic tricks—talking. Just talking. But by way of what they said, making an audience full of people they didn't know, strangers to each other even, laugh. There was just something about the whole idea of it that fascinated me like nothing else.

In an hour, what felt like the shortest hour of the week, *Toast of the Town* would be over. Me and Mae and whoever else would sit and talk about the program, maybe carry on about taking a trip to Hollywood to see how the stars live, or maybe riding down to Times Square to catch one of the Broadway shows we'd just seen a number from. We couldn't, of course. We couldn't afford a trip to California or a Broadway ticket any more than we could afford to buy a brick of gold resting on a bed of diamonds. In our hearts we knew we'd most likely never visit any of those places or see any of those things for real. But that's what *Toast of the Town* and Ed Sullivan were for. They were for dreaming.

After cleaning the dishes and straightening some, I would leave Grandma Mae and go back home to find my father actively involved in a pass out from a binge. Booze, or smoke, or pills. Besides the dope, my father had picked up the habit of going days without washing, weeks without a shave or haircut. On good days he looked like something that'd just come from hopping freight trains. On bad ones, he looked more animal than man.

In our apartment, in the living room, on the mantel above the never-used fireplace, was a picture of my mom. My father's guilt kept it standing there. There was no time when I came in for the evening when I would not kiss the picture, say good night to my mom. As I would go off to bed, in my head or in my heart, I could hear her giving me the same good night she did when she was alive: "You're a special one, Jackie Mann. Don't let nobody ever tell you otherwise."

I knew my mom meant well. I wished I could've believed her.

≈

NADINE RUSSELL WAS THE FIRST GIRL I'd ever noticed. The first I'd noticed as being something besides, something more than just another kid. I was approaching twelve years old, an age when boys realized girls—once naturally disliked—were real quickly becoming a source of fascination. Still too young to understand sexual attraction, my feelings for Nadine were of the same variety as my as-of-yet un-understandable desire to stop at newsstands and stare at pictures of Joan Bennett and Veronica Lake and Lauren Bacall as they glamoured at me from the covers of movie magazines.

Black women never shone from the covers of movie magazines. Black women didn't get to be movie stars.

Although Nadine had been attending school with me for as long as I could recall, there was just suddenly a day when I felt a creeping need to be in her presence, to see her big doe eyes and pudgy cheeks that for some reason I couldn't stare at long enough or hard enough. Just knowing I would see her each day at school juiced me with anticipation. She made me want to wash properly, brush my teeth, and make sure my hair was well groomed. She made me want to do things that previously, with all the love in the world, not even my mother could get me to do. She also made me feel very ashamed. Her father had a civil-service job—good, steady pay, at good government wages. Around my way, that made their family equal to uptown royalty. In her eyes, my raggedy clothes and worn shoes must have made me look like the poorest of the poor. And when the other kids would joke at me, call me names, what hurt bad only hurt worse if Nadine was around to hear their abuse and witness my crying. Her watching me break down cut deeper than anything the kids had to say. She would watch, but Nadine never joined in, never name-called, never so much as laughed. Sometimes, even, she looked very sad about what was happening.

And those times, when Nadine was showing a little sympathy for me, whatever it was a grade school boy feels for a girl, I felt for her.

I was coming home after doing chores at Sergeant Kolawole's. Like every night when I came home from working, I was coming home tired with just enough energy to eat before sleeping. Inside the apartment my pop was where he always seemed to be: taking up space on the couch. Hunched over the coffee table, his body was trembling and he moaned some. Experience told me he was coming down off whatever high had given him altitude. I left him to work things out with himself and went for my room, moving quietly, as most times Pop was an emotional minefield. Trouble was all a misstep ever got me.

As I passed him I caught Pop's face in the shine of the lamplight, his cheeks marked up with the slickness of tears. The shakes, the moans; Pop wasn't crashing, he was crying—his tears dripping down onto a photo album spread across the table. I went cautiously closer, curious the way you're curious at a car wreck, flinching every time my father made a move. But that night he was harmless, clean of liquor but high on memories fed to him by the photographs.

Pop lifted his head, looked up at me, his eyes as weak as the rest of him. "Jackie?" he asked as if not quite recognizing his own son. Then, "Jackie," he cried at me. His hand came up, stretched out. "Come here, boy. Come to your pop."

I did as told. Fear, not compassion, driving me to the man.

Pop took me in his arms, hugged and held me.

He stank. His clothes, gone days without change, reeking of the Thunderbird he sweated, were a pandemonium of odors. The closest I'd been to my father in years. All I could think of were his smells.

"Look here, Jackie. Look at this." A shaky hand sort of pointed at a picture of a man barely familiar to me—young, strong, handsome, and smiling. Fifteen years earlier? More?—standing on a beach somewhere tropical.

Pop started to ramble a story to me. He told me how he used to work on a transport, how he used to sail all over the world. South America, the Caribbean, and the Orient. As he dragged his fingers over picture after picture, literally trying to touch his past, he told me of all the things he'd seen, all the faraway countries he'd traveled to, each more spectacular or mysterious than the last. Maybe they'd been that way. Maybe the years, or the drugs, or the oppressiveness of his present life made them seem better than they ever really were.

He told me of the women he'd had. Sparing little detail, my father told me of the exotic beauties he'd sexed at apparently every port of call. I did not blush with shame at his stories. I smiled with pride for the man my father used to be.

He turned the page of the photo book. There was a picture of my mother. No matter that it was black and white, aged and faded, as beautiful as I remembered her, I never recalled seeing her *so* beautiful. I had never seen her so young and alive as she was in the photograph.

My father told me how he met her, and how once he had, all the other women he'd ever known could find no traction in his head or in his heart. He told me how much he loved my mother.

Love.

Coming from Pop the word sounded as foreign as Chinese.

He spoke it with no difficulty.

And then he told me how he'd promised to give my mother a house, a home, a family, and a decent life. But in those days, for a black man, making such promises was just telling lies. After he quit the boat to settle down, with what little education he had, he couldn't find good work. During the Depression he could barely find work at all. After his accident he didn't want to work, couldn't bring himself to try. That's when he started taking Relief.

I never thought my father as being much of a man, but every man has pride. He took aid, but every time the money crossed his palm it tore him up inside just a little bit more—the knowing that he had become so much nothing, he couldn't do the one single thing a man is truly supposed to do: He couldn't provide for his family. The shame made him run to the bottle, and the drinking made him need his relief all the more. A snake eating its own tail. It wasn't his body that was broken as much as his spirit. The world had ground and ground and ground him down until a drunk, an addict, and an abuser was all that was left of the young and smiling man in the pictures in the photo book that were on the coffee table Pop cried over.

For the first time, I understood my father. I didn't forgive him for the things he'd done to himself and to me, or for letting his wife—my mother—scrape and scrub herself six feet underground. But I understood him.

And I cried for him.

My father gathered me up in his arms, his grip weak. "It's all right, little Jackie," he told me. "You'll see. You'll see; everything's gonna be all right."

We sat, huddled close, until Pop fell asleep. Or passed out. I got up and went to bed but lay awake thinking of what my father had shown me of his life and of himself.

I woke up the next morning early, believing what Pop had told me: that somehow, from now on, everything for us was going to be all right. To celebrate that, I made breakfast. I didn't just pour cereal into a bowl. I made up some pancakes as best I could, scrambled eggs, fried some ham. Imitating Grandma Mae, I did it all up right. The first meal of the first day of everything being better.

I laid out the food on the table just as my dad walked in.

I looked at him and smiled.

He looked at me and screamed: "What you doin'! What the hell you doin' makin' all that goddamn noise first in the mornin'?"

I had to dodge flying plates and utensils, my father's swinging fists as I cut from the kitchen. I ran from the apartment, outside, not wearing a coat in the cold, but not wearing any bruises either. At the moment that had become my main, my only concern.

I went to school and after that I went to work at Sergeant Kolawole's and after that I went around the neighborhood doing whatever I could to keep myself from going home.

Eventually I had to.

Inside the apartment: Pop on the couch as always. Shaking and moaning. Not from memories this time. This time from whatever jag he was riding. He didn't notice me when I came in. He just sat and shook and moaned. Whatever was left of that man in the pictures in the photo album—young and strong and happy—was gone for good.

———

THERE ARE A COUPLE OF TRUTHS I came to know at an early age and have kept close my entire life. The first I learned one time, one of many times; I was getting made fun of at school over my clothes, or how poor I was, or about my pop and his drinking, or one of a hundred other things wrong with my life. Out on the playground, kids crowded around me, forming a wall of snarling and laughing voices as their fingers pointed in my direction, a group sign in case anyone had any doubts: Yeah, it was me they were mocking. Their laughing did the double chore of making me feel both hurt and angry. But I was too scared to so much as take a swing at any of them for the things they were saying. Standing up for myself was liable to get myself beat down. Standing there and taking what they were giving me was the safe bet.

Li'l Mo stuck close and tried to get the other kids to back off. Unlike me, Li'l Mo never had a problem getting scrappy if a little scrappiness was required. But Li'l Mo was just one against a whole mob of kids. They ignored him and taunted on.

I wanted to run and hide, but the way the kids were pressing in on me I had nowhere to run to. I wanted to cry, but crying would only give the crowd fuel. Not knowing what else to do, I did the only thing I could. I said, and I said loud for all the kids to hear: "Yeah, that's right. I'm poor. Know how poor I am? I'm so poor I can't hardly afford to pay attention."

They shut up. For a second every one of them was too surprised by my outburst to do anything but be quiet.

I kept on. "Hell, I'm so poor I can't even afford to change my mind. You know how poor I am? My shadow's got a hole in it."

I was doing bits I'd heard from the comics on *Toast of the Town*. I was doing them in their style with their timing. I was doing a stand-up routine.

None of the kids knew what to do, what to say. How were they going to make fun of me when I was making fun of myself?

"Y'all want to know why my pants is so short? 'Cause it'll be long before I get a new pair."

And just like that, the little verbal lynch mob went from being quiet, back to laughing. Only, their laughter had changed. They were laughing when I wanted them to, when I said so. It was me who was controlling the situation: You want to make fun? I'll show you how to make fun. You want to laugh? I'll give you something to laugh at.

"You know my pop is thinking about getting married again. He don't even love the girl. He just wants to keep the rice people throw. And you all talking about my pop, sayin' how he's got a drinking problem. That ain't true. He drinks, he gets drunk, he passes out. No problem."

The bell rang. Time for class. The kids ran off, but unlike most times they weren't chasing me down the hall trying to get their last few jibes in. This time they kept calling to me: "One more, Jackie! Just tell us one more joke! Please, Jackie!"

They said please to me.

What made it all good was that when the crowd of kids broke up, there among them was pretty Nadine Russell giving me a warm, wonderful smile.

THE OTHER TRUTH I LEARNED, I learned on a Saturday in July. Summers were long and hot in New York City. Hot in the way the sunlight kicked off all the windows, reflected down to the sidewalks, where it would congregate and turn the hard streets to a hot goo. They were long in the way the heat was dodgeless. It lingered across the drawn-out day until sundown and the night that was only some-what cooler than the day before it and the hellish morning ahead.

Indoors was just as sweltering as out. Apartments were con-verted into walk-in ovens, and the little old General Electric fan with the frayed cord that everyone seemed to own put up a poor, losing battle against the still, stifling air.

There wasn't much in the way of public swimming pools. Pub-lic pools, at least, that were friendly toward coloreds. Sometimes someone would take a wrench to a fire hydrant, jam a crate up to its nozzle, turning the whole of it into a fountain for us kids to splosh around and play in. For me the sound of summer will always be the sound of water spilling over concrete and laughing children. It was a sound that could be heard on any uptown street between June and August. Who needed a heated indoor pool, a water slide? Not us Harlem kids. Us Harlem kids had a city hydrant.

Sometimes we had it.

Other times the pounders would come 'round, kick away the crate, take a wrench back to the hydrant and shut it down. They would say it was city property and we didn't have a right to mess with city property and it was a waste of water and there might be a fire and there wouldn't be any water to fight the fire with.

That's what they said.

What it translated to was: "Knock it off, niggers."

It was that kind of Saturday, full of heat and lacking in things to do. Me and Li'l Mo and a couple of other kids from the neighborhood were sitting on a stoop, hot, getting hotter, trying to figure a way to get cool.

"Aw, hell," I said, never having been schooled at home not to swear. "Let's just go to the movies." In the day, the movies weren't just a movie. The movies were some cartoons and a short and the coming attractions and *then* the movie. Maybe a double bill. The movies were an all-day indoor event. All day, indoors and with, as the kicker, air-conditioning. Icy-cool, man-made, fan-blown, refrigerated air.

"How we 'posed to do that?" one of the kids asked.

"How do you go to the movies?" I asked back. "You get a ticket and you go."

Li'l Mo said for the group: "I ain't got no movie-ticket money."

Movie-ticket money, back then, ran maybe a quarter. To a poor black kid, it might as well have been fifty dollars. But to a kid who spent six days of seven slaving away at any job he could find, a meter of that hard-earned cash was a small price to pay for being cool and seeing a movie to boot. Maybe two movies.

"Shoot." I was already up and moving. "I'll buy the tickets. Let's just go."

I got to the corner, was waiting for the light to change, when I noticed I was waiting alone. Li'l Mo and them were still sitting on the stoop.

I walked back.

I asked: "What?"

"You was going to the movies."

"Yeah. Let's go."

"But how we 'posed to—"

"I told you"—I cut the boy off—"I'm buying the tickets."

With a cautious disbelief, Li'l Mo wanted to know but asked like he was afraid to find out: "You buying . . . for all of us?"

Four of us. A buck in tickets. I knew for a fact I'd put three dollars in my pocket when I went out that morning. Three dollars to eat with, and get a Coke or ice cream with. Three dollars to ride the subway with. Three dollars to escape staying home with Pop, who may or may not be getting high in one of a dozen different ways.

To the boys: "Yeah, all of you. Now, you coming, or you Negroes just going to sit on that stoop?" I'd heard some of the older men in the neighborhood calling each other Negroes when they were irritated with another's behavior or lack of smarts. Using the word in that way made me feel like I was a little better or sharper than the other kids. It was a feeling rare to me. I liked it.

Let me tell you: You've never seen so much collective joy in your life as what Li'l Mo and the others displayed. They were all laughs and cheers and good nature, and I had to race to catch up to them as they hightailed it to the theater. I bought them all tickets. Candy, too. What's another fifty cents total among boys? We sat and watched the cartoons and a short and the coming attractions and the feature. And the second feature. That we sat for hours and the only black faces projected on the screen belonged to subservient mammies and backward natives who were no match for the Great White Hunters didn't matter. All that mattered was that the temperature was low.

The next day, Sunday, was like most: me staying out of Pop's way until it was time to go to Mae's. A good meal, good stories, *Toast of the Town,* then home again.

Monday was a whole new thing. As soon as I got to school, kids, kids I barely knew or kids who only days prior were having at me for being the poor boy with the addict dad, where giving me: "Hey there, Jackie." "How you doin', Jackie." "Need any help with your homework, you let me know, Jackie." Very quickly it had gotten around that I'd sprung for movie tickets and candy without so much as flinching, like I was Charlie Bigbucks. And just as quickly everybody and their brother were angling to be the next to get some of my goodwill. It was nice, regardless of the reason, the sudden and heavy attention I found coming my way. What made it nicer was that the smiles Nadine gave started going from warm to hot.

That—that right there—was the other truth I learned: You can't make people love you, but there isn't anybody who doesn't like a man with money.

Almost nobody.

One afternoon, after school, Nadine had smiled her way into getting me to take her for ice cream. Late for the date, I came rushing into the apartment to load up on cash. I went for my room, opened the door, started to make for my money jar.

I got stopped by the sight of Pop sitting on my bed.

The room was dark, his head was hung low, but from what I could see, Pop was in rough shape. Going dry and deep into the DTs, he was desperate for a drink but beat back the need in favor of waiting for me. The effort so great it made his muscles jerk and sopped him with his own sweat.

But he just sat there.

No matter how much he ached for a brace to get himself right, Pop just sat with his eyes locked on what he held in his hands: my little jar full of money.

In a heartbeat a story told itself: Pop wakes up from a bender that he tries to dope himself back into, but the house is drug-free and his pockets are empty. He goes scavenging through my room, looking for bills or change, looking for whatever I've got that spends, anything that'll get him so much as a nickel closer to a fresh shot of liquor. But what he finds . . .

What he finds . . .

Pop raised his head slow, as if the rage it contained almost made it too heavy to lift. And that same dry-drunk anger boiling inside him distorted his face, made my own father almost unrecognizable.

"What dis?"

"Pop—"

"WHAT DIS!" His voice was summer thunder.

". . . It's money."

I didn't see the jar coming, much less have time to juke out of the way. For a jittery drunk marking time with the shakes, Pop had some speed to him. Speed and accuracy. The jar caught me between the eyes dead, solid perfect. My father, the Cy Young of boozers. When I came to I was lying down, looking up at my room that was slouched over at a funny angle and was newly decorated with fuzzy edges. My hands sort of moved around by themselves, and my mouth did its own talking in a language that to this day I've never heard again.

And into all that stepped my pop, towering above me Japanese monster movie–style done over in an angry black.

"Don't you never," Pop said—said as best he could through his struggle with sobriety, "don't you never let me find you was holdin' out on me. You'll be sorry, boy. Tell you that. You hearin' me?"

I responded some way or other in my new tongue.

"You be damn for sure sorry."

No more sorry than I already was.

Blood from a gush where the jar smacked my forehead ran down into my right eye, made it flutter.

Pop left me like that: stretched out and bleeding. First he took the money; then he left.

—————

THERE, AND GONE. Onstage, then off. They were a good act. They were a flash-dance act; two middle-aged guys and a younger one tap stepping at lickety-split speed. Race onstage, then race right off. There and gone in a flash. Between the racing they filled their show time with a few numbers done yowsah style, working up a big sweat that rolled down over their bigger smiles—do you likes me now, massa, do you likes me? Buff-shined patent leathers sliding over parquet. The screech of metal, then tickety-tac, tickety-tac. Some hand claps thrown in. Beat-bobbing heads to go with the shining ivory. A hesitation step when you think you can second-guess the rhythm, a tease, then the screech of metal again. Tickety-tac, tickety-tac. Strictly vaudeville by way of minstrel show. Strictly opening fare. How about a nice hand for the Will Mastin Trio? Now bring on the headliner.

Still, they were a good act. They were on *Toast of the Town,* so they must have been good. Good but not great, the same way Teresa Brewer was good but not great. The same way Al Hirt—trumpet-blowing, New Orleans jazz Al Hirt—was good but not great. The same way David Frye was good but thoroughly unrememberable. Anonymity was waiting to collect them all.

Except, the trio wasn't completely forgettable. Will might have been. So was his partner, Sammy Davis. But the young one was pretty much like something you'd never seen before. Standing center stage between the two older men, Sammy Davis, Jr. was black lightning; human energy. A little man, he was concentrated entertainment. Put a spotlight on him and stand back. Song came busting out of him. Dance came bursting out, steps that were im-possibly good and impossibly fast. Steps that made the other two of the trio look like they were standing still if moving at all. Legs, feet twisting, sliding, gliding in ways that made you say: "He can't, he can't do that." Then he'd do it again just to prove you wrong. I watched with the same breath-held viewing I gave to high-wire acts. Sammy Davis, Jr. had that kind of abandon. He worked without a net.

Ta-da!

Orchestra up.

Sammy and the rest of the trio bowed within the confines of the picture tube. The speaker of Mae's Philco pulsated real-time as the audience exploded with applause for them. As the audience applauded for *him*. For Sammy. And they applauded in the same vigorous way they did for the white performers. Ed stepped over, shook hands with them. Shook hands with *him*. Same as he did with the white performers. Adulation without distinction, that's what black entertainers got on TV. Sammy got it. The rest of the trio got it just for being around. Pearl Bailey got it. Got a sponsor-be-damned hug, too. Billy Eckstine and Sarah Vaughan got it. Ed wouldn't think of not giving some to Nat King Cole. "Always a pleasure to have you on the shew."

"Thank you, Ed. The pleasure is mine." "It's always such a thrill to be able to perform for you and the audience, Ed." "Ed, I'd just like to take a moment to thank my many fans across America for their support." They were articulate. The black entertainers on the show were always articulate and well spoken.

Well spoken. You would hear that from whites sometimes: "I saw Nat King Cole on *Toast of the Town,* and he was so well spoken." It was clubhouse talk for acceptable. They were well spoken. They did not "sound" black, so black entertainers were acceptable. To a point. A point much further than other blacks of the day could ever hope to reach. To see that, to be a young boy and watch blacks on coast-to-coast coaxial broadcast television being treated as equals, being treated better than most, it was like bearing witness to a miracle. To be a young man and watch that on TV made me want. I wanted to not "sound" like a black. I wanted to be acceptable. I wanted to be well spoken. Well spoken. Spoken white. I got a dictionary from Mae. I read it and I learned words. Big, long, white-sounding words. I took a master class in talking white. Television taught me. Droll Jack Benny taught me. Dry Jack Webb taught me. Smooth and cool Steve Allen taught me. My final consisted of me standing before a mirror practicing all I had learned.

Ready? Begin.

Ed, I must tell you what a distinct pleasure it's been appearing on your program this evening. I can only hope that at some point in the future I can look forward to returning to your stage. And, if I may, a sincere thank-you to all my fans wherever they may be viewing.

Pass? Fail? Didn't matter. I had no idea what do with my new skill. No matter how I sounded, no matter how my new voice made me feel, I was what I had always been: a poor black boy from Harlem. But then, so had Sammy Davis, Jr. once. And now he was so well spoken.

THE SCHOOL YEAR was a day from ending. I was twenty-four hours from completing the eleventh grade and the start of the summer vacation. My plans for the next three months centered around working six of seven days just as I had for each week of the six years that had passed both too quickly and too slowly since my mother had died. I planned on staying out of my father's way the best I could. I planned on spending whatever free time I had spending whatever extra money I had on Nadine Russell.

Li'l Mo changed my plans.

He showed me an ad in the *New York Post*.

I read it.

I said to Mo: "You must be out of your mind."

"Twenty-five dollars a week," Mo said back. "That sound crazy to you?"

No. That wasn't crazy. Twenty-five dollars a week back then was good money Rockefeller-style. It was the rest of the ad that made me think Li'l Mo was suffering a spell.

**Wanted: Men 18+ to work logging camp in the
Pacific Northwest. Earn $25 a wk and up.**

The ad gave an address where, and a time from when to when you could apply if you were out of your mind enough to apply in the first place.

Mo pointed to the part where it said $25 a wk and up.

I pointed to the part that said men eighteen and older. "You and me are seventeen."

"Twenty-five dollars a week." Mo echoed the ad by way of argument. "And up."

"And the Pacific Northwest? That's up in . . ." I wasn't sure where it was exactly, but my ignorance just confirmed it was way far away from anywhere I'd even been close to before. "That's way the hell far away," I went on. "We're supposed to just pick up and go off to wherever?"

"Okay, so this here camp is way off somewhere, an' we gotta fake how we eighteen an' all. But why shouldn't we try an' go out to there? You got somethin' better to do for the summer?"

I had other things to do, but they weren't much better.

Mo saw me starting to hesitate my way from no to yes, and his selling went into high gear. "How long till school start up again? Three months? Twelve weeks. That's . . ." Mo did some math, taking a little time with it. Math and Mo were never very friendly with each other. I would've helped out but got along with numbers no better than Mo did.

"That's near about three hundred dollars. Now, I been your friend too long an' too good not to know what three hundred dollars means to Jackie Mann."

Money meant a lot to Jackie Mann. But . . . "Eighteen? We're not—"

"We tell 'em we eighteen. Them loggin' people don't care how old we are long as we can cut wood."

"And what do we know about cutting wood?"

Li'l Mo waved his hands clearing the air of my bad ideas. "The ad said they want men. Didn't say nothin' about being no log-cuttin' expert."

"You telling me your folks are just going to let you go?"

"My folks could use some of that three hundred." Li'l Mo was getting annoyed. The bother of talking me into something so obvious was, objection by objection, wearing him to the core. "My family knows I ain't no little boy no more."

"I'm no little boy either."

"Not sayin' you are. But I got a sister an' a little brother that need takin' care of. I ain't afraid to do what I gotta to help out."

"You don't think I help out around my place?"

"Help what? Help buy your pop's booze, help pick him up after he drinks himself down?" No slip of the tongue, Mo threw that jab with a boxer's timing, quick and sharp. He threw it so it hurt.

"I help out plenty," I said. "I'm the man of my house."

"Then why don't you be a man an' help yourself to some cash. I'm going down to apply for this here job. You coming, or aren't you coming?"

Was I going, or wasn't I?

I went. Not so much because I wanted to go wherever and cut trees, or even because I wanted that money I knew would feel so warm and spend so well. I went because I wanted to show Li'l Mo the man I was.

The recruiting office was in Midtown. Afternoon of the morning of the day the ad ran, and already there was a string of people stretching from the office door. Boys way younger than Mo and me. Old men whose years were surpassed only by their desperation for a job. We waited among all of them—a millipede of people doing a slow shuffle for the office—thinking there was no way there'd be anything left for us by the time we applied. That's if they didn't just toss us on our black behinds for trying to pass for eighteen. We shuffled . . . we shuffled. . . . Men came out of the office smiling. Men came out of the office crying. We shuffled an hour and a half of the day away. We shuffled like a bunch of characters waiting to see the wizard who'd grant us the great and good favor of giving us work. But once inside the office, all that happened was we got

looked up and down by one of a number of white fellows sitting behind one of a number of desks. He asked when could we start work.

For the both of us Mo said: "Right away."

The white fellow filled in a couple of slips of paper, handed one
each to me and Mo, told us to be at Penn Station nine o'clock sharp
in the A.M. in two days' time. Those slips of paper were like tickets,
he told us, so don't lose them.

Just like that me and Mo were lumberjacks.

Just like that . . . except, I had to tell my father.

That first day after I got the job I didn't tell my father anything.
Would he let me go? Would he not let me go? If I just went, would
he even notice I was gone? I worked at convincing myself that if I
was man enough to go off to wherever and cut trees, I was man
enough to tell my father about it. A few hours of kicking around the
logic of that, and I was as unconvinced as ever.

I decided against telling my father just then. I decided instead
to tell Nadine that I would be leaving. My good-bye had purpose.
Nadine and me had been going steady for a couple of semesters.
She was my girl. She got taken to movies as my girl. She got taken
for sweets and ice cream as my girl. As her guy, I got the privilege
of publicly holding her hand and kissing her in private. I got little
else. And over time I got less and less satisfaction from hand-
holding and kissing. As I matured, I wanted other things. When
I held Nadine's hand I thought only of petting her thighs. When I
kissed her, I imagined undoing the buttons of her home-knit
sweater, peeling it back, and peeling back the shirt underneath, revealing breasts I'd watched ripen one school year into the next. She
was my girl. I felt entitled to explore my girl. But I'd never had the
courage to try, and Nadine had never offered. I was left with my
adolescent wonderings of how she looked raw. Like the old bum
woman Mo and I had seen bathing in Central Park? Like that but
with skin that was smooth, not ashy. Firm without sags. Certainly,
but I wanted to see for myself. Now I had a way into Nadine: the

lumber job across the country. The way it happens in some war movie—soldier going off to battle, maybe to come home again, maybe not—I was determined to give Nadine a good-bye that would make her want to offer herself to me. If I wasn't a man in age, if I wasn't a man in the way I approached my father, I at least wanted to go to the lumber camp a man in experience.

Two blocks south, one block east. I made the walk to Nadine's building. From the street I called up to her apartment. City communication. I used to throw little rocks up at her window. Once I broke one. A new window cost twelve dollars, and Nadine's father went two weeks without letting her see me. I called up to her window. She opened it and leaned out. Her breasts, pert in their youthfulness, shouted down to me. One minute later we got comfortable on the stoop of her building. After a little talk I began my performance piece. I would be going, I told her, to the Pacific Northwest to do hard work for good money. The twelve weeks I would be gone turned into "Who knew how long." The work would be dangerous. There was the possibility I could get . . . I let that hang. No need to frighten the girl, my girl, too much. All that got wrapped in the promise I would return home, return to her, as soon as possible and that while I was gone I would think of her daily.

At the end of my talk she asked me how much I was supposed to be earning.

I told her.

She repeated the sum toward a building across the street. She took my hand in hers, told me that she hoped I would be all right out . . . wherever, and that I'd come back as soon as I could.

I kissed her.

She kissed me.

I kissed her.

She kissed me.

I kissed her again, and slid a hand across her waist to her stomach, then started it on an upward journey.

Nadine made a motion to stand that came off as being very casual. From above me she told me she would miss me and hoped that I wouldn't be gone too long. I got a quick, final kiss on the cheek. She went inside.

Twenty-five dollars, she had repeated wistfully when I told her how much I would be making a week. For all her hand-holding and friendly kissing, it was the only emotion she had shown me. She was my girl. I had been her boy. Just then, for the first time, I understood the nature of our relationship. Not in the way intended, Nadine had matured me.

Next day. My last day of school. That night I had dinner with my father. Anyway, we sat at the table eating at the same time. The way he spaded down his meal I could tell it was a grass high he was working off of. But if he was straight enough to eat, I figured he was straight enough to talk to.

"Pop," I started, "I've got this real good opportunity to make some money. Real good money. I could be making twenty-five dollars a week. More than that." I hit the money theme hard, figuring that angle to be the most attractive to my father. The more I made, the more he'd get. "Probably a whole lot more than that. And I could send it back regular. That's the thing, I would have to send it back. The job's in . . . it's out in the Northwest. But like I said, I can have the money sent back regular, and it's only going to be for a few—"

"You ain't going nowhere." Between mouthfuls of food, I could barely make him out.

". . . Wha—"

"You ain't going nowhere."

"But . . . it's twenty-five dollars a week. More tha—"

"Don't care how much it supposed to be. Need you around here."

Need me? Need me for what? To day-labor for the money for his drink and drugs? To make sure his supply was fresh when he was too strung out to go cop his own? I'd had years of that already. I was sick of every one of them.

I sucked a breath. I said: "I'm going."

"Better shut your mouth, boy."

"I'm not a boy. I'm eighteen. Just about. I'm a man, and I can do whatever I wa—"

I was on the ground, I was holding my stinging face and crying before I even knew my father had landed the first blow.

I looked up at him.

His fingers went to his belt. One tug, and it slithered from around his waist. The leather of it creaked in the twist of his hands. Light jumped off the metal buckle, distorted to look huge by my frightened eyes.

I'd been hit by my father before, taken everything from a mindful spanking to a good punishing. What he gave me then was a beating. He rained a thrashing on me I'd never previously known. The first smack of the belt, the buckle clipping my head, drove me farther to the floor. The second and third cut easily through my pitiful defense of outstretched hands. All I could do about the blows that followed was curl in a ball and take them. Any of that high talk I had about being a man, about doing as I pleased, was battered from me lash after lash. The sound of the belt cutting through the air, the crack of the leather and thud of the metal on my body was answered in full by moans and whimpers. It was an ugly duet that got lost under the din of babies crying, blues singers and trumpet players out on fire escapes, girls laughing, and car horns arguing with each other. The sounds of my beating got lost among the sounds of the city—just another noise.

As much from being worn out as from having burned off his anger, my father eventually stopped. Sweating, huffing, he dropped the belt down by my face, gave me a good look at his tool of correction.

"Whatcha got to say 'bout being a man now?" he said at me. "Whatcha got to say now?"

I didn't have anything to say. I was shaking too hard to even speak.

I heard Pop lumber from the kitchen out to the couch and lower his tired-from-giving-a-whupping self down into it. I heard a bottle of booze get cracked open. Pop got to drinking. He drank the rest of the night, not moving from where he sat and me not moving from the floor. It was dawn by the time the juice had dropped him into a stupor.

I got off the floor, packed a few things, went and waited on the stoop of Li'l Mo's apartment.

Later that morning, Pop still passed out I imagine, me and Li'l Mo went off for Penn Station.

———

EXCEPT FOR THE SUBWAY, I'd never been on a train before. Except for most of Manhattan, I'd never been anywhere before. Now, at seventeen, I was traveling clear across the country to do work I knew nothing about. The ride itself was, to that point, the most amazing experience of my life; besides just the thrill of the journey, the bald-faced joy generated by each mile traveled opposite of my father. The rhythm of the *California Zephyr*—the gentle swaying, the steel wheels rolling over the joins of the rails in a syncopated beat—lulled you into a relaxed and mellow condition over the nearly three days it took to travel to Washington state, which me and Li'l Mo came to find out was specifically the Pacific Northwest the lumbermen were talking about in their ad.

Along the way America passed just outside the Vista-Dome: city melting into farmland blending with plains, desert, and mountains. To a young man who'd only had the world projected to him thirteen inches diagonally in black and white, it was a wondrous thing. It was almost worth being on the receiving end of my father's belt just to have the chance to see it. For the final leg north, we had a change of trains in Los Angeles. It was a short stop. Long enough for a hot dog and Coca-Cola but not nearly long enough to see any of the city. Not much of it, at least. I did steal myself a minute to go outside of Union Station. L.A. was different from New York. Flat. With few buildings of any height, there was nothing to block out the sunlight. Spread out. It stretched as far as you could see and had room to grow. That was my first impression of Los Angeles: nothing but sunshine and possibilities. I tried to catch sight of the Hollywood sign. I just wanted to look at it for a second or two. Look at it and know that while it was shining down on me, it was shining down on all those wonderful, glamorous stars that made Hollywood their dreamland home. I couldn't see the sign from where I was, wasn't even sure which direction to look.

I went back in the station. Me and Mo got on our train and finished our journey north.

WE GOT OFF THE TRAIN in Seattle, not only me and Mo, but us and a few dozen or more other men—young to late-middle-aged, mixed in race—who had collected along the way. Men who I could tell were going where we were headed for reasons besides just the fact they de-trained the same place as us. I knew where they were going because, also same as us, they looked poor and desperate. They looked like they would travel halfway—or all the way—across the country just to earn money.

Coming out of one of the train cars was a white fellow, young, but still a bit older than me, struggling with a suitcase. A big one. The guy would've been just as well off carting a Frigidaire with him from wherever he came.

Don't know why I did it—he was struggling like I said, and maybe I figured it wouldn't hurt any to make a few friends since I was all of the U.S.A. away from home—but I went over to the fellow, asked: "Use a hand?"

He looked up at me, sweaty in face, red more than white from all the effort he was putting into things. "That'll be the day when I need help from a coon."

He said it plain and simple. The white fellow said what he said about not needing help from a coon and went right back to struggling with his suitcase same as if all that'd passed between us was a quick conversation on the time or temperature. The comment was nothing to him.

Men from the lumber mill gathered us up into some trucks and we all got driven to the camp. As we made our way I saw that Washington was a whole other kind of joint, the exact opposite of the city. The air was scented with rain and pine instead of exhaust and soot. Trees instead of buildings. Grass instead of people. And what people there were, I noticed right off, were almost all white. Wasn't as if I wasn't used to being around white people. New York brimmed with them. But just about everywhere you went in the city, where you saw a white face, you could turn around and see people of color. All colors. Black people, brown people. People from the Orient and India. Up there, up there in Washington, there was me, there was Li'l Mo, there were a few dozen more blacks who made the trip, and that was it. Realizing my isolation, thinking of the man I'd tried to help with his trunk and the slur I'd gotten as a thank-you, I was just then beginning to think that summer would not pass quickly.

We drove a long way, drove until what city there was got left far behind. Drove until it seemed—having already ridden a train farther west and north than I'd ever been—like we had just about run out of America to drive through. We drove until there was nothing but trees, thick and lush and tall; brown and green pillars you'd have thought were holding up the sky. It almost seemed a shame to cut them down. I figured my first paycheck would help me get over the concern.

We arrived finally in the city of Everett. We arrived at Pemberton Mills, the logging camp where we'd be working. And a camp is what

it was, not much more. A building where all the milling and ship-
ping was done, another that served as offices. There was another
where we would eat and gather for anything we needed to gather for.
Sprinkled around all that were the cabins where we would bunk
down—koogies they called them. Long, narrow structures like railroad flats. Able to fit ten men, they were good in size, but they were
hardly big enough to house the trouble that came with mixing unfamiliar whites and blacks in them together. In the climate of the day
it would've been better, safer, to segregate the white and black workers. For both races it would have been just one more comfort of
home. But for some reason the management had the bright idea to
jumble everybody together. Some kind of Pacific Northwest liberal-
ism, I figured at first. The more I considered the subject, the more I
thought the owners didn't want all the blacks in one place for fear
they might come up with some crazy, militant plot to overthrow the
Anglo world from a cabin in a logging camp.

So, instead, the races got stirred. Me and Mo, maybe because we
had signed up together, got assigned to the same koogie along with
another young black named Kevin. Three of us, which meant as we
walked into our cabin there were seven pairs of white eyes to give us
some broiling stares.

Me and Mo and Kevin just took them, happy for the moment
that was all we were taking, picked out three beds, and put what belongings we had down. It was a simple act we very instantly found
out was strictly wrongheaded.

"What you niggers doin'?" a white boy said more than asked,
and said with all the casual menace he could put together. Following
so quickly after the complimentary slur I'd gotten back at the train
station, I had the feeling black-hating whites were going to be easy
to come by.

This black-hating white was tall and thin, pale so the blue/green
veins that laced his arms—raised up and pulsing hot—were as easy
to read as lines on a Jim Crow map. All roads led to trouble.

Again the white boy wanted to know: "What you niggers doin'?"

Li'l Mo and Kevin said nothing to that, having no strong desire to respond to being called niggers. At the same time, I had no strong desire to get handed a beating for not answering a question that was, real obviously, directed at us.

I said: "Picking out bunks."

The long, tall white boy seemed to find that funny. He laughed.

The other whites laughed.

"No you ain't. That ain't the nigger section. Ain't no niggers allowed over there. Now, you best pick up all your darkie shit, move it out of the white section and on over to the nigger part of the cabin."

Sure. That'd be fine. But nobody bothered to tell us just where exactly the non-white part of the koogie was. We three blacks gathered up our things, took a guess, and moved over to another bunch of bunks. We guessed wrong.

"That look like the nigger section to you?"

And the chorus of white boys started in again with their cackling.

We moved again. Me leading the way, then Kevin. Mo brought up the rear, deliberately slow about it.

"Naw, that ain't the nigger section."

More laughing.

I was getting the idea; far as these boys were concerned, there was no place for us. Inside the koogie or anywhere else.

That wasn't quite true.

"That's where you niggers go. Over there." The white boy pointed at the far corner of the koogie. "Now, you all coons just move your bunks on over there." He laughed again.

The other white boys laughed.

I wasn't sure if any of them had traveled up together, or even knew each other previously. I didn't think so. I figured instead they were just seven white strangers who'd formed a fast friendship over the mutual pleasure that came with the opportunity to rough around some blacks.

Me, Mo, and Kevin stood heads down but not moving. At least, outside of some nervous twitching from me, not moving for the corner where we'd been directed.

"You all hear what I'm tellin' you?" The white boy wasn't chuckling anymore, wasn't laughing. Neither were his new gang of pals. They were popping their knuckles, twisting their fingers, squeezing their fists. . . . Their hands, impatient with all the taunting, anxious to get in on some of the fun.

"What? Y'all too stupid to move a bunk? Lemme show you how to move a bunk." The tall white boy grabbed up the bunk closest to me, slung it for a corner of the cabin, slung it hard so that it crashed to its side, the mattress and linens flying off. "That"—the white boy huffed, breathless from the physical explosion—"is how you dumb-ass niggers move a bunk."

"Maybe we're dumb, but you're the one doing the moving for us." I was trying to be funny. I was thinking a laugh might just lighten things up. If I had been thinking at all, I would've kept my mouth shut. As it was, I just sounded like I was trying to be wise.

For a long couple of ticks nobody said anything, everybody stunned silent by my unintentional uppitiness. It would take the white boys only a moment to recover. It would take them only a moment to decide they needed to hammer some obedience into me. My body, working one step ahead of my thoughts, started to go for a bunk and move it over to where the other was strewn in the corner—the nigger section of the cabin. I refused to feel embarrassed or humiliated by my actions. My thinking? I could get beat at home. I didn't need to travel cross-country for more of the same. So if moving a bunk kept me bruise-free . . .

I heard more fingers cracking. Not the whites'. Now it was Mo's fists that were getting impatient. He wasn't about to do any bunk moving. He was fixing to have a go at these boys like he was Charlie Bad-Brother, all set to mess them up, solo if he had to, one-hundred-percent-style.

The tall white boy saw what Mo was doing, saw the fire stoking in him, and got with a peckerwood grin. Nigger wanted trouble? Fine. He'd give the nigger trouble.

Violence was coming. It was crowding up the joint, shoving aside logic and reason.

"Hey!"

All of us, black same as white, turned and looked. In the door was another man. White. Tough-looking. Not tough as in big and beefy but like he'd spent a lot of years doing the kind of hard labor that gives the whole body durability. He had on a shirt, the camp's logo sewn on the breast.

"What ya doin'?" the man in the door asked, his voice a mixture of annoyance and Southern drawl. The drawl made me think the annoyance came from him almost being deprived of the chance to lay in a few I-hate-coons-too licks.

For whatever reason, because no one else did, I started to answer the man. "We was told t—"

"What ya doin'?" the camp man asked again, ignoring me and talking directly to the tall white boy directing the confrontation.

"Just having some play with the niggers," he said all happy with himself. He might as well have been recounting fishing stories with drinking buddies. "Niggers don't know where niggerville is. I told them to put their bunks—"

"Ah'll tell yew where their bunks go." The camp man came down hard with that, using his voice as a cleaver to cut the boy off.

The boy started up again. "But he was—"

And again he got shot down. "Their bunks go jus' where they were." Tone underlined the camp man's words.

The white boy sucked at his lip, grumbled: "Shit."

The camp man took a step for the boy. One strong step that the boy backed from. Maybe propped up by his cackling gallery he thought he was big enough to stir up trouble with a few far-from-home blacks, but under his pomp of rage the boy was just a boy, and knew better than to try the same with this man.

The man: "Yew say somethin'?"

"No, sir." The white boy's eyes flitted around the cabin as if trying to keep track of a buzzing fly.

All the other white boys did some looking around. They looked around, looked down. Generally they looked pretty stupid. Their leader getting corrected took the fight out of them.

"All right then," the man said just strong enough not to invite any challenge. "Le's git this heyah place cleaned up, and ah don't wanna heyah about no mo' trouble outta this cabin."

The man, whose name, or at least the name he went by, I would later come to know was Dax, started back to whatever he'd been doing before taking the time to referee a race riot.

Kevin, the other one of the three of "us" said as Dax passed: "Thank you, sir."

"Don't yew niggrahs think nothin' 'bout it," he said without even looking at us. Then he was out the door.

Not more than a couple of hours in Washington and my work trip was turning into a living classroom. I'd thought Dax had done what he'd done, stopped the fight, because he was a decent person. He wasn't. To him me, Mo, and Kevin were nothing more than a few niggers. Not people to be treated equally, just animals that shouldn't be treated badly for no good reason.

THE WAR WAS OVER. The boom was on. Families left cities. Suburbs were born. Houses weeded up across the country, giving birth to entire towns overnight. Cedar Hill. Cockrell Hill. Levittown. Lakewood. One hundred houses a day were started at each. One hundred houses a day, and still not enough for all the people who rat-raced after their piece of the American dream: hi-fied dens and pink-flamingoed lawns. The camp ran full throttle six days a week to fill the demand for lumber. Dawn to dark the forest rang with the sound of chopped trees screaming as they twisted and snapped against their trunks before thudding dead to the earth. There were a dozen different tasks to be done, each tagged with their own slang: donkeys, donkey punchers, skidders, whistle punks, high climbers. They all sounded unique and exciting. They all amounted to the same thing—moving trees. Chopping trees and moving trees. Milling trees and moving trees. Clearing the land of every tree that stood. Nothing fancy about it. The sweat was ordinary. The muscle ache was the same that came with any other grind. The only thing special about logging was that you learned to respect the boss. The boss *was* the trees. Douglas firs, Sitka spruces, western red cedars, Port Orford cedars. Some three hundred feet tall and over a thousand pounds. When the boss got felled, when it was being skidded, you learned to get out of its way. Get out or get hurt. Hurt if you were lucky. Otherwise all you got was dead for your twenty-five dollars a week.

Twenty-five dollars that we didn't really get anyway. Every worker had a passbook, and at the end of each week a company man would write in it what we earned to be settled up at summer's end. We never got cash. The company men figured if you didn't have cash you couldn't get into any trouble. You couldn't go into town and get drunk. You also couldn't take what you earned and run off in the middle of the night. All you could do was keep working. Keep up your respect for the boss six days out of seven.

On the seventh day we rested. We spent the mornings gathered in various worship groups praying or singing or whatever. Once religion was out of the way we sat around playing cards, smoking, paging through mail-order skin magazines. For lack of booze, a few guys shook up a cocktail of Aqua Velva and Kool-Aid. Some got high off the mix. Some got a free ride to the hospital.

Almost always we stayed segregated. You might see the occasional white with blacks, or the rarer black with a bunch of whites. Mostly the races kept to themselves and the whites—generally the southern whites—made it plain they wanted things that way. You could hear them talking together about something or other—the weather, a story about back home, how somebody earlier in the day, not paying attention, almost got taken out by the boss. They'd be talking about nothing in particular; then you'd hear it from them, the word: nigger. Nigger or coon or jig or darkie. You'd hear the word in a sentence, not spoken in anger, but used as if it were just another part of the language. Apple. Sky. Boat. Nigger. That was the frightening thing, how easy it came to them. How commonplace their hate was. How rooted racism was in them. They were good whites, and we were black dogs and that's all there was to it.

Race mixing was not encouraged. Race mixing was not tolerated.

There was one young fellow from Michigan, white boy, who didn't much seem to care if someone was white or black or otherwise. He'd sit and talk and spend time with one person as equally as he would another. One night he got taken—got dragged—out into the woods by some other whites. He was found the next morning naked, freezing, and spilling blood from where he'd had a fat, coarse tree branch repeatedly, violently shoved into his butt-hole. All the management had to say about things was: "Should've known better than stir up race trouble," then sent the fellow back to Michigan.

Race mixing was not encouraged. Race mixing was not tolerated.

After spending most the day resting up from the week that'd passed, getting ready for the week to come, we'd all go to the main hall for dinner, eat segregated, then go back to our same color-correct groups and spend the evening entertaining ourselves with songs and music from guitars and harmonicas and Jew's harps. I couldn't play any of those. I couldn't sing. I could tell jokes, though. That I could do. I would bust up the boys with some bits

I'd heard from comics on *Toast of the Town* and observations about working at the camp. It was enough to give everyone a fair laugh. I guess I was funny. Anyway, I was funny enough to get some notice. One Sunday after joking around, Dax pulled me aside. He told me he was putting together an amateur show for the following Sunday, a chance for the guys with talent to entertain the ones without. He'd heard me telling jokes and asked if I wanted to do a few bits. I didn't even have to think about it. Just the idea of being in front of a crowd, having people hoot and clap for me same as they did for the TV comics, gave me a jazz.

"Real glad to hear that," Dax said. "Figure we ought have one of you for the rest of the colored boys."

The next couple of days got spent trying to work up a routine. Excitement kept me from thinking of much else. Not thinking of much else almost got my head taken off when I got into "the bite of a line," the snap of a tow cable that sent it flailing like a steel whip. To this day I believe ducking my father's blows gave me the speed to dodge the line. Most of it. While I was getting stitches where the cable had torn my shoulder, I made the obvious decision to save my joke-arranging for nights as I lay in bed. I'd mumble bits to myself while my worn-out body begged me for sleep.

Sunday night came around. The main hall was packed with people—workers, management. Everyone wanted to see the show, support their friends. That, and in the middle of a forest in Washington State with no money to spend and nowhere to spend it, an amateur night was the best and only bet. Some of the boys in the camp were not untalented, and the ones Dax had picked for the show were very good. Good singers. Good instrument players. The excitement I'd been feeling through the week got dialed over to nervousness, only then the gap between being funny for a few people and being horribly unfunny for several hundred becoming obvious to me. I felt something tapping against my leg. I looked down. It was my shaking hand.

Then all of a sudden it came time for me to take the floor. I got introduced, went out to the center of the room. Whatever applause there was died off. Maybe nerves were making me supersensitive, but I became aware of an odd split second of quiet between the clapping and my telling a joke. It was an emptiness that, in my mind, just hung in space, waiting to be filled. I filled it with some bits from the television comics, jokes old and hackneyed but funny enough to coax out a few laughs from the audience. Then I went into some bits about life at camp, the hard work and long hours and how we were rewarded for it all with some writing in a passbook and bad food. Basically I made fun of the whole operation.

The laughs started coming in waves.

And when I did impressions of some of the workers and managers—the way someone talked, or exaggerated one of their mannerisms, mugged their facial expressions reminiscent of how Pop used to mock the neighbors on one of his weed jags—the joint went nuts with screams and hollers.

From the corner of my eye I caught a glance of that tall white boy, the one from our koogie that wanted to beat in my head for not knowing the route to "niggerville." The tears in his eyes said he couldn't laugh any harder. Everyone was busting up.

Everyone except for Li'l Mo. Mo wasn't laughing. He didn't seem to find it too amusing, me clowning around in front of a bunch of whites. But as I finished up, all that was in my mind was that a room full of people—some who didn't know me, some who out-and-out hated me—were applauding me.

Dax had arranged for a special dinner after the show for the performers, a thank-you meal of steak and potatoes and a hunk of pie. I went back to the kitchen and got my plate same as the rest of the acts. The steak still sizzled when the cook plunked it down. Juice percolated from the skin of the potatoes. I started outside so I could get to eating while it was all still hot.

"Jackie," Dax called to me from a table. "Where yew goin'?"

"Outside," I said.

Dax sort of laughed a little. "What in tha hell for?"

Because I was hungry and I wanted to eat. I was going outside because I was black and everyone else was white. Blacks didn't eat with whites, and it never occurred to me that things should be any other way.

Apparently it should have. Dax waved me over to a spot next to him. "C'mon over heyah, Jackie. Eat outside, tha flies'll git in yer food."

As I sat down, as I cut into my steak and chewed on the first hearty mouthful, I remember Dax's hand coming down firm on my back.

"Funny as hell, boy. Where'd you learn to get so funny?"

<hr />

THE AMATEUR SHOW was four or five days in the past. I was working a skid trail trying to keep my mind on the boss and off the applause that was still ringing in my ears and the taste of the steak that was resurrected with my every swallow. As I worked at that chore, a Jeep came around driven by one of the camp managers. He stopped below my station, called me down from the line. I went to him, smiling, thinking he had something good to say about my act. Five days later and I'd still been getting the warm hand from people who'd seen me. Not this time. When I got close enough to read the manager's face, it told me and told me plain that whatever he had for me wasn't pleasant.

"Get in." Two words. To the point. And when the second I spent trying to figure out why was too long in passing: "Well, c'mon, boy. Get in. Let's go," the camp manager prompted again whip-cracking-style.

I started climbing into the Jeep. The manager barely waited for me to finish before pulling away.

I got ridden back to the administration building. I got walked to an office. Inside was another camp manager, looking less happy than the one who'd driven me. With him were a couple of frowning policemen.

"These here men are from the police," the manager told me in case their blues, badges, and guns weren't hint enough. "Your father's looking for you. Says you run off from home."

Most of the time Pop was too lit up and strung out to find his way from the couch to the floor. But somehow across the length of the country that smoker was able to stretch out and point a finger at me.

The manager said: "These officers are going to take you back to Seattle, put you on the first train for—"

"I don't want to go home." I tried to sound firm about it, but the only thing greater than the begging in my voice was the pleading. "If I go back home my pop's going to—"

"You're not eighteen." The manager didn't care a thing for my plight. He demonstrated his non-caring by not so much as looking my way. "You're not eighteen, you can't work. We'll get you on the train, we'll get you home." To further elaborate on his non-caring, the manager picked up some papers from his desk, stared at them. His furrowed brow indicating that the papers, and not me, now had his full attention.

I started to go with the policemen.

I stopped.

I asked the manager: "Where do I go to get my money?"

"You're not eighteen, you can't work. You can't work, you can't get paid."

Jammed between the two cops like a public enemy, I got walked to their prowl car and put in back. It was a long drive to Seattle, and on the whole of it there was no conversation among me and the officers. Once there, at the train station, I was left with a ticket for New York. Probably the lumber company paid for it. Taken out of what they owed me, they got off cheap.

Nearly three days back to the city. Outside the Vista-Dome, mountains melted into desert, which blended into . . . I had no money. A porter took pity on me, snuck me some leftovers from the dining car.

At the changeover in Chicago I gave consideration to getting off the train and running off to somewhere to do . . . something. Then I thought about how well I'd get along in an alien city, pockets empty, no one to feel sorry for me and slip me food. I got on my train and finished my ride to New York.

When I got to Penn Station there was no one there to meet me. I had no change for the subway and was too scared to try fare-jumping.

I walked home.

When I got to our apartment my father was high or drunk or some other form of passed out. On the couch. Right where I'd left him months ago. I went to bed.

In the middle of the night, on a jag, Pop busted into my room and welcomed me home belt in hand. His rant was something to the tune of: "I'll teach you to run off! I'll teach you to think you're somebody!"

For the next twenty minutes he taught me well.

part II

*T*here *was something floating in the Tallahatchie River. Bloated by water, gnawed by fish, it was hard to tell what it was.*

What it was was a body.

The body was Emmett Till.

Emmett Till was fourteen.

Was.

In August of 1955, Emmett had gone from his home in Chicago to Money, Mississippi, to spend the end of the summer with relatives. Money was rural, a township of barely fifty-five. Other than that, there was only fresh air and open fields. It should've been a good place for a kid to spend a summer. Would have been. Except that one day, at a tiny grocery store, young Emmett said something lewd to a white woman. Maybe he did. Maybe he only whistled at her. Maybe all he did was look in her general direction. Whatever the fact, as far as the upstanding white citizens of Money, Mississippi, cared, Emmett might as well have slapped her down and raped her. So that night two men—Roy Bryant and his brother, J. H. "Big" Milam, Milam being particularly nasty by even the rest of the town's reckoning—went 'round to Emmett's uncle's looking for "that Chicago boy." The two men strong-armed Till into their pickup and took him off into the dark.

Three days later that bloated, fish-eaten body was found floating in the Tallahatchie River. It was missing one eye. Its head had been crushed. A seventy-four-pound cotton gin fan had been necklaced around the body's throat with barbed wire. The olive to the cocktail: a bullet to the boy's head.

Bryant and Milam were arrested. Bryant and Milam were put on trial. A jury of twelve white men spent a long and labored hour and seven minutes deciding the two defendants were innocent despite what a parade of eyewitnesses had to say otherwise.

An hour and seven minutes. That included lunch.

The only punishment Bryant and Milam came close to receiving were the paper cuts they might have gotten from counting the four thousand dollars they were paid to recite the crime in Look magazine. Recite without fear of further prosecution. Double jeopardy. They were free to say what they pleased. What pleased them was to describe how on a muggy summer night they took Emmett Till down to the river, told him to beg forgiveness for whatever he'd supposedly done to the white woman.

He wouldn't.

Emmett told the two men that he hadn't done anything. He told them: So what if he'd talked to a white woman? Talked? In Chicago he'd kissed plenty of white girls, and he'd kiss plenty more if he felt like it. Fourteen-year-old Emmett Till, alone in the night, told two white, Southern men that he was just as good as they were.

So the two white, Southern men stripped Emmett, beat

Emmett, made Emmett carry the gin fan to the river. One of the two men shot Emmett in the head.

"What else could we do?" "Big" Milam recounted. "He was hopeless."

In the middle 1950s, in America, for most black people, a lot of things seemed hopeless.

March of 1956 to July of 1957

There was no other thing. No other way. I was going to be—I had to be—famous. I decided that. More rightly, the circumstances of life decided it for me. I turned eighteen, graduated high school, got a job with Li'l Mo at a moving company because it was the only job either of us could get, and I needed something more regular and better paying than the piece work I'd been doing. I worked the job almost a year, carrying other people's belongings down from one apartment, piling them into a truck, hauling them across town, then up into another apartment. Dressers. Beds. Tables. Boxes loaded with dishes and books and knickknacks—heavy like they were full of bricks. Heavy until you could barely lift them. But you did. You lifted them because moving them was the only way to get paid. You lifted, you got your money, and you wore the ache of the job long after it was done. You went home, slept a little, you woke up too early, you went out into the day and did it all over again.

At the end of that first three hundred some days I took a look at my future. I didn't see much waiting for me, and what I did see wasn't much good. The prospects for a black man in the fifties were limited to being famous or to being nothing. To be something other than one of those two, a doctor or lawyer . . . not that it couldn't happen. It could. It did. For some blacks. But to want to wear a white collar was little better than wanting to walk on the moon. Beyond that, without higher education that I couldn't afford if I wanted, couldn't get if I could afford, I was looking at a life sentence of manual and menial labor: sweeping floors and shining shoes and polishing cars and stocking warehouses. Moving furniture. I was looking at a future that looked just like my past.

But to be famous . . .

You'd see famous blacks on TV and in the movies, out on the playing fields: Harry Belafonte, Dizzy Gillespie, Ms. Lena Horne. Jackie Robinson and Sugar Ray Robinson and Bill Bojangles Robinson and . . . And famous blacks got to go where they pleased, do as they pleased and got treated just about as if they were white. You saw their pictures in the paper or a magazine, saw them at this party or that in fine clothes, drink in one hand and the other draped around a white, and the white didn't have any problem being near— being touching-close to—a famous black. Sure they didn't. I'd learned that a good time ago: You've got money or status and real suddenly no one gives a thought about being around you. And the more I saw of rich blacks and famous blacks, the more it filled me with ambition. Ambition that burned hot, burned away all else and left only what mattered: want. I wanted to be rich. I wanted to be famous. Not such a crazy dream. Althea Gibson had emancipated herself right out of this very Harlem. So had Dizzy. So had Sammy D. So could I.

With absolutely no other skills, and based solely on having made schoolkids and fellow tree cutters laugh, I figured—brashly, desperately—comedy was my best chance for mating my twin desires. Best, only. Neverminding the fact that I could list the truly famous black comedians of the world on a three-fingered hand, I blindly started a road.

First: I needed an act. Easy. I stole one. I watched *Toast of the Town*. Different from before, just sitting and enjoying the show, I studied it, the comedians, their style and mannerisms. The best bits I borrowed. Re-borrowed. Most of the jokes were already public domain—common in form, old in existence. It's the way comedy was:

generic lines presented by pleasant guys with good timing whose suits were more unique than their acts. Using the jokes, I bargained with myself, was just temporary. Once I got going I'd work up an act of my own. As I'd done when I was teaching myself to be "well spoken," I did time in front of the mirror in my room. I watched myself as I mimicked Will Jordan, Myron Cohen, and Alan King. Lots of Alan King. Thirty-seven times he was on Sullivan. His act I got to know real well.

Thing number two I needed was a club where I could perform. Easy. There was one joint in all of New York that was *the* joint: the Copacabana. I'd never once been in it. I'd barely been near its neighborhood—tony Midtown—but I knew it was *the* joint because whenever Sullivan would ask one of his in-from-Hollywood-between-pictures guests where they might be seen around town, when he asked a name comic or an even bigger name singer where they might be found doing a drop-in, the answer was most always the same: the Copa.

So one afternoon I took my ignorant self down to Fifty-ninth and Madison, knocked on the locked front door of the club. Waited. Knocked. Waited. Pounded. Waited. Pretty soon a tired-looking white fellow opened up, tie down, sleeves rolled high, and hair combed over a bald spot that just made it more noticeable rather than less.

"What?" he wanted to know.

"I'd like to speak with the manager, please."

"What?"

"Are you the mana—"

"What!"

"I'd like to work here, sir."

"Doing?" His body held a position that was half out/half in the doorway, like he was just itching to get back to whatever he'd been doing before I'd come around. If I'd burst into flames I figured there was only a fifty-fifty chance I could hold his attention.

"I want to perform," I said, as if it should be obvious. "I want to go onstage." Adding to it: "I'm a comic."

The guy with the comb-over made a whole lot of comments regarding my intelligence and the legality of my mother's marriage at the time of my birth. Then he told me to get lost. He didn't quite tell me that, but the meaning was the same.

What had I expected? Had I really figured to knock on the door, wave hello, and wind up onstage at the Copacabana?

Yeah.

Yeah, I guess I had, my vision limited with blinders of me taking bows before a laughing, clapping, loving crowd of people. I'd figured the only thing I had to do was show up, and all that would be waiting for me. I'd figured very, very wrong.

But the same arrogance or naiveness, stupidity maybe, that sent me to the Copa kept me from quitting things then and there. So I wouldn't kick things off at the Copacabana. So what? There were nothing but clubs in the city. If the Copa didn't want me, I'd take my act elsewhere. I took it to the nightspots strung along Fifty-third Street. Took it to clubs in hotels, their fancy bars and cocktail joints. I took it to clubs on the East Side, the West Side, coffee-houses and dives on both sides of the Village. I took it around for nearly a month, and I got turned down for auditions just as fast as I could find new doors to pound on. Nobody was taking what I was selling. Nobody was hot for a comic—for *one more* comic—coming their way. A realization was catching up to me: A whole lot of people in New York wanted to be in show business, and a whole lot of clubs and coffeehouses and nightspots were sick of seeing them come around.

I worked my way down to the Fourteenth Street Theater, down other than just locationwise. Down meaning I'd busted through the bottom of the barrel of respectability. The Fourteenth Street Theater was left over from vaudeville. A dinosaur that didn't know the rest of its kind was off marking time in a boneyard. Specializing in cheap beer and bad burlesque, it was a hole of a joint where comics and singers and novelty acts could go and do their thing for what constituted an audience. Between acts the theater showcased strippers. Or, depending on how you looked at things, between strippers the theater had acts so married guys could go home and tell their wives they were out seeing a show and not be lying about it.

I came around looking for the manager. I got a guy named Ray. I asked for an audition, asked with all the confidence I had left, trying to sound like a young man who was going to light up the world and not just another kid who wanted to crack funny but couldn't get stage time anywhere else.

Ray didn't seem to care one way or the other. He told me to come back two weeks from Sunday, to be at the theater at seven o'clock, then was done with me.

Two weeks.

They passed, but they took their time about it, me spending nearly every minute of every day refining fantasies about going on-stage, what it would be like up onstage, what my life—my gorgeous new life—would be like following the Sunday that was fourteen days and counting to come. But prior to being reborn, there was my real and current life to be lived in its two main components. There was my dad—always around and always high. Always ready to abuse—and there was my job at the moving company. I never had much of a build, always slight. Standing six one but never tipping out at more than one seventy, I wasn't made for lifting furniture. Except I was black. That was about the sole requirement for manual labor.

One time Mo and I were on a job, the fellow we were moving had a big . . . thing. Still don't know for sure exactly what it was. Like a chest of drawers only longer. Not as tall. Solid wood. Heavy. Of course it wouldn't fit in the elevator, so me and Mo had to haul it downstairs. Six flights, and on a New York–hot day. Hot like little sister. The heat, the weight of the thing, the sweating they made you do, didn't help my grip any. Also didn't help to have the guy who owned the piece at the top of the stairs barking down orders drill sergeant–style. "Don't drop it! You boys be careful and don't drop that!" Like if he hadn't told us we would've thrown it down the stairs for lack of knowing better.

"Don't drop it! Don't you drop that!"

His voice kept pounding my ears. The stifling air kept choking my throat. Hands wet, slick on the wood. Back screaming at me, arms crying. My foot caught a step wrong. No way to keep steady. I let my end drop. The piece hit the stairs. Not hard. Too hard for the cat it belonged to. He flew down the steps at me; he came fast and he came swinging. The side of my head took his punch and lit off fireworks inside my skull. When my eyes stopped rolling and fluttered open, I was where I'd so often been: on the floor, again. My face turning red under the black, again. Looking up at my attacker, trying not to cry, trying to take what I'd been given like a man. But my version of stoic was trembling and going teary-eyed. Again.

And while the man was raging at me with "how dare you" bits, cursing my useless Negro—not the word he used—self for dropping his expensive whatever, Li'l Mo stood watching him. Watching and balling his hands into tight, angry fists the same way he had back in the logging camp when he was ready to have a go at that redneck and his redneck clan. He was set to lash out, strike a blow against the oppressors. Li'l Mo was ready to start the revolution.

From my spot on the floor I gave Mo a look that told him to cool it. Only thing starting trouble would buy us was more trouble. Wasn't worth it. It was never worth trying to fight The Man.

Day over but not done, wanting to be alone, I gave Mo some story about needing to be somewhere to do something and went off walking, kept company by my stinging face and angry thoughts. I wanted bad to have at that white cat for slapping me. I wanted to fist up my hand and smack him right back. But hitting him would've gotten me fired. At least that. I hated my job, but I needed my job and had affection for the money that came with it. It's hard to have pride when lust and greed get in the way. Especially when your skin color is a permanent factor. So I took the man's slaps. And so what if I did? Real soon I'd be in a place where that white guy, where anybody, wouldn't be able to give me the back of their hand again. Real soon. Less than fourteen days.

Into my own thoughts, my eyes missed a two-by-four that had been tossed out in the alley I walked. My foot caught it, got tripped up, and I went over. As I flew for the ground, my hands jumped out to take the fall. Waiting on the pavement to meet my right palm was a piece of broken glass. Small, but just big enough to gash my flesh and start up a flow of blood. I sat on the dirty ground, pants torn at the knee, bleeding. And my face still hurt.

I looked up.

Sitting in the alley was a brand-new 1956 Packard Caribbean, a chromium wonder. Parked. Lifeless. Not doing a thing. Nothing except mocking me. It bragged of things I would never have: a near-six-grand touring car that I couldn't afford in a lifetime of trying. Whitewalls, white leather interior, and a tri-tone paint job—eggshell, sky blue, tango red—fresh-polished to a mirror shine. And that grille, that chrome-dripping grille that was like a big fat smile that came with a ridiculing laugh. A laugh directed square at my face: See me, Jackie? See what you can't have you poor, dumb, useless—

The two-by-four was in my hand. The two-by-four was all over the Packard. It smashed and spider-webbed the windshield. It de-sideview-mirrored a door. A swing and a hit; the hood ornament was sent out of the park. And then the grille. Then I went to work on that stupid, shining grille. The wood tore at the chrome, peeled it back, dented it in, beat down the bulbous points that were excess for the sake of excess. I beat them, but what I was doing was smacking back the white man who'd smacked me. I smashed the headlights, but I was giving it to my dad after taking it for so long. I pounded and pounded and pounded the car, but what I was really doing . . . What was I doing?

I stopped.

After the hammering of wood on metal the alley was horribly quiet. All of New York around me and the only thing I heard was the sound of a dog barking deep in the city, the sound of my heart beating in my chest. I heard the sound of the two-by-four clunking against the ground. All of New York around me, and I felt like every citizen was listening to the sound of my deep breathing and racing feet as I busted from the alley, from my victim: a Packard that had the misfortune of being in the wrong place at the wrong time.

SUNDAY. FINALLY SUNDAY. I hit the theater around five-twenty, spent a solid forty-five minutes cooling my heels before the joint opened up enough to even let me in. That got followed by another thirty minutes of standing around waiting for the show to start. When it did, fifteen people sprinkled a house that sat two hundred. I was scared I was going to get thrown on first. How was I supposed to do any kind of a show for that non-crowd?

I was burning calories with worry over nothing.

The seven o'clock hour passed and so did the eight with lots of acts going on and me still marking time.

After nine. The house was closing in on half full—as full as it was likely to get. The audience—all men, slobbish, and in a class somewhere between middle and low, warmed up and fairly sober even with the beers they downed at a pace—was peaking. The moment was ripe for me to take the stage, display my skills. I didn't. Instead, up went some singers, a couple of comics, specialty acts, dog acts, a guy who recited lines from a play, and strippers. All kinds of strippers. Every shape, size, and age equally represented. Except the good-looking kind. Those the theater apparently banned from the premises. The men in the house didn't much care. The men in the house gave the women drunken salutes, and in thanks the women peeled their clothes with a smile and a tease before letting them fall away altogether. It made the boys happy, and the boys made the girls happy, and everybody was happy except for me. I was just standing around watching the crowd get half as large and twice as loaded and plenty more hot with every comic and singer and dog act that went on taking up good and valuable stage time that could be better enjoyed with more stripping.

I tried to pin down the emcee, get a rough idea when I might—might—be going on. Scared mice were easier to corner. His best estimate, when I could get any out of him, was: "Soon, chum. Real soon." He said the same thing to some old guy with a banjo when he asked when he'd be going up.

Ten o'clock got to be eleven and twelve. The audience got cleaved. One and one-thirty cut their size again. The strippers had been through two rotations and a half, but to the boozed oglers who remained, the girls were new and unfamiliar, and with an alcohol makeover they were nearly beautiful.

At about two-thirty, when I was tired by just the thought of the full day of moving furniture that was waiting some five hours away from me, the emcee came over, said: "You're next, Jake."

"It's Jackie," I started to say. But just that quick, after standing around all night, I suddenly had to wrestle with my stomach, which decided it was nervous and had to empty itself. Sweat-slick palms clutching gut, I took up a spot in the wings. Occupying my future space onstage was a girl whose talents lay in her ability to unbutton buttons and unzip zippers nearly in rhythm to music. Nearly. And when she'd finished the job the house would belong to me. I tried to snapshot every second that passed as I waited. I wanted a museum-quality collection of memories of this event, this moment of personal history. I wanted it well documented in my mind, easily recallable in complete and exact detail for the day, for the certain day, when people would say to me: Tell us, Jackie. Tell us how it all began.

So, let me tell you: It began with the stripper ending her act, taking a couple of well-milked bows waiting for crumpled dollar bills from the audience that would never get tossed her way. The boys were drunk, but not so drunk they would pay a cent more than cover to peep what the girls were shaking. This one finally got to bundling her clothes and heading offstage with hot and not particularly well-hidden grumbles for the boys and their cheap, cheap ways.

The emcee took the stage, his stroll arrogant in its laziness. Never mind he was bringing on acts at a burlesque house past two in the morning, he was above his station. "Ooookay," he said slow and soft and dead tired, his too-good-for-this manner infecting his speech as well. "This next guy is a comic. How about some applause for Johnny Mann."

Close enough.

I hit the stage and I hit it fast. I hit it with all the energy the emcee lacked and enough left over to juice Staten Island. Applause. A very little. Then it was gone. And there was that void again, the same emptiness between the claps and my first joke that was waiting for me when I'd performed back at the logging camp. I raced to fill it with my borrowed bits. Bits about the crazy people in "my" neighborhood, about the mother-in-law I didn't even have. Bits on my dad the drunk that I hadn't written but still rang fairly true. Bit after bit after bit. Nothing. No laughter. No grins. No matter my daydreams, at some point you dig the reality of things: You're doing time at two in the morning for a handful of drunks who want to see naked women. A stand-up show doesn't figure into any of that. There wasn't a laugh to be bought in the house. But the worst of it, beyond the no-laughing, the people didn't so much as notice me. They didn't laugh, but they didn't boo. They didn't clap, but they didn't heckle. They didn't care. I was onstage trying to live a dream, trying to accelerate my life, and no one gave a damn. Drinks got ordered, conversation got passed around. I got ignored.

Confidence went away. Shakes and flop sweat took over.

After a lifetime-long three minutes onstage—two shorter than they had given me—I limped off.

The emcee brought on a stripper.

Her the boys gave attention to.

The exit. I couldn't move myself for it fast enough. I crossed past Ray, the house manager, not saying anything to him, figuring nothing needed be said. But as I rushed for the street, he said something to me.

"What?" I asked, hearing him but not believing what I was hearing.

"Mondays," he said again. "You can start going up on Monday nights."

For a second I got some positivity back, thinking maybe I'd been funnier than I figured.

"I was good, huh?" I asked.

Ray shrugged at me. "Gotta put something on between the whores."

———

GRACE KELLY WAS GETTING HITCHED to a prince, and that was perfect. The 1950s were the American dream; they were the American way of life lived as a dream. The U.S. was *the* all-powerful nation top to bottom. The president was the guy who beat Hitler, and the company man was the former G.I. who'd hit the beaches at Normandy. That we'd only been able to stalemate the North Koreans was a side issue. We were aces. We were prosperous and we were powerful. Madison Avenue told us so in the way it pitched us Plymouths and Geritol and Betty Furnessed us into buying Westinghouse. At home every man wanted to be king of his prefabricated castle, and every woman wanted to be a queen at least for a day. And as if the wish of the people willed the dream real, one of Hollywood's most glamorous starlets was turning herself into honest-to-God royalty. She wore a wedding dress and he turned out in some princely looking getup; chest full with spaghetti, shiny star-shaped medals dripping from a rainbow of ribbons. Made you wonder how he could've fought in enough wars to have won them all. But then, you gave it some thought and realized he hadn't fought any wars. He was a prince. Princes don't fight in wars. Princes send other guys to do their fighting for them. And he was a prince of a tiny country you could barely find on a map without trying three times real hard. Tiny countries don't get into wars. Tiny countries are liable to get themselves overrun. So all that spaghetti, the gold trim on his uniform, the sash slung beauty queen–style diagonally across him was, like Sergeant Kolawole and his freedom fighters, all make-believe. Except, he really was a prince. Prince enough he got to marry Grace Kelly. Many, many years later, she would die tragically the way lots of beautiful and famous people did, which would make you suspect there was a price to be paid for being beautiful and famous. But that would be many, many years later. At the moment, televised around the world, Grace Kelly was marrying Prince Somebody from a small country, and as I watched with the rest of the planet, all I thought was it must be so marvelous to be beautiful and famous: Here was a woman, who had everything in the world, getting the rest of it.

She had all that. What I had was a moving job that filled my days and something like a home life with my father to return to at night. But my *life* became the Fourteenth Street Theater. Whatever else it wasn't, the theater would always be where I first broke into show business. It's where I first met people who, same as me, had a blinding desire to be on television or to be in pictures—a known face and a household name. They wanted to be something more than what they were. Some had talent, some were just shining themselves. Time would tell which I was.

Performing on Monday nights was what Ray started me with. In truth, it was Tuesday mornings before I took stage. Same as when I'd auditioned, the Monday crowd didn't amount to more than a bunch of man-aged boys who'd come for the clothesless women and used the acts in between as an opportunity to refill their glasses.

Didn't matter.

By the time I went on, it was usually me cracking bits to the cleaning crew.

Didn't mind.

Not at first. At first I was happy just to be able to perform regular, work my act in front of bodies instead of a mirror and for a cut of the door on top of that, though most times my take didn't cover round-trip fare on the subway.

Didn't care.

I was in show business. I was an entertainer.

I spent more time at the theater than just the Monday nights/Tuesday mornings I went up. Every night I could I'd go down, hang out. Mostly I was hoping one of the scheduled acts would do a no-show and I could grab their spot. On average there were fifteen other guys sniffing around with the same bright idea. But I'd also watch the other acts, the ones I liked and the ones I didn't. If I liked them, I wanted to mimic their style and presence. I wanted to parasite anything I could from them to make me a little sharper. And the acts I didn't dig, I wanted to know for sure what I didn't like about them—what made them tired and unfunny, what it was that kept them at the theater long after they should've moved up and on, or gotten out.

The goal of my observing was to get me from Mondays to a spot on the weekend, Friday or Saturday night. Those were the prime gigs: The house was decent, a cut of the door added up to something more than pocket change, and, most important, it was a whole lot easier to get agents and managers and talent scouts to come around then than at past two A.M. on a weekday morning. And those were the people you had to have in your life—the ten-percenters, guys who opened doors, cut deals, and made noise. They were the ones who, real easy, could jump an act from clubs to television and from television to fame.

Over time, some of the acts at the theater who couldn't take not going anywhere quit coming around altogether. Because of them falling out, me getting a little better, slow and steady I made my way from Monday nights to Tuesday and Wednesday nights. Wednesday mornings. Not much after that I actually was getting stage time at night instead of the crack of dawn. I was making progress. I was feeling good, and I was feeling proud. I felt that way for the first few months. For the next few I felt content. After eight or nine months I felt nothing but worry. At some point I realized I'd stalled. I wasn't going anywhere. I wasn't moving any closer to Thursday nights, and for sure no closer to a weekend spot.

Worse, I wasn't getting on at any other clubs. The Fourteenth Street Theater wasn't any kind of a battering ram when it came to knocking open other doors. At some places having the theater as my only credit hurt me more than helped. And not having an agent or manager to do my hard selling for me only made me come off all the more desperate. I was going nowhere, the fact of it proven to me by the new faces around the theater; the fresh acts trying to break in. Wasn't very much earlier I'd been fresh. Wasn't very much earlier I'd been snickering at acts who'd been hanging around too long, had bottomed out, thinking: Why the hell don't they just toss it in? Maybe apprehension had me reading things that weren't there, but it seemed a lot of the smirks on the lips of the new faces were saying the same about me.

≈

ANYWHERE, were there any couple of people who could be any more not alike? Poor, black, from Harlem. White, Jewish, from

Williamsburg. I wanted to be a comic and she wanted to sing. I had no family to speak of and little education. She had manners, and a mother and father who actually cared their daughter was up late trying to make a life in show business. The only ways me and Frances Kligman were similar were in the desire to succeed and the belief—not counting the fact we seemed to have a permanent gig showcasing the least desirable joint in town—that we would.

The clearest memory I have of Fran, the first thing I think of when I recall her, she always smelled like food. Not that she stank of it. She carried the aroma of someone who lingered in a kitchen over shared stories as she prepared meals. The smell reminded me of Mae. That odd cocktail of things—the scent she carried, our differences, and our shared desire—was foundation enough for me and Fran to form a fast friendship.

We'd hang together at the theater, we'd talk, and at some point we voluntarily took up the chore of looking out for each other. Palling around with me would keep other guys from so steadily pressing up on Fran, trying to get the girl to give them the time of day. Fran was nothing if she wasn't a looker. Sandy-haired, maybe a little plump, but God-gifted in all the right spots. The wolves were constantly circling, eager to get a little play. I didn't blame them; I just kept them back. For her part, Fran kept me honest as far as the strippers were concerned. It was hard to pay them much attention when Fran was staring at me big-sister-style. Good thing for it. What the girls lacked in looks they made up for with jigs. Real easy they could Venus's-flytrap a young man from a good bit of what little pay he earned. A very good bit.

So, us two had a nice little groove. We would get to the theater early, catch the other acts, joke to each other about the ones we thought corny, give a just about honest critique of each other's sets, maybe grab some late food, sit and talk, sometimes for hours. It was very much as if, minus the sex, Fran and I were having a relationship. Not as odd as it comes off. We were different from each other, and mostly unknown to each other, but at the same time unsuitable for almost everyone else we met. Sometimes, when you're friendless, the next best thing is a stranger who knows you well. Frances came to know me very well. She was probably the only person I could be myself with, open and honest. Even at that, we both did everything we could to avoid one truth: Neither of us was making it in show business. The reality of things was plain, but like two people sharing a sin, we didn't talk about it. Most times we didn't. But one time, one night after a string of go-nowhere nights—bad audiences, bad pay—when I was walking with Fran after a show, we couldn't help but talk about it.

I was counting my cut of the door. It didn't take but an instant.

"What'd you get?" Fran asked.

"Dollar thirty. Bad enough my career's dead, I'm not making enough to bury it good." The city was never entirely still, but at that hour, very late, or very early, it was mostly quiet. Almost at rest. It was always incredible to me that a place with so many souls could become so nearly silent and empty. At those times, walking the streets was no different from walking through a Hollywood movie set, blocks of false fronts and empty structures built up to look like something. Just facades. It was the people that made the city.

I asked Fran: "What'd you get?"

"Same."

Too much of a sweetheart, Fran was never much at lying. "C'mon. I can take it."

A hesitation, not wanting to hurt my feelings. "Three."

I was split in my reaction to that. Ray had given her a buck and change more than me, figuring, figuring wrongly, it might be good for a little play with Fran. It wasn't fair and the reasoning behind it was off, but even so, a buck and change? I knew that didn't even begin to compensate Fran's talent. And if she wasn't getting what she deserved from a guy who wanted to make time with her, what chance did I have of ever getting my due?

Fran, seeing my heart sinking, tossed out some cheer-up bits to keep me from drowning in my own misery. "It's only because I get that same handful of guys coming in to hear me. They come, they drink, so Ray swings me a little extra."

We stopped walking for a second under the shine thrown down by a streetlamp.

"He does it 'cause he wants to swing you a little extra in the back of his Chrysler."

"I'll be careful, Dad." That came with a smile.

Warm as the smile was, it was no good for making me feel better. Of its own free will my mouth opened and heartache came spilling out. "Christ, Frances, I'm . . ."

"You're what?"

What was I? What word was there to describe the hurt of failure forming inside me? "Sick. I'm sick of my life, sick of spending my days moving furniture and my nights trying to get boozers to listen to jokes, and for what? For pocket change? For goddamn . . ."

My hands caught my falling head. I could have cried just then. Except that Fran was a girl, and, friend or not, I wasn't about to cry in front of a girl, except for that . . . So I did some dry crying. I wailed without tears. "I just want to make it, Fran. I want out of this life. I want—"

"What do you want?"

"I want to quit getting beat down." I corkscrewed against the defeat tearing at me. "I want to quit taking punches. Long as I can remember I've had people pushing me around, treating me like dirt, treating me like a nothing. All my life I've been nothing. Worse than that. I've been a black nothing."

"Don't say that."

"You ask my pop, he'll tell you. You ask any white person on the street, they'll tell you what I am."

"Including me, because I don't think that. I don't think of you as black, and I certainly don't think of you as nothing."

I quit my pity for a tick, looked at Fran. I wanted to read her, wanted to know if she was saying things to say things or if she meant her words. Even in the streetlamp's bad light she was obvious. She was honesty.

I had to break off my stare; embarrassment juked my head away—her being so strong and me being so weak.

I asked Fran, I looked across the street, but I asked: "Why do you do this, hang out all night just to get in a song in front of drunks? You're not like me. You have a good home life."

She laughed a little. "No. Yeah, I've got a real nice life. Nice parents, live in a nice neighborhood. I should meet a nice Jewish boy, have a nice wedding, move to a nice suburb and just . . ." Fran laughed again, this time pained. It was like the hurt I'd been feeling had infected her. "You know something? As much as you don't want your life, I don't want that: a house on Long Island with a couple of kids and a dog, and a Buick in the drive. I don't want any of that the worst way I know how.

"What I want is to be onstage, in front of people, performing. I want to sing. I . . . I need to. And if that means it's at the Fourteenth Street Theater at twenty past two, better that than trying to figure out what flowers to plant in the garden and what towels go with the bathroom tile. I know that's got to sound . . . I've got a thousand other choices, but I can't help it; I can't help the way I feel. I feel—"

"You feel like you were born different."

Fran shot me a look, slightly hot, as though I'd just announced her secret shame to the world. But after a beat her stare softened. She said: "Sometimes I feel that way."

Fran went quiet. The sound of her voice was replaced by the dull hum of life: the few cars that rode the avenues, the sound of them echoing through the skyscraper canyons. A siren went off somewhere we couldn't see. A guy at a newsstand talking to another guy who was waiting for the early edition to get thudded down from the cruising *Post, News, Herald Trib,* or *Times* trucks was going on about *them,* and about how he was sick of *them,* and how the president should do this or that about *them* before it's too late.

Fran said: "Let's go down to the Village tomorrow night."

I shook my head to the idea. "I hate that."

"Hate what?"

"Going to the clubs down there, seeing people doing better than me."

"Come on. It'll be fun. We'll catch a couple of acts, get us both jazzed up again. Jackieeeeee"—dragging my name out—"don't make me go down there by myself." Fran tossed me more of that smile of hers.

Fran was okeydoke, the kind of girl you thought of as one of the guys. Except when she smiled. When she smiled she was all woman.

". . . Okay."

"How did I know you were going to say that? I better run and catch my train. I'll talk to you tomorrow."

"Wait up." I held out a couple of bucks. "Here. Grab a cab."

"Jackie . . ."

"You can't ride the subway this time of night."

"And I'm not taking the little bit you hardly make."

"You don't get home safe, we can't go to the Village." I tossed back that smile she'd given me.

A little hesitation; then Frances traded the money for a kiss on the cheek.

"I love you, Jackie," she said.

I watched Frances hop a Checker for Williamsburg.

I spent forty minutes underground waiting for the uptown local.

———

TIME. PLACE. DIDN'T MATTER. New York. The modern age. Didn't matter. Didn't, but maybe it did. Maybe it mattered more.

New York City, 1956; eight million people. You are one in eight million. So, maybe the instinct to not be alone, the need for tribalism, mattered more even among the millions, even—especially—in New York. A voice by itself is nothing. A voice timesed and timesed and timesed again is a shout not to be ignored. The city was a collection of tribes trying to be heard. The Chinese had Chinatown pressing right against Little Italy for the Italians. The blacks took Harlem. The Puerto Ricans were left the crumbling west side of Hell's Kitchen. The rich had Park Avenue. The rich had the Upper West Side. They had the Upper Es and Wall Street to work on, and Fifth Avenue and all of Fifty-seventh to shop along. The establishment had established itself all over the borough.

There wasn't much Manhattan left for the rest looking for their tribe: the headstrong, the independent. The not-like-yous. Young, disillusioned America that wasn't buying into suburbia and *Father Knows Best,* or tail-finned automobiles and Automats and automatoning on commuter rails—nameless, faceless, soulless—to do the corporate job for the corporate pay somewhere waaaaay down the corporate ladder. They didn't go for duck and cover. They positively didn't think much of Norman Vincent Peale. They *did* believe television rotted the brain, all commies weren't bad, and if they were, they weren't as bad as Pat Boone stealing from the Negroes. They were the new tribe migrating from all points of Bohemia. They staked their claim south of Fourteenth Street, north of Houston and between Fourth Ave. and the Hudson River. Greenwich Village. Ground zero for the East Coast cultural revolution. The Village cribbed every fresh artist, every new musician, and every cat and kitten who desired to be one. Poets, actors, writers, painters. The Beats. The Beat boys, turtlenecked and goateed. The Beat girls, sporting sloppy Joe sweaters and drainpipes that ran a few inches short of their flat Capezios. The uniform of non-conformity. All in black. Always in black. Black was the color of the middle-class rebellion, an uprising waged by finger snapping to free verse in the cellars, the coffeehouses and jazz joints that choked MacDougal Street. They came to the Village wide-eyed and truly believing that theirs was the poem, or painting, or performance piece that was going to make the status quo sit down, shut up, and take notice. And if not, at the very least maybe they could score some good drugs, have some loose sex, and just generally be hep.

In that scene, in that craaazy scene, Fran and I could pal around stare-free. *Down there* a black kid and a white Jewish girl were routine. *Down there* men and men were routine, same with women and women, and men and men who dressed like women, and any other combo you could dream up. *Down there* everything was cool, so every once in a while *down there* was where Fran and I would hang in the clubs: The Village Vanguard, Upstairs at the Duplex, The Bitter End, Bon Soir. Dark little dives and slightly upscale cabarets that featured talent both famous and fresh. None featured more of each than The Blue Angel. The Angel it was called. A night at The Angel was a night of digging Eartha Kitt, or Julie Wilson, or the ever-sultry Lena Horne. Nichols and May were around doing their comedy bits. Mort Sahl was breaking in his act, toting a newspaper and V-neck sweater like he was Charlie Harvard. You worked The Angel you had real talent. You worked The Angel you had more than just a dreamer's chance of hitting it big.

I didn't work The Angel.

I felt queer about that joint, felt about it the same as you'd feel about a woman you dug but knew in your heart you could never have. Catching a show there was a harsh reminder of how far away success was, the distance from my seat in the audience to the stage. Nothing in my life ever seemed any farther. And the irony of the agony: As much as I hoped one day The Angel would figure into my future, I never figured doing nothing more than watching a show would kick my life in a whole new direction. But it's when you're not expecting things that you step off a curb and get yourself side-swiped. I got hit hard.

Frances and I were at The Angel catching acts—a few singers, a few comics—me having a good time despite washing each performance down with a straight shot of jealous envy. It was a good way through the show when the emcee stepped to the mike, did a preamble, and brought out the next performer.

She took the stage.

I can say this: I can say at no time in my life previously had I ever seen anyone—anything—so beautiful that they actually caused me pain. Pain from the fear that the desire I instantly felt would never be fulfilled.

She was easily, in my mind, the loveliest woman I'd ever seen: black but light in tone, coffee with cream. An unbroken mile of perfect flesh. Her face and features were smooth and rounded, small and delicate—childlike, which made her wide eyes look all the wider. Just above her lip on the left side was a tiny mole. A beauty mark. It was the only thing about her that even came close to being a blemish.

I can't say what I was feeling when I saw her was love. Still more kid than man, I didn't really know what love was. My mother had showed me some. Grandma Mae. Pop had taught me everything it wasn't. But what this woman made me feel was all brand-new. She was everything my heart had ever dreamed of.

I didn't know her name, hadn't been paying any attention when the emcee'd brought her up. I sat and listened to her set and longed in ignorance. Her voice was high in pitch but rich, stopping way shy of being shrill. In range it was full and captivating, the last sound sailors heard before a Siren lulled them to eternity.

Fran's elbow poking at my ribs got me down off my cloud.

"Pick up your tongue, buddy."

I shut my gaping mouth and went back to staring at the woman onstage.

The second she finished her set, I was first up out of my seat clapping like I was trying to slap my hands off my wrists.

As she left the stage she gave a thankful smile to no one in particular, to the audience in general, but I claimed it for my own.

Fran tugged me down into my seat. The emcee took back the mike.

He said, and I listened real careful: "The kitten's a canary. She something, isn't she? Clap the hands, snap the fingers. Thomasina Montgomery!"

I was back up on my feet, back to beating my hands. Yeah. She was something.

OUTSIDE THE BLUE ANGEL, outside the entrance. I was waiting. It was getting late. I was getting tired. I didn't care. I was waiting for Thomasina, and I would keep on waiting even if the end of time rolled around before she came out of the club. Fran, trouper that she was, kept watch with me though we'd been standing out in the getting-cooler-by-the-minute air for a good long while. I would've thought that we'd missed her, that Thomasina might've already left and headed home, but the instant she quit the stage I paid up and dragged Fran outside just so there was no chance of her getting by me.

Unless . . . was there a back way out of The Blue Angel?

"What are you going to say to her?" Frances yelled over to me. She stood a little ways away, giving me all the space I'd need to try whatever I was going to try with Thomasina . . . Miss Montgomery. . . .

"I'm going to . . . I'll tell her . . . I've got a line for her."

"A line?" Fran found that funny. "Okay, Mr. Poitier, you give her a line."

Truth is I didn't know what to say. I wanted to sound cool, not cuckoo. Complimentary, not off the cob. But what do you say to a woman who's probably been tossed lines by every Charlie who'd ever caught her act, every guy who's seen her walking down the street? In my head I tested all my best bits: Excuse me, miss. I'm a little offended, were you going to pass right by me without even flirting a little? Are your feet tired, darlin', 'cause you've been running through my mind. Your mama must've been a bee, 'cause you've got a voice like honey.

Your mama must've been a bee . . . ? Oh, that's good. I wouldn't even talk to myself after hearing that. How about I really get her to think I'm a joker? How about: Your daddy must've been a camel 'cause I love your humps.

The door opened.

She walked out.

Her good looks got multiplied at short range. She was younger looking, too. A lot. Eighteen if a day.

I started to say hello to her. She looked in my direction and I got caught up in those doe eyes. All my lines got aborted down to "Hi."

"Hello," she said. One word riding that soft, high voice of hers. One word. In an instant I heard it over and over a thousand sweet times. After that I was no good for anything but standing where I was and watching the girl hail a cab, get in, and be gone from my life.

Gradually Fran's voice started to reach me—a light working its way through the all-encompassing shroud of Thomasina.

"You didn't do anything," Fran said.

"What do you mean I didn't—"

"You didn't do anything, that's what I mean. Except for standing there and looking goofy, you did nothing."

"I said hello."

"You said hi, and soft as you did I'd have figured you were trying to keep it a secret." A big, bright smile. Frances was having the time of her life.

"I'm moving slow." I tried to make it seem me letting Thomasina disappear into the city was all part of some genius plan. "I'm not trying to scare the girl off, you know? Let her get familiar with me first. Take things gradual."

"You take things any more gradually, you'll get in your first date around nineteen seventy-five."

"That's not funny."

"I just hope you're still young enough to give her a show, and I'm not talking about your comedy act."

Sarcastic: "You're a good friend, Fran. Really. You really are."

She took me by the arm. "C'mon, Sidney," pulling me toward one of the endless number of Village coffeehouses, "let's go float your hopes in some Joe."

As we walked I looked back up the avenue and made a promise to the vanished taxicab: One day I would be with her. One day I would be famous and successful, and I would be with Thomasina.

"YOU'VE GOT PERSONALITY, you know how to tell a joke . . . You've got talent."

SID WASN'T A SHORT MAN, but being five foot six didn't qualify him as tall. He was hunched slightly, lacking a good amount of hair, had glasses that didn't seem to help his vision, and he didn't look his age—which is to say you couldn't figure if he was older or younger than he appeared. What Sid Kindler also didn't look like was the guy who'd help yank me out of the Fourteenth Street Theater and set me on the road to becoming one of the most popular young black comedians—one of the most popular comics, period—at the close of the 1950s.

First time I met Sid he was hanging around backstage at the theater. Saw him. Didn't give him much thought. There were always people hanging around backstage—other acts, friends of other acts, friends of the house who got snuck in so they could get a better look at the strippers as they came bouncing offstage. I was sitting on a stool in a corner, slightly turned toward the wall—back to the circus of people around me so I could run through my set. Regulars in the theater knew when an act was rehearsing; they faced a wall or a mirror, body gestures got exaggerated, and their lips moved but in silence. And when an act was trying to get themselves together, you left them alone. Everyone left me alone. Sid was the exception. He circled around me, swimming a bit closer with each sweep, giving me a good looking-over same as you'd give a museum piece you dug but didn't quite get. Finally he stopped and stood and stared. Not knowing who he was, not feeling like talking, I let him have his gawk. He took it. Going on a couple of minutes, he took it until, a fly doing a slow crawl over my flesh, he became unignorable.

"Is there something you wanted?" I asked but not too harshly. He was working on my last good nerve, but he was a white man working on my last good nerve. My black self had been conditioned to offer white people, in all circumstance, every nicety.

"You talk too fast."

I started again, slower: "Is there something—"

Shaking his head: "Onstage. You've gotten in this habit of talking fast, racing through your routine to get to the next joke 'cause you're not getting a laugh. Half the reason you're not getting a laugh is 'cause you're talking too fast for the schmucks out there to hear what you're saying."

What struck me out of all that, beside the immediate sense that he, whoever *he* was, was right, I had been rushing my act, was something he'd thrown into the mix but thrown in casually. He'd said I'd gotten in the habit. He'd said it like he'd caught my act before. Not once or twice, but a bunch of times. He said it like he'd been studying me.

He said: "And you change up your routine when it's not working, throw out one of your closers. But then you got nowhere to go, no jokes to top it with. That's why it's called a closer; you close with it. Changing up might buy you a quick chuckle, but it won't help much in the long run."

"Anything else?" I was sarcastic with that.

He missed it. "A couple of new bits wouldn't kill you. A couple of new bits that aren't somebody else's. That thing about going shopping with your girl, holding her purse while she's looking around—heard that on Steve Allen three weeks ago."

"I know. I wasn't . . . I borrow jokes sometimes. It's only . . . when the act is a little slow."

"It's a crutch is what it is, okay for when you're first starting out. How long you been doing stand-up?"

"A year. A little more."

"Too long to be doing other comics' bits. You've got to have your own jokes, your own voice. You do if you ever want to get out of here." To that he added humbly: "Hope you don't mind . . ."

"No." A lie. His comments were needles no matter they were on the mark. Maybe more so because of it. The fact that I was still at the Fourteenth Street Theater told me loud and clear my act had problems. I didn't need to hear it from some Charlie off the street. But he wasn't poking me to poke me. He was laying things out to be helpful, not harsh—your favorite uncle giving you tips with your Little League swing. You couldn't hardly get hot about that.

He stuck out his hand. "Sid Kindler."

"Jackie Mann," though I was pretty sure he knew exactly who I was. We shook. Forget how he looked, Sid had just about the most solid grip I'd felt since I was at that logging camp.

Without at all working his way into things: "You have any representation?"

"Representation? You mean like an agent?"

"Agent. Manager."

"There was a guy once I paid twenty bucks up front to rep me."

"Did he get you anything?"

"He got my twenty bucks."

A bit of a smile, then: "I'd only take ten percent, and that's after I start getting you work."

"Thought there was so much wrong with my act."

"You've got minuses, but you've got pluses. You're a good-looking kid, comfortable onstage . . . sorta."

"I'm well spoken," I said with a beam of a smile. My one honed skill. I was excited to offer it up as a sales pitch.

Sid shrugged, about as impressed by that as if I'd said I'd mastered the art of making ice cubes. Getting back to what he'd seen of my act: "You've got personality, you know how to tell a joke . . . You've got talent."

In all the times I'd been trying to get laughs, from when I was a kid in school until my Fourteenth Street days, no one had ever once told me that: You have talent. Somebody might've said I was funny, or good with bits, but so's the office drunk at the company Christmas party. I'd always thought I was talented. Told myself I was. But when you're the only one saying so—especially when you're the only person saying so after you've just finished a set for six bodies at the crack of dawn—you have a way of sounding like Charlie Denial trying to make yourself believe the not-true. For the first time it wasn't just me trying to convince myself of things. With those couple of words, "you have talent," I wasn't alone in my belief anymore. At the very least, I wasn't alone in my delusion.

"Listen, Jackie, I handle some acts, nobody too big. Nobody big at all to be honest. But I think . . . I can do something with you. Definitely get you some road work, get you time on some real stages. And when you're ready, I've got a few favors I could call in, a couple of city rooms that'll give you a look. When you're ready," Sid stressed. "You don't have to say anything now, but give it some th—"

"Yes!" What was there to think about? Go with Sid, or go with another of the hundreds of agents who never came my way? "Yes, sir. I'd be honored to work with you."

"Honored's a little thick, but I'll take the yes."

From his pocket a business card got produced and handed over. Nothing special about the card. Nothing fancy. Flat black lettering giving Sid's name and office address. Just a card. To this day, yellowed, worn, I still have that card.

Sid said: "Come around tomorrow and we'll talk about things. After ten and before five and not between noon and one. Thanks, Jackie."

He was thanking me?

Sid got going for the stage door.

As he started away I got a hinky feeling that shoved aside all my excitement as if Sid was the last lifeboat on a sinking ship and he was about to sail off, leaving the unlucky to drown. A little bit of boldness crept into my stomach.

Boldness.

I barely knew what to do with the feeling other than make sure Sid didn't take another step.

"Mr. Kindler," I called at him.

He stopped, turned back.

"Could you wait one second, sir?"

"Wait for—"

"Just one second. Please."

A stripper came offstage, clothes bundled in her arms. The path she took to the dressing rooms swept her right past Sid. He gave her no notice.

"All right."

I juked my way around backstage, running an obstacle course of milling acts and half-naked women, my head jerking around looking . . . looking . . . looking for . . . "Fran!" Like I'd been doing with my jokes, she was in a corner, singing quietly to herself. "C'mon."

Panicked, afraid she'd missed her cue: "Am I on?"

"You've got to meet somebody."

"Is this a fix-up? I don't have time for that. I need to go over my number."

Forget it. My hand to Fran's wrist. I yanked her back the way I'd come. I'd explain things to her same time I explained things to Sid.

"Mr. Kindler"—I started in before me and Fran had even finished covering the distance—"this is Frances Kligman. Frances, Mr. Kindler."

"Sid."

". . . It's good to meet you." Fran was real noncommittal with that thinking—fearing—this was my idea of a date for her.

"Mr. Kindler's an agent."

"Sid."

"Ohhh . . ." Some smiling rode with that. No longer Sid-the-potential-boyfriend. Fran flashed ivory to Sid-the-potential-agent.

"Fran's a singer."

Sid nodded to that. "Seen her. Heard her. Nice voice."

"She's real talented."

"She's very talented."

"Think you could, you know, agent her, too?"

"I'm not looking for singers. I'm looking for comics. A comic. Nice to have met you, Miss Kligman."

Sid started to turn away. I stopped him with: "But I can't leave her here."

"Leave her?" Behind his glasses Sid's eyes did acrobatics, got narrow, scrunched together. It was a floor-show version of trying to figure what I was talking about. "It's New York City, not Siberia."

"It's a burlesque house, and you said I could spend the rest of my life here. Same thing could happen for Frances."

"Nothing's going to happen but good things. She's a"—looking past me to Frances—"you're a very talented young lady."

"You said I was talented. You said I was talented, and you said I could spend the rest of my life here."

"What I meant was . . . What I was trying to . . ." Sid took a second, a breath, then got back to his point: "I don't need a singer right now."

"It's all right, Mr. Kindler." Fran was being gracious but had to work to keep her smile going. "I understand. Thank you anyway."

I went a little light-headed: blood pressure dropping. Anxiety rising. I said to Sid, to the man who was throwing me a lifeline: "I can't work with you unless you work with Fran, too."

Fifteen or twenty people backstage, maybe forty out in the house watching a harmonica act hack up the stage. They all got drowned out by my heart grinding like a bad gearbox.

Fran broke up the ugly noise. "You don't have to do that for me."

Have to? I didn't even want to. But Fran was my friend, and instinct told me friends were supposed to stand up for each other. The words just came pounding out of my mouth riding bareback on emotion.

"So I don't take her on"—Sid laid things out, made sure he was understanding me—"you won't *let* me take you on?"

"I just thought you . . . I'm just saying . . ." My thinker was doing double time trying to conjure a way to make everybody happy—stand firm but back down without looking to Fran like I was caving in. I came up idealess. There was a reason I was telling jokes onstage instead of working at the U.N. I figured that was my career right there; not many percenters would let a late-night comic tell them how to do business. My good luck, Sid wasn't one of them. He tossed his hands in the air—defeat meets frustration. "All right, I'll take the singer, too."

"Fran? You'll take on Fran?"

"You got another singer? God help me, you don't have another singer."

"No, no. Just Fran."

"Just Fran. Just Fran is enough." Sid took out another card, handed it to Fran along with the same spiel on when to come around to his office. He lamented: "A comic who squeezes me, and a singer I don't need. My lucky night."

My lucky night. Sid had gotten me off a sharp hook. In the moment I'd stood up for Fran. She was my friend. And being my friend, without thought, I'd done everything I could to swing Fran a piece of the good fortune that'd stumbled in my direction. I told myself there was no other way things would've happened.

I was telling myself a lie.

The truth . . .

The truth of it was I wanted like nothing else to get out of the Fourteenth Street Theater. The truth of it was I wanted it so bad, so hard, so deep, if it'd come to it . . . if it had come to it, I would have left Frances right where she was.

Fran was strictly sunshine and smiles, not hardly believing in the span of a couple of minutes the two of us had gone from burlesque acts to, if nothing else, burlesque acts with an agent. Sid got gratitudinal hugs and kisses smothered all over him.

Done with us, afraid if he didn't get out of the theater and get out fast he was going to end up with more acts he had no use for, Sid left as he'd come in: quiet and unnoticed.

Fran wrapped me up in herself. Between tossing out excited thank-you bits and quick riffs on how life was going to be so much better now that we had an agent handling things for us, she put her lips to mine.

Across the backstage area, near a lighting board, some union guy—hair buzzed marine short, once big muscles Jell-Oed fat—locked a gaze on me and Fran. Me hugging Fran. Fran kissing me.

He dipped his head toward the floor and spat.

≈

I WENT 'ROUND SID'S OFFICE. After ten and before five and not between noon and one. It was a small space on an upper floor of a building just below Midtown. That's about as descriptive as you could get with the place unless you went into detail about its dull wood paneling that complemented the dull wood furniture. There were some framed headshots on the wall. I thought I recognized a guy in one of them. The office did not jump up and down and yell show business. It did not have the luminescence of entertainment. All it had was Sid's name stenciled across the glass of the door, and below that: TALENT AGENT.

He offered me a cola and sat me down. We talked. Not about show business or my aspirations. Not at first. At first we just talked about whatever, beat the chops on this or that. Sid asked me where I was from. I told him. I told him about growing up in Harlem, told him I was without a mother and just about without a father, a little about my logging days and some about my moving job and my history on Fourteenth Street. Those were pretty much the Jackie Mann highlights.

Sid told me about him. Like me, he was from New York, White Plains. He was a widower, had a brother and a niece he adored. Other than that he had his work, having fallen in love with show business years and years back when he once caught his uncle's vaudeville act. Sid had wanted to be a performer. He discovered that he had no talent. He discovered that no matter he had no talent, he was able to finagle himself bookings. Sid figured if he could book a no-talent like himself, he ought to be able to strike gold booking acts with real skills.

Not quite gold.

Sid cared about his clients, thought of them as more than ten percent. He was concerned, wanted to know if his acts were well or not, happy or not—outside of show business—and if not, why. Sid gave a damn about people. Giving a damn about people, their feelings, keeps you from being a good agent. Anyway, he made a comfortable living.

Done with the getting-to-know-each-other jazz, Sid asked: "What do you want, Jackie?"

The question sounded a little nutty to my ears. If people ever asked me what it was I wanted, it was rarely. Even so: "Sullivan." The answer ready without thought. "I want to do the Ed Sullivan show. I want to be famous."

"Interesting."

"What?"

"You would say it that way. Not that you want to be funny, you want to be the best comedian around. You want to be famous."

"I do." No embarrassment. No shame. "I want to be famous."

Sid nodded. He didn't judge. He'd asked me what I wanted, and I had told him. Whatever answer I'd given, as long as it'd been honest, would've been okeydoke by him.

We talked some more business. Sid told me again that he had a number of rooms where he thought he could get me booked, that he had road clubs and how he thought they would be good for working on my act, and he did expect me to work on my act. He didn't want any laziness, didn't want me just parroting other comics' bits. He wanted an act who would go at things as hard as he would.

I okayed that.

Then he told me about some of the acts he handled. Some of the names I'd heard of, they worked around at a few of the Village clubs. Most of the names were new to me. The point Sid was trying to make without coming right out and saying so was that he wasn't hardly the King of Entertainment.

No. He wasn't. But he was the only guy in the business in the whole of New York City who wanted to have anything to do with me. So when he started to ask me the second time if I was sure I wanted to work with him, very much like the first time I cut him off with: "Yes."

We sat for a tick.

I asked: "So, now what do we do?"

Sid held out his hand. I took it, shook it.

He said: "We're in business."

MY LIFE BECAME VERY OKAY. Not great. Not by any means. But when I started working with Sid it got better than I could recall up to that point. There were, as Sid'd promised, those pocketful of clubs where he booked myself and Fran. Real quick the Fourteenth Street Theater became part of our past. He got us our police ID cards. Cabaret cards. We should've had them when we were working the theater, but didn't. At that time, the standing law was you couldn't work a club or cabaret, any joint in the city that served booze, without one. To get one you had to go through the N.Y.C. Police Department. The idea, cops controlling the cards kept the riffraff out of the clubs. Riffraff, according to the ordinance, was "Anyone convicted of a felony or of any misdemeanor or offense." Riffraff was also "Anyone who is or pretends to be a homosexual or lesbian." Even in New York, if blacks had few rights, gays had none. To the law they were no different, no better than criminals. Made me thankful all I had to worry about all day, every day, was being a nigger.

Me and Fran got our cards, got booked, got work—one type of club more suited for Fran and another for me. She did spots at the St. Regis, the Drake Room . . . the hincty joints. I was strictly downtown, the coffeehouses and cellars of the Village. That killed me and Fran palling around. But what's good was I was working clubs that not a month before the only way I'd get into was by lining up and shelling out my green same as every other Charlie off the street. Now I was the guy the Charlies were paying to see. Now I was working my bits on the same stages as Sahl and Kitt, Nichols and May. Working those stages, yeah, but still at the crack of dawn. My location had improved, not my hours. My act I was working on.

The times he could swing it, Sid would be in the house, watching, taking notes. After sets we would have a very late dinner/early breakfast, and Sid would break things down for me: how this joke or that went over, do I need to move it up or back, or toss it altogether. I appreciated Sid taking an interest, that I wasn't just a cut to him. I appreciated most, for the first time in my life, having something besides a pillhead for a father figure.

When we could, Fran and I would get together, talk about how things were going for us, what famous face we'd caught up close. Fran had me beat with a young Barbra Streisand.

That was the thing about the clubs: After the jazz of your first few weeks of working a real gig faded, after the late nights, the low to no pay, and the reality of you being just one more guy in the city full of people trying to sing or dance or joke their way to a better life, there were still the surprises: who might be doing a drop-in, what big-time so-and-so was in the audience checking out acts. In those days, in New York, when stars were made in the depths of the city, there were always surprises.

"HI," SHE SAID.

I jumped up from the spot where I was sitting backstage. Sitting. Drifting. Killing time till my set. I jumped up and banged my head on a shelf just above me, tipped it, and got caught up in a shower of electrical cables.

The times previous we'd crossed paths in the clubs, if I'd ever spoken two words to her, they were *hel* and *lo*. But in my head we'd been through a thousand conversations. In every one of them I was movie-star cool, and she was wide-eyed and pining. Then she says one word to me, "hi," she says, and I go Charlie Klutz right in front of Thomasina Montgomery.

"Are you all right?" She was laughing a little, but concern came through her smile.

Her teeth were a little less than absolutely straight. Just a little. Other than that the girl was perfect.

Rubbing my head: "Wasn't anything." After you've been hit by flying booze bottles, no, it wasn't.

"You're funny."

Great. I was a clown to her.

Thomasina picked up on me taking the comment wrong, added: "I mean onstage. I've seen your act."

"Really?"

"You sound surprised."

"I never fig . . . I didn't think you knew who I was, let alone you'd watch my act."

"I've seen you around, heard some other people say you were funny. Besides, I'm a healthy young girl. I like to watch a handsome man perform."

Well, let me tell you: My tongue went slack and flopped around inside my mouth. The whole of me took on a general retardation. I stood there, hoping against hope Thomasina wouldn't notice how she was drugging me.

"I'm Thomasina. Tommy."

"Jackie."

A beat.

"So . . ." she said.

"So . . ."

"I guess this is where you ask me out."

Holy . . . Was this for real? Was it really happening? After all my dreaming and wishing and imagining, was this girl really swinging me a little attention? And if all those fantasy bits I'd swapped with Thomasina—Tommy—were finally going to come true, then at the very least couldn't I play my part?

Turning up the charm star-style: "Yeah, but since we both know I'm going to ask you out, I was just going to wait for you to go ahead and say yes."

"But since we both know I'm going to say yes, I was just going to wait for you to go ahead and pick a place." She didn't miss a beat with that. It was as if we'd been swapping snappy-clack our whole lives.

I offered up: "The Five Spot?"

She came back: "I'm already there."

THAT I'D NEVER PREVIOUSLY been to The Five Spot didn't matter. Everybody knew, you wanted to show someone you were hep, The Five Spot was where you cruised. It was a jazz hang down on Bowery where "new" jazz and "progressive" jazz were being experimented with in the same dead-serious style the brain boys had experimented with the atom at Los Alamos. It was a kind of music I never much dug. Raw, unstructured, to me it sounded like someone threw a drum kit down some stairs, then tossed a horn and a cat after it. But in the day, everybody grooved to the noise. It was the music to which the Beats recited and the white niggers slummed. Jazz was the sound track to the times, and the sound happening then was especially fierce and wild and ignorant of rules. Bip-bop is what Monk called it. Bebop is what it got called. It's what Dizzy and Sonny and Mingus and the Prez played, and none of us understood, and since we didn't get it, it had to be deep, daddy-o. So people went to jazz clubs same as congregations went to churches. When the sermon was over, maybe you didn't get God any better, but you felt a whole lot closer to Him.

Out on the street, in the cold, a stack of people waited to get into The Spot. A twenty to the guy at the door got me and Tommy inside in under half an hour. We got a table at the back of the house, the house being so small, the back was practically the front. We were just far enough away from the stage that we could carry on a conversation. Not far enough away that some jazz artist on a xylophone—and don't ever make the mistake of not calling them artists—sent some stink-eye our way for not listening while he was trying to school us.

To hell with him. I was with Tommy Montgomery.

We had a few drinks and smokes—you weren't hip without sticks—and Tommy brought me up to speed on the short history of Miss Montgomery. She was a Philly girl, younger than even I had originally figured—in some states me just smiling at her was skirting the law—but already a veteran. She'd won her first talent contest at eleven, been playing clubs in Pennsylvania and Jersey since turning thirteen, and laid her first sides at fifteen. She'd even managed to squeeze in backing up the Godfather of Soul. That gig didn't last long, and what she said—or didn't say—about the man made me think there was more than just music to their relationship.

The thought of it, the thought of her with him—no matter how big a star he was, no matter at the time I didn't even know her— made me somewhat but very instantly jealous. I knew then if I hadn't already fallen off the deep end for Tommy I was taking a fast run at that cliff.

Tommy turned the questions to me, and I ducked and dodged some. Did a Philly girl need to know I was a dirt-poor Harlem kid? Did a nice young lady from a good home have to hear about the pharmacy of a father I had waiting sprawled out for me? I wasn't trying to lie to her about who I was . . . what I was. I was just trying to hide it a little.

Changing tracks, Tommy asked: "Why do you want to be a comedian?"

I shrugged. "Probably for the same reason you want to be a singer."

"That's not an answer."

"I want to have a life, and it's the only way I know how."

"You don't have a life now?"

"Not like the one I could have."

"And you could have . . . ?"

"Nothing but glad hands and backslaps. A life of getting what you want when you want it. You get to be somebody and nobody pushes you around. And if they do, you push them back. You push them hard."

I realized my tone and volume had jacked. I realized I was ranting, and that Tommy was staring.

She said as soft as I'd been harsh: "You've got a lot of anger in you."

I went soft, too. "I've got a lot of anger in me because that's where *they* put it."

"Laughing in the . . . What do they say about comics? Laughing on the outside, crying on the inside?"

"Crying on the inside, getting laughed *at* on the outside."

"And that's why you want to be a comedian? To not get laughed *at*? To get even?"

A guy on a bass finished up what seemed like ten minutes worth of solo, and the place broke out into hand claps and finger snaps, not so much because he was good but because that's what you were supposed to do when a jazz artist finished ten minutes worth of solo.

I asked Tommy: "Why do you sing?"

"Because I have something inside me that I want people to hear, some part of me that's worth listening to."

"There are parts of you that are worth looking at, too."

"You're not listening to what I'm saying." Tommy was just slightly sharp with that. Comedy is about timing, and when a girl like Tommy—a girl who lived for song—was telling you what music meant to her, it wasn't time to be cracking wise.

First date. I was turning it into our last and only.

Tommy: "I want to say something with my music; I want to speak to people. That's important to me. If you don't have something to say when you're up there"—she flipped a hand at the stage just beyond us—"what's the point of going on?"

"You talk like . . . I'm just telling jokes. I'm not delivering the Ten Commandments."

"It's whatever you want it to be."

"Yeah? Well, I want it to be my ticket to a better place. That's plenty."

Dissatisfied with my answer, Tommy aimed her attention at the quartet, their riffs suddenly more interesting than anything I had to say.

I WALKED TOMMY HOME, west from Bowery, cutting through Washington Square Park, then up Seventh Avenue. The distance from The Five Spot to her apartment helped warm the frost that had collected between us. I could barely feel my steps on the concrete. The drinks, the jazz, the secondhand smoke from the reefers toked back at the club . . . Tommy: They all got jiggered into a cocktail that got me good and lifted and very nearly spoiled me for any other kind of a kick.

"Jackie . . . Jackie!" Tommy's bodiless voice called to me from some other place.

I stopped. I turned around. Tommy's voice had no body because she was standing in a doorway ten paces behind me. I was so far gone on my trip, I hadn't even noticed she'd stopped walking.

"This is my apartment."

I just sort of nodded to that incidentally, didn't say anything, as if it was nothing but normal for a guy to leave a girl standing.

"Are you all right?"

I was flush and I was sailing. I was a man in love. "Yeah. Fine."

I walked back over to Tommy and stood.

She stood.

I kept standing.

We both stood around.

Twenty-some years old. I might as well have been in high school.

Tommy broke up our mime act with: "How come you never asked me out?"

"I did. Tonight."

"Before tonight, and you didn't ask me. I asked you."

A hesitation, then: "I wanted to. Almost did a dozen times. I just figured you must've had all these guys after you."

"All what guys?"

"Well . . . you're this big-time singer—"

"Big-time?" If she'd been in the audience watching my act, Tommy couldn't have caught herself a bigger laugh. "Coffeehouses, a couple of clubs. That's getting over?"

"When you're on the outside looking in . . ."

Tommy stopped laughing. She gave me a serious study. "Is that the only reason you wanted to go out with me, because you think I'm some kind of celebrity?"

"I wanted to go out with you because before I met you, before I even knew you existed, for my whole life I've been in love with you."

That was some swinging poetry. It was the kind of jazz a guy doesn't normally try to put over on a girl, and for sure not on the first date. Maybe it was part of my leftover high that got me talking that way. Maybe. Or, maybe it was the straight-from-the-soul truth. I figure it had to have been, because the way Tommy x-rayed me looking for any sign of a come-on, a play, or an angle, if I'd been giving her any less than what I felt in my heart she would've bounced my black behind all the way back to Harlem.

When she was done looking me over, when she was done checking me out and sizing me up: "Would you like to come in for coffee?"

"We had coffee."

"Coffee's not what you're coming in for." With that, a smile. A smile more mature than her years.

Just so you know, just so you don't think otherwise of the girl, nothing happened between me and Tommy that night. Nothing much other than that it was the most wonderful evening of my entire life.

Sid was a man not without abilities. Chief among them, as far as I cared, was the ability to work small-scale miracles. He was able to swing me some decent stage time. He was able to finagle Fran a recording deal. Deal was, some little label would press and promote a single as long as the total expense didn't top five hundred dollars. Five bills to cover studio time, session musicians, plus the pressing and the promotion with whatever was left. It wasn't a money gig. At best, if things worked out, it would be an opportunity to get Fran heard outside of clubs. Still, there was enough excitement to go around: Fran's first deal, her first record. The first real break for either of us. We couldn't help but feel it was the beginning of all things good.

The five hundred dollars didn't leave enough cash to hire a producer. Sid would be at the session to make sure things ran smooth. I would be there just to be there, to share Fran's moment.

The little bit of studio the budget allowed knocked the glamour right out of the gig. Nothing fancy. Not the Brill Building or anything close to it. A place on the West Side near the old Tin Pan district. Dirty walls, carpeting decorated with coffee stains. Butts. Everywhere, all over the floor, were cigarette butts smoked right down to the filters. Who in the hell, I wondered, smoked so much?

Like a musical zoo, the space was full up with booth after recording booth of acts laying down tracks glimpsed through glass windows as you passed. The zoo had many creatures. Milk-faced acts, their eagerness busting through the soundproofing; seasoned acts, relaxed and steady—one more session for one more record. It was a job, and there's nothing special about doing your job. Nervous acts. Nervous not because they were new to the music scene. It was opposite of that. They were nervous because they'd been around too long, gone hitless too many years. They were looking at last chances, failure blocking the road ahead, defeat racing up from behind. The truth of things made them sweaty and pasty as they paced their tight little booths—rats desperate to find a way out of their traps. Bad as their I-ain't-gonna-make-it mojo was, as thick as it floated through the studio, it got the big igg from Frances. For the minute, she was still riding high.

Sid got Fran checked into her recording space, introduced to the session musicians. She gave them enthusiastic hellos. The enthusiasm didn't catch. They were by-the-hour guys. Pay-me-and-I'll-play boys. A first-time singer showing up, smiles and ideas about breaking big . . . ? Nothing new. Where's the money, and what's the music?

The music, the song Fran was going to record, was "Let There Be Love." It was a light little number, a popular tune with some jazz phrasing. Framed only with piano, snare, bass, and xylophone, it left plenty of room to showcase a good voice. It would make a real nice cut for Fran.

She did a rehearsal with the musicians, did another, did one more, and everyone seemed to be on the same page. There were some instructions passed to Fran from an engineer. Fran nodded to them. The engineer set the tape rolling, the musicians played. Fran sang. From the engineer's booth me and Sid listened, my pant legs used five or six times in a couple of minutes to dry my sweaty palms. I was that nervous for the girl.

Fran finished the track, and it was good. She laid down another one, and it was good, too. A third that was as good as the first, and when she finished that one I read the worry on Fran's face, and on Sid's. The tracks were good . . . and that was the problem. They were good and nothing more. Not sensational. Not unique. They didn't make you want to jump up and run out and buy the wax after hearing them. I was Fran's friend, maybe her best friend, and even to me she sounded no different from any other girl singing just another song. The thing she had going for her onstage—magic, spark, style, whatever—was absent from her now.

So Fran took a little time, studied the playback, asked for a couple of adjustments from the musicians, then laid two more tracks back to back. Like the first three, they were good, that's it. On the next track you could hear stress starting to do things to Fran's voice. Her range got trimmed a little, whatever bounce and spontaneity she had sounded forced, thrown in as an "oh, yeah" afterthought. The number was getting worse, not better. All those spots in the clubs, all those early mornings at Fourteenth Street she'd spent sharpening her craft, didn't matter. Done night after night, year after year, working a stage got to be as demanding as singing in the shower. It got to be routine. The here and now, this recording session: That carried weight. The weight was making Fran choke.

Sid called for a break, ordered up some coffee and sandwiches, gave Fran and the musicians time to regroup. While they were recharging, I saw Sid talking to the guy who managed the studio. The session was going long and it would probably go longer. No doubt Sid was trying to work out a financial arrangement to get Fran whatever time she needed to get the cut right. The look on Sid's face when he was done dealing told me the negotiation hadn't gone very well. He said nothing about it to Frances. For her he was all smiles. He wasn't about to let the expense of things jam up her thinking.

Break over, Fran and the musicians headed back into the booth, laid another track. Same as with the others, it was good and only good. Maybe not even as. The next track Fran busted, and one right after the bassist blew. They were all starting to go stale, the musicians getting sloppy and Fran getting tighter.

The studio manager came 'round again. He didn't say anything, just tapped a finger on the face of his watch. Sid nodded. He got the guy's meaning. More than four hours we'd taken up space that had been booked for two. From his pocket Sid slipped some cash—his own, nothing he'd been fronted by the record company—and pressed it into the manager's hand. That would stretch things some. Not much. Forced into laying out the situation, Sid took Fran aside. Hushed words were passed: There was time for one more take. After that it would just be a matter of picking the best of the bland.

Weighted with reality, slow motions took Fran back to the booth. She paused, breathed deep, then signaled the engineer.

The tape rolled.

Fran stepped to the mike. . . . Real quick she waved the engineer off.

The tape stopped.

Fran left the booth for the hall with no destination in mind.

The session boys did some eye rolling, some head shaking. Their every expression said, and said with much aggravation: "C'mon, girl. Just sing, girl. Lay your freaking track so we can go home, girl."

Sid and I stepped into the hall. At the far end was Fran standing very much by herself smoking a bummed cigarette. I don't think I'd ever seen her with a cigarette before, but she worked it with a level of intense concentration as if, right then, smoking that stick was the most important thing in her life. Even at that, with all the effort she put into the action, it seemed she wasn't participating in what she was doing. She rolled the cigarette in her fingers, stared at it without really seeing it, same as you can stare at your hand and not notice your flesh. She was in some whole other place.

I started for Fran.

A hand gripping my arm pulled me back. Sid, telling me without saying so it was no good talking to her. What Fran had to work out she had to work out on her own. There was nothing Sid, or me, or anyone else could say to her, nothing we could do for her except leave her be. This was her session. This was her moment, and her moment was tearing her apart.

Dragging hard, Fran killed her smoke. She jammed the butt into an overflowing ashtray, spilled its contents onto the floor adding to the collected remains of cigarettes smoked in frustration, fear, and deep thought. My previous question was answered.

Fran came striding up the hall and once more into the recording booth. Strong, sharp eyes leveled at the boys. She said: "Follow me, and don't get lost."

They straightened up. Their looks went from "C'mon, girl" to "Yes, ma'am."

There'd been nothing in that cigarette except tobacco, but the smoke, the time with herself, the time to get straight, was all that Fran had needed. This was her session. This was her moment, and she wasn't about to give in to it. She was going to own it.

A nod to the engineer.

The tape rolled.

Fran stepped to the mike. Fran sang. She sang like she was singing for the very first time, full of virgin joy. She sang like she'd been singing all her life, rock-solid confident, flowing through the song as loose and easy as she'd previously been tight and con-strained. What was missing, what Fran had been lacking before, was there now with every word of every verse. She felt the music. She didn't work it, didn't force it, she just felt it, the groove and the vibe, and let us—the listener—share the sensation. Eyes closed, you could hear her sly smiles and sense the dance of her hands in the air as she conducted herself through the phrasing smooth as drawn butter, as effortless as running water. Just standing there listening, you could feel her delight.

Done, last riff played, we all broke out in claps and whistles. *That* was the one. *That* was the one by a long street. The boys, the previously jaded session players, couldn't give Fran enough cheek kissing. They knew soulfulness when they heard it. From Sid she got a bear hug, and the same from me. In my arms I could feel the whole of her trembling.

Sid palmed me some cash, whispered: "Get her home. I'll take care of things here."

Arm still around Fran, I walked her from the studio to the street. Each step she gave me more and more of her weight. By the time I hailed a cab, the grip of my hands was the only thing that kept her from melting.

"Williamsburg," I told the driver.

We didn't make two blocks before Fran folded into me, broke down into tears. What once were trembles turned into sobs. For nearly five hours she'd given everything she had. The last track had taken everything she had left. You don't carve off a hunk of yourself and not feel it. From the West Side all the way home she kept up her crying. From the West Side all the way home I held her.

At her parents' apartment I eased her from the cab, walked her up the steps of the brownstone to the building's door. Fran looked to me. The bad light made her drained face all the more pale, her washed-out eyes puffed and blurry.

She said: "That last one was good, wasn't it?" I don't remember Frances ever sounding so lost and desperate.

I put a hand to her cheek. "Better than good. That was the best I ever heard you. The best."

Fran worked at a smile, gave a kiss and a thank-you for my words. But truthful as I was, my saying she'd been great didn't make her believe. Yeah, she'd sung beautifully. Yeah, she'd bled song. But even at that I knew she wondered if she couldn't have given just a little bit of a percent more. Her singing meant that much to her. She loved it, and the love hurt. That's the price she paid—one of them—for being born different.

Fran faded into the building.

I got back into the cab and it took me to Harlem.

TOMMY WAS HEADLINING at Bon Soir. She was closing up her run, so I went down to catch her act. She was great as usual, great sounding and lovely and all that. Last night of a stand was always pay night, so we had to wait for the waitresses to tip out and the club manager to do his count and the paperwork before Tommy could collect her money. While the manager was doing his business we hung out in the showroom—me and Tommy, the act who opened for her and the backing musicians, the bartender and the waitresses. Maybe a couple of others. The wait got to be a while, so the piano player—his name I don't remember, but I think it was Scott—got onstage and started fooling around some, playing little bits of this tune or that. Somebody, one of the bar backs, called for "Let's Fall in Love," and he played it and then someone else called for "Lazy River," and that got played; then he started on "A Sinner Kissed an Angel," which was real popular just a few years prior, and people started to sing, but no one was sure of the words and we all started making up funny lyrics until finally Tommy went up onstage to set us all right but ended up hamming up the number—doing it Ethel Merman–style—and we all fell out laughing because none of us had ever heard Tommy purposely trash a song before, and she did it hysterically, big and broad and brassy and so funny that people started calling out songs for her to goof on. She did a couple— Scott's boyfriend and the bass player backing—then swapped the mike with the other act, then one of the waitresses . . . anyone who wanted to hit the stage and do a send-up of Judy Garland or Julie London or anybody else who rated a laugh. The manager came out of his office, count done, but by that time no one was in a hurry to get paid. Our little group had taken on size. One of the waitresses' boyfriends had come by to walk her home, a couple of people had called friends and told them to come down, a reefer got lit, next thing there's a party going on. The manager must've been feeling it because he opened up the bar and started pouring liquor on the cuff and then we were all drinking and smoking and singing and laughing and Tommy took the stage again, did another number, and somebody started going: "Jackie, get up there, Jackie" like I could sing, so I just begged off, but Tommy came down off the stage and took me by the hand and yanked me back up with her. Good luck refusing that. We spent a second trying to figure out what number we could duet before Scott just started playing "That Old Black Magic," which I barely knew the words to. My contribution to the song amounting to little more than *That old black magic ba da da a spell/ That old black magic something something so well . . .* I had to do vocal gymnastics to keep up with Tommy, who tutored me to a fall-out finish. Then the two of us started in on "No Count Blues" and got as far as the third verse before we couldn't keep from busting up and our audience couldn't keep from busting up and started clapping and whistling and hooting and hollering and Tommy and me milked some hammy bows as I announced that the two of us would be performing a limited engagement at the Copacabana with, as special guest opening act, Mr. Frank Sinatra . . . provided his audition for me and Tommy went well. More laughing and clapping, and then me and Tommy gave up the stage, sat wrapped up in each other, blowing hot in each other's ears, and watched another round of songs that went on until well past morning when all of us finally tumbled out of the club smiling and laughing and feeling good. Back at her apartment, still smiling, still laughing and feeling good, me and Tommy tumbled into bed.

"SCREW OFF," I told the boss man, the guy who ran the moving company—large guy, furry with hair. If you'd been of the mind, you could've used him for a human-skin rug. "Screw off," I told him.

In my head.

I'd been fantasizing about quitting the company since the day I first started working there. I had the scene conjured down to the detail: me walking into big boss man's office, thanking him for the long hours and lousy pay, telling him how the next time I had anything to do with him would be when his little outfit was moving me from uptown to downtown, or from Harlem to Hollywood. Then I'd be out the door, no looks back.

No more daydreaming. I was striding over to Seventh Ave., the company office, to hand the boss man back his job. Didn't need it. My life was in a comfortable groove. Thanks to Sid and his mini-miracles, I was working clubs regular. I was getting spots earlier. My act was getting stronger. I was making money. Not great money. Steady money, but that made it good money. Good enough the clubs were the only work I needed. By that time I was going into the moving company only three days out of five, and the little dough I'd lose not going in at all would be missed zero.

So, boss man, "screw off."

In my mind I said that.

What I actually said when it came time, all I had nerve enough to say was I wouldn't be coming in anymore, and followed that up with a very polite request as to if it would be all right to have my last check. Sir.

I went away hands empty.

Before I left the place altogether, I stopped down to see Li'l Mo. He was in the garage with the trucks, big machines, backs open and empty, waiting to go out on a job and get filled. The filling would take a lot of long and hard hours.

Screw off, trucks.

I caught up to Mo, told him I was out.

He nodded his head to the news, said nothing.

I tried to tell him, to share with him my enthusiasm over how things were working out for me in the clubs, how Sid was really helping me to—

"So what, you're quitting. You don't hardly ever come around anymore anyhow. You ain't working, how you gonna be quitting anything?"

"I'm just saying this is a good thing. I've wanted this as long as I can remember." I tried to get Mo to grab on to some of the excitement I was pitching around. "If you knew what it was like to be up onstage . . . You remember back in that logging camp, how I got even those rednecks to bust up? When people who are supposed to hate you are clapping and—"

"I'm glad for you," he strained. "All right? You go tell your jokes. I gotta go move the man's shit."

Mo crossed to one of the trucks, crossed quick like he had something important to do. From the way he stood around when he got there, it didn't seem he was doing much but getting away from me.

I couldn't understand the way Mo acted, couldn't understand why he should be resentful of my doing well.

The other thing I couldn't seem to do was collect enough energy to care.

FRAN'S SINGLE GOT RELEASED. After the expense of the recording session there was no money behind it, no promotion, and little air play to go with it. Even as a redheaded stepchild, the song charted in the top sixty before it went away.

IT'S THE SAME AS WITH YOUR FIRST CAR, or kiss. Your first girl-friend. They're with you always—always in your memory, and the memory always good.

Thursday night. The Village Vanguard. Late in the show. That clear it is to me. I was doing a bit, almost a throwaway line, about a guy I saw at a restaurant smoking *while* he was eating. What's the point of that? To give your food a nice hickory-smoke flavor? Guess it's just for people who are too busy to barbecue. Me, going into a gravelly voice: "Just gimme some raw meat and a pack of Camels. I gotta go."

An applause break is what comics call it. It's when you say something so funny the audience has got to do more than just laugh. They've got to sit and whistle and clap while they get themselves back together: catch a breath, dry their eyes that are pouring with tears from the thing you said that was so damn hysterical. That night—Thursday night. Village Vanguard. Late in the show—with that line I earned my very first applause break. And like I'd do so many times with the breaks I'd earn in the years that followed, I stopped and I stood and waited for the people to finish clapping, deep breathing, and wiping their eyes. I stood and I waited and I soaked up their applause and affection.

Affection.

Affection that I had otherwise gone most my entire life not being familiar with any other way. Affection and adulation and admiration and appreciation. They loved me. For saying something funny a slew of people I did not know, had never met before, had no attachment to, loved me.

Can you understand why a guy, alone, backed only with the wits in his head and the mike in his grip, would go up in front of a pack of people and dare to impress them? To stand onstage, not spinning plates or spitting nickels. Talking. Just talking. But what you say and how you say it has a way . . . It has a way, and it affects people so that they can't help but laugh. They cannot help it. When you can do that—when you can make people want you strictly for the things that come spilling from your mouth—it is a feeling like no other. Not like drink or drugs. Not even like women. It's a high that goes unmatched, and that you're forever forced to chase.

≈

TIME SPENT WITH TOMMY was spent in the clouds. Time spent with Tommy was time spent free of my father. Still living at home, any reason was reason enough to be away from him. Being with Tommy was more than enough. Over a bunch of months the two of us had put together a relationship that worked despite our differences. She was a walk-in-the-park chick, a stay-at-home-and-snuggle girl to my staying out late and cruising the clubs. If there was a scene to be made, I wanted to make it. I wanted to be in with the in crowd. Tommy wanted nothing to do with them. We were opposites, yeah, but me and her were opposites attracting at speeds up to one hundred miles an hour. Point of impact: love. What we got from each other is what we gave to each other. Tommy gave me a sense of being, a sense of worth. Except that I tried to make her feel like a princess every moment I could, I don't know I gave Tommy much of anything. Didn't have much to give. She loved me just the same.

And jokes. That was the other thing Tommy gave me, jokes for the act. A couple of times she came up with some bits she thought were funny, pitched them to me. Because I was her guy, and it's the kind of thing a guy does for his girl, I used one once. It got no laughs. It made her happy I'd even tried it. One thing more Tommy and I didn't have in common: what we thought was funny.

"You're not laughing," I said.

"It's not funny," she said back.

On the Zenith in her apartment: Milton Berle in drag, flopping around onstage in glorious black and white. It did nothing for her.

I tried to school Tommy in Caesar and Gleason and Kovacs and Berle. She didn't particularly go for them. She especially didn't go for Berle, taking to his show about as well as a Muslim to a Jolson concert.

Tommy, head laid over my chest as we sat on her couch, gave more attention to something across the room than to what was on the TV.

"This is classic stuff."

"A guy in a dress?"

"Yeah, a guy in a dress. It's funny. Everybody loves this bit."

Tommy, dry: "If everybody else loves it, it's funny?"

"I'm just saying if a lot of people like something, there must be a reason. Come up with a bit that goes over big, that's how you get somewhere."

On the Zenith: Berle swatting some stooge with a purse. The studio audience was busting up. And right then thirty-five million people around the country were busting up with them.

Tommy not included. "A lot of people like something, so what? Doesn't mean it's good."

"Okay, yeah, but . . . It's like . . ." What was it like? "It's like blues and popular music, right? Blues is better music; it's real music, but nobody digs it."

Tommy's head came up off my body and her gaze got trained on a spot right between my eyes. "*I* dig it." A bullet couldn't have hit harder. "And I'd rather be doing something that's real than something that's just popular."

"I'd rather go somewhere."

"You want to go somewhere? Go to hell!"

Discord jamming itself between me and Tommy. Sometimes opposites attract. Sometimes they just slam into each other.

She got up quickly and started to move away. I was steps behind her. As worked up as she was about what I'd said, I was the same about her not seeing my meaning. Firm, I took her arm in my hand. Gentle, I pulled her to me.

"Baby, I'm not saying it's right. That's just the way it is. Like with Uncle Milty; that's the way comedy's always been; that's the way it's always going to be."

"So one day you'll wear a dress?" Her eyes were hot. Her chest rose and fell against mine. She was angry. Anger made her sexy. Sexier.

"If they were paying me the kind of bread they're paying him . . ."

Tommy's hands went to her skull, her fingers wide and groping, trying to swallow it whole. She moaned at me: "Jesus, you make my head hurt!"

She wasn't kidding about that. The girl was migraining bad. You could catch her temples throbbing without even a hard look.

Weak, tired, Tommy bled from my hands, went back to the couch, back to watching the comic-in-a-dress. She didn't laugh or smile; she didn't do anything more than soak in monochrome light. Compliance and protest in the same act. She gave in to me, but giving in was the same as slapping my face: Here, I'm watching. I'm faking like I care. Happy?

I wasn't happy. I hadn't meant to, but I'd hurt her. Hurting Tommy was the same as taking a razor to a part of myself—her pain was mine.

Tommy was done talking to me, but the conversation was only stalled, not over. From then on it would be with us always—art versus commerce. *Being* something versus *saying* something. For Tommy and me the argument was our bastard child that could never long be left alone.

—————

"CBS? CBS!" I would've said it again if I could've come up with one more version of surprise and excitement. Instead, I gave some surprise and excitement to: "Friday? This Friday!"

Sid: "Jackie . . ."

Fran got grabbed up in my arms, swung around Sid's small office.

"CBS is coming to see us!"

"I heard," Fran squealed, eyes shut to keep from going dizzy.

"Jackie . . ." Sid's voice barely reaching me where I was.

Where I was was a Sunday night a couple of weeks, or a month's time in the future. Where I was was onstage with Ed Sullivan, who was trying—trying hard but not getting the job done—to quiet a busting-up audience after I'd just finished my first coast-to-coast television broadcast. And let me tell you, just as fast as that daydream had come into my head, it was suddenly too small for me. A guest on a program? How about my own program? How about the *Colgate–Jackie Mann Variety Hour*? How about the *Gillette–Jackie Mann Cavalcade*? My fantasies didn't care that up till then Nat King Cole was the only black to ever have his own television program, and he had to be one of the biggest stars in America to get it, and once he'd gotten it America got his black behind off the airwaves fast as they could. The King was a star, sure, a natural talent, but the Land of the Free and the Home of the Brave . . . they'd rather catch Lassie.

Maybe I had that history working against me, but my daydreams were tougher than anything reality could put in my way. "CBS! This is great, Sid. Isn't this . . ."

I let Fran down. She slid out of my arms, woozied to a wall, and steadied herself. I didn't really register any of that, though. I was looking at Sid. Sid didn't look good. For all the excitement I was throwing around, Sid looked just about sick.

"What?" I asked, scared to ask any more.

"It's . . . The thing is . . ." With all the effort he put into getting just that much out, Sid made talking come off as torture.

"What!"

"They're coming to see Frances. . . . Only Frances."

Just like that.

"I didn't want you to hear it secondhand. I didn't want . . . You and Frances are best friends, and I didn't want you to think . . ."

Just like that. For a moment I'd let my fantasies come alive, and just like that they were grabbed from me and made useless. My eyes dodged Sid and Fran. I couldn't look at them, was too embarrassed after the little show I'd put on, giving off girlish shrieks from thinking for even one hot second that some television executive or talent scout would ever want to be in the Jackie Mann business. Why would they? Why would anyone want to have anything to do with . . . with a little black nothing.

I hurt. I physically hurt. A razor-wired mile of humiliation wrapped around me and I twisted in it. As bad as from any pounding I'd ever received from my father, his punches to the head were soft next to this blow to my soul.

Voices.

Voices above me. Fran and Sid. I heard them from the bottom of the pit where I'd sunk.

"Can't you talk to them?"

"I tried. I tried to ta—"

"Three minutes. You tell them to watch just three minutes of Jackie's—"

"They know Jackie, know about him."

"Then they know he's funny. So what's it going to hurt for them to watch a couple of minutes of—"

"It's not that they don't . . . What they said . . . They told me they don't—"

I mumbled: "They don't have anything for Negroes." The truth. I got tired of them talking around it, so I just said it. "It's not about being funny, Fran. It's about being Negro. They're not looking to put Negroes on TV, are they, Sid?"

". . . No."

No. You better believe they weren't. But if I were Lassie . . .

Fran didn't hear any of that, or if she did she didn't care. "You talk to these guys, Sid. You tell them that if they don't look at Jackie, then they don't—"

I had to jump in, cut Fran off before she did a hara-kiri job on her own career.

"What's the big deal?" I tossed out, nonchalant despite my internal bleeding. "They don't want to see me, they don't want to see me. Why force 'em to sit through the act?"

"Because they won't look at you otherwise, that's why. Because it's wrong. It'd be one thing if they didn't think you were funny, but they won't even do you the courtesy of sipping their comp drinks while you tell jokes."

Frannie was civil rights before civil rights had a name. The idea of holding your ground against bigots had been branded into her by the hot memories of her father's embarrassed looks as he was politely, coldly, shamefully turned away in front of the watching eyes of his family from "exclusive" restaurants and "restricted" hotels. Exclusive. Restricted. Fran had grown up speaking the secret code of anti-Semitism. She'd grown up learning not to flinch from it the way her father had. And now she was about to equal-opportunity herself right out of an audition.

"Why are you making a stink over things when I'm not? CBS doesn't want me, I'll sell my act to NBC. Besides, it's not as if I don't love it in the clubs."

"Sure you do. You love the clubs, the smaller the better. If you had things your way, you'd book yourself right back into the Fourteenth Street Theater." Fran wasn't buying my I-don't-care bits. Not even a little. I kept on selling. Had to for her sake. For her sake I worked my deceits, told her how the audition was no big deal to me. How another one would come along same as a gypsy cab, and how CBS'd be sorry when someone else snatched me up. I told Fran I almost felt bad for her having to sing for some guys from the biggest television network, pen poised over paper, ready to sign her up.

With my sad little show I was able to lure Frances to the notion of not quitting the audition. My lies were obvious, but so was my desire that she go on.

She would, on a condition: "You'll be in the audience?"

"Wouldn't miss it."

Then we all stood around some, talking about what a real good thing this audition was going to be for Fran. I smiled a little. Acted happy. One more lie.

Pretty soon Fran excused herself, said she wanted to go home and pick out a dress, some numbers, rehearse them. . . . Generally she wanted to start the process of getting ready for the biggest night of her life. One more round of congratulations to her, and Fran left.

The second she was out the door Sid started talking, not wanting to let the dead air get any staler. "Like you said, to hell with them if they don't want you." He still looked ill. "Sooner or later NBC's going to—or ABC. They're the ones really shaking things up—they'll get a look at you, and they'll go nuts. These CBS suits, they don't know what they're missing."

God bless Sid. He was a worse liar than I was.

FRIDAY NIGHT. The Village. The Blue Angel. The vibe: good. The crowd: good. The CBS talent scouts seated among them. Sid was juiced with a nervous excitement proud-pop-style. I was a little cuckoo myself, dizzy and light-headed like I'd been downing smoke from a jazzman's cigarette. It wasn't anticipation that had me feeling that way. Part of me was not right, feeling something I'd never thought I'd feel for Fran. No matter it was her big night, there was part of me that was a small percent jealous. I tried to drive the feeling away with thoughts on how happy I was for Frances. I tried real, real hard.

Eventually the house went dark and the show started, and, eventually, after some warm-up acts, Fran took the stage and did her set. I half expected her to throw the audition, to take a dive: If you won't watch Jackie, then I won't *let* you watch me.

She didn't. Forget about her tensing up at her first recording session, that night Fran was nothing but a songbird.

Set over, the audience went nuts with itself. The CBS guys were all smiles.

After the show Sid borrowed the club manager's office and had a powwow with Fran and the two talent suits. I settled in for a wait while they talked business. The wait turned out to be a short one. Of course it was. How long did it take to tell Fran she was sensational, you loved her, you wanted to pay her big money to put her on television?

Not long at all.

The two CBS guys came out of the office first, backslaps and broad smiles, high on happiness for finding a piece of talent so obvious, the blind could've spotted it. Then came Sid. Then Frances.

Fran crossed to me, wanting to say something. She said nothing, knowing whatever thing she said would be the wrong thing. She kissed me. She left.

The next time I kissed Frances she would be a star. The next time, and the last time.

*T*here was a picture in Life *magazine of a cute little girl with cute little curls in mid-skip of a jiggle-belled jump rope as she played on a quiet suburban sidewalk somewhere in Middle Americaville. It was a perfect image of a perfect time to be a kid, too young to know there were ever such things as the Depression or the Second World War. Too young to know about dust bowls and death camps. For the kids of the 1950s, there was only Davy Crockett and Captain Video, Hula Hoops and Flexible Flyers. There was only fun to be had. As it should be. Kids should be having a good time, playing, laughing, and all that. Kids should be kids. What they shouldn't be is martyrs and heroes, frontline soldiers of a civil war.*

Nine were.

Nine kids who just wanted to go to school and get some education. Problem: They wanted to go to Central High School in Little Rock, Arkansas. The government said they could. The law said they could. The good white people of Little Rock said different.

Said?

How about they screamed. How about they called the kids

niggers. Goddamn niggers. Lousy coon niggers. Frenzied, faces red and twisted with blind hatred, foaming from their shrieking mouths, they called the kids animals.

They called the kids animals?

The kids, armed with just books and pride, tried to do some learning.

The mob of whites chased them off.

But the children tried again.

The National Guard chased them off.

But the children said they would try again.

The governor said, go on. Try again. Try all you want. He would keep chasing them off. That, or let the mob have at them.

Ike didn't care for that, the laws he was supposed to be upholding getting ignored by the troops of redneck governors. Ike sent in the big boys: one-thousand troopers from the 101st Airborne.

The mob quieted up.

The National Guard stepped aside.

The governor backed down.

The children integrated Central High School.

Nine kids. Nine kids who just wanted to learn. They weren't trying to start anything.

For all their non-effort, what they helped start was the civil rights movement.

August of 1957 to February of 1958

S id and I were having a sit-down. The topic: the future of Jackie Mann. A future I felt I was rushing toward at a slower and slower crawl. Getting turned down for a look-see by the network, having my best friend walk away from an audition with a holding deal; that sock popped the wind from me.

Sid did what he could to set me right, never trying to cheer me up by overselling my prospects or promising me the impossible. With Sid it was strictly what he could get for me, why he thought I should take it, how it would help me down the line. Plain, simple, and regular. Sometimes too plain, too regular, and I'd find myself wanting more. A lot of times I'd want more. More, or bigger, or better: this club over that one. A theater over a club. A radio spot over both. And over all that I wanted Sullivan.

And when I got that way, my wanting in full bloom, Sid started up with his cautionary jazz: Don't get ahead of yourself. Don't rush. You've got one shot at things while you're climbing the ladder, one chance to impress the bookers and talent guys at each rung. If you slipped, down was the only destination. So don't do something to do something, do it when you're ready.

I listened to Sid.

Tried to.

But his counsel was no match for the rat of stagnancy that was making a meal of me and the sense that failure was creeping close, ready to mug me from behind. The pair were becoming a constant of my life that were wearing me out, wearing me down. Twin abuses filling me with a fear of my future: at best a life sentence of coffee-houses and Village clubs. At worst—at the very worst—back to carting furniture by day, back to carting home the high of choice for my father at night.

"We need to get you on the road." Sid talking. "Get you in some clubs in big markets. You're getting strong. I think you can handle it, opening for a few names. These aren't one-nighters I'm talking. You go out, you're going to be out for a while. I got ins in Chicago, Philly. Hell, we haven't even had you in Jersey yet. I can put you in the Five Hundred easy. They're all class houses, pay top dollar. Three hundred a week for starters. Most'll throw in a meal."

Three a week. Three and food. By far the most I'd ever made to that point. But Money was starting to seem lonely without sister Fame.

Sid could tell the talk of the road work was doing nothing to prop me up. He started to do a hard sell for what would end up being the last leg of the tour, a stand at the Fontainebleau in Miami Beach. It was class, it was good pay, it was a hot house, it wasuzuzuzuzuzuzuzuzuzuz . . .

Sid talked. I drifted, let my gaze travel out the window. Hazy. Ugly. Raining. Below, an intersection. Water had puddled around a clogged sewer drain. A guy—gray suited, anonymous like the man in the Sloan Wilson book—tried to leap over it. Didn't make it. He landed right in the puddle, much deeper than it looked, and ended up splashing water all over himself. He stood where he was, sour, wet, and getting wetter. All around, people pushed by him, past him. They couldn't care less he'd messed hisself, that maybe he had some important meeting or maybe a first date he was going to miss for looking like a rag. All the people cared about was that the soaked, gray-suited man was in their way.

They were New Yorkers.

They had places to be.

I jerked around, breath held. Something Sid'd said snagged me, spun me. Exhilarated me. Almost. The blisters from the last time I'd been burned by premature enthusiasm were fresh enough I was shy of letting myself get jazzed on the quick again.

I asked him: "What did you say?"

"I'm not making any promises. But if things go right—"

"What did you say, Sid?"

"The guys at the Fontainebleau, they have an in. You do well there, they told me they'll talk to Jules."

Jules. That's all the more he had to say, and I dug his meaning exactly. Jules. Jules Podell. Jules ran the hottest nightspot in town. What Sid was saying, just by saying his name, was that if I went over in Miami, if I did right, I had an in at the Copacabana.

<p style="text-align:center">~~~~~</p>

WHAT'S THE OPPOSITE OF INDIAN SUMMER? Did it have a fancy name, or was it just early fall? No leaves turning yet, many weeks from an icy chill, not even October but the air was going crisp. The climate being cool, the sun being bright, made for a special kind of weather that juiced you with some Mother Nature–made menthol. Taking a deep breath was taking in a lungful of tingly vitality. Days like that, the city begged to be walked around in, leisurely enjoyed at a stroll's pace: Get out there, boy. Don't let life pass you by. Days like that, New York City seemed just about perfect.

Still, beautiful as the day was, it held a creeping frost.

"All you care about is money."

We were having the conversation. We were having the conversation *again*—the one about which was more important, art or commerce. Show or business. Whether it was better to be good or make it big.

If I wasn't hip to it before, Tommy made her thinking real clear to me. "You think money's everything. You think it's everything, but it's not."

We were starting to have the conversation with near regularity. Over meals, before lovemaking, after watching other acts—Tommy would want to know if I thought they were talented, or just popular. One night after she'd finished a set, the audience sending her off-stage with extra-strong claps and whistles, she beelined for me, faking lament, worrying that if people were digging her, she must not have any depth anymore: "I don't know, Jackie. I don't know. I think I'm selling out."

The comments were sharp, never subtle. Tommy's remarks never needled, they hacked at you razor-style. But even at that, it wasn't as if she was trying to be smart-aleck about things. To her, for me, it was a kind of therapy, especially in the months since those boys from CBS treated me as if I were a one-eyed albino. Day by day I wanted nothing more than to increase my stature, elevate myself to a place where slicks in suits had no say over me. They could hate me, they could despise me on their own time, but I wanted only to be so big that to my face they could do nothing but love me. Notions that didn't sit at all well with Tommy.

"Why are you always on this trip: If I were a star, everything would be great. If I were rich, life would be fine."

Arguing wasn't how I wanted to spend my last days with my girl before going off on the road. We were walking on Sixth, bundled mostly in each other and kept warm by our steamed words, after a matinee showing at the Ziegfeld. As if I didn't already have Tommy hot enough at me, same as every other Charlie in America I'd guaranteed myself a standing reservation in the doghouse by insisting we take in a film staring European sexpot Liliah Davi.

"You're telling me," I told Tommy, "folding money's not better than trying to get by on fews and twos? You get some green, you get some juice, there's nobody who doesn't respect you."

"Why would you want their respect? Why would you want to minstrel your way into having a bunch of ofays who hate you pretend they don't?"

Yeah, okay, on a level, maybe, Tommy had a point. Maybe. But it was the point of a girl who grew up in the pretty, pleasant German-town section of Philly. The point I was trying to make came hot off the streets of Harlem. I was arriving at a truth, one I'd been putting the dodge on for the sake of our relationship. Like myself, Tommy was born different. She had something inside her that made her unlike other people. The problem was, the thing that made Tommy different from others also made her different from me.

"You don't get it," I told her. "You come from money."

"I come from parents who worked hard and gave me and my sister what they could."

"They gave you a good life, that's all I'm saying. I want to be able to do the same. Get a house somewhere nice, a quiet, tree-lined neighborhood. We could do the whole scene: picket fence, swing on the por—"

If she'd taken a bullet, Tommy couldn't have stopped any deader. If I'd smacked her, she couldn't have looked at me any more shocked, her pretty little eyes never so wide.

She asked: "We?"

"What?"

"You said we. *We* could do the whole scene."

A hundred times I'd mind-riffed on a thousand different combos of the future of me and Thomasina Montgomery. Me and her shack-ing up, married up. Married and living in the city, or upstate. Kids got blended into this fantasy or that. But the one thing every varia-tion had in common was us. The two of us together. Me saying "we"—to her, surprising—was just talking out loud about what I'd already worked over again and again and again and again.

Still, letting your main know you sit around pipe-dreaming on domestication is strictly a no-no.

Backpedaling: ". . . I was just supposing. I wasn't saying any-thing." Trying not to backpedal too far: "Not that I wasn't saying anything at all, I was just . . ."

I quit there. No point going on. I didn't own Tommy's attention anymore. It belonged to something that had caught her eye. Up the avenue, an appliance store. A crowd, mixed black and white, pressed up to the front window, hypnotized by the chorus of images projected from a display of televisions.

Me and Tommy walked for the crowd, bobbed around trying to watch what they were watching. No good.

I asked a brother: "What's going on?"

"News film. Little Rock."

All the more backstory he needed to give. Looking between shoulders, I caught some of the monochrome horror show. Black children trying to go to school. Blocking their way were bayonet-flashing National Guardsmen—protecting the lilified school from the young invaders—and a gang of whites lynch-mob crazy. Yelling. Screaming. Some rocks got thrown. And through all that, through the wailing voices and hurled slurs and the stench of violence, past the Guardsmen who would just as soon let the mob loose on the "niggers" as muss their uniforms trying to stop them, the children quietly walked up the stairs and into the school to do some learning.

I said to myself, but out loud: "Why in the hell would anybody let their children go through that?"

The brother I'd questioned didn't care for my comment and let me know with a "Negro, please" twist of his lip. "I expect so your children won't have to."

Done with me, the brother moved off.

Tommy, her stare zigzagging past bodies to the TV, said: "It's terrible."

"Yeah." On the TV: Some crazed whites chased down a black who just happened to be out walking. They beat him bloody. From what I could see, they beat him until he was just about dead. "It is."

Tommy kept standing where she was, kept juking her head

around, trying to grab a look at one of the sets. Maybe that was her way of showing support.

So I let her. For a while.

Pretty soon I gave a tug to Tommy's sleeve and I headed off and she followed. Since I couldn't do much concerning America's race issue standing around in front of an appliance store, I figured I should bust my conk on problems I could solve. Like coming up with some new bits for my set.

⁓

MY FATHER WAS MOSTLY SOBER, or as close as he got anymore. He was sitting at the kitchen table. Eating. You could call it eating. You could call it shoveling food in the general vicinity of the hole in his face.

His level of communication, the sum of hospitality he could extend to his son as I entered the room, amounted to: "Want some?"

I went to the table. I ladled out a bunch of whatever it was Pop was having—maybe rice and chili—onto a plate, sat. We had a meal together. No eye contact. No words. Our only conversation the dueling of his spoon and my fork against our plates. Anyway, it was our version of having a meal together.

I said: "I'm going away for a while."

"When you come back, bring me a—"

"Not coming back. Said: not for a while."

That paused him for a tick. "Whadaya mean, a while?"

"Might be a couple of months. Might be more."

"You ain't goin' nowheres." He said that like it was a simple fact he knew to be true: The sky is blue. Water is wet. I wasn't going anywhere. He said it, then shoveled more of the slop toward his mouth.

I ate some more, too, then I corrected my pop. "I am going away. It's going to be a few months. Might be more."

"Where? Where do you think you goin'?"

"To do some clubs on the road."

"Nightclubs . . . ?"

"Philadelphia, Milwaukee, Chicago. A few other places. Going to end things up in Miami."

Pop didn't care for me explaining things to him. Heating himself up: "Work a few times in the city, you think you somethin' big. Think you somethin' special. Ain't nothing, Jackie." He just about snarled. "Jackie . . . Know why I name you Jackie? 'Cause tha's a girl's name, and tha's all you are." He just about laughed. "You nothin' but a sissy little—"

"I'm a good comic."

"Ain't nobody gonna pay to see yo nigger ass!" Pop's anger flushed his black skin. His chest pumped short, hot breaths.

I stayed quiet, the quiet only making Pop all the madder.

A few more scoops of food. After that I stood from the table, took my plate to the sink, and put it with the others Pop had left there for me to wash.

To him I said, even in tone: "People will pay to see me. They'll pay this time, and they'll pay more next time. And I'm going to take their money and get me some nice things, a nice apartment. And when I get that nice apartment, I'm going to leave you here."

"You ain't gonna—"

"I'm going to move so far away, all you'll be is some black man I'm going to have to think hard about to remember."

"Ain't goin' nowheres! Not gonna let you go nowheres!" Pop clutched at his spoon, ready to use it for something besides eating.

"It's already happening. Sid's booked me into—"

"That Jew? That Jew done this?"

"Don't you talk about him that way."

"That Jew got all up in yo head an' poison you against me."

"You don't talk about him like that!" For the first time since I'd walked through the door, hard as I'd tried to keep cool, Pop had finally managed to edge me up. I didn't care what he had to say about me. There was nothing else he could add to the volume he'd written. But I wasn't going to let him talk on Sid. "He's more a man than you are. He's a *man,* a decent man, and that right there is one whole hell of a lot more than you'll—"

"Learn yo nigger ass!" Pop came at me; the spoon, having completed its transformation from utensil to weapon, led the way. But for all his anger, Pop's move was powerless, the lumbering and incoherent charge of a perpetual addict, his actions as exaggerated as they were slow. It took little effort to sidestep him, grip him by the shoulder. It took even less to push him away. So little that the conservative energy I put into my defense sent Pop to the floor.

It wasn't that I'd suddenly gotten tough with myself, gone Charles Atlas and was paying back some sand-kicking bully. It was just that I wasn't a kid anymore. And same as I no longer believed in imaginary monsters under my bed, I knew my pop wasn't a demon, just a sad old man who no longer had a hold over me.

From the floor he looked up at me with a hurt that was greater than his little bit of physical pain. His kid—his weakling kid—had just shoved him down. Whatever manhood Pop had left had just taken a beating.

I said to him, said very clearly in the same manner used to communicate with an animal that doesn't have the capacity to dig your lingo: "Sid has set up some club dates. I'm going with him on the road. I'll send you some money for rent, food. Use it for booze. Use it for whatever. I don't care. Not anymore. But I'm going, Pop. I'm going away."

The last time I'd told my pop I was going off on my own I spent the night on the floor—belt-whipped and bleeding—and slinked away while he was passed out. This time I would pack a bag and walk out the door when I was good and rested and ready.

THE IDEA OF GETTING DRESSED UP and going out to a club for a meal and a show is laid up in the same burial ground with the notion of *not* buying a car because its tail fins aren't big enough.

But used to be . . .

Used to be a guy would put on his sharkskin, his lady would get dolled up in a beehive and pearls, then head off for a night of adult entertainment. Adult meaning steaks, some drinks, and a smoke before settling in to watch a name act from so close, you had to dodge the sweat that flew from their hardworking showbiz bodies as they gave and gave and gave until you had no choice but to jump up and put your hands together.

And real suddenly I was part of that. Sid had pulled his strings, and I was part of the High Life opening up for talent I'd previously been no closer to than my TV screen.

Week one: Club 500 in A.C. opening for Buddy Greco. Good Guy. Nice Guy. A guy who never knew how to do a show that was less than one hundred percent. Sid figured Jersey to be a good place for me to start things off: out of New York, out of the Village with its Village clique and coffeehouse scene but still near enough the city to be "my" crowd, the kind of people I'd been cracking jokes for since I'd first hit a stage and with just enough boardwalk tourists mixed in so as to tell me what would and wouldn't fly beyond the bridges and tunnels.

Sid came along, would be along for the whole tour. He told me he wanted to get out of the office, that every now and then you've got to go shake hands with the owners and the bookers. The hidden truth: He wasn't along glad-handing, he was hand-holding. Mine. He made the trip to be sure everything was okeydoke for me.

But I didn't need a minder. I was a professional. The three bills a week I was earning said so. Not that there weren't things to learn. I learned when you're an opener you've got to get your audience, get 'em big and get 'em fast. The suits in the seats didn't pay to see you, had probably never heard of you, didn't want to know you (GUEST

ACT FOR YOUR LAUGHING PLEASURE was all the more billing I got one week). You opened, and you were just a little something to let the lobster thermidor digest before the real action started. So with all that working against you, there was no easing into the act; there was no moseying to your good bits. They all had to be good, and they had to be good from the first word from your mouth or you had twenty minutes of two hundred people giving you the igg while they tried to flag a waitress to freshen their drink.

I'd open my sets with local bits—bits a comic makes seem local, like he'd actually taken the time to find out something "unique" about the town he was playing: "Boy, you people in Nowheresville, you all drive like the speed limit is just a suggestion. I don't want to say there's a lot of construction around here, but the state flag should be one of those orange cones." Follow that up with a quick platitude supporting a position nobody could argue with: "Is it just me, or is this Khrushchev cat crazy?"

Wait for the applause and whistles to die off.

Then a joke about the obvious just to keep Mr. and Mrs. White America from getting too nervous. "I guess you can tell from looking at me . . . I'm a New Yorker." Then into my bits on my relatives—nobody couldn't relate to jokes about relatives, even though my bits were made up. Some made up. Some borrowed. Sid kept on me to write more of my own stuff. Get my own voice. I told him I would. Eventually.

Mix in some charm with all that, plenty of personality, timing, and talent, add an olive, and you're a comic.

Each night that cocktail did me well, Buddy pulling me back up onstage and milking some extra applause out of the audience for me. Each set I got a little more confident, and confidence was the mortar that cemented my act.

Six nights and our stand was done. On the last night I said my good-byes to Buddy, told him what a talent I thought he was and how I'd love to work with him again.

Buddy, turning to Sid, pointing at me: "Remember that, pallie. I'll need a witness a couple of years from now when I come looking to open for him."

Good Guy. Nice Guy.

The following week: a two-week stand at The Latin Casino in Philly, opening for Janis Paige. She was a different kind of act from Buddy. Slower, more mellow. Torchy in her singing. Coming hot off my week in A.C. my act was tight as a harp string. Opening night I whipped the crowd into a stir Janis had to work to follow and even at that didn't follow very well. The next day Sid came 'round to tell me that Janis's guy had come 'round to tell him to ask me if maybe I couldn't tone things down some. And Sid added that Janis's guy told him to tell me that Janis was asking me in the kind of way that would get me asked right out of the club if I didn't comply.

Something else I was learning: As opener you could be as good as you pleased just so long as you weren't better than the name on the marquee.

The next night I took a dive. I was subduedly humorous, and I was that way the next four nights, twice on Friday and Saturday, and the same the week after.

Philly done, me and Sid trained our way to Cleveland, where we did a week at the Empire. After that we railed it up to Milwaukee for an eight-show stand at the Riverside.

Five weeks.

Thirty-five days.

I was noticing something. The nights, after the shows, sometimes I would notice myself feeling . . . depressed is how I guess I would call it. Having a club full of people laugh at you, clap for you, is a high hard to come down from. It's not made any easier spending the dark hours by yourself staring at the bad art hung on the wall of your hotel room. After being loved, the empty room had a way of making you feel all the more lonely. There was Sid to spend time with, but Sid, friend that he was, wasn't what I needed to keep me lifted. There was liquor, but that was a habit I didn't want to learn. There was Tommy. As often as I thought of her, after a show, lying on a bed, staring at a ceiling, I thought of her all the more. Thinking of her was a tease that made me desire her voice. And calling her, hearing her voice . . . that just made me feel lonely all over again. Sometimes, when I got that way, I would allow myself half a drink, then some sleep. If I was lucky, Tommy is what I'd dream of.

After Milwaukee was Chicago opening for Vic Damone, the Jr. Sinatra, at the St. Clair. His wife, that looker of an Italian actress, was in attendance every night. And every night, as her husband sang, she would cry nearly out of control. She must've really been crazy for the cat.

I worked those Chicago shows. Worked them hard. I honed and trimmed my act. Made it tight, then got it tighter. I was a fighter at camp. That week in Chicago was my last week before hitting Miami, before taking a shot at getting into the Copa by way of the Fontaine-bleau.

It would also be the last week in my life of never having been al-most lynched.

MIAMI WAS A JEWEL, a vacation paradise split between art deco ho-tels and beach resorts. Home to the rich, retreat of the stars, play-ground to anyone with dough enough to toss around. Miami was Hollywood east. Vegas with shoreline. Glitz, glamour, surf, and sun.

And it was territory to some of the biggest white trash, pecker-wood, black-haters in all of America. And why shouldn't it be? Florida is as far south as south in America gets. Virginia, the Car-olinas; Florida is below them. Mississippi, Alabama; you still got some southward traveling to do before you hit Florida. Florida is straight down.

So is Hell.

The similarity didn't come to me until much later.

From the moment Sid and I stepped off the train the signs of racism were all around. Literally. WHITES ONLY. COLOREDS NOT ALLOWED. A pleasant one written up: NO DOGS, NO NIGGERS.

They'd take dogs before they'd take blacks.

There were other signs, subtle, but obvious: the way some blacks walked the hectic station head down and gaze turned so as not to risk locking eyes with a white; an innocent act so often confused with being uppity, defiant, and in need of being taught a couple of things. The few blacks who did speak with whites started every sentence with "Suh" and ended them the same.

In a nutty way, for these people, white and black alike, this way of living—the postings that told you which water fountain and bathroom to use, the choreography of where to look and how to speak—was strictly normal.

I was not naive. No black in America was naive to life in the South, and after my time in that logging camp I knew there were people who couldn't hate blacks more if you'd raped their mother and shot their dog. But what was going on in Florida, it was bigotry as a way of life. It was racism as a tradition. It wasn't hidden in a cold stare or reluctant service at a place of business that was so slow in coming, you were long gone before it got to you. This racism was out in the open and proud of itself.

It took me and Sid a good few minutes to flag a porter. Even though to a man they were black, when they saw me they figured I had no money to tip with, or that if I did was too tight to part with it anyway. That's how deep Jim Crow had his hooks in that burg: He'd taught us to hate ourselves. Finally, me standing apart from Sid, he was able to wave down a redcap to take our bags to a cab.

Getting a taxi to take us to our hotel was a whole other adventure. Like everything else in Miami, there was black and there was white. The white cabs—the cabs with white drivers who took white passengers—weren't about to take me anywhere, and the colored cabs weren't allowed to take us where we wanted to go—hincty and restricted Miami Beach. Twenty dollars over the meter paid up front got a white cab to run us to the Fontainebleau. The back door of the Fontainebleau. The only door they'd let me in.

From there things only got all the more cuckoo.

"Your police card."

"Police . . ."

Joe Fischetti was the entertainment manager of the Fontainebleau. From his hand I took the card he was holding out to me, stared at it like if I stared at it hard enough for long enough I might be able to figure why I needed the thing.

Joe explained: "The beach area's got a curfew."

"A curfew in a nightclub zone? That's like having restrictions on cheese at a deli."

Joe didn't much smile at my bits. "A curfew for coloreds. You don't have a card, the police can arrest you on sight. Can and will."

I looked to Sid.

Sid, who'd obviously held back a few items from me concerning the Sunshine State, just shrugged and mouthed "Copa" at me.

The Copa. My reason for putting up with this nonsense.

Finishing his primer on sub–South Florida, Joe told us we'd have to work out something with the cabs. Probably get two—one for me and one for Sid—back and forth from Miami to Miami Beach.

I told him we were already cozy with the regs regarding the transportation system.

Joe, apologetic but matter-of-fact: "I don't make the rules."

The rules: I could work the Fontainebleau, perform at the Fontainebleau, but there was no way in hell they'd let me stay at the Fontainebleau. Instead, I got put up at the Madison across the bridge from Miami Beach in Miami proper. Proper as in: Away from the ritzy hotels was the proper place for coloreds to stay.

The Madison wasn't a bad joint. Wasn't a good joint, either. Leaking pipes came standard with each room. The cold water was freezing, the hot was only warm. Housekeeping seemed to have taken the Emancipation Proclamation very seriously. Other than that, the roaches didn't much have a problem with me moving in.

I looked to Sid, shook my head.

"The Copa," he said to me.

The Copa was becoming my mantra.

I told Sid he didn't need to suffer staying with me, that he should go find himself a decent place on the beach.

Sid told me that rednecks weren't any bigger on Jews than they were on blacks. That gave us both a laugh. The only one of the day.

We took a rest.

That night we got in our separate cabs, went over to the Fontainebleau, where I was opening for Mr. Mel Tormé. The voice, *that* voice, the voice you know. Don't know it, get familiar with it because me describing it would be nothing but words thrown at you. The man owned a skill and an ability and a talent that is beyond verbal description. He was to jazz and scat what The Swoon was to standards. Mel the guy, he was a hipster. As swinging offstage as he was on. Mel didn't go in for any of that black/white nonsense. He was cool, and cool was color-blind. One night he got into a real beef when he wanted to have dinner with me in the hotel restaurant. The management nixed it. We settled for steak sandwiches backstage.

The shows were good. They were just about great. Maybe my best up to that time. We might have been in the heart of Crackerville, but crackers couldn't much afford to populate the beach hotels. Instead, we got the well-to-dos, East Coast intellectuals and New Englander liberals come down for a few days of surf and sand. The audiences were smart, classy. In particular the crowd Mel pulled in were hep, progressive whites catching a primer on jazz and scat to prove how broad-minded they were, plenty receptive to the colored cat who warmed them up for it. I wished very desperately that Tommy could have been there to see me, to see those shows. Of course, if Tommy had been there, she wouldn't have been able to see my shows because the management wouldn't't've let her into the hotel because she was black. Other than that, I think she would've been very proud of her man.

Saturday night. Last night of the stand. Late. Second show done and backstage meal downed by Sid, Mel, and me. Mel and I did our good-bye bits before he headed up to his room. Sid and I were ready to trek back to Miami, the city of. We called the cab company, the one black one we'd arranged to pick me up on the beach.

Sid and I waited. Sid was excited. Joe thought I was a sensation and promised to put in a word with Jules Podell at the Copa back in New York. Well, let me tell you, that was all I needed to hear. Racist, bigoted, Jim Crowed to the eyeballs, I'd put up with a city that was all that and more if it landed me at the Copacabana.

Sid and I waited. Excitement faded. Sid was looking end-of-the-tour tired. I told him to go on, hop a taxi, head back to the Madison.

"A little fresh beach air isn't going to hurt me any," he said, indicating he didn't mind waiting any.

Sid and I waited. Excitement died. I couldn't take the guilt of his slogging through the wait anymore.

"Sid, you've been with me every night at every show since we hit the road, you're staying with me at that flophouse passing for a hotel . . . the least you could do for me—since you're doing everything else for me—is go get some rest when I ask you."

Sid "no"ed that, said he was fine. His drowsy eyes said otherwise.

The back-and-forth kept up until I just about pushed Sid into a taxi and sent him on his way.

I went back to waiting for my cab. A colored cab.

I kept waiting.

Fifteen minutes turned into thirty. So what? So I'd call for another cab. Only, the admiral-suited flunkies at the door weren't about to let me back in the hotel—back in through the *front* of the hotel—no matter that the laughs from my set weren't even cold yet. Ego wouldn't let me beg my way past a couple of uniformed Harveys who would've been hard-pressed to scrape up the ready cash to so much as buy a ticket to catch my act. I figured I'd take a little walk, find a phone somewhere.

That was the plan.

But the warm night, the post-show booze I'd put down that lightened my step, applause still hot, still rippling through my memory and the good feeling the sound brought with—it all got together to make my head swim and my judgment poor. As I walked, I didn't mind walking. Enjoyed the stroll. I figured, since I had my leave-this-darkie-alone card from the police, why not just hoof it back to the Madison? I could probably make it in the same time it would take to find a phone and get a cab—a black cab—to pick me up. Yeah. Walking seemed like the right idea.

Shortly I was lost. Not completely. The combo of liquor and euphoria had distracted me and I'd wandered along a couple of wrong turns. I could see the glow of the beach hotels beyond some trees and make out the low skyline of Miami, but somehow I'd gotten on a road that took me away from one without exactly heading toward the other.

A dark road.

Okay.

Okay, I thought. I'll just head back the way I came. Head back, find that phone, and call that cab.

So I did that, started heading back, not much concerned, figuring I could untwist myself. If I thought of anything, I thought of the laugh Sid and I would have over me getting all fouled up trying to play Charlie Trailblazer.

And I wasn't much concerned when a pair of headlights came up over a rise behind me, caught me, swept over me as a car rode past.

A car. Just a car.

The car kept on for thirty, forty yards . . . then its taillights went from dull to bright.

It was braking.

I got concerned. Just a little. Just a . . .

The car sat, didn't drive on and didn't roll back. I didn't move, either. The only exchange between us was the idle of the motor and my shallow breathing. Beyond that there were no other sounds I can recall. Just myself and that car.

The little white lights above the bumper blinked on. The car crept back toward me.

The warm night went hot.

I got real concerned.

Real concerned, but I remained still. My mind active—lickety-splitting through a dozen things I should maybe do instead of standing around—but my body able to accomplish nothing.

It was just a car. It was just . . .

The car—a cream-colored thing. Make and model hidden beneath dents and rust—came parallel to me. Inside: three men. In the dark I couldn't well make them out except they were three white men. Two up front, one in back.

The one behind the wheel drawled at me: "Boy, watcha doin'?"

"Going home." I had to work the words out, and when they came they came nervous.

"Say he goin' home." That didn't sit too well with the guy next to the driver, who repeated my words for the others.

The driver stated: "Ain't no niggrahs live roun' heyah."

"I don't live—"

"What that, boy?"

"I don't live here. I'm from out of town."

"Say he ain't from roun' heyah." That was the guy next to the driver again doing a cracker translation of what I'd just said. The third one, the one in back, kept quiet, did nothing more than slouch where the seat met the door and chew at something that seemed to be permanently lodged in his mouth.

"Nahh, he ain't no local niggrah." They talked past me to each other. They talked like I didn't exist. "Ain't no local niggrah stupid 'nough tah be walkin' roun' at night when he ain't supposedta."

I started to show them my police card, tell them how it was "okay" for me to be out after dark.

"Ah don't give uh damn 'bout no card." The driver shut me down.

The one next to the driver darted an arm out the window, snatched the card from my hand.

I offered no resistance. Fear stupefied my reactions.

Looking over the card casually, without regard: "Say he can stay out past curfew."

"Why yew sucha special niggrah? Yew tha Jesus niggrah?"

Nigger came out of their mouths with as much ease as anger. And just as that word was easy for them, there was a word that, in that moment, was becoming untroublesome for me: "Sir? No, sir. Nothing special about me, sir. I work at one of the—"

"Get in tha car."

Miles and miles away a train sounded. I remember that. I remember very clearly the sound of that train.

"I . . . I think I can just walk back to—"

"Boy, git yer ass in tha car. We all take yew where yew need tah go."

The third one, the one in the back, pushed open the door. It stood gaping, waiting to swallow me whole.

I was not stupid.

I was not so stupid as to think there was any good to come from getting into that car.

I was not stupid.

I was not so stupid as to think running was any better an idea. To run was to be chased. To be chased was to be caught. To be caught was to be . . . Three of them. I was alone.

I was not stupid.

I got in the car.

And as I did, for lack of anything better, I held out a little hope these three might actually take me where I needed to go—to Miami, to the Madison, to a room with vermin that dodged leaking pipes of cold water that would be the most beautiful room I'd ever been in.

Sure. Maybe they'd take me there.

"Close it, boy. Close tha door."

I closed the car door. I closed in the smell of alcohol and sweat. The alcohol came from them; their every breath exhaled the stink of cheap beer downed in large amounts that got the drinker good and high. The sweat came courtesy of all of us. The rednecks sweaty with anticipation. Me, fear.

For a while we drove. Didn't know where we were going, except I knew we weren't going toward the city or the beach. Beyond the car was darkness, peeled some by the headlights to reveal only desolation ahead, and some by the occasional flash from a rural street post. In those flashes I caught glimpses of my companions. All had buzzed hair, the driver's blondish. On the back of his neck, acne scars that disappeared down under the collar of his shirt. And there was something wrong with his ear; a hunk of it had been chewed and torn off same as a mutt that's lost a dogfight.

The passenger was red. Red in hair. Red in flesh.

Man number three, the one in back with me, was thin. Nearly rail-thin. Except for a pot of a stomach that sloshed itself out from under a plaid shirt he wore unbuttoned for better viewing of the miracle of his thin/fat self.

This one, the thin/fat one, eyed my threads, guzzled from a

Schlitz can, then got around to asking: "Whuh yew all fined up for?"

"I told you."

"Yew ain't said shit, niggrah."

It was coming to seem like nigger was the standard close to every sentence.

The car rode rough. There was a sound coming from the engine. An unhealthy one. I had never owned a car, but I figured, probably, the oil had gone unchanged for longer than it should have and whatever it was that oil lubricated was going dry and grinding. I let out a little hysterical laugh that was disguised as a hiccup. I was thinking about the redneck's car. That was quite funny to me. I hiccupped again.

I said: "I work in town."

More beer. "What tha hell yew do with that git-up?"

". . . I'm an entertainer."

Laughs and cat calls in redneck stereophonics.

"Entahtainah? Yew some big stah, boy?" one of them asked. Couldn't tell which. Their mumbled ignorances stretched out in a slow drawl were selfsame.

"Like that niggrah Jew, ain't yew, boy?" The thin/fat redneck sucked more beer. Got a little higher on the booze. Got a little higher on his hate. "Bet yew jus like that niggrah Jew. Think yer sumthin' special. Think yer so goddamn . . ." He drowned the last of that beneath a swallow of beer and gave me instead an angry stare.

From the front of the car: "Maybe he oughtta entahtain us."

". . . I could try to get you tickets to the show. . . ."

"Yeauh. He oughtta entahtain us," the thin/fat one said. He said it quiet, said it soft. Said it like a guy who was saving his energy for things besides talking. He said it again: "Yeauh, he wanna entahtain us, don't yew, boy?"

The car tire hit soft shoulder.

Gravel pinged off the fender.

I jumped.

The redneck next to me smiled.

The driver was angling for a gas station. Closed, dark. The car stopped. Rednecks one, two, and three got out. I stayed, a death-house inmate who didn't want to leave his cell, the cell being better than what was waiting.

One of the rednecks, I think the driver: "Well, le's go, boy." He clapped his hands the way a master calls his dog. "Le's get tah en-tahtainin'."

I inched along the seat. I inched out of the car. That was all I did.

"Gowon over in tha spotlight." The red redneck pointed to where the car's headlights bounced off the wall of the garage. "Gowon."

Reluctant steps took me into the light. It filled my eyes, made the rednecks silhouettes.

One of the outlines: "Le's see yew dance, boy."

Their shadow arms bobbed up to their mouths and back down. More beer to fuel their fire.

"I don't . . . I'm a comedian. I don't dance, I tell—"

"Ah ain't tryin' tah heyah no niggrah joke-talkin' shit. Now, le's see yew dance."

I danced.

There was no pause, no inactive moment that I tried to pass off as defiance. I lifted a leg, then the other. Did a little shuffle step. Small motions. Tiny movements. My father's belt, whipping me to the floor, never delivered such total degradation. I didn't care. I didn't care if the three rednecks stood and laughed and pointed all the while I was humiliating myself. The only thing I cared about was ending the night alive. So I danced.

But all my halfhearted self-shaming did was stoke them. Where's the sport in beating down something that is so willing to be beaten?

"What is that shit?" one of the outlines demanded. "What tha hell kinduh coon shit is that suppostuh—"

"Niggrah's too goddamn good tah dance," from another of them.

"No, sir. I'm . . . I'm not too goo—"

"Thank's he's so goddamn good. All these niggrah Jews gettin' tah thank they so goddamn . . ."

Their rants, if ever, no longer even bordered on a kind of logic. They were just an excuse to hate out loud, dirty talk and foreplay before an orgasm of violence.

A beer can got tossed away. There was business to be gotten to.

One of the rednecks stepped from the dark to the light. The thin/fat one. He stood there. He looked at me, barely able to stand my sight, his face twitching with little jolts of scorn. A hand into his pant pocket. It came out, fingers shiny, kicking brass moonlight. Brass and slightly reddish. Rust. Rust or dried blood.

Terror racked the whole of me with a fierce nausea, made every part of me fail simultaneously. My heart labored. My muscles went loose and weak. My stomach and bowels demanded to empty themselves.

Thought useless, instinct stepped in and drove me back. I stumbled—toolbox among my feet—fell against the wall of the garage.

The redneck sneered at that: Look at the nigger, too stupid to even run away good.

The other two rednecks stayed back. The other two were going to let the thin/fat one have his fun.

Me, against the wall, crouching tighter, trying to will myself through it. Trying to wish myself out of backwoods Florida, north to New York, to the arms of my Tommy.

"Tommy," I screamed, my mind and voice spasming along with my physical self. "Tommy!" Hands frenzied, flailing, clawing at the wood I was pressed against. Pain. Hot, sharp pain. Palms warm, wet. Blood from splinters. Kept clawing. I kept—

Cold. In my hand: something smooth and cold and heavy.

The redneck: standing over me. Like my father, liquor-sick,

standing over me. Racist bile drooled at me, broiling and incoherent. Didn't matter. Words didn't matter. Words had become nonsatisfying. Hate is what mattered. The hate was real and ready to go to work. Thin/fat redneck's arm jerked back, the brass knuckles bouncing car light, flashing a warning: Here we come.

He swung down.

I swung up. The cold and heavy thing I gripped moved by terror, not courage. I swung. It whistled, chopped air. I swung. I swung until something interrupted my arch, the connection vibrating up my arm from hand to shoulder. Simultaneously there was a squooshy crunch—a soft melon getting hammered. The follow-up sound: dead weight hitting ground.

No sound after that. Nothing from the redneck I'd just pounded. Nothing from the other two.

From me, movement. My weapon tossed aside, used, now useless. A delirious scramble forward, eventually up to my feet, my body drove itself for the road, away from the gas station and the remaining rednecks.

The remaining rednecks right behind, not smart enough to chase me down with the car but closing just the same. As quick as fear moved me, rage moved them. Them. Two of them. One to hold me while the other strung me up—the minimum number required to perform a lynching.

My brain, useless up to that point, a slave to my instincts, got off the bench and back into the game. My brain told me sticking to the road, keeping with a straight-ahead run, was only good for getting me caught and killed. My brain told me to veer for the brush, to lose my hunters in a thicket of trees.

My brain fucked me up.

Just off the shoulder—a fence, the wire barbed. I hit it, hit it at speed and got thrown back and down, the fence keeping a good slice of my cheek.

From the ground I opened my eyes. Looking straight up, I saw dark sky and stars. I turned my head. I saw angry, huffing red-necks.

One of them, the one who'd been driving the car: in his hand a board. In the board nails. Dull, dirty, and bent. Useless nails. Good for nothing. Nothing but killing.

The sight of it—the redneck, the board he held, the seething drunken fury that held him—the sight of it all made my body thrash, marking my grave with a dirt angel. It made me want to puke, piss, and cry.

I started in on all three as the redneck started for me.

I just didn't want it to hurt. That's what I prayed for. Painless-ness. Other than that, on the ground, basting in my own filth, I was resigned to things ending. *Please be quick. Please be painless.*

The redneck stepped close to answer my prayers.

From up the road, sound: the low whine of an engine, the dull hum of tires over dirt. The combination of noises snatched the at-tention of the rednecks from me.

Whiteness broke the horizon. A car came up over a rise, came toward us . . . kept coming . . . then slowed to a stop, its head-lights a pair of big eyes staring at the situation. A beat. A couple of beats. The headlights went from regular to bright, those big eyes giving some serious consideration to what was what. When it was done figuring things, the car's door groaned open. Someone stepped out.

My eyes, the eyes of the rednecks, were too washed out to see much more than it was a man, fair in size.

He said to us in a normal tone of voice that carried in the dark and isolation as a shout: "What are you all doing?"

"This heyah niggrah took uh pipe tah Earl," the redneck with the board with the nails said, using the board—his judgment stick—to point at me even though I was the only "nigger" in the vicinity. "We fixin' tah learn him how we handle thangs with niggrahs down heyah."

The redneck raised the board. The demonstration was about to begin.

But it didn't. The redneck's arm got caught, got stopped mid-swing by the stranger's voice.

"Leave him be."

The redneck looked back at the man, hearing but not believing what he'd heard. "You heyah what Ah said? Tha niggrah beat our friend with uh pipe."

He left out the part about his friend wanting to bash my head with brass knuckles.

"Ain't no niggrah gonna git away with beatin' uh white."

The stranger didn't seem to care about any of that. The stranger just said again: "Leave him be."

The two rednecks swapped looks, making sure they equally understood as little of what was happening: Someone was keeping a colored who'd had the nerve to instinctively fight off a lynching from getting the back-road justice he deserved?

That just wouldn't do.

The redneck double-clutched the board in his hand, his thoughts obvious: Maybe two men were in for getting beat down.

There was a standoff brewing over me, over my life, and I was nothing more than an audience to it all.

The redneck took a step for the man. One step.

Then we heard the click.

Blind from the light, me and the rednecks couldn't see it, but there was no mistaking the very distinctive sound of the hammer getting cocked on a gun.

The thing of it is, when there's a disagreement and one guy's got a lousy board with nails and the other's got a gun, the pulling of the gun will end all manner of conversations and keep an equal number from ever getting started.

The redneck's grip on the board slackened along with his will to use it.

The figure, the outlined man to me: "Let's go, boy."

Despite the fact my life was being saved, for a moment I lay where I was.

The outlined man again: "Come on. Get up. Get in the car."

For a black man whose troubles had started because he couldn't catch a cab, suddenly everyone wanted to give me a ride.

I got up. I walked wide past the rednecks, mouths shut but their eyes delivering sermons on hate, for the savior car. Stepping from the glare of the lights, my head snapped Stepin Fetchit–style like I'd just been mule-kicked.

The stranger: "You keep quiet, boy, and get yourself in the car."

For both our sakes I did as told.

The stranger got back behind the wheel. Keeping the lights keyed on the rednecks, keeping them blind, he backed . . . backed . . . then pulled the car into a tight U-turn and sped off the way he'd come.

The stranger: "What were you doing?"

I didn't answer that. Couldn't answer. I was no good for talking. I was no good for anything but sitting and shaking.

The stranger, again: "What the hell were you doing?"

I turned and looked, focused on the man who'd just saved my life. But staring at him did little to calm the cuckooness of the scene. This man who'd just stood down a couple of blood-crazy whites was black. Same as me, darker even.

My senses, which had deserted me, started to return. I felt chilled and I *felt* my fear. I looked like hell, and the stink of my own foul matter started to choke me. The shame of my circumstances made me cry. The shame of me crying made me cry all the more.

The stranger: "Are you listening to me?" His voice a hand slapping me steady. "What the hell were you doing?"

"Noth . . . I wasn't . . . walking."

"At night? In the middle of nowhere?"

"I wasn't nowhere when I started." Calming down some. Just some. "Got lost. I was at the Fontainebleau, and I was walking back to my hotel in the—"

"You were at the Fontainebleau?" His tone told me he had the same hard time believing me the rednecks had.

"I work . . . I'm an entertainer and I was . . . Couldn't get a cab, so I—"

"So you thought you'd walk from the beach back to Miami." The stranger did some blank-filling.

"Then those three . . . there were three of them . . ."

"Stupid."

"They were going to kill me." I used a quiet voice to distance myself from the near-certain reality.

"Stupid."

"Worse. Animals. Dumb, ignorant—"

"Yeah. They're ignorant animals, but you . . . you're just plain stupid."

That got me. That brought me all the way back. "What?"

"Walking alone at night in these parts. Might as well just wear a lynch-me sign."

"I got lost. I told you, I got lost. Sure as hell wasn't looking to get picked up by a bunch of . . ." I felt a hurting. The hurt became a specific pain. Fingers to my cheek. There was a warm and continual ooze of blood. "Oh, God . . ." My almost-death came vivid again.

The stranger handed me a handkerchief. His contempt didn't cancel out his compassion, but his compassion didn't keep him from giving me a good verbal smacking. "Must be a Northern black. You from up North?"

"New York."

Shaking his head, talking as if we were some species just beyond his level of understanding: "All you Northern blacks . . ."

"It's my fault? This is my—"

"You don't think. None of y'all up there ever—"

"Think about what? Think about getting strung up? No, we don't. But 'us all' up there don't have crazy yokel-billies running around with nothing to do but drink and lynch."

"Yes, sir. In the North you have everything nice and quiet and polite. *You* don't get uppity, and *they* don't change anything."

I sat for a moment looking at, but not really seeing, the lights of Miami as they finally drew nearer.

A thought got with me. "You were driving alone. You're getting on me, and you were out driving by yourself."

"I'm not by myself." He patted the gun that lay between us.

"If you weren't out by yourself, you wouldn't need a gun."

"There isn't a time in his life a black in the South doesn't need protection. And I've got a long drive. Heading back to Mississippi from a regional conference."

"You a salesman?"

He laughed a little at that. Then thought. Then reconsidered my question as not being so funny after all. "In a way. We're not really selling anything. We're offering. Offering blacks—"

"Blacks. You keep saying—"

"*They* called us colored and Negro. Black is what we're starting to call ourselves. Same as they're white, we're black. It's who we are, what we are. And what we're offering blacks is dignity, equality, and the chance . . . the *right,* the right to be treated just the same as white folks."

"Who's 'we'? Who's doing the offering?"

"The N-double A-C-P."

My turn to do the laughing.

"Don't think much of us," the stranger said.

"I think you think you're doing some good, but if you figure issuing some proclamations and giving after-lunch speeches is going to do anything—"

"Demonstrations, boycotts, voter registrations—"

"Do anything more than get a bunch of peckerwoods riled up . . ."

"You don't think it will?"

"I've had a taste of this bunch firsthand."

The stranger nodded at my cheek. "They do that to you?"

"Didn't do it shaving." Not ten minutes fresh from almost getting killed and here I was doing bits.

"They cut you?"

"They chased me into a fence."

The laughing swung back to the stranger.

"Doesn't matter how I got cut, it hurts!"

"Yeah. It hurts. You know what I've seen?"

"What have you seen?"

"I've seen old black women thrown to the street just because they refused to ride in the back of the bus, and I've seen men hauled from buses and killed for the same thing. I've seen schoolchildren, boys and girls, beat for demonstrating for better books and better classrooms. I've seen men who are so afraid of being strung up for looking wrongly at a white woman, they step out into the street rather than brush past them on the sidewalk, while the same time white men practice back-door integration on our women.

"I've seen Emmett Till."

Emmett Till. They beat him because he wouldn't cower, and when he wouldn't grovel they killed him. Emmett Till. Fourteen years old.

I danced.

I turned my head, looked out the window as if there were something in the dark that needed to be looked at. All I saw was my own face reflected back at me, guilt and disgrace its strongest features.

"And with all that," I said to the image and to the stranger, "with all you've seen you really think you're going to get these people to give you anything."

"No. They're not going to give it to us. We've got to earn it: sitting in at lunch counters where they say we can't. Staying on the sidewalk when they think we should be walking in the street. We earn it by holding up our heads and looking white people in the eye. We earn it by standing up for ourselves."

"Like that Martin King in Alabama? All he ever earns is a free beating and some jail time."

"If you know another way . . ."

"I know another way." Looking back to the stranger now, selling him some of my religion. "You make it. You make it so big and so good that white people can't stand in your way if they wanted to, and they don't want to. What they want is to see you, be near you. They want to line up and pay their hard-earned money just to spend a couple of hours in your presence."

"And that's what you're doing, making it big."

"Better than taking a billy club to the head."

"Then how come you were walking back to Miami instead of staying at a beach hotel?"

The sting of that made me forget about my cheek. I sat there, not answering.

The stranger drove.

There was a stillness to the rest of the ride. The road a little rough, but the car found a pace and rolled in a smooth rhythm that almost forced you to ease yourself. Around us there was only dark and quiet, and it all seemed wrong somehow. I felt as if the whole world should be going crazy in the wake of my trauma, people out screaming how and why could such indignities happen to Jackie Mann? But there was just the dark and the quiet. I was a victim alone. The world couldn't care less and did just that.

Eventually we got to Miami, the Madison.

"You going to be okay?"

I nodded. I think. I don't remember. My mind, rattled beyond functioning, was completely focused on the suddenly monumental job of opening the car door. "Thank you."

He shrugged. "Sure you would've done the same for me."

Not knowing any other way to conclude things with the man who saved my life: "Good luck."

"Same to you. Who knows, you doing it your way and me mine, maybe we'll meet in the middle."

I got out of the car and the driver drove off. I had no doubt he'd make it back to Mississippi all right.

I went into the Madison. Sid was in the lobby looking as anxious as a guy could. The second he laid eyes on me he started in with his panicky bits.

"Jackie, what the hell . . ." Seeing my blood: "Are you hurt?"

Was I hurt? I had gotten it in my head I had joked my way to being somebody, only to be reminded in the harshed manner I was still just a little black nothing. Was I hurt? I hurt like hell.

"Where were you? I've got half the Miami Police Department out looking for you. I called every hotel on the beach, in the city. I've been driving all—"

"I just want to get some rest."

Sid didn't ask any more questions, didn't say anything beyond that. He bought me a drink, bought me an entire bottle, then sent me off to my room.

I drank.

I threw up.

I drank.

I got in the shower. In the cold, rust-brown water I stood crying. After ten minutes I slid down the chipped tile wall and sat in the tub, crying. After forty I turned off the water and just cried. When I was done with that I told myself, told myself several times, that what had happened was a good thing. It was good because I had learned; I had gotten some real-world, near-death educating. The lesson was I still had a lot of getting big to do. I had to grow so large that I would never be near the backwoods of Florida, any backwoods anywhere, ever again. I rededicated myself. On the floor of a tub in a pool of gritty liquid I swore to myself that Jackie Mann would be the biggest thing going. Whatever it took, he would be the biggest thing.

I threw up again.

I drank some more.

I went to bed. I could have slept just about forever.

Sid woke me the next morning, having made arrangements—by instinct—to get us an earlier train out. I was very glad for it.

As I packed up I realized I still had the stranger's handkerchief and no way to get it back to him, as I didn't know who he was. I tossed it.

Sid and I made the train.

We got out of Florida.

All I thought as I rode was that every mile traveled carried me a mile closer to home, closer to Tommy. I knew that when I was with her, without her saying a word, without an action, she would have a way of making every single thing in the world good again.

—————

TOMMY SAID TO ME: "I've met a man."

Rednecks with their boards with nails and their brass knuckles couldn't have hurt me more. What Tommy delivered was a hit to the heart.

Right away Tommy saw my ache and clarified herself. "No, no. I don't mean I've met another man. I met a man, an A&R man for a record company. Small label. New one. That's all I'm saying, baby." She took my hand in hers, squeezed it, let me know through strong physical contact that our relationship was just as solid. Tommy was giving me extra sensitivity that morning. She knew I'd had a rough time of things my last week on the road—the proof in the bandaged cut on my face—but not the details of why. I spared her those. It spared myself from having to relive events.

With her touch my pain died off. But the memory of the moment of having "lost" my girl was a fear that wouldn't fade.

Tommy said: "I really want you to meet him, Jackie. This company, they've got some really good ideas about music. I don't mean just about a record. About putting together a look and a sound, a whole presentation."

"Slow up a tick. Where did you meet this guy? Through an agent?"

"At the Vanguard. He just came up to me, told me he liked what he saw, and wanted to work with me."

Call me Charlie Green-Eyes. I got real skeptical real fast. Maybe I didn't exactly have years in the entertainment business behind me, but I'd put in enough time to whiff the stink of a player when he was stepping to my girl: some Harvey rolls up on her at a club, tells her he's in the record business, tells her he can help her out, tells her all she has to do is come back to his office, or hotel suite, or—what the hell—let's just go out to the alley behind the club and . . . talk about the future.

I said, and I said plainly and obviously: "I don't dig this character."

"You haven't even met Lamont."

"Lamont? I don't need to meet *Lamont* to not dig *Lamont*. Coming around telling tales, trying to talk you out of your slacks."

"He's not like that. The man is all business. The only thing he cares about is my voice."

"Yeah, your voice and how high he can make it go."

"You're jealous."

"I'm not—"

"You are. You're jealous." Tommy smiled with that, thinking me cute.

I wasn't trying to be cute. I was trying to be serious.

"Yeah. Okay. I'm jealous," I admitted. "How am I not going to be jealous when some low-rent Harry Belafonte is trying to load his banana in your boat?"

Smiling more, thinking me cuter, Tommy dipped her head, looked up at me with her doe eyes. Her teeth separated a little. Her tongue darted out and wet her lips.

I felt my blood rushing from one end of my body to the other.

Tommy said: "I'm not a little girl, Jackie."

Young, sweet. Possessing an innocence without being innocent; no, she wasn't a little girl. Tommy was nothing but woman.

"Don't you think I'd know if a man was trying to romance me?"

"I . . . probab . . ." The look Tommy tossed me made concentrating a full-on chore.

"And don't you think if I thought a man—a man besides you—was trying to romance me, I would send him walking?"

". . . Yes . . ."

"So you've got nothing to worry about, do you?"

". . . No."

"No." Tommy moved her hand, cupped her small fist in my palm. The fit was nearly perfect. "Jackie, I want you to meet him. I think . . . I think he could be really good for me. Not just for my career, but for my singing, for the kind of music I want to do. I want you to be okay with it. I want you to be part of it. Would you please? Would you meet him?"

Walking over hot coals. Sucking on broken glass. Was there anything for any reason that I could have ever refused Tommy?

No.

"You know I will. If it's that important to you, I'll have a sit-down."

She leaned over and touched me with her lips.

How long had we been steady? How many times had I kissed her? I still needed a moment to recover.

When I had: "You didn't tell me."

"What's that?" Tommy's eyebrows popped up.

"The label?"

"It's new. Small."

"You said. What's it called?"

"Motown."

⁓

"I'm not trying to make you nervous or anything, but this is huge; this is the next step for you. The Copacabana."

Sid was talking, up and animated, moving around his office. I was listening but looking out the window at Manhattan—the buildings, the skyscrapers. The people. One point seven million people shoved onto an island two and a half miles by twelve and a half. We worked among each other. We lived among each other. We were anonymous to each other. We were all just background and extras to someone else's life. Every other person in this city had their own concerns. I had mine. My hand into my jacket pocket: I felt my concern.

I let my attention drift back to Sid. . . .

". . . Hard as Hades for an act to get into the joint, especially . . . they're not exactly Negro friendly. But after the shows you put on at the Fontainebleau, the word's out, from Mel, from Buddy. Emmis: You're one of the hottest openers around."

But I couldn't stop thinking about Tommy.

"Tell me about your wife."

After a second of not doing or saying a thing, Sid went behind his desk, fell into a chair as much as sat down.

"I'm sorry," I said. "I didn't mean to—"

His hand came up and swatted down. "Let me tell you about Amy. Amy is the most beautiful woman I ever met. What man doesn't say that about the woman he loves? But as far as I care, you'll never meet a sweeter, kinder woman than Amy is.

"I remember a week—we were still just dating—I'd been working late. Two, three o'clock in the morning every night, going to clubs, watching acts. By the time I got home, got to bed, got up, and got to the office, I didn't have time enough to sleep, let alone eat a decent meal. So I come back to my apartment one morning, open the door . . . Jackie, there is this smell, this gorgeous smell: eggs, toast, coffee. All hot and ready to eat." Sid's smile was resurrected by good memories. "Amy had the super let her in, cooked all that up for me, and didn't even stick around for a thank-you kiss." His smile went Vegas bright. "But don't think I didn't track her down and give her one. That's just the kind of woman she is."

"You keep saying . . . is."

"I know I do. And I know she's passed. I'm not trying to trick myself into thinking she's still alive, but . . . but you know something, Jackie. She is. She is alive right here." He tapped his middle finger to his head. "And here." His finger went to his heart. "There isn't a day that goes by I don't remember something about her, or I walk by this corner or that and don't recall something she'd said or something we'd . . ."

His smile went away. His color left him.

"I lied to her, Jackie." Sid sounded like he was making a death-house confession. His eyes got slick. "She told me she was going to a picture with a friend, and I told her . . . A pipe." The wet in Sid's eyes turned to running water. He was hurting. I didn't know if I should cut him off, or if this was the kind of hurt that every once and again a man forever mourning needed to allow himself, so full with his own pain, if he didn't let it out, misery would pull him under. Drown him. I let him go on. "That's the thing that makes it so . . . If it was a drunk driver, a crazy with a gun, but a pipe falls off a building from thirty stories up, who are you supposed to get mad at? Where are you supposed to put your anger? Just a pipe falling off a building. If she'd left five minutes earlier, ten minutes later . . . I lied to her, Jackie; that day she went to the picture. I told her that I'd see her later . . . and I lied."

I turned my head some to give Sid a bit of privacy to compose himself. And to brush away my own tears.

The point of my question-asking hadn't been to drag Sid to the verge of breaking down. But in that breakdown I found the solution to my concerns.

I said: "I'm going to marry Tommy."

As quick as it had gone, a smile came back to Sid. Not on purpose, I was making him do emotional acrobatics. He pulled off every one of them. "Oh, Jackie, that's . . . that's great. I can't tell you happy I am to hear it. You have a date? And don't tell me you're doing a Vegas job. The girl deserves big, and you've got to give me a chance to lose a little weight so I can fit back into my cutaway."

"There's no, uh, there're a couple of things I have to do first."

"Do? Whadaya need to do? You're getting married, not landing on the moon. Get a church, reception hall . . ."

"I need to ask Tommy."

". . . Yeah, well, that you need to do." Sid took a minute to chew around a question, come up with the best way to spit it out. "Look, Jackie, I'm not trying to be a dark cloud, but what if—*if* mind you— but what if she's not as hot on the idea as you are?"

From my coat pocket I pulled out what my hand was clutching: my concern. A box. I popped it open.

Sid gave a low whistle.

Sid said: "Holy cow. Get a load of that rock." He took the engagement ring from the box, held it up, admired it. In the setting was as big a stone as a guy pulling in three hundred a week most weeks could buy. And back when most families were making less than five grand a year, that kind of green could buy a lot.

"You think it's too big?" I asked.

"Depends. If you're Elizabeth Taylor, no."

I was so deep in my anxiety, I couldn't figure if Sid was joking or trying to hip me to my overdoingitness. "I can take it back. The guy at the jewelry store said if there's any reason I—"

"Forget the ring, would ya? It's nice and all. It's beautiful. But it's not the ring Tommy's yes or no-ing." That got punctuated by Sid putting the ring back in the box, handing the box to me. He tossed off: "But if she doesn't, I'll marry you." A beat. "I'm happy for you. I really am. I think about the times I had with Amy, the good and the bad." Another beat. "They were all good. You look back, they were all good. All good, and all too—" Abruptly Sid quit the thought he was working on and went back to another. "Okay. The Copa." He stared at the contract on his desk, used it to help him focus. "It's one week opening for Tony Bennett—yeah, Tony Bennett—Tuesday through Sunday. Two shows Friday and Saturday. Same rate as Miami. Not a bump, but it's good in-town money. Ah, heck, it's the best in town—" As quick as he started, he stopped.

Sid brought his head up from the paperwork. He looked at me, looked at me with eyes trying to communicate the most dire thing any one man ever shared with another. "You love somebody, Jackie—you love somebody, then you grab them up with both hands, hold on tight, and you don't ever let go. Not for nothing, and not for nobody. And if you love somebody, if you truly . . . pray you die before they do."

<hr />

A LITTLE BETTER THAN A FURNISHED ROOM—a single with a bathroom. Shower, no tub. A kitchenette. A window that opened without too much sticking and gave me a decent view of the alley below. That's it. Nothing more, nothing special. The cubby I was moving to was less than six blocks from my then current apartment. Three blocks east, two and a half south. But those almost six blocks would be a world away from my father. He had devolved into a hermit, never went 'round the neighborhood, hardly even left the apartment. His two states of being were high or unconscious. I could've relocated to the stairwell of our building and never seen him. Five and a half blocks? I might as well have been moving to China.

I carried a couple of packed bags for the door. My father watched with the same dull sadness of a dog that knew it was about to be left alone for a long, long time.

"What am I supposed to do?" he mumbled.

"Same as before. Get loaded. Get tight." I didn't even look his way. "I'll swing you money same as always."

He said something else to me, but it got lost under my exit-slam of the door. I was wasting no time getting out. I'd already had most of my life wasted by that man. My emancipation wasn't about to get delayed with the fakery of a drawn-out scene played to ease his pain. There, there, Pop. It's all right, Pop. Let me put on the performance of both our lives for you, Pop. I had nothing but a wordless good-bye for the man who brought me into the world and took my mother out of it.

My new apartment was small. Had to be. Paying for two places, Pop's and my own, I couldn't afford much. But it was just big enough to hold all the independence I'd never previously owned. Wherever I went in the tiny space, there *wasn't* my father. I didn't have to tread softly when I got up in the morning or came home late. His drunken rants went unheard, and his odor was nowhere to be smelled. Instead of always cooling at Tommy's, I had a place I could bring her. I could paint the apartment any way I wanted, put in whatever furniture I pleased, stock the refrigerator with any kind of food I liked. . . . Out of all the choked space had to offer, that was its best feature: It came with prerogative.

The morning after my first night there I woke up happy. The next morning I woke up the same way. By the third day I was simply content, the unburdened ease I felt quickly becoming a constant of my life.

The fourth day Grandma Mae brought 'round a plate of oatmeal-raisin cookies as a welcome to my new digs. They were still warm. Since I'd starting working the road I'd had to take a pass on our traditional Sunday night gatherings, so it felt especially good to see her and to have my own place for her to visit. I gave her the grand tour of the apartment. I spread my arms, said this is it, and the tour was done. Still, being able to reverse the favor, entertain Mae, made me feel grown-up and a man. Over the cookies we talked. I told Mae about the stars I'd worked with and all the places I'd been—Philly and Chicago and Milwaukee. Concerning Miami, there were parts I left out. Mae listened to me, dug my stories the way I used to dig stars telling tales on *Toast of the Town*.

And I updated Mae on Tommy, hinting a little about my hopes to marry her. Hinting right back, Mae hoped that one day I would make my plans real. She told me how important family was, how the greatest success any man could have was being a good husband and loving father.

Joking, I told her I'd have to take her word for it.

Mae said she understood; she knew I'd never had much of a home life. But she added to that, different than strangers, in spite of what passed among them, she was raised to believe that family always took care of family. She eased into saying that no matter the things my father had done, the kind of man he was, he was still my father and deserved, if not my affection, then my compassion.

And all at once I got edged up. Even coming from Grandma Mae, hearing that I owed my father—my drinking, hitting, hating father—any more than a good-bye got me nice and agitated. Hadn't he been the one to abuse me every chance he got every way there was? Wasn't I still supporting him, giving him money for grub and rent that he was only going to waste on booze and drugs?

And that, Mae told me, as calm as I was hot, was the problem: I supported my pop, I gave him money, but if I left home for good, there would be no one to take care of him. I brought him his basic needs, food and liquor, and that kept him from having to wander the streets in a stupor, looking for something to eat or a way get high. I cleaned his clothes, cleaned the apartment. That kept him from living in his own squalor. Mae had kept an eye on him while I had been away, she'd do the same in the future, but what my father needed, she told me, was family. He was nothing better than a full-grown infant, and Mae made me think that without me he would be nothing at all. She did not ask me to return to my father. She knew if she did, for her alone I would have. But that was a commitment she could not force on me. Mae asked only that I do what was in my heart, then left me to think.

And I did.

I thought of all the punches I'd taken, all the nasty names, all the hard put-downs, all the rage that man had given and given and given me. That man.

That man.

My father.

I thought of him alone, preferring dope and drink to food and shelter. How long before those choices killed him? I didn't care. I didn't want to care. I just wanted to leave him to himself.

But I couldn't. I couldn't because my mother wouldn't leave him. She would not let him be even if it . . . even though it killed her. I hated my father for that, murder as far as I was concerned. I hated him, but not as much as I loved my mother. And to love her, to honor her . . .

I swore at myself. I told God to damn me for feeling anything in any way for that no-good louse.

I repacked my bags, I moved back those five and a half blocks to again be with Pop. The action cost me a month's rent. That, and my freedom.

⸺

THE PHONE RANG . . . rang . . . rang . . .

"Hello?"

"Fran?"

"Jackie!"

"Get you at a bad time?"

"I was just cooking some."

"I can call you back if you're—"

"No. Absolutely not. I want to talk to you. Feels like forever."

"Been on the road."

"I know. How was it?"

"It was good. Kinda fun, you know? Haven't traveled that much, so that was a gas. Did a week with Buddy G, a week with Vic Damone, Mel Tormé—"

"What's he like?"

"Strictly star: big, but nice. That's the way I want to be if I ever . . . when I, you know, get over. Big, but decent."

"And the Copa. Sid told me you're opening up at the Copa."

"Next week for Tony Bennett."

"Jackie, that's great. That's so sensational! It's going to be a terrific stand, I know it is. I'm supposed to be in L.A. next week. I should cancel."

"No."

"I can talk to—"

"What are you talking, cancel?"

"It's your big night."

"First of plenty. I'm going to be regular at the Copa from now on. You can catch me next time, so don't get crazy rearranging things. What are you doing out in Los Angeles any—"

"Wait. Hold on a second. . . ."

". . . Had to take something out of the oven."

"Sure you don't want me to call you back?"

"No, no. What were you—"

"What are you up to?"

". . . Nothing . . ."

"How's nothing going to be going on with you? You've got that big deal—"

"Oh, yeah. It's huge."

"Bigger than my deal, since I don't have one."

"You know what it's like? Signing up with CBS is like having another dad. These guys are into this grooming thing: I've got to wear my hair this way. I've got to dress that way . . ."

"It's television. You've got to look good."

"I don't look good now?"

"Don't even start with that. You know I think you're a doll. I'm just saying for TV you've gotta look—"

"I'll tell you right now the day they try and tell me what songs to sing . . ."

"They won't, and quit trying to make the whole gig sound worse than it is, because it's not bad at all."

"How's Tommy?"

"She met some record guy out of Detroit, wants to sign her to a deal."

"On the level? Oh, that's terrific, Jackie! She's a good kid. She deserves it."

"Sure. It's sensational. She's got a deal, you've got a deal. Everybody's got a . . . What are you laughing at?"

"I was thinking—you remember that, uh, the first time you saw Tommy, at The Angel. You're standing around outside the club all night waiting for her."

"That was a real riot."

"Then she comes out and you tell her . . . I don't know what you said to her. Nothing. Then she gets in a cab and she's gone and you're just standing there. . . ."

"Anytime you want you can quit with the laughing."

"You should do something about that in your act."

"Sure. I'll do a bit right up front: Good evening, ladies and gentlemen. Say, have I told you what a big dope I can be?"

"It's personal, Jackie. It really happened. I just think doing bits that are real are fu— Ow!"

"You okay?"

"Burned my finger."

"I should let you go."

"Yeah . . . I sort of need to finish this up. But call, all right?"

"I will."

" 'Cause I want to get together with you. You and Tommy both. I really want to. . . . Can I tell you something goofy? I know you're going to think it's goofy with all the other stuff I have going on, but . . . sometimes I miss the Fourteenth Street Theater. You ever miss it?"

"Parts of it. Sometimes, I guess I do."

"But you know what I mean when I say I miss it? I don't, you know, miss the drunks. I don't miss the no pay. I miss—"

"I know what you mean."

"I knew you'd think I was a goof."

"No, I don't, Fran. I don't think you're goofy at all."

. . .

"So . . . you're going to call me, right?"

"I will. I'll call."

"Okay."

. . .

"Jackie, I love you."

"I love you, too."

Fran hung up.

I hung up.

———

AROUND THE CORNER from Grand Central was a Horn and Hardart. I waited there for Lamont Pearl. He'd given me a call, wanted to talk. I wasn't particular one way or the other about meeting the man but for two things: Tommy wanted me to have a sitdown with him, and whatever Tommy wanted, Tommy got. Thing number two: I wasn't so far away from being a starving artist that if a Jehovah's Witness wanted to buy me a free lunch I wouldn't've found a space in my day.

A cup of coffee occupied my time. Just over the chatter of people swapping noontime clack, the sound of quarters plinking into and rolling through the automats—soups and sandwiches and hunks of pie being debated over—a radio played. The news of the day: Albert Anastasia—Al the Mad Hatter, Big Al, Albert the Executioner—while getting his hair cut had his head bullet-pierced over at the Park Sheraton. The mob handling mob business. A brutal, bloody murder . . . and we all hung on the newscaster's every word. No more clack. The quarters quit plinking. Maybe those Mafiosos were all a bunch of ruthless, criminal dog-killers, but they were as much a part of the city as Times Square and Lady Liberty. They murdered, they stole, they extorted. They added a phantom tax to almost every good and service in New York. But they made for great copy, so we loved 'em. The bottom line of it all: Doesn't matter how you're famous as long as you're famous.

And then he came in.

Lamont came into the diner moving with the kind of assuredness that simply took over the joint even though he didn't look the kind confidence came to naturally. He was half a foot under six. His features carried the baggage of the punches he hadn't slipped as a daydreaming prizefighter. Working an assembly line of a Ford plant had taken all the tenderness from his hands. You'd never've thought he was the type of guy who would help create a whole new sound so fresh, so smooth, no matter it was black, white America would beg to have it poured down their throats. And maybe it was exactly because he didn't fit the bill that he was one of the advance guard who snuck in under the radar on the way to reshaping the musical landscape.

Taking a chair, Lamont thanked me for meeting with him, especially on short notice as he was heading out of town.

I tossed him a dry version of my Jehovah's Witness crack.

"I get the feeling you don't like me very much."

"Don't flatter yourself," I nonchalanted. "What makes you think I like you at all?"

A grin. "Save the daggers." Lamont waved over a waitress to pour him a coffee. She went away smiling from his dollar tip. "I can guess where your head is. Regardless of what you might think, I'm not trying to take Tommy away from you."

Yeah, there was that. But I also didn't care for Lamont's tailored suit, or the just-polished shine on his expensive not-from-this-country shoes. I wasn't crazy about the way the roughness of his hands was hidden beneath the soft kick of fine gold jewelry. His self-confidence, his sureness . . . What I didn't dig about him was that he had everything I wanted. I didn't care to add Tommy to the list.

Lamont did what he could to ease me of that fear. "The two of you make a handsome couple. Real fine. You going to marry her?"

". . . How did you—"

"If I were you, I'd marry her. If I were you, I'd already be married to her. You're a lucky man, Jackie." A sip of his coffee. "Thing is, woman like that, I don't think I could stand to be away from her."

"I'm not planning on being away from her."

"You're not going to do road clubs anymore?"

"Sure I am."

"Sure you are. Need those clubs to get established, to work the act."

"You going to manage me now?"

Again Lamont smiled. The cat was unfazeable. He had, I noticed, a habit of brushing his thumb back and forth over the tips of his fingers. Back and forth. He kept it up like he was collecting pay for it. "I'm just saying; you're away working clubs, you're away from Tommy."

"She can come with me."

"She could. She could." More coffee. "That'd be a shame."

"A shame for us to be apart, a shame for us to be together . . ."

"The shame is that it would be the end of her singing career."

"It's not the end of anything. I'm not asking her to stop singing."

"You said you were going to take her on the road with you. She's traveling with you, how's she going to sing?"

"That's not the . . . I'm not saying . . ."

Same as a by-the-hour lawyer, Lamont was putting me through my paces. What God had held back from him in height and looks, He'd doubled down on in smarts.

"Look, Jackie, of course Tommy could still sing. Here and there. At least till you have a kid. And even then, maybe, she might still have a shot at things. Somehow. The point is: There aren't that many opportunities for us." He said "us" in the way black people say "us" to each other when we're talking about *us*. "Not a lot of chances to make it, and make it big. That's the idea behind Berry's record company."

"Berry?"

"Berry Gordy. Founded Motown. Founded it on the concept of creating a look and a sound and a style that's so unique that it can't be ignored, not even if they wanted to." He said "they" in the way black people say "they" to each other when we're talking about *them*. "You do that, you make it large, then you don't have to be dependent on some ofay in a high office to give you your due. Dig my meaning?"

I dug. Lamont was preaching to the converted.

He said: "And Tommy is due. She rates it. She's got the voice, the look. She's got the talent. But you take her away from her singing now, she may never make it."

Well, let me tell you: I could've hit him. I'll say it free and plain: I could have reached across the table and hit Lamont Pearl. If *I* take her away from her singing. I. Me. My fault: Marrying Tommy was no different from flipping the executioner's switch.

I could have hit him, but his words bounced around inside me, bounced around until they landed on the truth: It would be my fault. I would be the one taking Tommy away from her singing. I would be the one tossing the first shovelful of dirt on her career. A day earlier I was so sure of myself that the future of me and Tommy was a future together. But after talking with Lamont, after hearing his slicked-up words, I didn't know what to do.

I said: ". . . I don't know what to do."

"When you don't know what to do, sometimes the best thing to do is nothing. Not for the minute anyway. There's time for the two of you after she's made it. After you've made it."

I fought logic with pure emotion. "I love her."

"Hey, man." Lamont's hands went up in a kind of surrender. "I'm not telling you how to play things. But what kind of love is that? Taking away everything she could be. No matter you want her to succeed, you know the woman; you know how devoted she is. You marry her, she'll never leave your side. No more clubs, no more singing. No more nothing."

"And you know that? You've been around Tommy, what, a hot minute, and you know—"

"Then tell me I'm wrong." Back and forth, his thumb across his fingertips. A sip of his coffee.

Unfazeable.

Lamont was no longer speaking any known language; he was just making a shrill sound that I could only barely comprehend: Career. Success. Failure. Marriage. Don't. Understand.

Understand?

"You understand, don't you, Jackie? Don't you?"

At some point I think Lamont offered a few pleasantries and said good-bye to me—must've—then left for Grand Central to hop his train.

I don't remember that.

What I remember is sitting in that Horn and Hardart a good, long time.

AT THE MOMENT The Village Vanguard was empty. Middle of the afternoon, dark in the daylight, the joint was closed for business. At night, when the shows were running, The Vanguard was as shoulder-to-shoulder happening as any cabaret in any piece of the city.

At the moment it was empty.

Empty except for Tommy and a piano player who accompanied her in "Speaking of Happiness," as she worked the song out before chairs upended on tables and a guy who was pushing a broom around the floor paying more attention to Tommy than to whether or not he was collecting any dirt.

I slid myself into a corner of the house.

I listened. I'd heard Tommy sing maybe ten dozen times. But this time I *listened*.

There are people who sing. Besides just in the shower, there are people who get up onstage before an audience, sing, and get paid for their singing. Maybe their voice is decent. Maybe they've got some style. Whatever it is, they rate as a singer.

There are people who interpret. Same as if they're changing French into English, they tell you what the song means, translate lyrics and melodies into a language the listener can understand: Love. Joy. Sadness.

Loneliness.

And there are people so gifted, they can make you feel those words, make them hack right through you like a surgeon's brand-new cutting tool. Those kinds of singers, they're not just giving you a tune for your money. They're injecting themselves into the song, making naked their emotions, slicing off some of their soul for your consumption. They are giving you a piece of them. And accordingly, whether you want to or not, you smile, you snap your fingers, you cry. . . . You do what their voice tells you to do. That powerful the gifted are. That special.

That's how I felt standing in the back of The Vanguard, *listening* to Tommy. I felt like when she was done with her number the empty chairs and the tables they rested on would jump up and start applauding the hell out of themselves.

But all that happened was—having heard her for the thousandth time, and for the very first time—without a word I slipped from the club same as I'd slipped in.

INSIDE HER APARTMENT, in the kitchen, across a table from each other, over coffee, me and Tommy sat. The conversation started a mile away from the subject. How was I? How was she? The weather. Been strange. Yeah, unseasonable. Hear what the Soviets did? Those Reds are crazy.

Then we got to what's what.

Tommy asked: "You talked to Lamont?"

I nodded to that. "Before he left town."

"What did you think?"

Editing myself: "Seemed bright."

"He is. He's got a lot of good ideas." Tommy followed up a sizable pause with: "He wants me to go to Detroit, work on some music out there."

I didn't say anything to that.

"I don't know how long I would be gone. A few months. Or more. Then I would have to, if I got a record out, I mean, I would have to, you know, go out. Support it." That was mumbled.

Beneath the table, out of Tommy's view, I clutched my little box with the very big ring inside.

"And with you gone, you on the road, I don't know when we'd see each other. . . ." She was climbing a mountain. Tommy had to stop, take a rest before pushing on. It was as if she knew where she was heading the air would be thin and things would be dizzying for all involved. "You're always saying how important career is, how important it is to make it. But if there was, you know, some reason . . . if you didn't think I should go . . ."

I sat there. I sat where I was, and if I sat for one second, I sat for a year. That's what you do when you're at a crossroads, the map you've been carrying is suddenly no good, and your compass is just spinning around no matter somebody's telling you what direction to head.

I put my hand to my pocket. In my pocket I put the box with the ring. "Of course you should go. Like I said, that Lamont is a sharp cat. He can do things, do some serious things for you. And hey, just because you're gone and I'm . . . Nothing's going to change for us. What do they say? Absence and all that jazz. A little absence, and you and me are going to be so crazy for each other . . ." That was all the more talking I could do before the sound of my own voice made me ill.

I looked up. Through all I'd said I hadn't had the guts to look at Tommy while I lied. But then I looked up.

Tommy's eyes were near tears.

"You okay, baby?"

"I don't feel . . ." Pressing a hand to her head, Tommy fought up out of her chair. "Maybe you should go."

"You want me to get you something?"

"I don't . . ." Clutching her head now, fingers trying to work their way inside. "Please, just go."

Tommy went to her bedroom, closed the door, but not so tight that the sounds of sobs couldn't creep out from behind it. I'd given Tommy what she needed: the freedom to be the star she deserved to be.

But what Tommy wanted . . .

What Tommy wanted was tucked away in the pocket of my coat.

A COUPLE OF DAYS LATER. Maybe three. Tommy was taking a plane to Detroit. We said our "see-yas," avoiding good-byes that would make the scene feel any more final than it needed to. Along those lines I put her in a cab but didn't head to the airport with her. She was just taking a little trip. No big deal. No need to turn it into some kind of a thing.

Tommy's flight was at two-thirty.

She left for LaGuardia at one. Lamont would be there, back from wherever he'd been, to get Tommy to Detroit. Personally.

When she was gone I did some walking around the city, window-shopping. I liked watches. Nice ones. I'd never owned one. A nice one. Didn't have the money. Not really. But they were good for looking at. Rolled by a tailor's and checked out some fronts. Suits I couldn't afford to go with the watches I didn't own. Stopped by a diner to grease myself. Basically I got back to the business of living my life.

I checked the time.

It was one-eighteen.

No good. It was no good me pretending there was any normal living to be done without Tommy, without at least seeing her off.

I hopped a cab. A twenty wagged in front of the driver got me to Queens in record-busting time. My legs busted a few more records getting me to Tommy's gate when I heard a call made for her flight to board.

I spotted her talking with Lamont. As I came up I caught a little of their conversation: "Demo . . . image . . . packaging . . ."

Lamont looked over, saw me. I heard: "Shit."

Tommy was all light and smiles as she flew into my arms. "I knew you'd come."

In an instant we were holding, hugging, kissing. Feeling good. Feeling all right. Feeling, at least, a lot of emotion. Some of Tommy's emotion, flowing from her eyes, soaked through my shirt and wet my chest. Tears so warm I felt them from one side of me through to the other.

"I don't want to go."

"What are you talking?"

"I don't want to leave you."

"You're not . . . It's just for a while." I went into my cheer-up bits. "Why are you making a scene? You're going to Detroit, that's all. It's only a balloon ride away. You have to go."

"Why? So I can be a big star? So I can make lots of money?" My own words spat back at me. They burned like acid.

I tried using reason to wear Tommy down: "You've got a chance, a real chance at things. After all the time you put in trying to get your music heard, somebody hands you your first big break and you want to throw it all away?"

One more time her flight got called.

"What I want is something that's real, that means something."

"I'm always going to be here for you. Doesn't get more real than that. We have time."

"Do you know that, Jackie?"

I didn't know that. I didn't know what I was doing, what I was saying. I didn't know anything except that I loved Tommy enough that I wasn't about to let her throw her career away over . . . over me.

"What am I supposed to do?" I asked her.

"Tell me to stay."

I hesitated. I said: "I love you."

She said it again, she pleaded: "Tell me to stay."

Tell her to stay? I could barely open my mouth to talk, and when I did all I could say, repeat: "We'll have time."

After the shortest of minutes Tommy withdrew from me. She went to Lamont, exchanged words. She looked back to me, gave a quick wave—as if anything longer would have put her at risk of more breaking down—headed out a door and across the tarmac, up some stairs into her airliner.

Lamont came over to me.

"I know it must hurt—"

"Get on that plane."

"But it's for the best."

"Just get on the plane."

Lamont did that. He got on the plane and pretty soon the stairs got taken away and the door was closed. The Super Connie got backed from where it was parked, it taxied, then sat up at the end of a runway, waiting there for me to do . . . something.

I did nothing.

The plane sprinted down the runway, flew for Detroit.

I went home.

part IV

Jackie Mason gave Ed Sullivan the finger. Live, onstage, on Ed's show—the show that he renamed after himself in 1955 just so there'd be no mistaking who was boss—Jackie Mason gave Ed Sullivan the finger.

Not really.

But Ed Sullivan thought Jackie gave him the finger. Jackie's set was running long. Ed, from offstage, was throwing Jackie hand signals to wrap up, get off. Jackie, nervous, started throwing hand signals back at Ed.

Jackie thought it was funny.

Ed thought Jackie was giving him the finger.

Ed banned Jackie from his show.

That got Jackie blackballed from television.

That killed Jackie's career.

In the late 1950s, still in its adolescence, television was already that powerful. With a shot on Sullivan or Paar or Godfrey, a club act could be a household name before the night turned to day. Without that shot they could be same as they always were, nothing but somebody joking or crooning in a smoky room after dark.

And television didn't just change the lives of the people on the tube. Things got changed up for everyone. Once TV went coast-to-coast, the whole country was running on the same clock. We got entertainment live. We got sports live. We got news live.

We got the world live.

Civil rights protestors getting hit with water hoses and attack dogs live.

Mob bosses pleading the Fifth live.

Updates on Sputnik and Ike's bum ticker live.

And all of a sudden the whole wide world wasn't two or three steps removed anymore. All of a sudden a cathode-ray picture of every major event—glorious, gruesome, or graphic—was part of your living-room decor along with your pole lamp, cloverleaf coffee table, and BarcaLounger. And all of a sudden you couldn't plead no knowledge of what was happening down South or up North or out West. Like it or not, uninformed bliss went the way of hoop skirts and ducktails. Reality was checking in.

There are talking heads who'll yadder about how America lost its innocence when television started shining its blue light on us. But a country that was stolen from her natives and built on the backs of slaves and coolies was never innocent in the first place. All we did was shed our ignorance. TV was that powerful. TV was that pervasive. But to take full advantage of it, you had to be part of it.

You couldn't be part of it if Ed Sullivan thought you gave him the finger.

March of 1958 to May of 1959

Frances Kligman was no longer Frances Kligman. Frances Kligman was Frances Clark.

CBS, who loved her so much when they caught her in the Village, loved her a little more after brow-beating the girl into de-ethnisizing her name.

I asked Sid about it.

He shrugged. "People don't mind watching Jews on TV, they just don't want to be reminded they're watching Jews on TV."

Sid told me Fran went hellion when the suits tried to get her to go with Clark, said she didn't care who else had changed their names, she didn't care how big they'd gotten with their new names. She was Frances Kligman, end of story.

It took a fifty-three-minute phone call from Dinah Shore to convince her changing her name wasn't the same as selling her soul.

Other than that little blip, it was strictly good news for Fran. She had a new record on the way. With RCA this time. Chances were it would land big.

CBS didn't care to take chances. They had plans for their new starlet. The suits had Fran hold off a month or so in releasing the record. They wanted her to break it somewhere she'd get noticed. They wanted her to break it on the season premiere of the Sullivan show.

Fran was in Los Angeles when she got the news and was beside herself with excitement. Why shouldn't she be? A new record on the first show of a new season of Sullivan. Besides the fact she was a sensational talent, that kind of exposure guaranteed Fran would be a hit. And the Monday after the Sunday she went on, Frances Clark would be a household name.

After she got the word, the first call she made from the coast was to me insisting that I be there with her at the broadcast. Just like the old days. Just like back on Fourteenth Street.

I told her I wouldn't miss it for anything. Told her a bunch of times how happy I was for her.

We hung up.

From the other room my father yelled at me that he needed a fix.

ARTHUR MILLER HAD MARILYN MONROE. The army had Elvis. I had my father.

I hated my father. There was no other way, no gentler way of saying things. I hated him, but I stayed with him. It was a nutty kind of syndrome of abuse: It used to be his beatings, the fear of getting beat, that kept me close. Now that he was harmless and pathetic, it was guilt. An unspoken oath to my mother made me feel guilty about leaving him to himself. I would care for him for as long as he lived. And as long as he lived I would never be free.

How many ways are there for a drunk to die? How many ways are there for an addict to end his life? As many nights as I lulled myself to sleep counting the means. The mundane: Drunk falls down. Drunk bangs his head. Drunk is too drunk to do anything except lie there and bleed. The sensational: Dope fiend killed in hail of bullets as juice joint is raided by narcs. The simply ironic: Boozer, user, loser—his heart gives out trying to climb stairs and he ends up in a heap where my mother ended up in a heap years prior.

None of those things came to pass.

No matter how much the dope and liquor affected my father, it could not destroy him. He'd built himself a resistance. The smoke, the pills: hazardless. Alcohol to him was the same as a tall glass of cool water. There was nothing for me to do but sit and wait and wait and wait for him to no longer be.

How many ways are there for a drunk to die? How many ways are there for an addict to end his life?

As far as my pop was concerned, seemingly none.

Pulling myself from my rant, I apologized to Sid for having to sit through it. I'd come around his office to beat the chops, and here I was going off on my dad—that stinking lush. That lousy, drunken son of a . . .

Again to Sid: "Sorry."

Sid sat wordless for a couple of ticks. He squirmed some in the chair behind his desk. "There's something you should know, Jackie. Something I should've told you first off . . ." He paused, took a look around the room, out the window. He didn't look at me. "I had a, uh . . . There was a time when I drank a little too much. Little too much, little too often."

I said: "Oh." I said it with surprise, said it with curiosity. Mostly I said it regretting I'd been talking about drunks dying in front of him.

"Forget little. I was an alcoholic. Still am. That's the thing about it: Once you've got it for booze, it stays with you."

Sid waited for me to say something.

I said nothing.

Sid said: "After Amy was . . . died, I fell apart for a while. You don't know how it hurt when she . . . You feel that way for a couple of weeks, a few months, you get to where you don't want to feel anything. That's where the drink came in." Absent of thought, he brushed fingers across the top of his desk. "When I hear you talk about your father . . ."

"You're different from my pop," I yeah, but-ed. "That guy, the way he treated me—"

"You don't think I abused my share of people?"

Right then I didn't know what to think.

"Never hit anybody. Was never violent."

"Well, then, you didn't—"

"There are all kinds of abuse. My brother, his wife; you should ask them how good I was to be around when I was soused. My clients, the ones whose careers I was supposed to be handling when I was bent over a glass at noon." His head dropped some. "It's no accident I've got no acts to my name, and the ones I do have are—"

"Are what, Sid? 'Cause, remember, me and Fran are two of them."

That got a little smile out of him.

From me, cautiously: "But you're cleaned up now. I mean, that's the thing; my pop just wants to stay in his bottle. You got yourself clean . . . right?"

Sid nodded. "Had a relapse once. Other than that, I'm a good friend of Bill W's. I'm only telling you all this, Jackie, because you should know. You should know that people aren't perfect. That I'm not . . . I'm telling you this because, knowing how you feel about drunks . . ." For the first time since he started this run, Sid looked at me. "If you wanted to quit things . . ."

In the whole of my life, how many people had ever been so much as decent to me? Sid included, I didn't need all the fingers of a hand to count them.

I twisted my wrist, read my watch. "I should get home to change. *We*," I stressed, "need to be at the Copa by six-thirty."

———

THE COPACABANA. The Copa. The object of my devotion. Icon of its era: upscale class. Big money-style. You read about it, you heard about it, but most workaday Americans would burn up a month's salary just paying for the cover, food, and drinks. And even if they could scrape up the green, they'd find once they got to the Copa, they couldn't get into the Copa. Forget that the club wasn't black friendly. Neither were the Stork, '21,' and most especially El Morocco. The Copa wasn't friendly to anyone who didn't have dough or juice or some combo of the two. The Copacabana was progressive that way: It discriminated against everyone equally.

Sid and I got out of the cab on Sixtieth and Madison, went for the Copa's doors—my freshly cleaned suit bagged up in plastic and slung over my shoulder. Inside we got a "Hey, howzit" from Jules Podell, who owned the club, and were given a quick introduction all around. The waiters, bartenders. I said a hello to them all.

Mostly I got back lukewarm stares.

We got walked to my dressing room, a suite in Hotel Fourteen above the club. Tony Bennett came 'round before I had a chance to stop over and greet him. He told me he'd heard great things about me, about my act. Said he was looking forward to a terrific stand together, and if there was anything he could help out with, be sure to give a holler.

He wanted to know if there was any way he could help *me?*

Tony was strictly decent. Around him I didn't feel like a kid catching a break but that I was among his kind, that I was just about a star myself.

He wished me a good show again, then went back to his dressing room to make ready.

Sid hung around some before claiming to want to go check the crowd. Truth is I don't think he wanted to infect me with his own nervousness. He left, tossing off good-luck bits on his way.

Me, I just put my heels up and relaxed. With a good quarter-plus hour before the show got started, I enjoyed the quiet moment. I riffed in my head about the time I'd come around knocking on the Copa's door and couldn't get past the guy with the bad combover, how in short order I'd be onstage, taking in laughs, claps, and smiles from an audience full of people who'd paid top dollar to see me.

Okay, they'd paid to see Tony, but I came along with the deal, so in a way it was *like* they'd paid to see me, too. Anyway, I assured myself it wouldn't be long before my name was at the top of the bill and there was no doubt who was shelling green to see who.

I thought of Tommy.

I picked up the phone and the long distance operator put me through to her hotel in Detroit. She wasn't in.

I flipped my wrist, checked my watch. Just a few minutes before the show. I reached over for a glass of water. It spilled on my hand. Or really, my hand was shaking so badly, I couldn't keep the water from sloshing out of the glass and onto me. I stood up to grab a towel, but my knees barely worked as supports. On top of that, taking a good, steady breath was turning into a circus trick.

Nerves.

Nerves that I'd been dodging all day were wolves closing in on me. Never mind the months on the road, forget all that other club work I'd put in. This was the Copacabana. I could play things cool all I wanted, for everyone else I could act as if tonight was just another show, but all I was doing was acting. The truth of it: Opening for a cat the size of Tony Bennett scared the hell out of me. Working the Copa terrified me. Maybe Sid's counsel had been right. Maybe I should've made sure I was absolutely ready for everything I did every step of the way. And real suddenly I didn't feel like a seasoned act but a frightened little boy who had no business thinking he could entertain people. I felt again what I'd so often felt inside myself, not special, just different.

I got myself from my dressing room downstairs to the backstage area—a space married to part of the kitchen. Jules Podell was watching the house from the wings, his fat hand swallowing a highball glass. He looked at me, saw my pale blackness, asked: "What's the matter, kid?"

I copped: "Just got some jitters. Guess I'm a little nervous. Honest? I think I'm going to throw up." I laughed some. At myself.

Jules smiled at me, smiled as if he were about to go all fatherly with some wise words from a longtime club owner.

He said: "What the fuck are you talkin'; you're nervous, you goddamn nigger coon?"

Right then I got hip. He wasn't smiling, he was sneering.

"I bring you into my club, feed you food, let you drink my booze, pay your nigger-ass good goddamn money just so you can cry like a bitch? 'Oooh, I'm scared,' " he mocked.

Why didn't he just reach over and slap me? I was better at taking slaps.

"You listen to me, you little black shit. I don't want to hear any of your fuckin' cryin'. You get your moolie jig ass out on that stage and tell your goddamn jokes. And be fuckin' funny."

Pep talk done, Jules took a hit off the glass hidden in his hand and wandered away, sick of my presence.

The waiters, the hired help in the kitchen, they went on hustling, filling orders, scooping melon balls. Whatever. Worse than laughing at me, I wasn't even worth their attention.

I stood around feeling Jules's verbal punches, extra fear now jiggered in with my nervousness. I had no desire to see how unpleasant the man could get should I be anything less than hysterical.

The announcer started in. I heard my name. I went out onstage. The applause I got greeted with was good. Good until the audience of suited, evening-dressed, jewelried, and beehived people got a look at my blackness. Then their clapping got dialed down to polite before it just went away.

I found myself standing at the edge of that gulf again—that quiet spot separating the applause, what applause there'd been, and the laughs from my first joke told. That night the spot wasn't just quiet, it was graveyard silent.

Between the audience's lukewarm welcome and Jules's sendoff, I was good and dazed. Couldn't help but be. My usual opening bit was swimming somewhere in my head, but I couldn't reel it in. Instead, winging things, I stepped into the gulf with: "Well, dig this crowd. Never seen so many dressed-up people in my life. Guess this is where Tiffany's goes when they want to buy jewelry."

There was the sound of silverware on china. A call to a waiter about a steak that wasn't done right. And there were laughs. A few. Most weak. Not that the line wasn't funny, but all those people didn't much know how to respond to me. Except for catching Nat King Cole on television, and maybe Sammy in the flesh right there at the Copa, they weren't hardly acclimated to watching a black on-stage. On *their* stage at *their* club. What was the world coming to? And trying to figure the answer to that question kept them from getting much cackling in.

Kept most of them.

From a booth stage left came the noise of an asthmatic bear hacking up a Virginia ham. Took me a second before I figured out it was a guy laughing. And that laugh was followed up by a bunch more little ones—other people in the booth jumping in.

Just as those laughs were dying down, I tossed out: "Classy joint, the Copa. I don't want to say it's pricey, but you know they've got three waiters at every table. One gives you the bill, the other two revive you."

Like before: The cat with the choker's laugh started up, followed by other laughs at the booth.

People looked, tried to ID the fellow who was having the good time. A little murmur worked its way across the room the way fire works dry brush.

I went into my next bit, tried to circle my way back into my act. "I'm not used to this kind of class. Didn't have much money growing up. We were so poor, when I was a kid I couldn't afford a second thought, only changed my mind once a year, and never had a new idea."

Now the laughs were strung together, the cat in the booth, the people with him, the whole rest of the crowd. They were easing up, relaxing. The fact that the fellow in the booth dug me made it okay for everyone else to dig me, too.

And that right there was all the more handicapping I needed. I got my stage legs back, my timing and my rhythm. Same as a fighter catching an opening, I knew I could take this bunch, and for the next twenty minutes I hit them with bits just as hard and as fast as I could throw 'em.

That show, that first one at the Copa, was a long way from being the smash I'd spent nights and waking hours dreaming of, but it wasn't close to the disaster it could've been. By the time I'd wrapped things, the audience was good and warm and ready for Tony, and that was all the more I needed to do. I got off to stronger claps than I'd gone on with, and as I went, the fellow in the booth yelled a few things at me. I was too jazzed to make out exactly what he was saying, but it wasn't "lousy nigger," so I figured it was a step up from where the night had started.

Sid was waiting for me backstage. "It was a good one, Jackie. You pulled it out. Almost lost it, but you pulled it out."

That's what I liked—that's one of the hundred things I liked about Sid: He didn't sugar-coat or soft-pedal. From him you didn't get underplay or oversell, you didn't get told half-truths just because he thought it was what you wanted to hear. Everything was straight from the shoulder. My set had been solid but nothing better, and that's all the more praise Sid laid on me.

Jules was another story. When he got backstage he was strictly smiles and warm hands. "Great set, Jackie. Really terrific stuff. That bit about your uncle, I just about bust a gut. You want somethin' to eat? After a set like that you gotta have an appetite. Hey, Nick, what are you doin'? Get Jackie a menu."

Was this the same Jules who just prior to my set had stopped yelling at me only because he'd run out of slurs? And the rest of the staff, the same people who had greeted me with nothing kinder than a cold stare, now jumped around like if I went unattended for more than a second, heads were going to roll fast and hard. I wish I could've believed all this goodwill getting tossed my way was on account of my performance, but my ego wasn't so swelled I didn't know the workmanlike job I'd done onstage didn't rate me the attention I was getting. Something else had thrown everyone's switch from nasty to nice.

Tony finished his set. The houselights went up along with a rowdydow from a well-pleased crowd.

Jules came back to the kitchen, where I was putting down the last of my New York cut. "Jackie, somebody wants to have a meet with you."

A fan wants to talk to me? Who doesn't have a minute for that?

Jules guided me from the kitchen into the show room. Along the way I caught an earful of congratulations tossed out from the tables we passed: "Great show, kid." "Dynamite stuff, Jackie." "Sensational. You were killing me." It was like the whole joint was infected with some kind of Dig Jackie virus. As I walked the room, I wondered if I could pay the Russians to release it into the water supply.

From Jules's trajectory I knew right off where we were heading: the booth. The booth stage left where the hard-laughing cat had been sitting.

Six people at the booth—it was the largest in the house—three guys and their dates, bottle blondes who most probably handed out affection on an hourly basis, and when you said good-bye to them it was with cash on the nightstand and a pat on the cheek as you slinked off into the morning.

Jules did a quick introduction. "Frank, Jackie Mann."

The fellow smack in the center of the booth nodded at me. He was a weighty guy, but not fat. Kind of pudgy. Kind of jowly. Other than he was a slick dresser—silk suit, silk shirt, silk tie—he was average-looking. Except for his nose. His nose was some whole other thing. There was a lot to it, and it took up most of his face. Not pointed or hooked, it arched from between his eyes, way out, then back in to land just above his lip. An arch: That was the best way, the only way to describe what was going on there. An arch.

The man, Frank, said: "Good meetin' ya, Jackie." His voice was slightly high-pitched and partly choked off like he was talking at me through a vacuum cleaner hose. It came off as a wheeze more than anything else and sounded especially funny slipping out of such a beefy guy. "Tell you this, you're a funny boy."

Boy. I didn't care for that. Didn't say anything about it, either.

Jules had plenty to say. "You bet he's funny. Wouldn't've hired him otherwise. Just about bust a gut listening to this kid, and I've heard 'em all. All of 'em, Frank. You remember that one time we had Martin and Lewis here and Lewis went off an—"

"Hey, why don't you go make sure the drinks've got enough water in 'em?" Frank rasped.

Jules left without a word more.

Whatever this cat's voice lacked in bass it made up for in authority. He talked, people listened. I made a note regarding that kind of respect: Get some.

All around, couples and parties at their tables sat, not paying any attention to each other, not saying a word, not wanting to miss a second of me having a talk with this Frank fellow. Forget about what I, or even what Tony had done up onstage. What was going on now, this was the show.

Frank wanted to know: "That bit about your old man not being a drunk . . ." He tried to recall the wording.

One of the other guys at the table jumped in and jumped in fast the way a lapdog jumps to its master with the morning paper. "He said his father's not a drunk, 'cause he can lay on the floor without holding on."

Frank gave a burst of that hearty-stifling laugh of his as if he were hearing the bit for the first time.

The other guys laughed.

The girls just smiled.

202 ~ JOHN RIDLEY

"Where'd you learn a rib like that?" Frank asked.

"It's not a rib, sir. It's the truth. My father's got passing out down to a science," I said very seriously.

Frank and his table did more laughing.

"If drinking were an Olympic sport, my pop would be the gold medal record breaker. The Jesse Owens of boozers . . . as long as he didn't have to run in a straight line."

Frank—face going from red to blue—waved a hand in the air, signaling me to stop before he choked himself out.

The other guys did the same. Threw in some foot stomps and table smacks just so Frank would know for sure how excruciatingly funny they found me.

The girls just smiled.

I stood thinking of my pop, the lush, who'd started this laugh fest. At least he was good for something.

Frank: "Have a siddown, Jackie."

There wasn't any room for me at the booth. It took about half a second to notice that, but it was apparently half a second too long with someone not making a move to accommodate me.

"Paulie, what the fuck ya doin'? Get the fuck up and let Jackie have a seat."

Paulie, whoever Paulie was, got from where he sat and did it like he was trying to earn a stay of execution.

I took the open space next to Paulie's lady friend.

A murmur flared its way across the room. I couldn't tell if the buzz was about me sitting with Frank or me sitting next to a white broad.

Frank. I hadn't caught a last name, and I couldn't figure who he was. The face was familiar. Vaguely. He kind of resembled George Raft but wasn't an actor. A movie mogul? My heart upshifted. Was I getting tight with a movie mogul? He was jeweled up like he had that kind of juice. The whole of the booth was pinky-ringed and gold-watched and diamond-stickpinned and pearl-strung.

While I was thinking, Frank said, said again: "You're a funny boy. How come I haven't never seen you here before?"

"Never worked here before, sir. Mostly done Village clubs, coffeehouses."

"Workin' with those long-haired freaks." Frank made it plain he didn't care for the Village crowd. "You don't do drugs, do you?"

"No. No, sir."

"Nothing but poison. You stay the hell away from poison." Frank killed the liquor in his glass.

"Yes, sir. I've spent a lot of time on the road recently. Just now breaking into the class joints."

Frank nodded to that, said: "I like how you don't have a foul mouth. Lot of these acts, specially the ones who work with them long-haireds, everything is fuck this, fuck that. Not you. I could bring my wife to see you."

"You could, Frank," Paulie chorused from his penalty box beside us in the booth. "She'd enjoy the show."

A red jacket appeared, replaced Frank's drink, was gone without a word.

I felt something brush along my thigh. I looked over at the woman I was sitting next to. Paulie's girl. She was staring at Paulie and sporting a dull smile.

Frank: "You ever worked Tahoe?"

"Lake Tahoe? No, sir."

"Got to get you up to Tahoe." To Paulie: "Remember me to talk to Momo about getting this kid into the club."

Paulie took out a pen and paper, wrote things down rather than chance them to memory.

I asked: "Who's Momo?"

Frank did a quick jump from sincere to sharp. "Somebody we know, that's who the fuck he is. Don't fuckin' worry about it."

I didn't worry about it. I was more worried about what else I was going to get besides a good talking-to for asking the wrong questions.

"Jules takin' good care of you and everything, getting you something to eat?" Frank, sincere again. I was getting hip to the fact that he was the variety of cat who would just as soon slap you as stroke you, and neither really meant a thing to him.

"Yes, sir. Had a nice New York steak."

Nodding a couple of times, then: "Well, I know you've got to get ready for the next show . . ."

I'd been in entertainment long enough to catch a cue when I heard it.

Getting up: "Thank you for your hospitality and kind words, sir."

That hacking laugh started up again. "Hospitality and kind . . ." Frank turned to the others in the booth. "You hear this fuckin' kid? Sounds like fuckin' Shakespeare." He laughed some more.

As always, I didn't care to be laughed at.

As usual, when the person doing the laughing had juice, especially when they had enough juice to get me into Tahoe, I didn't say or do a thing about it.

Frank put out his hand and I shook it, and shook the hand of the girl next to him and the other guy at the table and his girl and Paulie's girl next to me . . .

I felt paper crumple between our palms. I looked at the woman and she looked back with a blank meaninglessness that advertised to all who watched that the only thing going on between us was a hand-shake.

I did a quick hand-to-pocket magician-style before shaking with Paulie.

I crossed back to the kitchen. Along the way, from a table: "You believe that? The kid knows Frank Costello."

Costello?

I stopped. My hands went slick with sweaty jitters, slipped over the back of a chair I used as a crutch.

Costello.

Frank Costello was a name everyone in the city knew. Most times, in the papers, it was tagged with the words alleged and reputed. Frank Costello. Why Jules was extra eager to make sure I was taken care of, why the room laughed when he laughed; the reason for all that was I was having a sit-down with the Prime Minister, one of the biggest Mafia bosses in New York.

I made it back up to my dressing room, fell onto the bed. Exhausted. The scene was turning into one long crazy carnival ride, and there was still the second show.

Sid caught up with me. I gave him the short version of me and Mr. Costello, his offer to help me out with Tahoe.

"Jesus," Sid said to that.

Yeah. I knew. Frank Costello was *the* Mafia fixer. It was widely, quietly believed he'd bought and paid for New York City starting at the beat cops and ending with the mayor. Even FBI hotshot Hoover—public gambler, private degenerate—was in Costello's hip pocket, carried around same as a good-luck charm. If the mob wanted to do business in the city, if the mob wanted protection from the law, the mob went through Costello. He did things the clean way: spread money around to avoid trouble. Still, if it came his way, he had no problem giving trouble a couple of bullets to the head to keep it down for good.

Sid gave a smile, weary and wary. "You've got a friend," he said, saying it all.

Sid headed down, got a table for the late show. In the few minutes I had before I went on, I unpocketed the piece of paper Paulie's lady friend had slipped me: Gina and a phone number.

I recollected on the girl. Not bad-looking. Very not bad-looking.

I projected a short bit into the future, thought about how I would feel after the second show—how I felt after a lot of the shows I'd done: worn out and hungry with an appetite food and drink did nothing for.

Lonely.

Lonely is how I would feel.

Gina and a phone number.

I thought about it. I thought about how good it would be to get sweaty with the woman. I thought about how good it would be, in an exotic way, to get sweaty with a white woman. With a white woman who was also making time with some guy who was the pal of some other guy who oozed respect. There was that; there was all that on one side of the scale.

On the other side was Tommy. Nothing more than the thought of Tommy, out there somewhere, thinking of me while I was thinking of her. Nothing more was needed.

I tossed out the paper.

I went down for the second show.

Even without Frank Costello leading the yucks, I killed.

MY NEW HOBBY was trying to get together with Tommy. You'd think in the age of air travel two young people making decent cash would have no trouble maintaining a fairly regular schedule of physical acquaintanceship.

You'd think.

In some five months time, Tommy made one trip back to N.Y.C. It was while I was doing two weeks in Cleveland. I made a swing through Chicago, talked about going up to see her in Detroit, but she was leaving on what Lamont had tagged the Motown Review, a traveling road show of fresh and as of yet unknown acts doing warm-up for Smokey Robinson and the Miracles, the newborn record company's first bona fide stars. The review was a solid idea as far as getting people familiar with new artists and make some cash at the same time. I may not have liked the guy, I may still have figured him for having eyes for my girl, but I had to admit Lamont knew his business.

The review was playing mostly down through the South and the Delta, bringing entertainment to blacks who otherwise didn't have much access to it. After my adventures in Bigotville I was nothing but worried for Tommy. But unlike my road dates, the revue played the chitlin circuit—black-owned clubs and venues—where performers got treated better than as if they were just field labor.

Tommy suggested to me I should try getting on the circuit. There was plenty of stage time to be had, the pay was good and the people appreciative.

Sure.

But black comics on the chitlin circuit didn't make it to the Sullivan show.

I told Tommy I was fine with my clubs.

The revue would be a month solid on the road, and by the time Tommy was done and free I'd be back out doing dates.

I missed Tommy. More than that, us being apart was a kind of torture. At first. But gradually over the months, on the occasions I talked to her, she sounded more and more content as the pain of separation was dulled. She was getting used to Detroit and being on the road. My fear was she was getting used to life without me.

I distracted my worries with constant work.

I needed the work.

Not so much for the money, although the money was sweet. Most times now more than four hundred dollars a week. What I needed the work for was the work itself. I was getting to be a solid performer, and every time I went up I was honing a style and presence, putting together an act that couldn't help but get laughs. And when I was really on, when I was clicking, I could barely do much less than kill.

But there was still something missing from my sets. I knew it. Sid knew it and would tell me so. What I didn't have was a distinctiveness that separated me from every other Charlie cracking wise. Jack Carter, Shelley Berman, Norm Crosby; except for my skin, I was no different. No better, no worse. No different. You could be as good as you wanted, you could kill as often as you wanted, you could get paid as much as the law would allow, but until you were selling something others weren't, you were just another guy trying to make funny. What I didn't have was a voice. The nutty part was: The one time in my life I needed to be different, and I was painfully the same.

I WAS MAKING A STAND at a club in St. Louis. I got a call from Sid, who'd gotten a call from the Cal-Neva in Tahoe. They were offering me a week starting in a month's time.

I asked who I'd be opening for.

"No one."

"No one? What do you me—"

"You're headlining, that's what I mean. They want to put you in the Cabaret Lounge. Not as big as the Celebrity Room, seats less than a hundred, but the—"

Hearing, but not believing: "Headlining? You sure it's me they want?"

"By name they asked for you, and on top they're bumping you up to five-fifty a week."

Small room or not, five hundred fifty cash-dollars a week to headline a show?

Frank Costello. It must have been Frank Costello coming through for me.

"Only . . ." Sid cut in with the spoiler. "The week they're offering is same as Frannie's debut on Sullivan. So I asked the booker to move you to—"

"No."

"Jackie, they said it was no problem to mo—"

"I don't want to chance it."

"Chance it?" Sid couldn't even begin to dig my lingo. "Chance what? You know same as me why they're making the offer. With a guy the size of Frank Costello in your pocket, you never had a better bet. Look, I'll get a message to him personally that—"

"My first gig headlining, a favor from some cat I barely know; I'm not going to let that pass. Not for nothing."

"Not for Frannie? Frances isn't nothing, Jackie. She's your friend."

Static. Between me and Sid, across a transcontinental landline, there was nothing but static that filled a pause that was less than a quarter of one minute but felt much longer.

Sid cut through it with "I'll book the date" and hung up.

Later, I would call, tell Frances that I couldn't make the Sullivan show. She did her "don't worry about it" bits, but the whole scene was a definite letdown for her. I told Fran how sorry I was I wouldn't be there. I told her I'd be watching and how happy I'd be for her, how proud I was of her.

What I didn't tell Fran: I didn't mention how that little piece of me that was jealous when she first landed her record deal, her CBS deal, in the dark and cold inside me, had grown like a fungus into something larger.

⁓

TAHOE WAS THAT OTHER SPOT in Nevada. Different from Reno, Las Vegas, it was more a place for the outdoorsy crowd—people who dug shushing the High Sierra slopes in winter, camping and boating in the warm months. Tahoe had few crowds, was light on traffic. It was the summer stock version of Vegas. There was gaming, sure, but it was gaming as an afterthought: Okay, we climbed, we skied, we did the water jazz. Guess we might as well drop five hundred at the tables. There was high living to be done, but it was high living done on the low profile.

The Cal-Neva sat on the north shore of the lake. Smallish,

ringed with bungalows, the joint itself was more lodge than hotel, parlor room than casino. Its novelty was—like the claim of its name—the border ran right down the middle of the swimming pool. You could sip highballs in California, then stroll on over to the Silver State to get a little roulette in.

I made the trip alone. Sid'd stayed in New York with Fran, had made a point of staying in New York with Fran. He was signifying to me.

I flew into Reno where I would get picked up and driven the rest of the way to Lake Tahoe and the Cal-Neva. When I got off the plane I didn't know what to expect, so I expected what I'd gotten from most of the hotels I'd played across the country: cold stares and reluctant handshakes from the very same people who'd hired me. A room somewhere off the property. A "thanks for coming, here's your money, now beat it, boy" attitude all around.

What I got was none of that.

What I got was picked up from my flight by some fellow driving a just-about-right-off-the-lot Cadillac Series 62, sporting a uniform and the works.

He was strictly: "How was your flight, Mr. Mann? Is this your bag, sir? Let me get it for you. Right this way, if you please." He opened the back door for me, stood holding it. Stunned, I fell into the car.

The driver drove. I rode. Anxious for a while. Expecting at any moment to get hit with the punch line to the joke.

None came.

Two hours to Tahoe. The smoothness of the Caddy, the rhythm of the ride; I couldn't help but ease up, settle back. I gave the inside of my eyelids a full examination.

When I came awake, we were cruising up the Cal-Neva's drive. Waiting for me was a clinging vine of uniformed laborers—luggage marines—to heft my bags, check me in, show me this or that. Make sure I was taken care of. Endless in number, hot to please, they reproduced faster than I could dole out tips.

One of the bellboys lackeyed me to my room. Nothing somewhere on the "dark" side of town. My digs were right there at the lodge. King bed. View of the lake. Same as any other patron. Better than most. The kicker: Unlike any other patron, the house was paying me to be there. The whole of it left me head-shaking stupefied.

But why? When I gave it thought, why should any of it—the car from the airport, the "yes, sir" service, the room—why should it rattle me? I was star quality. I was headline status. I was breaking through. I was seeing light at the end of the long tunnel I'd crawled from Harlem to stardom. I was right where I deserved to be.

I wished Tommy were there to share it with me. I wished Sid were there to enjoy it with me. I wished my pop were there so I could take it all and rub it in his face.

He wouldn't've cared. He would've just wanted to know where the bar was and if the juice was gratis.

And then, almost as an "oh, yeah" afterthought to everything else, there were the shows, my reason for being in Tahoe in the first place. The cabaret was small—if you did some pushing and shoving, you could get maybe fifty people in there, so by default there wasn't a night during the week the room wasn't packed. And there wasn't a night during the week I didn't kill. The management helped by building me up with some fresh-smelling propaganda: the new sensation straight from the Copacabana in New York. A favorite opener for Buddy Greco and Tony Bennett. But more than the hype, I was just having good shows. My timing was on, my presence was a definite. My self-confidence was treetop high. Maybe I hadn't found my voice yet, but from the way the crowd howled things up, the voice I owned spoke just fine.

Thursday night. After the show. I was on my way back to my room, when this fellow stops me with: "Jackie."

"Yes?"

He was a short guy. Plump. Round. He looked as if, under his clothes, he were trying to smuggle gelatin across the border. "Jilly

Rizzo." He said his name like saying it should mean something to me.

It didn't.

I tried to put a little "yeah, and . . . ?" on my face. He didn't catch it.

Jilly said: "He wants to talk to you."

"Who?"

I got tossed a look that was good and queer: How the hell could I not know who the hell he was talking about?

"Frank," he said.

"Mr. Costello's here?"

He was trying to be patient, that was plain. But it was also plain this Jilly was a cat who didn't have much patience for the uninitiated.

"Sinatra wants to talk to you."

FRANK SINATRA FILLED THE ROOM.

Not physically. Not hardly. Sporting an orange sweater over a white turtleneck with brown slacks, he was just a guy, somebody's fashion-senseless uncle. About as imposing as a plate of sauceless spaghetti. He was rounding into middle age, heavier than he'd been as the crooner from Hoboken. Balder. A combover took care of that. He was getting with lines on his face, the middle of his forehead resembling a tilled field. But all those defects were shingled around eyes that were sky blue. Blue and sprouting crow's-feet.

What could barely fit into the room wasn't the man himself but a combo of legend, myth, and good PR. There was the story of a man going from Swoonatra to Charlie Has-been to Chairman of the Board—star of movies AND records AND television AND any other form of entertainment shy of writing haikus. Pal, drinking buddy, and messiah to some of the biggest stars and hardest livers that Hollywood ever turned out. Not so secretly the same with a slew of Mafiosos. There were the bobby-soxers paid to take a dive, the "wrong door" raid he pulled with the Yankee Clipper, trying to dig a little girl/girl dirt on M.M. that nearly landed them both in jail. There was the Oscar, the brawls, the face-punched reporters . . . And there were the love affairs.

There was *the* love affair. The off-as-many-times-as-on-again one he had with Ava Gardner—hot, hard, and violent, trips to the hospital as often as trips to the flower shop. Made my beefs with Tommy look like a Mormon holding hands with a Quaker. Word on the street: After Ava kicked him to the curb for good, Frank tried to off himself.

More than once.

That a star his size should want to check out over a chick, over any one chick . . . that's love.

The other thing filling the room was Frank's voice. His legendary voice. Still rich. Still as deep and as expressive as the day he first cut a side.

At the moment it was expressing some of the foulest language I'd ever heard at some poor Harvey, withering, drenched with his own perspiration. A sweat balloon that'd sprung a leak. The guy was too scared to move, to blink, to look at Frank, or to look away from him. All he could do was stand there and take it. Lots and lots of *it*. From what I could pick out between variations on a theme of "fuck," apparently someone had won and won good at the blackjack tables. Probably counting cards. Frank the casino owner didn't much care for the fact that none of his employees saw fit to cut the guy off before he walked out with a bundle.

"What the fuck do I pay you for, to hand some other fuckin' crumb money—my money—you stupid fuckin' guinea!"

The cat on the receiving end sputtered. I couldn't tell if he was trying to talk or starting to cry.

"I ought to give you one." Frank curled a fist to end any confusion as to what the one was he was thinking of giving away was. "I ought to just haul off and . . . Go on, you lousy fink. Get the fuck out of here!"

The cat wasted no time in obeying.

"And I don't mean out of my lodge, I mean out of this fuckin' state! Don't stop. You hit fuckin' Canada, you don't fuckin' stop!"

I doubted if he'd stop before he hit Iceland.

Done with the man, Frank crossed to a bar and did some mixing—went straight to it as though me and Jilly were vapor.

Jilly said: "Frankie . . ."

"What!"

"You wanted to see Jackie."

He looked up, looked at me.

Let me tell you: I picked up sweating right where that other guy had left off.

"Howzit, Charlie?" Frank's smile couldn't have been brighter, his voice any more even. It was as if what had just happened—the yelling and the screaming—had happened a couple of years prior if at all. Moving toward me, hand out: "How's your bird?"

"My . . ."

His handshake was firm but friendly. "Want some gas, Charlie?"

I didn't know what I was agreeing to, but, ". . . Sure."

As he headed back for the bar: "What are ya drinkin'?"

"A Coca-Cola will be fine, Mr. Sinatra."

Frank laughed.

Jilly laughed.

But different from most times when people busted up over me—at least when I wasn't onstage—they weren't laughing at me. They were just two guys having a good chuckle.

"It's all right, Charlie," Frank assured. "We're all eighteen. Have yourself a little of Mr. Daniel's."

"Thank you, Mr. Sinatra."

"And what's with this Mr. Sinatra jazz? I'm strictly Charlie, same as you."

He was so relaxed, unassuming. Talking with him, talking with Frank, was the same as talking with any other non-superstar guy. Just another Charlie in a sweater, a fellow who could've been getting ready to watch a ball game or rake leaves. The normalcy of the moment made it seem all the more unreal. Not that his being around should have been completely unexpected. That Frank owned the Cal-Neva was common knowledge. You got that plain enough from the sign on the road leading to the joint: WELCOME TO FRANK SINATRA'S CAL-NEVA LODGE. But who figured he would frequent a Tahoe lodge whether he owned the place or not? And who in the hell would ever have figured he would want to have a sit-down with me?

As he handed me my drink: "Haven't had a chance to catch the act yet, but I hear you're puttin' on a real swinger of a show."

"Yes, sir. They've been real good."

"Yeah. Momo said Frankie C was ravin' about you, didn't he, Jilly?"

"Said you was a hoot."

"So I told him let's get this kid in here. You ever meet Momo?"

Meet him? Last time I even asked about this Momo guy, all I got for my trouble was a verbal smacking. "No, sir."

"You've got to meet him sometime. Sammy's a real good guy."

"Sammy?"

"Sammy. Sam Flood."

"Momo," Jilly said, once again growing impatient with my rubeness.

"Sure. I'd love to meet him someti—"

"So how's everything? Everybody treating you decent?"

"They're treating me decent. I don't think I've ever—"

"Nobody's giving you any trouble, are they?" The way he kept cutting me off, I got the feeling Frank could carry on a dialogue just fine by himself. "'Cause you've got the run of the joint, Charlie. Anybody says different, you tell me." A cloud fell over Frank. He became a very dark man. "You tell me, and I'll tell them and tell them so they don't forget."

"Yes, sir, but I haven't had any problems. None at all. Everybody's been real fine. Like I said, real fine."

"Swell." And quick as it'd come the cloud sailed on. Frank was all sunshine again. "Listen, you know I've got a piece of the Sands in Vegas. I'm gonna talk to Jack about gettin' you in there."

Just like that. With a word, with a mere wave of his hand, he was offering me a slice of my dreams with the same non-effort that anyone else would offer a glass of water.

"The Sands in Vegas? You're . . . you're giving me the Sands?" The plane had crashed. I was thinking: My plane had crashed before I'd even gotten to Tahoe. My plane had crashed, I'd been shredded and burned and killed, and I ended up here. I'd been a good little boy, and I'd gone to heaven.

"I'm not givin' you anything you didn't earn by knockin' 'em dead from my stage, Charlie. How do you think it's done anyway? Connections. Who you know. Now you know me." Frank got with a smile, big and toothy. He liked being benevolent. He dug being the king. "Have to slot you as an opener, but we'll make it worth your while. Jilly, how much we payin' Charlie?"

"Five-fifty."

"Five-fifty? Why you lettin' me be so tight with the kid? How's he supposed to pitch dames livin' on the cheap?" To me: "How's seven-fifty sound, Charlie?"

"That's just . . . I'd do it for free."

"Let me tell you somethin': You're only worth what you say yes to. You say yes to nothin', you're worth nothin'. Vegas or not, you do it for real money, you do it for keeps, or you don't do it at all."

Some swinging lingo. But you don't rise and fall and rise again without learning a few things.

Frank said: "Glad we had a chance to talk, Charlie. I'm expectin' big things out of you."

I thanked him for his time, trying to be cool, trying to sound one-star-to-another.

I followed Jilly for the door.

"Pallie."

I turned back.

Again Frank insisted to me: "I'm expectin' real big things from you."

Then the king gave me his blessing: a salute with his highball glass.

⸻

Sunday night. On the West Coast rebroadcast of the Sullivan show, I watched Shelley Winters get an intro from the audience, Peg Leg Bates do a tap number, and sandwiched between shtick from Reiner and Brooks and Japan's Fujiwara Opera Company was Frances Kligman as Fran Clark doing a swinging version of "In Other Words." She gave the tune all it was worth, brash and brassy but never overbearing. If she was nervous, I couldn't tell. If she carried any stage fright, it didn't show. She wasn't some little girl doing late-night spots on Fourteenth Street anymore. She was a star in the happening, crossing the sky and heading straight for Fameville.

Monday morning. The trade papers had nothing but orchids for Fran. She was a definite sensation.

Sunday night and Monday I tried to call Fran, congratulate her. I couldn't get through for all the busy signals.

⸻

Back in New York. Back in the city. The city more hub than home, a base of operations. It was where I went when I wasn't working the road. It was where I went to wash my clothes and read mail and take care of Pop and maybe see Tommy.

Maybe, but not likely.

New York had become her hub as well. Detroit was her home. Especially once she started working on her first record.

So we'd call, usually missing each other. We were missing each other a lot. We were not speaking to each other with greater regularity. I would leave messages for Tommy at Motown. Pop, when he was sober enough, would remember to tell me when Tommy called. When he was sober enough.

He was hardly ever sober.

I often missed messages from Tommy.

I did my laundry, read my mail. Got ready to head back out onto road America, worked on some new bits.

As I wrote, Pop came 'round. Didn't say anything, just shadowed the door to my room. I let him stand there. Didn't talk to him much anymore. Didn't talk to him at all anymore. Not if I could avoid it. But after a while of him staring at me, grating on me: "You want something?" I said it neutral, not knowing which version of my pop I was talking to. High Pop. Jagged Pop. Strung-out Pop. Crashing Pop.

He said: "Goin' again soon?"

"Yep."

"Seem like you always goin' off somewheres."

"Seems that way."

"Doin' it a lot. Goin' off a lot. Guess things is workin' out for you."

"I guess." The Dodgers had just moved from N.Y. to L.A. I wondered if I should do a bit on that.

"You always goin' off and . . . and . . . always goin' off . . . Workin' a lot . . . Wha's that like, bein' up in front of all them people? Wha's that like?"

"Nothing. It's nothing at all."

"I figured it must be . . . all them people . . ."

I turned, looked.

Sweaty. Bleary-teary eyed. Little tremors snapping and popping all over his body. It was crashing Pop. Dried-out-and-in-need-of-a-hit Pop. Harmless Pop.

Blubbering his way back around to: "You goin', and I get to feelin' alone . . ."

"City full of people out there. Clean up. Go meet some of 'em."

"Yeah. I'm thinkin' . . . I'm thinkin' I'm gonnahhhhhmabbaaa . . ." He mumbled off into something, then mumbled up into: ". . . to tell you that . . . you workin' so much now, goin' to all them cities and doin' good for yourself . . . just wanted to tell you—"

"Tell me what? What are you going to tell me that you're only telling me 'cause you're dry and talking crazy? What do you want to tell me that you won't even remember you told me tomorrow, when you're lit up? What do you want to tell me that doesn't matter, doesn't mean anything 'cause it's only the drugs, or lack of drugs, or the need of drugs that's keeping you talking in the first place? So what, what are you going to tell me?"

My father didn't say anything to that. He just looked like I looked on the any number of times he stretched out and smacked me for no good reason: hurt.

Eventually he faded from the room. I heard him rummaging around the apartment. I heard a beer get popped open. A snack to him. To him it was just an appetizer.

I kept writing.

———

I HAD EXPECTED to see her. Not that day. Not that morning. After-noon, really, for the rest of the city. But following a night of working the clubs, post-noon was still morning for me.

Anyway.

I hadn't expected to see her that day, sitting alone, looking tired, thumbing a copy of *Look* magazine, as I got breakfast—lunch—at a diner on B'way. But I always figured sooner or later I'd cross with

Nadine Russell again. I'd lost track of her, or she let me lose track of her after I'd returned from that logging camp years back. She'd made it plain her affections stretched only to the end of a dollar bill, of which I had, apparently, not enough.

In the time when I had gone on to do piece work, she'd gone to trade school to learn typing or steno or shorthand, to become a career girl at either of the two companies in all of New York where a black woman in those years might actually be able to have a career. Didn't matter, really. A career wasn't truly what Nadine was working toward. What she wanted was a man. A man with good prospects ahead of him and a little cash making noise in his pockets. Name a better place to find one than working in an office tower. Okay. Fine. Except, her man would have to be a black man, and every black woman was looking for such a black man and there weren't hardly enough black men to go around in the first place. Factor in the lack of prospects for men of color . . . Nadine was eating alone for a reason. She was looking tired for a reason. No man meant her temp life as a career girl had turned into an unlimited engagement. No one to take care of her, no one to buy her nice things, take her to dinner and a show. No one to come home to, or to make her feel special for no special reason. Nothing waiting for her but a job of memo typing, taking dictation.

And I was happy for that.

Nadine had seen me as a man without means, and how could such a man fulfill her ambitions? Jackie, the hey-boy. Jackie, the moving-company guy. Only, I'd turned myself into Jackie the rising comic and pal of celebrities. Jackie, the cat who earns a whole lot more than your average black and still had room to grow. No doubt Nadine knew this. No doubt she'd seen me written up somewhere, one of the Negro papers, heard talk about me from whoever she kept in touch with from the old neighborhood. She knew I'd made it, and I knew it must be killing her, and, honest, I couldn't wait to take the cold truth and wash her smug mug with it. Oh, I had the moment well rehearsed. When we met I would feign non-recognition, a quizzical look billboarding my face that reorganized itself into pleasant surprise when Nadine reminded me of her name. Oh, Nadine, how you been? Really? That's just swell. No, I haven't heard of them, but I'm sure they're a nice little company to work for. Yeah, well, you do look a little worn, but I'm sure once you move up some . . . Really? That long, and no promotion? Me? Okay, I guess. Yeah, opening for this star and that star and me, me, me, and yeah I'm earning a lot of money, and I guess I'm making it big, and I guess you should've been better to me. I guess you'll find a black man who's doing as well as I am to call your own.

Someday.

Maybe.

Nice seeing ya, Nadine.

Yes, I had the script written and ready. But hell if I was going to cross the diner and acknowledge Nadine. I waited for her to notice me. Waited through the tail end of my breakfast and another cup of coffee and another couple of eggs, scrambled.

I loved that about New York: You could order any food you wanted any time of the day without the what-the-hell-is-this-boy-doing-eating-breakfast-for-lunch look you'd get tossed anywhere else in America. It was going to be a sweet day all around.

Finally, Nadine finished up, finished with her food, reading her magazine. She stood. She moved through the diner, out the door to Broadway. She fell in with the foot traffic that was heading the direction she needed to go and walked.

She had not even noticed me.

Or . . .

No. She'd spotted me. She'd spotted me, but the embarrassment of having let me go only to watch me explode while she was sweating away workaday-style with so very little to show for herself kept her from so much as glancing in my direction. She was probably out on the street now, crying, cheeks streaked with five-and-dime mascara as she trudged back to all the nothing she had.

Yes. That's how I chose to believe things.

———

THE DREAM I'D BEEN HAVING was a bad one. It was about a black guy who was trying to wander home. That's all he was trying to do: just get home. But on the way home there were nails like claws, and shiny knuckles that wanted to tear him to shreds and beat him down. Pretty much they wanted to end his existence. And the guy kept thinking someone was going to come along the road he walked and save him from taking a thrashing. Save him from getting killed.

No one came. The guy was all alone. The guy was as good as dead.

The thing about the dream: A lot of times I would have it while I was wide awake.

———

I LEFT NEW YORK for five weeks on the road that would culminate with me opening for Eddie Fisher at the Sands in Las Vegas.

———

DEFINITION MADE LAS VEGAS a city. Reality said it was a town. Barely. What it was was a district that had sprung up along a railroad stop and, south a ways in Paradise Township, about half a dozen hotel/casinos along the Los Angeles Highway. Later on they would call it The Strip. The city—the town—being in the desert, was hot in temperature except at night, when it was cold, and during the winter when it was freezing nearly all the time. It was full of sand that was unstoppable from being windblown through every crack and crevice, dusting every object indoors or out. It had no factories, no major industry. It had no reason for being.

Except one.

You could gamble in Las Vegas.

You could gamble in a lot of cities. You could gamble all over the state of Nevada. But Vegas added a couple of wrinkles to the trick: flashy carpet joints with free meals if you lost enough. Big losers got their rooms comped, too. For spice there were showgirls who went topless and free juice handed out by cocktail waitresses wearing barely more than the ladies in the chorus. Las Vegas passed out the drinks with a wink and a neon tease, not to be nice but because it knew the more you drank, the stupider you got. The bigger you bet.

And if somehow all that wasn't enough to get you to get yourself to the high desert, Vegas had one last card up its sleeve: entertainment. It was live entertainment capital of the West. Hollywood might have been where the stars shacked, but Vegas is where they shined. Onstage and in person. And there was nowhere they shined any more hotly than at the Sands. Subtitled "A Place in the Sun," ultramodern by design, the hotel/casino to beat all hotel/casinos made her presence felt in The Meadows from the day its doors swung open: You pulled up a slick circular drive under three narrow beams that shot from the hotel, then ninety-degree-angled straight into the desert floor as if the building itself were staking a claim to the city. Forget the old-fashioned cabin-style wood-and-stone construction, you were welcomed into the joint by chrome and glass and marble letting you know this was the up-to-date way to lose your money. And just in case you still weren't sure about things, there was the sign. Fifty-six feet tall, every inch of it burning with lights that boldly, simply, in scripted letters read: SANDS. No doubt at all. This was *the* place in the sun. It was one big slice of all I ever wanted. All I ever dreamed of.

If nothing else, what made it that way was the Copa Room, sister to the club in New York. And same as the club in New York, the Copa was where anybody who was anybody—Marlene Dietrich to Noël Coward—wanted to be. Working there made playing the empty desert of Vegas better than bearable. It made it an event.

But for all the Hollywood celebs, all the palm trees and neon, Vegas was still strictly Hicksville. Hicksville is where Jim Crow called home.

"Sorry, Jackie."

Jack Entratter was sorry.

Jack Entratter was the entertainment coordinator of the Sands, the fellow who handled the Copa Room for the casino. At six foot three, he was a hulk of a man, weighty, and sporting several chins. He would've come off as a monster except that he was a fairly decent guy. Maybe by nature, maybe because he was humbled by the gimp a childhood illness had left him. Either way, you kinda believed him when he said: "You know, I've got no problem with things, but it's policy. We just don't allow coloreds into the casino. You understand, don't you, Jackie?"

Sure. I understood. It was the same as it was a lot of places. I could entertain. I could make good money. I could stand onstage and take all the applause an audience could dole out, but after that I was expected to be gone, and be quick about it.

"If it was left to me . . ." Jack was getting in all his apology bits. "But we can't make any exceptions." He modified himself. "Except, one exception."

I knew the exception. But then, Mr. Entertainment was an exceptional cat.

Jack looked from me to Sid and back again, helplessness in his face, then held up his hands in a show of things being completely beyond him. In case I couldn't read all that: "There's nothing I can do."

And there wasn't. Didn't matter Jack was taking orders from

Frank Sinatra himself. Sinatra may have been a part owner in the Sands, but that didn't make him boss, just slave to the paying customer. The paying customer didn't want any blacks in the casino, the paying customer didn't get any blacks in the casino.

Sid and I thanked Jack. Sid and I left.

The Sands was good enough to provide us with a car while we were in the city. We'd need it. It was a good trip between the hotel and the part of town known as Westside. The "Negro" side. The side where we would be staying. And the whole of it made the black section of Miami come off like the French Riv. Small, rundown shacks for houses. Beat-up cars that were ten years old the day these people bought them "new." I didn't see any schools, or a hospital. I didn't see anything you could call nice or decent. Westside seemed to lack everything except poverty. Poverty was all over the place and plentiful.

We checked in at Mrs. Shaw's, a boardinghouse where out-of-town blacks stayed, famous and otherwise. Stayed for about twice what it cost to room at one of the hotel/casinos. If we could've roomed at one of the hotel/casinos. We couldn't, so we paid Mrs. Shaw's prices. End of discussion.

Sid got stares—a white fellow staying in a colored rooming house—and I gave the stares right back: The cat's with me, so lay off.

We got our keys and went up to our rooms. They were unattractive.

Same as I did whenever Sid was with me in a city that wasn't progressive, I told him: "I'm a big boy. If you want to head back to The Strip . . ."

Same as he did every other time, Sid waved me off, tossed out a few excuses. "Clip joints with neon trim."

Time to kill, sitting around, we talked some about the upcoming show, did a back-and-forth about which bits I should go with. That got followed up with a little yatter on sports, weather.

Then, Sid, from left field: "I was talking to Frances."

"Yeah," I said.

"Yeah. You know her new record's a smash."

"Hear it all the time."

"Yeah." Sid took a beat, went on with: "CBS is giving her a special."

"That's great. She's a great kid. If anybody deserves—"

"It's a pilot, really. If it does good numbers, they're going to give her her own show, a variety thing. Fatima's all set to sponsor."

I rolled my tongue around in my mouth, wiped away the bad taste that was forming.

One time. One time Frances was on Sullivan—one sensational time—and now she was *this close* to becoming Ed in a dress. My jealousy broke its leash.

Sid told me: "You should call her."

Thinking of me skipping her debut just to play Tahoe: "She's on her way. She doesn't want to hear from me."

"She forgives you."

That hurt some. Hurt a lot, Sid cutting deep to the truth, that I needed to be forgiven. But I did. I knew it, Fran knew it, Sid knew it.

Sid tried to soften the comment. "Frannie knows how much working Tahoe meant to you. It's what got you to Vegas, and you and I both know what a break it is doing shows here. So does Fran." Pause. "She misses you, Jackie. If you would just call . . ."

"I did. You know I did, and I couldn't get through, so don't act like I didn't."

"A couple of times after she did Sullivan, but other than that, how hard did you try?"

The question didn't get answered, but the truth, the truth that Sid and I both knew: not very. It wasn't fear of Fran's reaction that kept me from calling. I knew she'd understand me picking Tahoe over her, or at least, like Sid said, I knew she would forgive me. The thing that wouldn't let me make the call was my own shame.

I said: "Tonight's a big night. I better rehearse the act some."

Sid didn't even bother making an effort to carry on the conversation. He said okay and left.

I didn't go over the act. I was too restless. I lay down and tried to nap. I was just restless in bed.

I went early to the Sands, leaving a message for Sid telling him where I'd run to.

At the Sands they would only let me into the Copa Room, and only through the back. For the moment that was okay. The Copa Room was all the more anywhere I needed to be. I sat in my dressing room staring at my reflection in the makeup mirror. I can't say how I felt inside—not like a man, but I wasn't a boy—but on the outside my face looked years worn. Permanent nicks from my father and his fists and belt and booze bottles and everything else he'd ever hit me with. A tattoo barb-wired into my cheek. Lines around the eyes, notches of worry, carved there night after late night spent in sleepless fret over my life, my career. Tommy. All that, and I wasn't even thirty. The thought of how I'd look in twenty-five more years made me turn away from myself.

A houseboy came 'round, asked if there was anything I needed.

Prime rib. Medium.

He went off to fetch it without a word.

I went out to the stage, looked over the show room—green accented with red—green walls, red chairs, green carpeting. Guys in red jackets setting the tables. I stood looking at the empty space projecting my thoughts a few hours into the future when the room would be packed with people eager to get entertained. Waiting to be entertained by me. Me opening for Eddie Fisher, at least. But even at that, I was far from Harlem, from the Fourteenth Street Theater, and not just in physical distance. I was on the opposite end of a ladder nearly impossible to climb. But I'd made it. Not to the top, but at least to this rung: the Copa Room in the Sands in Las Vegas, Nevada. And in my heart, regardless of whatever big dreams I'd been carrying around in my head, I knew where I was was farther than I ever really thought I could go. But I still wasn't where I wanted to be. I wanted to be able to walk out the doors and into the casino. I wanted to be headlining. I wanted Sullivan. I wanted the pilot Fran had. I wanted a shot at my own show.

I wanted.

I wanted.

With everything I had, I wanted more. That was the thing; for all its shine, success was nothing but a cheap back-alley score. And same as the hot bottle cap habit I'd witnessed my pop fix so many times, the more you got, the more you wanted. The more it *made you* want more. I could feel all my dreams getting twisted up. I could feel my desires becoming diseased: that it should matter so much to me to be fawned on out in a casino whose only affection was for the money you dropped, that I should have envy and jealousy for the best friend I'd ever had . . . I couldn't make sense of how I felt. I couldn't stand how the dope of need made me feel. The other thing I couldn't do was quit that jag if I'd wanted to. And I didn't want to.

I went back to my dressing room. The houseboy brought 'round my rib, wished me a good show. Time was I could never have eaten before I went up. Nerves would have worked on whatever was in my stomach every second I was onstage, made my gut sick.

Not that night.

That night I knew everything was going to be fine. The worst I had to endure in my ascent—from drunk hecklers to rednecks wanting to put a rope around my neck to other points along the way mostly bitter and bad—was behind me. What was going to happen in the Copa Room was the beginning of my true beginning: me hitting the stratosphere star-style.

The prime rib went down easy.

Sid was in the room. So quiet he was, I didn't even hear him enter. I looked up, he was there. I told him what I knew to be fact:

"It's going to be a good one tonight, Sid."

He was slow to respond. When he finally wrenched his mouth open he closed it up again without saying anything.

"What?"

Sid looked away from me.

"What is it? Fran? You hot at me over Fran? Look, I said I would call her."

". . . No."

"I'll call her right now, do all my make-up bits. That make you happy?"

"No, Jackie. It's not . . . You should . . ." He practically turned his back to me. "Just have a good show." Sid was hiding something. Trying to hide something but not doing much of a job of it.

"What's going on?"

"Nothing. Nothing's going on."

"Where'd you learn to lie, in a convent?" My biggest fear: "Did they cancel me?"

"No."

My second biggest fear: "Are you sick? Are you o—"

"Just have a good show. The show's the thing; that's what's important. Anything else . . . it can wait."

Sid had done a lot of hemming and hawing, but he hadn't answered my question about him being ill. I went to him, took him by the shoulders, and spun him around, my compassion and concern coming out rough.

"Tell me! Whatever the hell it is, just tell me!"

For a tick or two, nothing. Sid tried to talk. The effort he put into it no different than lifting boulders. Sheer force of will was the only thing that got words out of his mouth.

He said: "They couldn't find you back at Mrs. Shaw's, so they told me. I wanted to wait until after . . . I know how much tonight means to you, but . . . They called from New York. Your father . . ." Sid trailed off there. That was it. That was all the more he could stand to give me. And truth was, it was all the more I needed to hear.

Dead.

For a while, for lack of knowing what to say, neither of us said anything.

My father was dead.

Then, from Sid: "If you want me to talk to Jack . . ."

"No."

"He'll understand. It's your father."

"Sid, I'm opening tonight. I'm going up. The show must go on, and that jazz. My father's dead, so what?"

Like he'd taken a rock to the head; that's the kind of stunned Sid looked.

"Yeah, so what? You ever see him around? You ever see him come out and support? You ever even seen him, Sid? He died, it's sad, but it's the same kind of sad as if some other Charlie I never knew got hit by a car crossing the street. I can't not do my act every time somebody who doesn't matter dies."

And with that I was convinced: My father didn't matter. I didn't care.

Sid didn't say anything about it. Sid just stared at me . . . stared at me. . . .

Sid left.

Eventually the house filled and it got to be show time and I went on, stepping back into that waiting void.

I had a good set.

I had a good set for the first three minutes of my six and a half. Then I got to the bits on my pop being a drunk. I fell apart. I didn't break down and cry, I didn't go fetal or anything. I just announced onstage that my father had died, which pretty much brought the laughs to a stop. Talking about real-live dead people in a comedy show tends to do that. There were a couple of titters, people who figured I must be doing the setup for one hell of a punch line.

I wasn't. What I was was real suddenly on a guilt binge that wouldn't shake. I went on about how my father was never there for me, how he abused me, how I will always believe he killed my mother. It wasn't like opening night in Vegas I wanted to rap about any of that, but my grief was a groove that I couldn't pull out of. I was nose-diving for the ground kamikaze-style. The whole ugly scene lasted a minute. Less than. But less than a minute of that kind of crazy talk was enough to smack the smiles off any crowd. For the next hundred twenty seconds I worked hard as ever, tried to grab the people back and leave something resembling an audience more than a wake for Eddie to face. I did it. Barely. I got offstage to confused and smattered clapping.

Jack was furious—me not only bombing on my opening night, but turning his joint into a morgue—until Sid pulled him aside, told him the bits I'd done on my father weren't bits. He was dead for real. It didn't take any of the heat out of Jack, but what was he going to do? He knew if Frank found out he was giving me trouble because my pop had passed, he would get what he gave me in spades.

While Sid and Jack made peace, I sat, sick and getting sicker by the second. Feelings I'd been trying to shove aside were hitting me hard. Feelings I wanted nothing to do with. Regret and remorse and sorrow and . . .

And what I wanted, what I needed was to drink or gamble or lose myself in Las Vegas, in the swamp of all the sin it had to offer. But the situation of the day prescribed that I sit backstage in my dressing room far from the lily whites. Sit, or go back to Westside.

I thought about calling Tommy.

She'd been busy. I'd been busy. It'd been a while, not long, but too long, since we'd last talked. I knew just hearing her voice would make things if not all right, at least better.

I wanted to call Tommy.

But Tommy was working on her record. In my frame of mind I was afraid of what kind of crazy emotions might come spilling out of me over the telephone. And after a week, two weeks—more than that—of not speaking with her, then hitting her with the news of my father, breaking down to her the way I'd done onstage—weak and weeping—what would that do to her? What would that do to her when she was trying to put together the biggest break of her career? When I'd done everything I could to get her to Detroit, why should I burden her with my craziness?

"Because she's your girl," Sid told me. "And when people love each other, they share with each other, their pain and their strength."

Sid was going eloquent, the truth he spoke earned at the expense of his own loss.

Backstage, through the walls, I could hear Eddie swell to the end of "Cindy, Oh Cindy." I could hear the audience applaud, whistle. He had gotten them back. He had used whatever magic he owned to make a room full of strangers love him.

Quietly, mostly to myself: "So many times I wanted him dead. I mean it. Not just that I wished some badness on him. I wanted my father to die. But now . . ."

"I know you must feel awful as hell, Jackie, but that'll pass. You've got to know, you've got to believe, wherever your father is now, he knows you love him. He knows, and he forgives you."

My head rose. I looked at Sid, gave a hollow laugh at his mis-understanding. "You're reading me wrong. All those times I wanted him dead, and he's got to wait until opening night in Vegas to finally do it. That son of a bitch. Dead, and he's still messing with me."

⸻

IRONIC. TRITE. Don't know which. Ironic, trite, me thinking Pop had waited until my opening night in Vegas to die. I gave him too much credit. He couldn't've been that slick if Hollywood'd written the script. The way it was: Years of drug abuse had weakened him. He had a . . . a seizure that hit him same as a stroke, left him mute and immobile. It took days—puddled silent, motionless on the floor of the apartment—for Pop to slowly, agonizingly, starve to death. Days more before his body was found. The reek of decay the only thing that made his passing even noticeable. From OD to discovery was over a week's time altogether. Over one week's time. Opening night in Vegas wasn't when he'd died, just when I got the word he was no longer alive.

Between Sid and Jack they were able to come up with an act to cover my remaining days on the bill. There wasn't much hard about finding someone who wanted to work two weeks at the Sands.

Nothing but a sack of mixed-up emotions, Sid got me back to New York. Grandma Mae, as she'd done years earlier with my mother, took care of most of the funeral arrangements, which, different than when I buried my mom, included finding enough mourners to give my father the semblance of having mattered to anyone. Mae put the word out she was cooking up a spread for the after-interment meal. That got bodies into the church.

The casket was closed. I didn't want to see my father. I didn't think anyone else cared to see him. I knew no one wanted to see his hands, fingers scraped raw to the bone from uselessly, feebly clawing at the floorboards for help as, day by day, he died.

Sid brought Fran by the services. The way he told it, she insisted on coming. She gave condolences. Despite knowing what kind of man Pop was, Frances came off as being truly sad, truly sincere.

Taking my hand, squeezing it: "It's all right, Jackie."

I knew she wasn't talking about my father. I knew she was talking about me being absent from her Sullivan shot. And in those few words, "It's all right, Jackie," she told me that no matter what I'd done, no matter what I'd done to her, nothing had changed for us. Just as before, same as always, she was my friend.

THE FRANKS—Sinatra and Costello—had heard about my father passing. After my performance at the Sands, they couldn't help but get the word. Both sent over wreaths to the funeral, some cash to cover any expenses I had.

Frank—Sinatra—phoned up with sympathy and support. We talked some, me hardly believing he would have time to waste on me. But he didn't seem to be rushing me off the phone: How you doing kid great I gotta go. Getting past my father, he talked leisurely, asked me what I had going on. I told him that in a couple of weeks time Sid had me booked into Slapsie Maxie's, my first ever show on the coast, that town west of Vegas where all the idiots lived.

Frank laughed at that. He gave me congrats, told me Maxie's was a hot joint—the audience most times peppered with industry types. A good show there could really break things for me. He added, as I would be in Hollywood anyway, I should run over to Ciro's and check out Smoky.

"Smoky?"

"Sammy. He's headlining with the trio. Kid puts on a swinger of a show."

I told Frank that would be great but had heard when Sammy did shows they were strictly SRO. Getting in was as good as impossible.

"Don't you worry about it, pallie. You just make sure you get yourself over to Ciro's."

Frank had spoken.

CONTRARY TO MOST PEOPLE who'd just buried family, hot on the heels of my father's funeral I turned into Charlie Party. I made the rounds to every club and nightspot, every hole that offered some combo of music or liquor or any other legal distraction. I filled every minute of the day with dance and drink, because when I left a minute open, it was the minute I thought of Pop and the thoughts were lousy.

It wasn't fair.

He hurt me. He degraded me. I didn't care he was dead. I had no reason to care he was dead . . . and I felt wrong for it. Guilt is what they called it. It seeped through me, and bop and booze did nothing to sop it away.

Get out.

I had to get out. Out of the old apartment I'd been in too long, out of Harlem. Out of the life I used to know. I found some new digs, Midtown digs, quick as I could and packed my belongings. My essentials and nothing more. No mementos. No keepsakes. No nothing of my father's. All that got sent to the garbage man. No more baggage slowing me down. I'd buried my father and now I wanted to bury my past in the next hole over.

The day prior to me moving out. Some last-minute boxing-up getting done. Li'l Mo came 'round the apartment. Not having made the funeral, it had been a good few years since I'd seen him, the last time being when I'd quit the moving company and he gave me looks and attitude like I'd been making a play for his sister.

I opened the door and there he was. He looked different. More than just the years. He looked serious. Very serious, but not as if over one thing in particular. He looked as if seriousness were just an emotion he carried 'round with him constantly, same as a watch or a wallet.

I smiled when I saw him, and he sort of did the same. We hugged awkwardly and passed back and forth remarks about how good the other looked.

I invited Li'l Mo in.

He accepted.

Then we kind of stood around for a moment or more. That quick we ran out of things to say to each other.

It was nutty. We were not more than five, six feet apart, but it might as well have been a mile. The two of us were traveling in different directions in life and picking up speed, and all the glad-handing in the world couldn't cover that in a short span of time we'd become not much more than just two guys who used to know each other. Strangers with familiar faces.

I thanked Li'l Mo for the sympathy arrangement he'd sent.

"I was sorry when I heard," he said. "Your old man was a—"

"Bastard?"

He smiled a little, genuine this time. "Still, ain't never nothing easy about losing folk."

I shrugged to that, not wanting to get into my complicated and double-minded feelings concerning my father.

Instead: "So, what's going on with you?"

"Got a job at the *Times*."

"The *Times*? That's terrific." I dialed up my enthusiasm. "That's perfect for you. You've always been a sharp brother, always had a head on you. That's sure to be the kind of gig where you could—"

"I load papers onto the trucks." Li'l Mo was flat and even about it. He didn't say it like what he did was a bad thing. He most certainly didn't say it like the job was any good.

I didn't much know how to respond, if I should modify my compliments or wish him luck getting the hell out of that spot fast as he could.

"But you doing all right, Jackie."

Underplaying: "Guess I am."

"Sure you are. See your name in the paper and whatnot. See you working at this club or that."

"Wish you'd come down sometime," I offered. "Catch a show."

"Yeah. Yeah, I'd like that. 'Cept, I don't suppose they'd let me catch a show at the Copacabana. Guess I could see you at the Apollo. Guess I could. If you ever played the Apollo." He slipped me that no different than if he was slipping me a knife.

I tried to get things going in a different direction with: "Well, I'll tell you, Li'l Mo—"

"Morris. I don't go for Li'l Mo. Not no more."

A half a mile got added to the gap between us.

Morris looked around at my collection of packed boxes. He said as much as asked: "Moving, huh?"

"Just taking it downtown some."

"We'll miss you up here."

"Midtown ain't China. And you know you can—"

"That's not what I'm saying. What I'm saying is we can't afford to be losing good brothers. Doesn't look right."

"What doesn't look right? That Negroes are making it, that they're moving up?"

"Moving up means moving out, leaving the rest of your people behind? It's saying you're not really a successful black until you don't have to live with blacks anymore. So, you—brothers like you leaving—it doesn't look right."

"So I should stay here just 'cause that'll look good to some other Negroes—"

"The word is black."

"And you don't think it looks good to other *Negroes*"—used in spite—"that I've worked hard enough I can live in a good neighborhood."

"Harlem's no good?"

"I didn't say . . ." Just then I realized how hard I was breathing. The effort this conversation took was the same as running uphill with lead in your pockets. "There's nothing here for me anymore."

"And how's there ever going to be anything here for anybody, when soon as they can the blacks who get over get out?"

"Come on with that. I can't help what other people do. I'm talking about me. If I go, if I stay; one person isn't going to matter one way or the other."

Morris nodded like he understood. Nodded, but said: "Not one person. One more person."

After that we were done talking. Done truly talking with each other. We pretended to go on a bit about sports, music. Subjects that were conversable but not combustible. But it was plain we were talk-ing just so neither of us would feel like we didn't do all we could do to keep up our false-front friendship.

With "Guess I need to be getting on my way," Morris indicated the game was over.

"It was real good seeing you Li . . . Morris."

We hugged again, awkwardly again, and Morris left.

I closed the door.

———

"IS THERE SOMETHING WRONG, JACKIE?"

Tommy was on the phone.

"No," I lied. "Everything's . . . everything is—"

"You seem so quiet."

"I'm just . . . you know, just . . ."

"If there's something you want to tell me . . ."

"Just a little tired."

I couldn't say for sure why I was lying. It wasn't as if my father passing was some particularly traumatic event Tommy needed shielding from, that sooner or later she wasn't going to find out he'd died. But my reasons for doing what I was doing were many, just not good. I didn't want to burden Tommy with my grief while she was putting together her record. I didn't want her worrying about me when her career gave her worry enough. The recording was coming slowly but well, she said. The song was sounding good, she said. She said she was thinking of going with a stage name. Tammy felt more girlish, sweeter, than Tommy, she said. So let her concern herself with all that and let me leave my pop out of things.

Truth was, at the minute, I didn't want anybody's worry. I didn't want any more sympathy, or people asking how I was holding up. I didn't want to have to try to explain my jumbled-up feelings over Pop's death. Most of all I didn't want to be reminded of or have to deal with those feelings myself. Denial was better all around. Better, especially, for Tommy. That's what I told myself anyway, told myself that what I was doing—lying—I was doing for her.

Tommy didn't get any of that.

All Tommy got from my quiet voice, from my distant and dodgy nature, was that she was being pushed away when, in reality, I wanted nothing more than to hold her close.

She told me in a week's time she would be playing at the Riv in Atlantic City. She told me how badly she wanted me to come down. Even if she couldn't see me from the stage, just wanted to know that I was in the audience. She told me how much she wanted nothing more than to be with me.

I told her the week she would be in A.C. was the week I would be working Slapsie Maxie's in Los Angeles.

Her opening night I sent Tommy flowers and a "break a leg" card.

part V

*H*ollywood was hurting. Hollywood was getting knocked around. A little wood box with a cathode tube was doing the knocking. Television, still mostly a New York thing, was snapping up Hollywood jobs and snatching away movie audiences. Hollywood hated television. Hollywood couldn't do anything about television.

The studios were having a rough go of things those years of wandering between their golden age and the time when they finally threw up their hands and started supplying the box with programming. So, with nothing else to do, Hollywood went on doing what it did best—putting up a fake front of glamour and significance. It kept sipping cocktails on the deck of a slow-sinking ship.

Hollywood, more an idea than an actual location, was still one big fat Roman orgy of liquor, pills, and passion. Price of admission: starhood. It was still a place where studio fat cats the size of Louis Mayer could keep out of jail and out of the tabloid rags one of his drunk stars who'd hit-and-run some poor Harvey stepping off the wrong curb. It was a place where every day at four o'clock all business at the Fox lot came to a *standstill while Darryl Zanuck was getting serviced down low by wannabe starlet #32. It was a place where Harry Cohn could take a chick like Margarita Cansino, pluck her eyebrows, electrolysis her hairline, give her a dye job, diet her into a sexpot, bury her Latina heritage, and wa-la—Rita Hayworth.*

Hollywood did a lot of that, a lot of wa-la-ing, star manufacturing. Constance Ockleman got wa-la-ed into Veronica Lake. Issur Danielovitch into Kirk Douglas. Betty Joan Perske became Lauren Bacall. Bernard Schwartz? Wa-la. Tony Curtis. Sometimes, because it was Hollywood and Hollywood did what it wanted, it performed its little magic act in reverse. Ava Gardner was born Ava Gardner, but studio PR flaks told the world her real name was Lucy Ann Johnson just so Tinseltown would get the credit for inventing the girl.

And when the dream factory wasn't constructing its own talent, it was overseas Shanghaiing stars and dragging them stateside: Brigitte Bardot. Gina Lollobrigida. Liliah Davi. Sophia Loren.

Hollywood, U.S.A. If they don't have it, they make it. If they can't make it, they steal it. If they can't steal it, they get the press boys to convince you you didn't want it in the first place. Its only true concern was generating fame, money, and power by any and all means.

In the whole of the world, was there any more perfect place?

June of 1959 to January of 1960

The Noon Balloon took me West. I hadn't been in Los Angeles since, years ago, a change of trains on the way to Washington State gave me a couple of minutes to try to spot the Hollywood sign. I couldn't see it.

Now, not too many years later, driving a rental from Union Station to my hotel, the sign—giant white letters that looked to me a mile high each—was plainly visible from where it sat on the hills that separated L.A. from its valley neighborhoods. The city was as I'd left it: sunshine and open spaces. In reality a bunch of suburbs—Boyle Heights and Silver Lake and Echo Park and Los Feliz and Inglewood and Brentwood and Westwood. And Hollywood—pearl-strung together by endless stretches of dirt roads, urban streets, and superhighways that would take you wherever you wanted to go: city or beaches or mountains or rugged countryside. There was all that in one place. There was so much. There was so very, very much. Everything about Los Angeles cried growth and opportunity. It was Outpost America, the far edge of our nation. It resembled the rest of the country but refused to adopt her cultures and customs, opting instead for a carefree existence. Because, maybe, of the heat from the always-present sun, because, maybe, of the weak scattering of trades other than the entertainment business, there was a particular ease and dreamlike manner overlaying the constant hubbub of its one true industry: getting famous and staying famous and grabbing back fame once lost. After the crush and crowds, the cold shoulder, get tough or get lost bump that New York continuously tossed you, the casual flow of life in the pueblo was a warm and friendly embrace that told you to slow down, relax. All things would come to you in their time. In *their* time. But somewhere, in some manner, it was there for me. It—everything Hollywood had to offer—was there, a hidden gift that only had to be found to be enjoyed.

For my two weeks in Los Angeles I made the Sunset Colonial my pad. The hotel was ground zero for a bushel of fresh-off-the-bus actor and actress types. It sloshed beefcake boys and bottle blondes. They'd headed west with a lot of ideas on becoming stars. Ideas, but not a single plan on how to reach their destination. With nothing better to do, they made looking good their business. Poolside became their office. They idled there sunup to sundown, plying their trade, waiting to get over.

Waiting.

They would wait as long as it took, or wait until the waiting broke them and sent them limping back to whatever life they used to live before hitting L.A.

I hit the Colonial. The cat at the desk checked me in in a very businesslike fashion. Businesslike right up until I let it slip accidentally on purpose I was working Maxie's, that I'd worked the Copa and the Sands, that I was a legitimate talent. Then the kid couldn't "Mr. Mann" me enough.

That was the nutty thing about Los Angeles, about Hollywood: different from the rest of America that was caught up in its race problem—either trying to beat people of color down, or lift them up to stroke their liberal guilt—the only color Hollywood cared about was green: You make money for somebody, you turn a profit and return a dividend, there isn't anybody who doesn't love you no matter what you are. The guy behind the counter was obvious in his hoping that I'd introduce him around, get him an "in" someplace where people with real juice congregated, so I got treated decent.

I got the same warm hand from the rest of the staff. Hector the valet; Rick the bell captain; and Doary White, a sweet young black girl, a maid at the hotel with a perpetual smile—similar in fashion to the smiles the starlets-in-training tossed me as they floated around the pool wearing something next to nothing. But their smiles were just show. I was hep enough to know the real goods they saved for the moguls and producers, the big-box-office actors who could traject their careers upward. All a guy my size would ever get was ivory from a distance. I didn't take it personal. In Hollywood, if you had nothing to offer, you were nothing; and people wanting things from people, that was just business. Truth of it was those poolside girls, women who in any other city would be hanging on street corners whistling at the cars that slow-rolled by, made me thank God I had a girl like Tommy.

Unlike the headline clubs I'd been working—me opening for some name talent—Slapsie Maxie's was a showcase room, a bunch of acts who filled a bill that ran on into the night. A good place for scouts, agents, and studio suits to catch a string of performers live. Deals—TV deals, movie deals, record deals—got made over drinks at the bar. Your career, your life; all you needed was one solid set to alter them forever. A truth reflected in the eyes of the acts who x-rayed the mingling suits desperate to find the one who would elevate them to a place just short of immortality.

I had three solid sets. My first three nights at Maxie's were strictly killers. People nearly choked, they were laughing so hard.

No one offered me any deals.

TV, movies—neither was ready for the next black sensation. They barely knew what to do with the colored acts they had. I waited at the bar alone. A fast girl waiting for a trick who never showed. I was just like that. I would have pimped myself easy, said anything, done anything to please any John with juice. There were no takers.

On the fourth night, the fourth night of killing again, the fourth night of again watching lesser acts take sit-downs with suits, I decided I needed to do something with myself. Something besides go back to the Colonial and look at my reflection in a dozen phony smiles.

Outside. I hopped in my rental, drove for the Sunset Strip—a tease of bright-light nightspots for drinking or dancing or just being seen at a scene. I got myself to Ciro's. Besides that it wasn't far from the Colonial, Ciro's was a cinch to find. All you had to do was look for the line of people waiting to get in. There was always a line when the top acts played the top nightclub in the West. That night the line was around the block. They'd come to see Sammy Davis, Jr.

Officially, the sign on the marquee read: THE WILL MASTIN TRIO FEATURING SAMMY DAVIS, JR., the other two of the three being Sammy's father and uncle. But the sign might as well have read: SAMMY DAVIS, JR. AND A COUPLE OF OTHER NEGROES. Sammy was a one-man show. He could sing, he could dance, he could do impressions, tell jokes, play instruments, do gun tricks . . . He could and would do all that. He would do it, and do it, and do it some more, then for an encore give you another hour's worth of dazzle. The show only ended not because Sammy got tired but because you were so worn out from watching, you couldn't take any more entertainment.

Mr. Entertainment, they called him. Like his B'way show, they called him Mr. Wonderful. That was no lie. But he should've been called Mr. You-Can-Line-up-to-See-Him-and-Wait-for-a-Bunch-of-Hours-but-That-Don't-Mean-You're-Going-to-Get-In. He drew a crowd that made even the audience Sinatra pulled look barely big enough to fill a Hoboken whiskey joint. Jesus couldn't sell out his water/wine shtick if Sammy was booked next door. All I could hope for was to maybe, *maybe,* get past the front door. But I felt like sucking up some Hollywood. Felt like trying. There were about two hundred other people cooling their heels outside making the same try. I walked for the club entrance, passing a bunch of recognizable faces. Stars. Mostly TV personalities. No one too big, but they were three times my size at least. If they couldn't get in . . .

At the door was a humorless guy, young, suited, hands folded before him, standing behind a velvet rope. Might as well have been a brick wall.

I said: "I'm Jackie Mann. I'm here to see the show."

"You and everybody else," the fellow said, nodding at everybody else in case I hadn't noticed them.

"I was told a ticket would be left for me."

"Yeah. A ticket. We got lots of tickets sitting around for jokers who show up last minute. You want one, or you want fifty?" The guy was good with sarcasm. He must've worked at it daily.

"Is there any way—"

"The way is for you to stand in line with the rest, and wait for whatever empty seats we've got."

I looked over at "the rest." Ten more people and they could've petitioned to become a state.

I walked away from the guy behind the velvet rope. I was replaced instantly by an older man complemented with a busty red-head who looked like he knew getting any play from her depended critically on getting the girl on the other side of that velvet border.

The good thing at least was Ciro's wasn't too far off from the Sunset Colonial. I could make the short drive back to my room, maybe read. Maybe watch some television. Maybe I could just sit around and watch night become day. Time was cheap to me.

"Mr. Mann!"

I turned. It was the fellow behind the velvet rope. Only he wasn't behind the velvet rope. He was running for me, sporting a sweat sheen that came from something other than the couple of yards he had to cover to chase me down.

Flustery: "Mr. Mann, I'm so sorry. I didn't . . . I was on vacation last week and no one told me that . . . We have your table, sir, if you'd just please come with me. Please."

Well, can I tell you: That last "please" wasn't asking, it was begging. The boy looked on the verge of tears, about to bust out crying for the job he'd lose if he didn't manage to get me back to the club. I hadn't wanted to, didn't even know if I should've used Frank's name first off. But it was plainly obvious it was the shadow of Sinatra that was putting the fear into him, not me.

I just rolled with it. "Sure, kid," I showbizzed. "Lead the way."

He did that, body shaking a little as he piloted me with quick steps past the what-the-hell stares of those still in line, and through the door. He went on with: "I'm so sorry. I didn't . . . I had no idea—"

"Don't sweat it, Charlie. We all make mistakes. You just keep up the hustle, you might still get a tip out of this."

The kid got me inside and over to another guy, older and black-tied, who was only slightly less nervous about things. He introduced himself as "Herman Hover. Forgive the confusion, Jackie. If you had just told Max here you were Mr. Sinatra's guest . . ."

I said, telling the truth but selling it big: "I don't like to drop names."

Herman was a pleasant-looking fellow, round-faced and plenty of meat to his features. Between his thin eyebrows and thick hairline was a billboard of a forehead. The tux he wore was cut nicely but didn't seem to fit him, like he would be more at home in Bermuda shorts and an open shirt flipping burgers at a backyard grill. He looked, basically, not like the kind of guy who would own the hottest club on Sunset.

Stepping aside, Herman swept a hand and welcomed me into his joint.

What a joint.

Saying it was plush was selling it short. Saying it was grand was an understatement. Silk tablecloths, the menus in French, and the captains all in black ties. Even the bar, satin seats and top-shelf gas, was strictly a boozer's heaven. The whole of it made the Copa in New York look like someone had set up a card table and folding chairs in their basement.

And the final touch: the girls. The Ciro's Girls. The hatcheck girls with their Ava Gardner dos, the cigarette girls whose skirts rode thigh-high over fishnets. They were, same as the sign next to the marquee promised "the most beautiful girls in the world," and by themselves just about worth the cover.

If you paid a cover.

When you knew cats like Frank Sinatra, all you got was a warm hand and shown in gratis.

The house was decent in size. The main room sat about five hundred, and another one fifty could fit in a banquet room that overlooked the stage. That night you'd have thought six times as many were packed, shoved, and jammed into every hole in the place. All of them, it seemed, stars. Rock Hudson, Anita Ekberg, Bob Mitchum, Kirk Douglas and his Mrs., Jimmy Stewart and his Mrs., Liliah Davi and a whole string of cats wanting to be her man. They flocked to her as if her sexuality had its own inescapable gravity. The whole of it was like a Mount Olympus reunion. Wall-to-wall gods. And they all just sat and talked and laughed and drank with no regard to the lookie-lous at the edge of the room—the regular people, the off-the-street Charlies who were somehow grace-of-God lucky enough to get tickets to the show—pointing and whispering at Hollywood in all its grandeur.

Herman walked me for a table. I figured, with that kind of crowd, a colored cat like me'd be lucky to get seated somewhere near my room at the Colonial. Except, we kept heading deeper into the room, deeper, until we were past front and center to just about ringside. There was a small table, and on it a little sign: RESERVED. Herman lifted the sign while the kid, Max, pulled out the chair.

Herman said: "In the future, Mr. Mann—not that I'm complaining—but for everyone's convenience . . . if you could just let us know when you'll be attending . . . We've held this table every night and—again, not to complain—but we certainly could have used the space."

"Next time? I'm not sure if any of this is happening this time."

I don't know if Herman got that or not, but he laughed it up as if he did. Max joined in, not to be left out.

Herman, followed by Max, did some if-there's-anything-you-need bits, then took off and were quick-style replaced by a riot of waiters, one to take a place setting, one to turn over the water glass; another filled it while another napkined my lap. The leader of the pack—dark-haired, dark-skinned, Mexican, I think—suggested a few late-night finger-things to enjoy with the show and I yessed them and he went away with his jacketed buddies.

I was alone.

In the middle of some eight hundred smiling, finger-waggling "luhv you, dahling" stars, I was some nobody Negro seated middle of the floor at a table for one. I couldn't've been more obvious if my hair was on fire. Right about then I got to wishing I was back in a re-stricted club shunted off to the side. That's not what I deserved, but no matter how much I faked things, compared to these folks, that's where I belonged.

A tap on my shoulder. I turned. It took everything I had to keep from blurting out "Chuck Heston!" and act like it was normal as sunshine at noon to have stars tapping me for attention.

He said: "Good to see you."

". . . Good to see you."

"What's going on?"

"In town. Doing some sets at Slapsie Maxie's."

"No kidding?"

"No."

"I get some time off from my picture, I'll have to come down and see the show."

"I'll leave your name at the door."

He caught someone out of the corner of his eye, was already smiling at them as he said to me: "Good to see you."

"Good to see . . ." I let myself trail off. He'd already moved on.

I was certain for a fact Heston didn't know me from Moses. But he knew Herman Hover had personally walked me down and sat me stageside at a sold-out Sammy Davis, Jr. show. No, he didn't know me, but he liked me for the people I knew. That's all that mattered to him.

If not before, at that moment I was very much in love with Hollywood.

Pretty soon the lights went down. There would be no warm-up act. The audience who came to see this show came in hot, wet, and ready. An announcer started in with an introduction:

"Ladies and gentlemen, Ciro's nightclub is proud to welcome to its stage the—"

After that the bodiless voice got buried under claps and whistles. Sammy Davis, Sr. and Will Mastin hit the stage and hit it hard Bojangles-style in their old flash-dance mode tap-stepping for all they were worth. They kept it up for a minute, a minute being all the more the crowd really wanted to see of them, then took a couple of steps back.

The announcer gave things another shot: "Featuring Sammy—" And one more time he got stubbed out, this time worse than before. Stars, the biggest stars in Hollywood, were on their feet clapping, screaming like goofed-up teenage girls as Sammy Davis, Jr. strolled out onstage. Strolled as if he had all the time in the ever-loving world. Strolled as if he were saying: "I don't care who you are, I don't care how big you *think* you are. My show, my rules." The crowd might have been full of showbiz glamour, but they were worshipers in Sammy's church.

"Black Magic" was his opening number. More applause as he started it, then people settled in to enjoy. Without pause Sammy ran through a few songs, a few dances. All the while his pop and Will Mastin just stood onstage motionless. A couple of cigar-store Indians. How desperate are you to be in show business that being scenery is okay with you?

Sammy wrapped up a set of numbers, sopped up applause, then slowed the show down a bit.

He stepped to the edge of the stage, said: "Thank you. Thank you so very, very much. On behalf of my father and Will Mastin, let me say what a distinct pleasure it is to once again have the opportunity to perform both here at the magnificent Ciro's nightclub, and for you splendid people."

So well spoken. That was the thing about Sammy. He'd come out doing a show that was part vaudeville, part minstrel, and all black lightning, then hit you with some talk that sounded as if he'd just a couple of hours earlier been knighted by the Queen of England.

"If you would be so kind as to indulge me for just a moment; while there are so many dear, dear friends in the audience tonight, there are a few whom I would be sorely remiss in not acknowledging their presence. May I introduce you to a man who is more than just a talented actor, more than just a friend. He is a man I consider to be my brother, Mr. Jeff Chandler."

Applause. The swing of a spotlight. At a table, a guy with features whacked out of stone and a thick wave of black/gray hair half stood from his chair, and just as halfheartedly did a little wave that was full up with humility: Aw, shucks, don't bother. I'm just an average big-time Hollywood star same as the rest of you. He threw part of that wave to Sammy, then sat down with himself.

"If there ever was *the* Hollywood couple, then these two kids are it. My dear, dear friends—"

Were any of his friend not dear, dear?

"Mr. Tony Curtis, and the ever so lovely, ever so talented Janet Leigh."

Tony was on his feet, playing not to the rest of his screen buddies, but to the handful of off-the-streeters who were whooping it up, drunk on the disbelief they were *this* close to showbiz royalty. Janet finally got to her feet doing a "what, for me?" bit, as if she were just then being informed of her celebrity status.

Sammy let the clapping die down, let the room get real quiet. "As you know, one of my most dear friends in this crazy business of show, the man who, if not for him, I would most certainly not be standing here tonight—Mr. Francis Albert Sinatra . . ."

I looked. Everybody looked. The group murmur: "Sinatra? Here?"

Before the murmur got out of control, Sammy cut it off with: "So, you know any friend of my man Frank's is a Charlie of mine."

My heart got a little speed to it.

"He's in town playing at Slapsie Maxie's . . ."

He was talking about me. He couldn't have been. But . . .

"And if you haven't caught his act yet, might I humbly suggest you do so before you're the last person on the planet who hasn't, because this young cat is a definite sensation. He is going places, and I mean that, babe. Ladies and gentlemen . . ."

Jesus . . . Holy . . . He was talking about—

"Mr. Jackie Mann!"

Next thing I know there's light washing out my eyes and the thunder of twelve hundred clapping hands in my ears. Clapping hands. Some whistles. For me.

And I just sat there. All the shows I'd done, all the minutes into hours I'd put in onstage, and the best performance I could come up with was to sit there wide-eyed and starstruck no different than some straight-from-Iowa kid?

No. Oh, no. Half my life I'd been working over one fantasy or another about a moment like this. If it never came again, I wasn't going to let it pass me by now. So, I did a Jeff Chandler—a little stand, a little wave, sending some of it Sammy's way, along with a look and a smile and a mock-scold wag of the finger that said: You know better than to make a big deal out of me, Sammy.

I sat back down, thought, over the fading applause, I heard Charlton Heston say: "Yeah, Maxie's. Kid puts on a heck of a show."

Chuck. The big phony.

Sammy got back to his act, got back to singing and dancing and impressions and instrument playing, and, and, and . . .

I couldn't pay attention to any of it, ruined for watching, too caught up in the brief moment when, like him, and thanks to him, I was a star. Riffing on that, trying to hold the receding past tight in my mind, I missed the next two hours of show. It was only Sammy's finale of "Birth of the Blues," so knock-your-socks-off, that was able to yank me clean of visions of my elevated self.

To a standing O and dripping with sweat from laying down a wall-to-wall performance, Sammy waved good night. The other duo of the trio exited, sweaty from having the nerve to stand onstage while Sammy did all the heavy lifting.

The houselights came up, and with them another buzz about Sammy and wasn't Sammy sensational and how there's nobody more sensational than Sammy.

On his way out Jeff Chandler threw me a wave, asked: "See you at King's?"

As though I had so many other things stacked up on my social calendar, I gave a thoughtful frown and a bit of nod that didn't commit one way or the other. "Probably see you there," I said, not knowing where or what *there* was.

I tried to flag a waiter, pay my bill.

The Mexican guy came by, said: "Everything is taken care of, Mr. Mann," and said it animated, like the biggest disaster of the night would be me trying to offer my own money for something.

I asked him about King's.

"Oh, yes, sir. Will you be going?"

". . . What is it?"

"King's Restaurant. Open all night." He looked over the exiting crowd. "And when you're a hardworking movie idol, you can't possibly go to bed before the sun comes up." That got salted with a little spite.

"Nice joint?"

"Sure, amigo. I go there all the time. Right after I finish a round of golf with Ike. I can't say the place is friendly to my people. Don't know how they feel about yours."

Maybe it was the hour, maybe it was a night of pinballing from table to table being a hey-boy for every famous face in town, but the waiter was feeling himself.

He said: "You should go."

"You just said—"

"Mr. Davis'll be there. They won't shoot you any trouble with him around. And it'll be good for us."

I didn't get that "us."

He explained: "Hell, they're not going to let the Mexicans in until they get used to the coloreds. If you go tonight, I figure one day, if it's still around, my grandkids might be able to eat at the joint."

CRESCENT HEIGHTS AND SANTA MONICA. King's Restaurant. I handed my car over to a valet and went for the door. I got looks but no trouble about it. Like Ciro's, King's glowed with a stellar shine. Celebrities hanging around smiling, idle-talking. Doing nothing but being famous with each other.

There was a crush of people to one side of the room. If you eye-balled them hard enough, you could make out, barely, Sammy Davis in the center of the swarm. I thought of going over, trying to say hello, but figured it would take at least half an hour to get close to him, and when I did I'd just come off as some gushing fan.

There were some open tables, but I didn't much feel like spending any more time at a table for one. There were groups that had open seats, but no one in particular seemed eager to have me join them. No one much looked my way. They buzzed from table to table pollinating each other with kisses to the cheek. They would flash smiles at each other, chat, but all the while their eyes kept rolling over the room, looking for the next—the next star or producer or personality who was loftier than the star or producer or personality they were currently smiling at. And when they found them, off they'd buzz again.

No one buzzed in my direction.

The goal was to move up the ladder, not down. A nod from Sammy or no, I was still just a club comic. A black club comic. I stood there with all those people, those people I wanted so much to be one with, but my existence didn't add up to anything more than, or more significant than, room dressing—a chair or table, a piece of furniture to be stepped around. The reality of my non-stature—the cut of it coming so close after being clapped for and whistled at by the same bunch who, now, didn't ignore me, they couldn't even see me—set loose a dull sickness in my body. A sharp sadness.

I started to go, and I wasn't slow about it. I couldn't be away from the joint quick enough.

Somebody said my name. Had to say my full name twice before it sunk in that anybody in the restaurant could be—would be—talking to me.

"Jackie Mann?" A clean-shaven fellow, suited, was moving for me with a hand out. If he was famous, he wasn't famous to me. He didn't act all celeb. His manner more shrewdish than starry. "Jackie Mann? Chet Rosen, William Morris. Caught your act down at Maxie's."

Sure you have, I thought. *Probably shared a table with ol' Charlie Heston.* But then he went on to compliment me on a couple of my bits, quote them.

He had seen my act.

He said: "You had a hot set. Just the way Sammy said, sensational. You've got real personality onstage."

". . . Thank you." My sickness was drying up.

"Who are you with?"

"I came by myself."

A smile. "Your agent, I mean."

"Sid Kindler."

Chet gave a little shake of his head. "What agency is he with?"

"He's on his own."

From his pocket, from a metal holder gold in color, Chet produced a business card. His name, the William Morris name, letters raised, were the same gold color as the case they'd come from.

As he handed the card over: "When it stops working out, give me a call. Good to have met you, Jackie."

Two pats to the shoulder, and he was done with me.

Nutty.

It was very nutty: "When it stops working out . . ."

Other than that, slightly reinvigorated by the encounter, I aborted my exit and stood at the bar some. At one point Janet Leigh came 'round and introduced herself, said she hadn't caught my act yet but hoped to.

Nice lady. It was all I could do to keep my eyes from straying below her neck.

I thanked her and told her if she ever came down to Maxie's, I'd make sure she was taken care of. As if she had to worry about that.

Miss Leigh returned to her table without offering any kind of invitation.

Eventually it got to be past three-thirty in the morning. Everyone was still having a smiling, cheek-kissing good time.

I wasn't.

I went back to the hotel.

Doary was there working late, or early, as it was very much the morning. She asked me where I'd been all night and I painted her a picture of me getting sat stageside at Ciro's, getting applauded by Hollywood royalty, of me hanging and swinging till just about dawn with all the stars in the sky—painted the picture with broader strokes and brighter colors than the slightly dull palate of reality.

Doary glowed and smiled, maybe the only real one in the whole of Los Angeles, and gave me congratulations. She asked me what it was like doing shows, being up onstage in front of all those people.

I performed my standard line: "It's nothing, doll. When you're a star, when the business of show is your life, doing bits in front of a crowd is nothing at all."

Telling me she would be done with her cleaning shortly, Doary said she'd love to hear more about my night.

I told her I was tired, some other time, then went up to bed.

⸺

I SHOULD HAVE STAYED IN LOS ANGELES, soaked up the sunlight and the starshine. Should have gone back to New York, worked some clubs, made some money. I should have, because if I had done either of those, if I had done anything other than go to San Francisco, I would have stayed ignorant. Ignorance has a way of making life so much simpler. You never feel stupid for the things you don't know, or hurt for lack of an education in finding out how wrong you've always been.

I got an education.

I got one that would twice give sense to the words of two women. The first time would be there, San Fran. The second would come years later when it all ended where it all began.

I DIDN'T HAVE ANY DATES lined up in San Francisco, hadn't planned to go. But people talk. Since my nod from Sammy at Ciro's, in the nightclub circles I was what people were talking about. Maybe among the stars of Hollywood I was an anonymous face, but to bookers I was building a name. Keith Rockwell, who owned the Purple Onion, called down. An act had fallen out and he needed someone to fill the bill and fill it pronto.

I had some days off and I never had a problem making some extra pay. I made the trip to S.F. from L.A. Made it by train, but I could have floated up the coast, my head having mushroomed to fit my new ego. When I did the city I was treated to more of that "Mr. Mann"-style of service I was getting addicted to along with the related highs that came with it. The hotel—the St. Regis—the restaurants where the club picked up the meals, were all five-star or four-diamond. Whatever I needed—to get driven here or there, to see sights or go buy this and that—nothing was too much of anything to ask for. I was unbecoming Jackie Mann. I was becoming Jackie Mann, direct from Los Angeles. Jackie Mann, sensation of southern California and friend to the famous.

The shows at the Onion were solid. The audiences in the Bay were smart, thoughtful. Like an upscale version of the Village, more than just coming to get entertained, they came to listen.

I did the week with ease, things having gone so well in San Francisco, my ego kept me where I was, eager to suck up a few more days of backslaps and of getting whisked around, wined and dined. Just a day or so more of getting drunk on thanks for coming up and saving the day as only Jackie Mann could.

What I got was just about inevitable. Cocked at such an arrogant angle, I was begging to get slapped down.

The club was Anna's 440. More a coffeehouse. A showcase room. I went to watch, not work. Really, I went to get slathered over, the uptown act going downtown to see how the other half got entertained. I had Keith phone up, get them to save us a table. He was sure to make a big deal out of it, let them know that Jackie Mann was coming 'round. When we arrived, I got nothing but the warm hand. "Hello, Mr. Mann" and "This way to your table, Mr. Mann." And if all that wasn't enough to make me feel tops, there was a comic on the bill I'd worked with a couple of times in New York. A guy who, used to be, had no time for me. When he heard I was in the audience, he came 'round before the show with a big smile and broad hug, told me how happy he was I was doing so well. He wasn't. He was putting on a performance in hopes, if I bought the act, I'd mention his name to someone who could help him down the line. The idea of the envy I knew he held and the bitterness of having to swallow it just to shine me for favors, the idea that I was even worth trying to shine in the first place, it was a cocktail that just made me all the higher.

The show started. There were comics, a couple of singers. The guy I used to know went on pulling out all stops to impress me.

Then Lenny Bruce went on.

When he was introduced, different from now, I didn't think one thing or the other. Never having heard of the guy, I had no expectations. Maybe that's why he hit me so hard.

He took the stage.

He took hold of the mike.

He said things.

More than just standing there cracking jokes, he said things, things about religion and politics and society and race and all the craziness that seemed to be erupting everywhere. Cool and relaxed, he eased across the stage, taking his time with his act instead of running from joke to joke. But when he got where he was going, he went at his topics vicious as a shark, uncaring that some might be offended, and just as happy if they were.

He said things.

About sex. He said a whole lot of things about sex, about having sex, about who we have sex with, why and how. He was graphic in detail. He was foul in language. Foul and raw in a way you didn't normally hear even in the coffeehouses. You barely heard it outside of smoky rooms and back alleys. Sick. They called his humor sick. But he didn't flinch, he didn't back down, back away, back off. He was assured in what he was saying and that he had a right to say it. He was so precise and so on target, it wasn't like he was swearing to swear, swearing to shock. It was like he was using the arch words of a whole new science. His talk, his lingo, was a mumbly-style scattershot delivery making it seem he was too cool to rehearse; his routine wasn't a routine—dragging out the last word of every sentennnnnce. Letting it hang theeeeere. Making you listen, maaaaaan. Making you think. Then he'd rapidfireatyouwithsomethingkeen. Something knife sharp. He made you be quick with him or risk getting cut.

He said things.

And the things he said were real. No made up little ha-ha bits about his mother-in-law, his fat aunt Ethel. If it wasn't going on in the world, if it didn't reference some event or emotion or outrage, if it didn't grate and bite, if it didn't make you sit up and take notice, then he didn't have time for it. He didn't want anything to do with it.

And on top of all that, he was funny. This sullen-eyed, side-burned, slick-haired wonder, the devil's jester, was funny. Insightful and funny. Clever and funny. Uninhibited, racy, provocative and . . .

After he got offstage, on came a singer, another comic, another comic . . .

I finally got myself up out of my seat, begged off Keith, told him I had to get back to the St. Regis. I left, but I felt like I was sneaking out, afraid of being spotted for the phony I'd suddenly been revealed to be.

What had I been doing? All that time I had worked myself up from burlesque to coffeehouses, from nightclubs to supper clubs, to finally circling around about where I wanted to be, what had I been doing? The jokes I told—compared to Lenny, compared to what he was laying out—were old and stale and tired. They were ordinary, unremarkable. They were indistinguishable from anything that anybody else might say. Anybody. Anybody with a little timing, a little skill, could pick up my bits, hit a stage, and have an act. I'd sold my audiences, maybe, on being likable. Conned them into thinking I had something to offer by having a personality, by being a "good" black who didn't scare them. Other than that, I was as unique as a slice of bread.

What made Lenny so different, he had a point of view. He had perspective.

He had a voice.

What he talked about and the way he talked about things, he put a stamp on every joke that made it his. He owned his material.

What Tommy had tried to beat through my skull since forever I finally got. You want to be famous? Fine. You want to live the high life? Who doesn't? But if you really want to make a mark deep and hard and forever, then you have to be unique. You have to be special.

So there I was in my hotel room after getting the warm hand all over town. There I was alone with myself and the truth: I was either a guy who told jokes and would get away with telling jokes until people got tired of my tired self. I was either that, or I was, like my mother used to whisper to me, special.

I don't know what time I'd come in from the club, but sunlight was working its way through the draped windows before I did anything besides just sit. I picked up a pen, some St. Regis stationery, and started to write.

≈

FRAN'S SPECIAL AIRED. A half-hour variety show. Her guests included Judy Holliday, and a young and very swinging Bobby Darin. Sid told me Fran had wanted me for the comedy spot. CBS had nixed the idea. CBS wanted a name. CBS wanted someone people would tune in to see. CBS got Louis Nye. I guess he was a name. Back then.

Fran sang three numbers including her newest record " 'Tain't What You Do." The song was great. Fran was great. The program was great and the ratings proved it.

Shortly, CBS announced their fall lineup would include *The Fran Clark Show*.

Fran had just become the newest star to light the heavens.

═══

THE HOUSEMAN, the gorilla in a suit, didn't know what to do. He didn't want to stand there, middle of the casino floor, all eyes on him, apologizing like a little girl who'd messed her dress. He didn't want to not apologize, because if word got around that he had given Sammy Davis, Jr. anything close to heat, he'd be in for twice what he'd handed out. So the houseman, looking past me, who he couldn't care less about, said: "Didn't see you, Mr. Davis," which came off as more statement than apology.

"You didn't spot the only colored Jew in the joint? Baby, I thought *I* had trouble seeing." Sammy tossed off the line without missing a beat, the chucker reduced to working as his straight man, good for being the butt of a laugh and nothing more. Hand still on my shoulder, Sammy was walking me away before he'd even finished the crack.

I didn't say anything. I was no good for talking. The bravado I owned when I walked out of the Copa Room and crossed the restricted floor for the gaming tables was spent. What the houseman hadn't scared out of me the rescue from Sammy had stunned quiet. I thought it best to play things cool, try to play them off, as if having big stars talk me out of tight spots was just about routine.

"Thanks, Sammy."

"Sammy? Oh, now we're chums? You know, I'm very upset with you. I give you a hello from the stage at Ciro's and you don't even bother to do a drop-by at King's Restaurant."

"You saw me there?"

"Chicky, I might have one good eye, but I can do a whooole lots o' lookin' wit' it," he joked Kingfish-style.

We arrived at the roulette table. People made space. Not like they didn't want to be around a couple of blacks, but more like Sammy's star power compelled them to give room.

I dug that.

I put my hundred on black.

Sammy put out five hundred dollars cash.

"Money plays," came the call from the dealer. He spun the ball.

"Sammy . . . Mr. Davis—"

"It's Charlie between us."

All around I felt stares, felt the press of flesh from the constricting crowd that buzzed same as a hive of excited white bees.

"I didn't mean any disrespect that night, but there were all those people wanting to meet you, all those celebrities, and I figured I'm just—"

The ball dropped.

The dealer called: "Twenty-two. Black."

The crowd gave a hiccup of thrill.

The bets were paid, I started to reach for my chips.

Sammy didn't. He quipped as he lit a Dunhill: "Well, if you're going to be cheap about things . . ."

His thousand to my two hundred. Casually as I could I moved my hand away from the table.

The dealer spun the ball.

People hurriedly laid bets on black just because, win or lose, they wanted to go back to whatever breadbasket or Bible belt state they called home and tell the folks they'd bet with Sammy Davis, Jr. They did it because they wanted to be like Sammy Davis, Jr.: able to toss around green as if green were nothing. I looked at all that money overflowing from the table. There was a reason Sammy was the only black they let walk the floor.

"Listen, Charlie, maybe I poured it on a little heavy at Ciro's, especially as I still haven't caught your act. But emmis, the word on you is you're sensational. And you know, and I know, if you weren't a colored act, you'd be twice where you are today."

The ball dropped.

The dealer called: "Thirty-one. Black."

Going on three deep, the crowd cut loose with an electric yelp.

Sammy moved for his chips and I did the same.

A cocktail waitress, dressed skimpy like all the cocktail waitresses, did a slow crawl past the scene.

Nodding at one of the drinks on her tray: "Sweetheart, who's the gas for?"

"It's for the gentleman over at the cra—"

Never-minding all of that, Sammy picked up the glass. "Tell him he just bought a drink for Sammy Davis, Jr." Tossing a hundred-dollar toke on her tray: "That's so you can buy the rest of that outfit." Chasing the toke with another: "That's so you don't."

The girl just about bust out of her bra.

Moving from the table, I stayed with Sammy, people clapping, applauding his one-man show. He headed from the casino for the guest rooms. I puppy-dogged along for lack of specific instructions on what else to do.

All eyes on us as we eased across the floor, the air around aromaed with more envy than resent.

"That was . . . You're a cool one, Mr. Davis, I'll tell you that."

He shrugged. "You win, you lose. Last time I checked money was for spending. Look, Jackie, you've got to quit playing Charlie Wide-eyed. You're strictly star now."

Hearing that from Sammy, I was flattered.

After seeing Lenny, I was honest. "I'm just a comic."

"Forget the humble bits. You're a Copa comic. A Sands comic, and that's a whole lot more than most. On top of that, you're in the club. FOF." He could tell I didn't even begin to get that. "Friends of Frank. Most exclusive club in the world, babe. And that membership buys you a whole lot."

"Sinatra, he's a hell of a guy."

"Oh, you done said a mouthful. Half the time you don't know if the cat is going to kiss you or kill you."

I thought of the first time I'd met Frank, of him tearing some poor Harvey a new hole, making him cry, then turning around and playing St. Francis to me.

"Yeah," I tagged.

"You heard about the party?"

The party? "No."

"The party. Palm Springs celebrity to-do some kitten was throwing. Frank's there, talks up a girl. Preps her with some gas to get a little hey-hey out of her. Only, bright eyes and short skirt doesn't want to hand out any hey-hey. Leastways, she didn't want to hand out any to Frank. Now, most cats would've had their ego bruised but just limped off bird in hand. And a star the size of Frank should've moved on the next broad same way you'd pick meat off a deli platter.

"My man did neither."

Sammy paused.

I felt the way I did when I was a kid at the movies anticipating the next chapter in a serial. "And . . ."

"And he shoved her through a plate window."

"Jesus. You're kidding me."

"I kid you not, Chicky. The scene was crazy. Bright eyes was lying there, bleeding up the joint. Judy Garland does a faint. Rock Hudson's screaming like a girl. . . . Frank? He mixes himself another drink."

"That . . ."

"That son of a bitch. Yeah. He can be that. The cuckoo thing is, as nasty as he can be, he can be just as swell. When I had my little . . ." Sammy swirled a hand near the left side of his face. "You know."

I knew.

"Frank dropped everything, drove out to San Bernardi-nowheresville just to sit with me in the hospital. Then the man gave my self-sorry-feeling behind the kick it needed to get back on the showbiz horse. And I'll tell you this: There isn't a cat alive who is more race tolerant than Frank. Let him find out some Harvey was giving you trouble, and see what his Irish is like. He's opened a whole lot of doors for this colored Jew."

We got to Sammy's room. Standing just outside was a girl, young, tight dungarees and T-shirt. Her makeup, bright, multicolored, and spatulaed over her cheeks and eyes, said she was a showgirl straight from the line.

A white showgirl.

You had to figure she'd probably been parked in her spot a good while, but the waiting hadn't worn her down any. The smile she gave were Vols. I and II on anticipation. She looked more than ready to personally autograph Vol. III.

"And, baby," Sammy added as a final thought to me but delivered right to the girl, "when these doors open, they swing."

Sammy opened the room door, sidestepped, and did a broad sweep with his arm, letting the girl in first, gentleman-style, for what would surely be some very un-gentlemanlike activities.

Kept company by the science Sammy had lectured to me, I walked back to the Copa Room by way of the casino. A lot of looks got sent my way, but no one said a thing.

＿＿＿

KANSAS CITY. Kansas City, Missouri. I was having an afternoon rest. I'd been up late, a jazz club after my show. I'd just eaten. Barbecue. If you dig that sort of thing, meats slathered with tangy sauces, K.C. has some of the best bbq to be had. I lay on my bed in my hotel thinking of nothing in particular. My life had reached such a point of steady ease that very little deep thought was required in being me. Sid booked my shows, I did my shows. I did them well and was paid accordingly. I worked New York. I worked Los Angeles. I worked Las Vegas. I worked the best clubs in each city. The only blip on my mental radar was television. As comfortable as I was, I knew I needed some national exposure if I was going to ever be *more* comfortable.

Sid kept telling me not to worry, television would come.

Alone in my room in the quiet, I had to be honest with myself: I was getting a little tired of hearing that.

The phone rang. I flopped a lazy hand to the nightstand, picked up the receiver. "Hello?"

"Jackie Mann?" The voice was tentative. It had an accent. Southernish. Missouri was a border state. There were a lot of accents walking around.

"Yes."

"Jackie, Ah'm, uh . . . well, Ah caught yer act last night, and that was some funny shit yew were talkin'. Ah jus' . . . muh wife an Ah both—"

"Thank you, I appreciate that. And thank you for calling." I said that last bit in a you-may-hang-up-now manner. The party on the other end missed my meaning.

"Ah was hopin' that, well, that . . . tha missuhs would surely luv tah tell yew how much she enjoyed tha show."

I didn't mind having fans. I could even deal with fans calling up to the room. But why did the ones who called have to be the lowest common denominator of fan?

I told him: "Now's not a really—"

"Wouldn't take up but uh minute. Tha missuhs, like Ah said, it would jus', yew know, mean uh lot. She surely does thank yer uh hoot."

Ego. My ego was working me. Tired as I was: "Just for a minute."

"Thata boy, Jackie. We'll see yew down in tha bar."

FIVE MINUTES LATER. The bar was barely populated. A few people. One couple. A guy at a table in the back waved me over with his glass. He was alone, no wife. Maybe he was the guy who'd called up. Maybe it was a convention of Jackie Mann fans. I went to him.

"Welllll, Jackie Mann," he drawled. "Hava seat, Jackie Mann."

I took a look around. "Where's your wife?"

"Oh, Ah expec' she'll be along in uh minute. Go on theyah, take uh chair."

Something about him . . . Something about him edged me a little. Maybe it was his way of talking. I never much cared for the sounds of the South. Maybe it was his breath that stank of liquor and his clothes of cigarettes. His clothes. The suit he wore was rumpled and out of style by a few years—the wide lapels telling as tree rings—but he sported it in ignorant pride, unaware it made him look clownish in the hotel bar with the Lacoste-wearing tourists and business travelers decked in miracle fabrics.

So he was a poor Southern white guy. So what? He was a fan. That's how strong my act was: Even poor Southern crackers dug it. I sat.

He said: "Ah wasn't sure if yew was actually gonna come on down. Some show folk, they're . . . well, yew read how they ahr in them gossip magazines. They jus' too good. They wouldn't take uh long elevator ride jus tah meet uh fan. But not yew, Jackie. Not—"

"I'm sorry, I don't think I got your—"

"Missuhs an me, we're not from heyah, yew know? Takin' uh little vacation. Had tah save up uh lot. Everythang cost these days. Everythang. Ain't like we got much."

I didn't say anything to that, not wanting to make the guy feel bad by agreeing with what was obvious about him.

"Then we get heyah, an tha missuhs wants tah see a show. Now, Ah ain't hardly got money for that, but when uh woman wants somethin', well, yew know how that is, Jackie. Talkin' about wantin' thangs, yew want uh drink?"

"It's a little early for that."

As if to prove how wrong I was, the guy gulped some of whatever was in his glass.

I made a broad show of checking my watch. That minute he had promised me this was going to take was stretching into ten.

"I'm not trying to be rude, but I really need to—"

"Dighton."

"I'm sorry, I don't—"

"Yew asked mah name, didn't yew? Dighton Spooner."

Taking out a pen, reaching for a cocktail napkin: "Mr. Spooner, why don't I just give you my autograph and then you can—"

"Don't mean nothin' to yew, do it, muh name. Yers didn't mean nothin' tah me neither. Tha wife wants tah go see uh show, an' Ah see Jackie Mann's at tha club, so Ah take her, an' Ah don't thank nothin' of it."

I started to get up. "If you could tell your wife that I'm very sorry I couldn't—"

"We're on vacation, like Ah said. Like Ah said, we're not from around heyah. Know where Ah'm from, Jackie? Ah'm from Florida."

I looked hard at the guy and I knew what it was that made me uneasy about him: his ear—messed up like at some point something had gnawed away at it. A rat. One of his own kind. I sat back down. The sudden lack of strength in my legs gave me no choice.

"Yeah, now yew startin' tah recall, ain't yew, boy?"

I recalled. The last time I saw that chewed-up ear I was taking a ride with three rednecks in the dark of Florida, heading for as much of a beating as they felt like handing me.

"Yeah, yer name didn't mean nothin', but soon as yew walked out onstage Ah recalled right off. Ah said: Goddamn, there that niggrah who squirrled away from us. Now heyah yew ahr entahtainin' jus' like yew said." He took a big, long sip of his drink. I could almost track the booze as it worked through his body, making him dark and sullen.

He said with narrow, spiteful eyes: "Big star and everythang, everybody clappin' for yew, laughin' at yew . . . A big niggrah star."

At night in the dark, when I was alone and he was with two others, this man was as terrifying a thing as existed. In the day, in the light, when I could see him for what he was—a cheap lush—he did not scare me. My father had cured my fear of drunks.

I started to regain some of my self. "Better step careful. We're not in backwater Florida now."

"Yew tha one ought tah be careful, niggrah."

A thought occurred to me. A bad one. I did a quick look around for any more of the white-trash trio who might have come to finish what they'd never properly started.

The balance of fear shifting back in his favor gave Dighton a smile. "Settle up, boy. Ah ain't got nobody with me. Jus' tha missuhs, like Ah said, an she's back at the motel." He gave our surroundings an overdone inspection. "Naw, we cain't afford no place like this."

He raised his glass to the waiter, signaling for another round.

Continuing: "Nope. Jus' me an tha missuhs. Don't much pal around with Jess no more. Yew rememba Jess? Redheaded Jess. After what happened that night he sorta got spooked. Spooked by a spook." Dighton grinned at his own cleverness. "Don't pal around at all no more with Earl. Cain't. Earl's dead. Earl's dead, an yew tha one that killed him."

I said nothing. My face danced with confusion.

"You killed Earl."

"I—"

"Well, whadayah expec', boy? Take uh steel pipe, put it tah uh man's head; whadayah expec' 'cept that he gonna die?"

In an instant the past was present. The thin/fat redneck was moving for me, hand brass-wrapped and ready to do work. I swung the pipe and could feel the resonance of metal on bone through its shaft and across my body. But even against a memory so real I protested.

"I didn't ki—"

The waiter came 'round, set down a fresh drink before Dighton.

As he moved away, I started again, guarded: "I didn't kill him."

Dighton sipped at his booze, savored it same as he savored the moment. He reached into a pocket and took out a clipping—yellowed and torn—that seemed to be as old as the jacket he pulled it from. In a grand gesture, a ham actor playing to the cheap seats, he held it to me.

I did nothing, my show of defiance, but only for a moment. I took the clipping, unfolded it. It was from a newspaper, and read:

AREA MAN KILLED IN ATTACK

A local man was killed late yesterday night in what witnesses called an attack by a colored drifter.

Earl Colmbs of Kendall was killed near North Miami by what police say was a single blow to the head from a blunt object.

Witnesses, Jess Rand and Dighton Spooner, both also from Kendall, said they were driving with the victim, when they came upon a colored man walking alone who appeared to be in distress. The three men stopped to inquire if the colored needed assistance, when the drifter swung a metal pipe, striking Colmbs in the head and killing him. The colored then fled the scene. Rand and Spooner, attempting to give aid to Colmbs, did not pursue the suspect.

It went on from there. The article dryly recounted the eyewitness's details, the police search for the colored suspect, mentioned Colmbs's survivors. There was no mention of the redneck's brass knuckles or their board with nails. The article had nothing to say about how the victim, poor, departed Earl Colmbs, and his buddies tried to deliver a lynching that night.

Still . . .

Still, I had killed a man. By accident, in self-defense, but I had killed a man. I don't know if what I felt was revulsion or guilt or sorrow despite the circumstances, but when mixed together it was a sickness that thrashed in the pit of my stomach before seeping through my body. Soon there wasn't a part of me that wasn't infected with the sense of murder.

Whatever the emotion, it was more than what Dighton felt. He seemed not to care about his dead friend but only to take pleasure from the state he'd reduced me to.

Fighting my own affliction, I tossed down the article. "That's not how it was."

"Tha's what tha papers say. Tha papers don't lie."

"It was self-defense. It was you three who—"

"Yew got anyone tah say otherwise?"

The man in the car, the one who saved me . . . What were the chances of ever finding him?

Dighton put an end to that train of thought with: "An no matter how yew say thangs was, how yew think uh Florida jury's gonna feel about it? What's tha word of uh niggrah against uh fine, upstandin' white?"

I considered that. Then I considered that if this redneck really thought he had the law on his side, he wouldn't be sitting across the table from me, boozing. The cops would already be putting iron on my wrists.

"You willing to take that chance?" I bluffed.

"Are yew? 'Cause tha way Ah figure, no matter what uh jury say, it ain't gonna be no good for some celebrity niggrah tah have this kind uh shit swimmin' around him anyhow. Know what Ah'm sayin'?"

That smile of his again. That goddamn smile.

I knew what he was saying.

The air was getting weak. Breathing was hard and thought would've been impossible except I was beyond thought. Nerves made my actions bypass my useless brain. As I had back in Florida, I was operating on instinct.

Instinct told me to get down to what was what: "How much?"

"Welllll, Ah ain't a greedy man—"

"How much to make you go away and stay away?"

"Ah was tryin' tah tell yew, boy—"

"Don't call me—"

"Boy, Ah was tryin' tah tell yew, Ah ain't uh greedy man, but that don't mean Ah don't like money. Ah like it jus' fine. How 'bout we call it five thousand dollars?"

The cat was pure hick. To most Charlies off the street, five grand was a fortune. I wasn't a Charlie off the street. I was raking more than seven hundred in a good week. Five thousand dollars wasn't letting me off cheap, but it was very affordable, especially when it came standard with the promise of staying out of jail and clean of headlines. Only, I didn't need him to know that.

Protesting: "Five?"

"Shit, Ah seen all them people at yer show. Ah read them Hollywood magazines. Ah know how show folk live. Five thousand ain't nothing."

"It's not the kind of money a man walks around with."

"Oh, Ah understand that." Dighton scribbled in the air at the waiter for the check. "Me, tha missuhs, we gonna be around for uh few more days. Ah'll give yew uh ring before we head on outta heyah."

The waiter brought 'round the bill.

Dighton started to fish out some money, stopped, looked to me. Again, that smile. "What the hellam'ah doin'?"

He left the bill for me along with the clipping saying: "Gowon an' make a souvenir a' that. Ah got lots others."

I CALLED SID, set him up with a story about having to do a quick purchase of this or that that I'd seen and loved and had to have right away, then hit him with the punch line of needing five grand. If Sid bought or disbelieved what I was handing him, I couldn't tell either way. He'd worked with enough talent who had their hidden bents that a sudden need for cash for one reason or another didn't get a rise out of him anymore. He Western Unioned the money out to me.

Then I waited for word from the shadow of my past. Making it through one day, through a night and a show carrying fear and anxiety was like trying to live a normal life with fire ants crawling over you: They were always with you, always tearing away at you. They were with me the second day, the second night and show. The third day of not hearing from the hick did nothing to calm my worries, but it gave me a little pinprick of hope that maybe he'd gone away. Maybe he'd gotten scared or lost his nerve or figured putting pressure on me would likely cause him more trouble than—

The phone rang. It was Spooner.

We met again in the hotel bar. He wasn't alone this time. This time he was with a woman, long and lean and plumpless. From neck to ankle she was a stick of a figure, no bumps, no curves. The secondhand clothes she wore—shirtwaist dressed in three-year-old Montgomery Ward fashion that would most likely get stretched into service for another two—said she was probably Mrs. Spooner. That she was anywhere near the man at all said definitely holy matrimony was involved.

I got in Dighton's eye line, waved him over to me. He waved me over to him. He was holding the cards. I went.

"Jackie," he said with a big show of excitement at my arrival. "There yew ahr." To the woman: "Told ya Ah knew Jackie. Didn't Ah say Ah knew him? Jackie, say hello tah tha missuhs."

". . . Hello" was all I could force from myself. I knew nothing of the woman except that she was with Spooner. That's all the more I needed to despise her.

Mrs. Spooner returned my greeting. Then she went on to tell me how much she had enjoyed my show, couldn't recall when she'd had herself such a good laugh. She told me, in a pleasant Southern lilt, that vacations, going out, were a rare treat, and that seeing me onstage would make their trip all the more memorable.

I wanted to hate the woman, but as polite as she was, as humble as she was, as different as she was from the man she'd married, all I could do was feel sorry for her.

Spooner, impressing his wife taking a backseat to the bitterness grown from the compliments she handed me, stood and walked me aside.

Alone together, away from the table, I handed over an envelope of get-lost money. The way Spooner eyed the cash I'd have figured he was going to get sexual with it.

Breaking up his revelry, I leaned close and hissed vicious. "You and me are even now, you understand? Blackmail's a crime. You come around again and jail's where you're heading even if I've got to head there with you."

"Yew expec' me tah think yew'd—"

"Yeah, I would." I was sharp about that. Sharp as a brand-new razor.

One long stare passed between us. There was some serious eye-screwing going on. As serious as the jail time I could do for murder or he could do for extortion. Spooner was the first to flinch, just a little, as he licked his cracking lips. He needed a drink. I could tell. But I could also tell he wanted to get away from me as much as I wanted him gone.

Wagging the envelope of cash: "This heyah's all Ah come for. Tah hell with yew" was his good-bye. He went back to the table and collected his wife.

I watched them go. To the side of the woman's left eye: a fading mark that looked something like a bruise.

I sat.

I stretched out my hands before me. All they did was shake. I calmed them down enough to signal a waiter. He came by and I told him I needed some liquor. What kind, I didn't care as long as it was strong.

My eyes closed.

A couple of deep breaths.

I'd made it.

I'd made it.

Five thousand dollars.

Spooner could have taken me for so much more. He could have taken my whole career from me, but I'd made it. I'd bluffed him and sent him off. Twice now I'd gotten away from him.

Still . . .

My mind was stuck in a groove of possibilities, and the nasty pictures it painted for itself—me in jail. Me in headlines. Me in ruins— is what gave me the worst of my jangles.

The waiter came back with my drink. I had to two-hand it up to my mouth. The second the juice hit my throat it burned hot, lavaed its way along my body, slagging all nerve endings, deadening all sensations. Halfway through my second glass I felt good and steady, and by the bottom of my third I wanted to smile. Were things really so bad? Were they? Trouble had come my way and I'd sent it walking. Jackie Mann had elevated himself to a place where he could buy his way out of a jam. Isn't that what the real stars did back in Hollywood? When situations went wrong—when they'd married the wrong person, when the wrong girl got pregnant, when they got busted smoking the wrong kind of cigarettes—didn't they just throw money at the problem and make everything right? When you looked at things that way, I was more the star than I thought I was.

Man, let me tell you: The liquor helped me think straight.

I ordered another glass of gas, understanding why Sid'd used it to ease the hurt of losing his wife. Finally understanding why my pop dedicated his life to the stuff.

MONEY GOT ME OUT OF TROUBLE. Money helped me bury the memory of trouble.

When I got back to New York, feeling free and alive after my near existence-ending experience, I used money as a green salve to numb my pain.

I took myself a march along Fifth Ave. heading out to burn cash the way Sherman burned Atlanta.

Suits. I didn't much need them, but I got them. I got them tailored. Cye Martin's. They were good. They had to be good. They were what Sammy wore.

Watches. I needed more than one watch less than I needed the suits. What I really didn't need was the Vacheron Constantin I had my eye on: $1150. I got two. I got a $900 Patek Philippe to go with it. If it shined, it was mine. I bought first and asked no questions later.

"Last time I checked, money was for spending," Sammy had told me. Only now was I hearing him loud and clear. He also told me I was strictly a star these days. You couldn't be a star without star attitude and star style. I was planning on stocking up on both.

Make it two Patek Philippes.

───

I SCREAMED AT THE CABDRIVER to pull over. He did. Not so much because I told him to as because my screaming made me come off as some kind of nutcase that chances should not be taken with.

More screaming: "Turn it up."

"What are you—"

"Turn up the radio!"

The hack driver grumbled Brooklyn prayers at me but increased the radio's volume.

I'd been expecting it. Not at that exact moment, no, but I knew Tommy had cut a record. I knew it'd been released to radio. I knew it had gotten some play, and I knew it was just a matter of time before I heard it.

My fists were shaking. Fists, because I was so excited for Tommy that on their own my hands had balled up until my fingers dug into my palm.

Tommy. My Tommy. And the picket-fence reception the radio got through the towers of Manhattan couldn't hurt the sweetness of her voice. A voice I was concentrating so hard on listening to, the song was half over before I could relax enough to enjoy it.

I ignored the cabbie, him barking at me that he didn't care how long I sat he wasn't about to shut off the meter, and listened.

And then the song ended.

And then I got excited all over again in anticipation of the disc jockey announcing her name, Tommy's name, my girl's name over the airwaves for all of New York to hear. And he did.

Sort of.

He said the name of the song, said something about how it was some fresh wax out of Detroit by a hot new sensation. Then he said a name I didn't recognize.

The deejay was wrong. He had to be wrong. I'd know my girl's voice anywhere, but the name . . .

I paid up the driver, forgot about wherever else I used to be going, and set out to find a record store. My legs moved to the rhythm in my mind: The deejay was wrong. He had to be wrong.

Tommy's disc was so new, I had to hit three stores before I found one that carried it.

The deejay was wrong. He had to be—

I checked the label. The deejay wasn't wrong. No matter how much I recognized the voice, the name wasn't the same. Tommy was going by Tammy. She'd said that. I remembered, vaguely, Tommy saying something about going by Tammy. Tammi with an "i." So that was a kick, but just a little one. What really slugged me was that along with her first, she'd changed her last name as well. Tommy, my Tommy Montgomery, was now Tammi Terrell.

I CALLED TOMMY. TAMMI. She wasn't at her apartment.

I called over to Motown. The woman who answered the phone told me she was in the recording studio and couldn't take a call, asked if I wanted to leave a message. I hung up.

I got myself out of the Detroit airport—only eighteen hours since I'd heard the record—got a cab, and headed the driver for Motown. This time it was me who had a surprise for Tommy. Tammi.

The cabbie took me where I was going. I didn't know what I expected, but I expected more than what I saw: a brownstone— small, plain—that looked a couple of late payments shy of being abandoned. In a window was what looked to be some schoolkid's class project, a handmade sign: HITSVILLE, U.S.A. Other than that, I wouldn't've known I was in the right place. Until I walked through the door. Black people. Nothing but black people. Black singers and songwriters, musicians, engineers. Black executives and ac-countants, and black secretaries. It was a sight not regularly seen in those whitewashed days: black people working together in a busi-ness setting. Black people owning and earning and achieving. That's just how rare it was; even if you were black, the sight of see-ing your own kind making it was enough to shock you. That's how conditioned we were.

"Jackie!"

I turned, looked. Lamont Pearl making his way over to me.

"Jackie, what are you doing, man? How long you been here?" He took my hand, pumped my arm like he was hoping I'd spit gold.

"Just, uh . . . I just walked in."

"You doing a show this week?"

"No, I was . . . had a few days off. Thought I'd fly in."

Impressed, or at least acting so: "Fly in? You're doing all right." Like he wasn't doing fine himself. If nothing else, and there was plenty else to him, Lamont knew how to stroke with the best of them. "And look at that suit. What is that, is that a—"

"Cye Martin."

"Yeah, that's sweet. That sure is sweet. Sammy wears those, you know. What am I talking, 'course you know. Read in the *Courier* you and Sammy—"

"Tommy around?" I said what I said stressing her old name. I said what I said to the point, trying to let Lamont know that maybe he had time for chitchat, but I didn't. But the effect of my attempt to take charge was the opposite. Lamont just smiled at me the way you smile at a kid playing soldier. His thumb made the rounds over his fingertips. Back and forth and back again.

"Sure, Jackie. Let's go find your girl."

Lamont walked me by rows of small recording studios. Little universes in a bottle. Passing the glass windows, you looked in on men and women, solo, in groups—their faces young and unfamiliar, hungry to be famous—recording, rehearsing, listening to playback, but all done in silence behind soundproof walls. It was if I were a god up high looking down on the festival of man.

I wondered if that's how the shadow boss, Berry Gordy, felt when he walked the halls of his little city, his Motown, his Hitsville.

Tommy/Tammi was in one of the studios with a lanky black fellow, clean shaven and with a neat, tight Afro. Almost in a Caucasian way, his features were narrow and angular, and in fresh-laundered slacks and shirt he was looking just a little too prim. A little too proper. A little too like a cat who thought he was slick and could get slick with any girl he cared to. The two of them were laughing. What at, I didn't know. Something funny he'd said or she'd said. A busted take that'd been replayed for them. Didn't matter. Whatever the reason, whatever it was, I didn't care for the sight of it.

Lamont rapped a knuckle on the glass. Tommy turned, looked blank-faced. A second, a couple of them went by before it sunk in it was me.

The very next thing, Tommy was in my arms hugging me, kissing me. I was doing likewise and at the same time shooting a look at Pressed Pants and Starched Shirt that said: Yeah, she's mine.

Between kisses, from Tommy: "What are you doing here? Why didn't you tell me you were coming?"

"A surprise, baby. You like surprises."

"When they're about you I love them."

As tight as we already held each other, Tommy tried to sink herself even deeper into me. Forgetting about Lamont and the Nancy boy in the booth, forgetting about everyone else in the building, Tommy and I spent a good moment exploring each other. Months and distance and separate lives had worked on us, but for all that changed what remained was intense. We were back together even if just for a minute. That was enough for me to hang my hopes on that whatever else and whatever more Tommy and I had to get through, we would arrive, one day, at a place that was our own.

Lamont broke the spell with: "Tammi, why don't you knock off for a bit, let Jackie take you for some lunch?"

He wasn't out of line with that. Not hardly. Except for maybe he'd called her Tammi with as much emphasis as I'd called her Tommy, if anything, he was doing me a favor cutting her loose for the afternoon. But something about his offer just caught me the wrong way.

Snide: "Really, Lamont? Is that okay; is it okay if *I* take *my girl* out to lunch?"

All I got from Lamont was more of that "oh, you little boy" smile.

From Tommy I got some stink-eye.

WE FOUND A SPOT 'ROUND the corner from Motown, a diner-type joint where everything came grill-cooked. The background music the constant sizzle of frying foods. We got a table, sat down, and right away I went to work on the menu.

"It all looks good. You know what you want, baby?"

Tommy wasn't about to let things go. "Why are you like that?"

Playing dumb to my own behavior: "Like what?"

"Why are you like that with Lamont?"

"Because he's always around you, always acting like he owns you."

"He's handling my career."

"You don't see Sid around me day-night-day."

"If he did, I wouldn't care."

"That's because Sid isn't trying to—" I cut myself off before I said something I'd surely regret. But I didn't stop soon enough that Tommy couldn't figure where I was going with things.

"Is that what you think? You think Lamont's just trying to sleep with me?"

"I didn't say that."

"Not by much you didn't. And if he was, do you think I'd let him just to get a record out?" Slow, Tommy shook her head side to side while a hand rubbed it. "You're breaking your own records. Doesn't even take you a minute of arguing to get my head pounding."

I tried smoothing things. "So I'm anxious to see you, I rush here and catch you smiling and laughing with one cat, I got Lamont doing bits about you in my ear, and I get a little hot. Some people call it love."

"Jealousy's what they call it."

"Only the ones who don't know what passion is."

That got five-eighths of a grin out of her.

A waitress came around. We ordered. The waitress left.

I said: "You look good, Tommy . . . Tam— I don't even know what to call you."

"How about you just call me baby?"

"You look good, baby."

That brought out the last piece of her smile. "You, too."

"Did you do something to your—"

"Braces. Just got them off."

"Your hair looks—"

"It's just a wig. With the traveling and all it makes it . . . you know . . ."

"I heard the record."

"Yeah?"

"Yeah. Heard it in New York."

"Yeah?"

"It was . . . I had to have the cabbie pull over, I wanted to listen so bad."

"I wanted to play it for you."

"I was riding along, and it comes on and . . . and I was shaking so hard. I was so excited, I—"

"I wanted to play it for you. I wanted to call you and . . . I was so nervous about it, about how it sounded. Then the next thing I know it's done, and it's out and—"

"You didn't tell me you changed your name."

"You didn't tell me your father died."

Well, that put the brakes on things right there. The waitress brought out our food, extended the quiet beat. I sat like a fighter in his corner figuring how I was going to approach after the bell.

The waitress left.

Round two.

Before I could say anything, Tommy said: "I'm sorry about your father. I know things weren't always good for you two, weren't good at all. But just the same, it must—"

Digging into my food, not wanting to talk about *that*: "This sure looks good. Hope you're hungry."

"No, I'm not. It must hurt in some ways losing him, and I'm sorry."

"So what's with the name change?"

Tommy/Tammi didn't care for being dismissed. For a second she teetered between getting up and walking out, and picking up a butter knife and going to work on me. She settled on: "It's a stage name. I told you I was going to change my name."

"Mentioned it once. Said you might; all you said was you might—"

"I told you, Tommy was too . . . Tammi: It sounds good; has a good ring to it."

"Tammi. Tammi with an 'i.' Tammi Terrell."

"Yes. It has a—"

"Terrell. Tammi . . . why Terrell? Out of all the names, out of everything you could've . . . Terrell. Why?"

Nothing from Tommy/Tammi.

"Why Terrell?"

"I got it from a friend of mine, Jean. I got it from her brother. It's their last name, Terrell, and he said I should take it. He said it would sound good, sound good with Tammi. It does."

"What else did you get from him?"

The crack not even finished, and she was up and out of her seat and moving for the door. I grabbed her wrist and she snatched it free like I'd wrapped it up in nothing more substantial than tissue. I reached for her again, not to grab her—couldn't hold her if I wanted to—but to say to her with a touch what my ass of a self was useless to say with words: I'm sorry. Don't walk away. I'm wrecked up, and please don't leave me alone with myself. Please.

She stood where she was so ready to go, so ready to get back to the life she was building without me.

She stood there . . .

She sat. For the longest time we were motionless across from each other no different from the two most unfamiliar people on the planet.

Eventually Tommy/Tammi—Tammi/Tommy got to a place where she could say: "That really, really hurt me, Jackie."

"I'm sorry. I am jealous, I'll admit that. I'm . . . I heard the record, heard the disc jockey call you Tammi Terrell and I thought maybe, you know, you had gotten hitched and you didn't tell me. I flew out here fast as I could; then I see you with those . . . those men, those musicians. *Musicians.* You know how they are. If they were any bigger sex fiends, they'd be sleeping with each other, and they probably are anyway."

Tammi/Tommy gave me nothing but blank face, and I realized I'd just wasted an explanation on a subject she wasn't trying to deal with.

"That's not . . . what hurt me, what I'm talking about. When your father passed and you felt like you had to hide it from me—"

"I wasn't . . . How am I going to hide my pop dying? I didn't tell you because I didn't care about him."

"This isn't about him, it's about you. You and me. If you loved him, if you hated him, you must have felt something when he died. And whatever it was you were feeling, you wanted to keep it from me."

"Yeah, I did. I did want to keep it from you. In the middle of everything else you're doing, in the middle of putting out a record, you want to deal with me trying to deal with my pop?"

"I wanted to help you with whatever you were going through. I wanted—I *want* to be part of your life, and you just pushed me away. Do you know what that feels like? To love someone, to think that they love you—"

"I do love you."

"And that's how you show it, by treating me like a stranger?"

First one, then a few, then came a rain of tears from her eyes. I don't think I'd ever seen her cry before. I was sure I hadn't. I would have remembered. Seeing her break down, knowing I'd caused it, it was the most painful thing I'd ever witnessed. It was a misery, seen once, I would never forget. I tried as best I could to soften the hurt.

"The thing is, the thing you've got to understand, I did it for you."

"That is so . . . That is just a bunch of—"

"If I had called you when my father died, would you have come to me?"

"You know I would have."

"Yeah. Yeah, I know it. You would've come, you would've held my hand, kissed away my ache, and while you're doing that, how're you supposed to cut a record?"

"Would you shut up about my record!" More rubbing at her head. "It's nothing! It doesn't mean anything!"

"You're the one always going on about me just wanting to be famous, about how I've got to realize what we do is special. It is special. Your singing is, anyway. I'm not going to be the guy to keep you from it, or to keep you from being the biggest star you can."

She started to protest.

"So that everyone can hear you sing, everyone can hear how special I already know you are. I'm not pushing you away, I'm . . . I'm pushing you forward. There'll be time for us."

At that Tammi/Tommy laughed, and it wasn't a pleasant laugh.

I took her hand. Across the table I kissed her tears. I said to her again: "There'll be time for us."

She leaned in, rubbed her cheek against mine. Was there ever anything so soft as her flesh?

Pretty soon Tammi/Tommy—Tammi. She was Tammi now— pretty soon she stopped crying, sat quietly; then me and her worked very hard at being a guy and his girl out enjoying a meal together. A couple of times, when we weren't working at it, when we just let moments happen—when she laughed at something I'd said, or I lost myself in her smile—things were as they used to be a few years prior when I was just a late-night comic and she was just a coffeehouse singer. But the moments came and went and did so real quick. It was becoming obvious that as much as we cared for each other, as time passed with us apart it would become more and more of a chore to make love stay.

We talked some. Updated each other on ourselves. Tammi asked if I was as close with Sammy Davis, Jr. as she'd read in a couple of the Negro newspapers. By way of answering I pulled her to a pay phone, dropped some dimes, dialed Sammy in L.A. He wasn't there. The housekeeper said he was in Chicago, doing shows at the St. Claire. Tammi said it was okay, she believed I knew Sammy, but said it like maybe she didn't. I got the number of Sammy's hotel in Chicago. Dropped more dimes. Dialed. I got put through to his room. After a couple of big hellos passed between a couple of Charlies, Sammy and I rapped for a tick about this and that and nothing in particular. I put Tammi on. Sammy and Tammi rapped for a tick about what a swell guy I was and what a talent I was and how he hoped "us kids" would go places in the near future. Sammy said his good-byes, "babe," and hung up.

I think for the first time Tammi was actually impressed by my growing stature.

We finished eating, sat some more until the time it took to come up with things to say to each other drew longer and outweighed the minutes we spent talking. A final question from her: Would I be in Detroit awhile? I told her I had to get back to New York, then hit the road.

There was nothing more to say.

I paid.

We left.

I walked Tammi back to Motown, walked her inside before I kissed her good-bye—long and deep and hard—for all to see.

I left.

I walked some, finally hailed a cab, and got in and sat down. It was more like I'd slumped down using all of the door to keep me nearly upright.

I felt in the pocket of my coat, felt the jewelry box I had brought with me from New York thinking that this time would be the time I took the ring from it, put it on Tammi's finger, and asked her to be my wife.

But as I sat across from her in the diner, I knew that the ring was nothing but a noose that would slowly, day by day, strangle her voice quiet. Like I'd said to her, I wasn't going to be the guy to do that. I meant it. Same as always, I was doing what was good for her.

I laughed as Tammi had. Yeah, I was doing what was good for her. And I was "good for her-"ing her right out of my life.

"Buddy," the cabbie wanted to know, "where you going?"

FROM DETROIT TO NEW YORK I had to do a stopover in Chicago, change planes. I grabbed some coffee, a sandwich. Waited. While I was doing my waiting, Sammy was doing the Jack Eigen show—a radio talk guy popular around town—plugging his stand at the St. Claire. The show played over a box near my gate. Jack and Sammy went back and forth with the same old showbiz gibble-gabble: what a sensation Sammy was, what it was like to be such a sensation. A little on this bit of gossip, or that—was it true, wasn't it?

I listened without listening.

My thoughts were on Tammi Terrell, with new teeth and hair to go with the new name. Slowly, she was becoming different from me. I wondered if I—same name but with fancier clothes, pricey watches, and an ever-growing appetite for fame—was becoming different to her. And I wondered, too, if you took two people, two people who loved each other, if you took them and separated them so that they didn't grow together, was there no helping that they would eventually grow apart?

In a moment the radio show that I hadn't been minding made me pay attention.

SAMMY: I love Frank and he was the kindest man in the world to me when I lost my eye and wanted to kill myself. But there are many things that he does that there are no excuses for.

JACK: Well, I've heard stories, we've all heard stories about some of his behavior—slugging reporters, the "wrong door" raid—but I put myself in his place. A guy that talented—

SAMMY: Talent is not an excuse for bad manners. I don't care if you're the most talented person in the world. It does not give you the right to step on people and treat them rotten. This is what he does occasionally.

JACK: That's something right there; you talk about the most talented person in the world. Let me ask you this: In your opinion, who is the top singer in the country right now?

SAMMY: Without a doubt, and I say this humbly, but without a doubt, I think I am.

JACK: Really? Bigger than Sinatra?

SAMMY: Oh, yeah.

Well, that was . . . What was that? How could he say all those things? It was true. I knew it was true what he'd said about Frank and his occasional reigns of terror. And as far as who was the better act, anyone who'd ever seen Sammy onstage knew that pound for pound nobody could outperform him. But how—no, *why*? That's what I didn't get. Why go on the radio and throw a dart at Frank, especially when Frank was the kind of guy liable to pick it up and stab you with it.

Yeah, well. It was Sammy's business, not mine.

I started to go back to thinking on Tammi, but they called my plane. I put off my thoughts on her until I got in the air for New York.

CINCINNATI WAS THE PLACE. As good a place as any. Better than most. Just about right for what I did. I didn't arrive there with any ideas in my head, no grand scheme. It's not like I thought: Cincinnati, that's where I'll do it. Maybe what happened happened because of seeing Tammi, of being reminded what, to her, was important. Maybe what happened happened because of the gig itself. I was working the Wildwood. Headlining. Sid had made the trip with me, something he did more and more infrequently. I was beyond the hand-holding stage. Doing the road, for him, was just a change of pace, a break from dealing with the craziness that came from running interference for Fran against the weekly hoops CBS made her jump through despite the high ratings for her program.

Maybe it happened because Cincinnati was nothing. That's not a knock against the city. I mean that strictly in terms of the shows; they were nothing. Nothing out of the ordinary. Nothing special. They contained very little sparkle in my post-Hollywood life. The opener would come out, do some numbers, I'd go on and fill an hour plus. Everyday as the sun chasing the moon. My first three nights I killed. Killing had become easy, same as drawing a shallow breath or falling asleep on a rainy afternoon. And maybe it was all those things jiggered together—the dull routine of performing, the non-importance of the shows themselves, Sid being there—that gave me the push I needed.

Maybe.

Whatever the reason, while I sat backstage that fourth night listening to the opener work his way through his set same as he'd done the night before and before and before, I took out of my coat pocket some dog-eared pages—stationery from the St. Regis hotel. It was an unnecessary gesture. I knew very well what was written on them. I'd read through them many times in the months since I'd been in San Francisco. But looking at the papers served a way of asking myself a question: You sure about this?

The opener went into his closing number.

The pages got folded and put back in my pocket.

Pretty soon I was onstage, the applause from my introduction trailing off. I let it die all the way out, and there I was one more time facing the quiet, familiar gulf between the audiences clapping and the telling of my first joke.

I paused for a second.

No. Not a pause. It was a hesitation. Nerves. Something I hadn't felt in a long while.

I hesitated, and then I said: "Thank you very much. I'm Jackie Mann, and I'm a Negro."

Little bits of laughter.

"I have to tell you that because I wasn't always a Negro. I used to be colored. As I understand it, pretty soon we're going to be calling ourselves black. We keep changing what we call ourselves all the time. I think we're hoping we can confuse white people into liking us: 'I hate them.' 'Who?' 'Those col . . . Ne . . . bla . . . never mind!' You know, things are really getting tense with all this integration. Down in Alabama, Governor Wallace says the only way there's going to be integration is over his dead body. Well, Governor, if you insist. Don't get me wrong, folks. I'm not trying to scare you. I'm not antiwhite, I'm just pro-Negro. I'm so pro-Negro, I won't even pick the cotton out of a bottle of aspirin. I hand the bottle right to the drugstore man, tell him: You put it in there, you take it out!"

People just looked at me, some of them trying to figure out what in the hell I was yammering about. Some of them wanting to know why in the hell I was yammering about race nonsense when they'd paid for jokes. They looked, but they didn't laugh.

Some of them.

And some of them did laugh. Some of them couldn't stop laughing for the world. And not just straight laughter, not the same programmed yowls I'd gotten for years now. This time I got nervous laughter, excited laughter. I got some did-he-really-just-say-that laughter. With each setup I was walking those people to the edge of a cliff, then using a punch line to snatch them back at the very last second. It juiced them, shook them up. It kept them dancing to my tune. I hit a couple of dead spots, yeah, but I was doing this routine as fresh as the crowd was hearing it, and that very fact alone gave me a hot, hard buzz as well. My act was a roller coaster, wild and bone-shakin', and we were all riding it together.

The ride was sweet.

OLY HAUK SHOT spittle bullets from his mouth. They seemed to travel just above the speed of sound, hitting me in the face a split instant before his voice smacked into my ears.

"The fucking . . . kind of goddamn . . ." White-hot rage had short-circuited his communication skills.

Oly was the owner of the Wildwood and chief among the non-laughing bunch who'd caught my show. He didn't like what he'd seen and heard. Didn't like it at all. And the trouble he had talking didn't stop him from trying hard as he could to express his displeasure.

". . . Paying you good goddamn money, and you stand up there and go on with some . . . some race-agitator shit!"

We were in Oly's office. Basement of the club. Even at that I figured any minute we were going to get calls from people a county over complaining about the racket.

"He was good." Sid, getting into things. Concerned about making Oly happy but backing me up. I could tell, in a fashion, he was glad an opportunity had come along for him to do something managerial. Something beside dealing with whatever new "problem" on Fran's show the network suits had imagined up so as to justify their existence. For him, going one-on-one with a club owner was like old times. "All I saw were people laughing."

"You know what I saw?" Oly fired some spit bullets Sid's way. "I saw half of them laughing. Maybe half. I saw the rest of them stone-faced. You know what I heard? The sound of them getting up and walking out, or coming to me wanting their money back, and that's"—at me again—"coming out of your pay!"

Sid started to say something, but Oly cut him off with "He wants to do that race shit, he can do it at an NAACP meeting. Tomorrow night I want jokes. *Good* jokes."

Done with our scolding, sent walking, Sid and I found a diner and got ourselves a couple of sandwiches. I took mine with a Pabst.

Sid was quick with "He doesn't know what he's talking about," trying to put the sound of Oly's voice out of my ears. "I've never seen you so good."

Time, short as it was, had taken the edge off the high I'd felt onstage. My drink dulled it further. "I don't know . . ."

"Jackie, how many times have I seen your act? And you're good, you're funny, but tonight you were . . ." For a second, in his head, Sid relived my show. "You were sharp, you were smart, right on target. When'd you come up with that stuff?"

"San Francisco. Been kicking it around for a while. Maybe I should've kicked it around some more. A couple of years more."

"The world's changing, Jackie. Comics, what they talk about, how they talk, that's changing, too. Tonight you were right where you needed to be."

"Oly isn't wrong. There were as many people hating my stuff as liking it." I caught Sid eyeing my beer. Shouldn't've been drinking in front of him. Shouldn't've been, but I took another sip.

"This time. Next time there could be twice as many loving it."

"Or twice as many walking out. Sid, I've always been . . . I've always been likable onstage." I was spouting the doctrine according to Chet Rosen. "And that's worked for me."

"And maybe what you did tonight'll work better. Jackie, c'mon. You look me in the eye and tell me the laughs you were getting didn't feel good to you."

Yeah, they felt good. A hot-shot straight-to-the-veins good, and my big scare was they were just as poisonous. I thought of Lenny Bruce, sharp and edgy. Sharp and edgy in a tiny basement coffeehouse for a handful of long-haireds. I thought of me, likable. Just

likable, but likable in the best nightclubs in N.Y., L.A., and L.V.
I was not the biggest comic around, not even close, but I had carved
out a place for myself, done it against the odds and in fairly short
order with room to climb higher. Was all that worth tossing away
just to claim I had some edge to me?

Saying what I was feeling: "I just don't know."

"You've got to forget about Oly, forget about . . . Yeah, people
are going to give you grief over that kind of act, but you had—"

"That's what I'm saying; they're going to give me grief and
they're going to stop giving me spots."

"You had a voice tonight. That's what we've been talking about,
having a voice."

I finished off my beer as if some booze in my system might give
me a little perspective.

The waitress gave us our tab, and I flipped out a twenty, told her
to keep the change.

I liked that. I liked being able to toss around money without a
thought to it.

I said: "Yeah, I had a voice, but that doesn't make it a good one."

L.A. AGAIN.

Ciro's again, but different from before. Instead of me in the audience, it was me onstage with Louis Prima and Keely Smith. Opening, but opening at Ciro's. And opening at Ciro's was better than
headlining most joints. It wasn't overflowing the way it was when
Sammy played, but the house was full. It wasn't packed with
celebrity flesh, but more than a few stars shone. Hollywood liked to
go out at night. Hollywood liked to be seen.

The shows were outrageous, Louis shouting his way through a
number as much as singing, Keely just about the only woman
around with lungs enough to keep up with him and the band—big,

brassy, and jive. Opening night was more like going to a party than to work, and there I was with a ringside seat for it all. As I sat and watched and listened, I believed I'd made the right decision post-Cincinnati, to just do what I did best: go up onstage and be likable, then sit back and drink down the nectar of the gods. Why blow it? I had worked hard. I had earned myself an unbelievably good life.

In short order it was going to be unbelievably better.

"LILIAH DAVI WANTS TO MEET YOU."

My jaw just about hit the floor. I don't mean that as an expression. I mean my hole flapped open so wide, the only thing that kept my mouth bone from smacking tile was the flesh of my face.

Second night at Ciro's. After the show. Me in my dressing room and Herman Hover had just stepped through the door to deliver a haymaker.

I asked the only thing I could think to ask. "Liliah Davi? Are you sure?"

"Are you kidding?"

"Well . . ." Well what? As unlikely as it seemed, Liliah Davi wanted to do a drop-by. What was there to even consider? "Well, send her back."

Herman started out, stopped, turned, and shared with me a smile that only men could understand.

Liliah Davi the European actress. *The* European actress, though her acting skills weren't the reason people—men in particular—flooded to her movies. Her breakthrough picture had been some kind of an art-house thing that nobody got. Liiiah made it an international sensation just by standing onscreen and breathing. She did as much by doing as little for the celluloid junk that Hollywood put her in once they brought her stateside. But, good films, bad films; it didn't matter. Put a diamond in the dirt and even a blind man could see it.

As I was flipping through my mental dossier on her, Liliah walked through the door. It was like sex was walking into the room. She was five foot seven inches of curves and kisses with a smile for a kicker that was pure sin. Dark hair, dark eyes, Perm-A-Tan skin. She wore a beautiful black evening gown. Taffeta, maybe. Dior. Givenchy, probably. Strapless. It was seemingly held to her body by the same sexual attraction that gravitated everything else in the known universe her way. For a capper, a slit ran the garment from floor to thigh that gave reality a running start on imagination.

"Mr. Mann?" Her voice rode her accent the way a flute rides a tune. She held out a hand—gloved to above the elbow—the way you see royalty do it, wrist bent, back side up and finger diving for the floor.

All I knew about greeting chicks on her level was what I'd seen in the movies. "Miss Davi." I took her hand, kissed it doing my best Cary Grant bits. "It's a pleasure."

"The pleasure is mine."

I waited for her to take her hand back.

She didn't.

I said to her: "I saw your last picture. You were fabulous."

"Some people say that I cannot act."

There was bait on that line. If she'd been just another movieland bimbo, I'd have distracted her with shiny words. But I was pretty sure this one was fishing around trying to find out if I'd blow her smoke or tell her true.

"I'm not sure it's strictly acting, but what you do you do better than anyone alive."

Her lips made a gesture—they parted slightly. They bent upward—but what you'd call it, I don't know.

She said: "I enjoyed your performance this evening. You were quite *sharming*."

"Really?"

"What I could understand I thought amusing." A slight pause. "But truly I enjoyed watching you."

I could feel beads of perspiration ripening on my forehead, and I willed them to stop. I didn't know for sure, but I was pretty certain that gorgeous stars weren't impressed by sweaty comics.

"Will you be long in Los Angeles?" she wanted to know.

"Just pretty much this week, with the show."

"Oh."

A beat.

Liliah said: "I won't keep you. I'm sure you are quite busy. I only wanted to tell you how much I enjoyed you."

I don't recall Liliah taking her hand from mine as much as I remember my grasp never having felt quite as empty as when I no longer held it.

"I will see you," she said as she floated for the door, the comment as inscrutable as the bat of her eyes that went with it.

And then she was gone.

I poured myself a glass of water and drank it down. I drank another.

I MADE A DISTRACTED WALK from Ciro's back to the Sunset Colonial. I was tired and I was preoccupied, my head rerunning the scene of me meeting Liliah over and over again. I sort of recall talking with Doary, who was cleaning, for a moment—her asking about the show and me telling her something or other but not really paying her much attention. Then I was upstairs, in my bed, wanting desperately to sleep but unable to do so. Liliah kept me awake.

It wasn't that I was obsessing on her. I never thought for a moment I could mean anything to her other than a good night's laugh. It was more that I was thinking about how utterly incredible it was to even meet such a woman. It wasn't that long ago I was sitting and watching her movies or slowing down at the newsstand when I saw a fluff rag with her picture on the cover, same as every other man in America. Now, unlike most men in America, I'd actually looked her in the eye, held her hand, and traded quips. I pinned a medal on my chest, thinking: I bet Lenny Bruce has never done that.

The phone rang. I'm not sure if it rang me awake from sleep or a daydream. I jumped, anxious, not startled. For one quick moment, for whatever insane reason, I thought it might be Liliah calling me.

"Jackie . . . oh, my God, where have you . . ."

It was the most moan-ful sounding voice I'd ever heard, filled with so much despair, I almost didn't recognize it.

"Sammy?"

"Why didn't you call me?"

"Call you? I didn't know—"

"I left messages. You didn't get—"

"I was doing my show. I came back here, came right up to my—"

"You've got to come over. Will you come over? Please?"

"What time is it?"

"Jackie, please." Some sobbing, then: "I've got to talk to you. I need your help."

My help? He needed my help? The idea of it was crazy, but how could I say no? I got the address, hung up. I looked at the clock. Five forty-three.

Twenty minutes later and I was navigating my rental toward Sammy Davis, Jr.'s home.

≈

SAMMY LIVED IN THE HILLS. The Hollywood Hills. The formerly all-white Hollywood Hills. Liberal Tinseltown talked a good game, was all for putting a better world up onscreen, but same as most uni-colored enclaves, they weren't about to do any handstands and tuba playing over a black guy moving in next door. Then Mr. Entertainment showed up. When Sammy Davis, Jr. decides to set up shop on your block, there isn't much stopping him. That was the kind of juice he had.

I pulled up into the drive and went for the door, but before I could ring or knock, it opened. It was Sammy, processed hair messed, a growth of beard, and looking as though he hadn't known sleep for a week.

Sammy said nothing. He just opened the door, then shuffled back into the house zombie-style. I followed him into a living room, big as my whole place back in New York, where he fell into a couch.

I didn't know what to say, where to start. "Are you . . . Is everything—"

"He's trying to kill me."

I did some quick looking around with a little ducking added in. I didn't need to haul myself from bed and drive all the way up into the Hills just to get my life ended.

Sammy said again: "He's trying to kill me," then added, "Frank's trying to kill me."

"Frank Costello?"

"Sinatra. Francis wants my hide."

"Why? What did you—"

"I didn't do anything. I didn't . . . A few months ago I was on the radio in Chicago—"

"The Jack Eigen show. Yeah, I heard. What were you thinking?"

Sammy took my words as well as a bullet. Going fetal on me: "You, too? Oh, baby, I'm dead."

"No, no, it wasn't that bad," I lied. "I didn't think it was that bad."

"Frank did. He heard about it and the man blew his stack. He put the word out: Nobody hire Smoky. I'm getting deals canceled, bookings canceled. He had me thrown out of a movie. I had a contract, Jackie, and he had me thrown out!"

"Do you want a drink?" I asked, not knowing what other remedy to offer and remembering how good some booze made me feel in my time of trouble. "How about a drink?"

"Oh, God. What am I going to do?" Sammy keeled over a little more, buried his face in a pillow.

I had to sit down. The situation was going to require some serious attention, and nothing in my life I'd ever seen, heard, or done had ever prepped me for dealing with star-level meltdowns.

"Look, Sammy, you're one of the biggest acts there is. Frank, yeah, he can cause you some trouble, but he can't take away everything."

Lifting his head up from the pillow: "Baby, if you think that, then you don't know the man. It's Frank's world. We just live in it." Back to the pillow his head went.

I offered the obvious: "Why don't you talk to him?"

"I've tried. He won't return my calls; he won't see me. He was playing the Fontainebleau when I was at the Eden Roc. I went over, and he wouldn't even take the stage until I was out of the hotel." Again, for emphasis: "He—wouldn't—even—take—the—stage."

"I don't . . . Sure, he's a little upset now, but he's not going to—"

"He's doing a picture."

"He's—"

"He's doing a picture and everybody's in it."

"What do you mean, everybody?"

"Dino, Joey, Angie, Peter—"

"Lawford? But he—"

"He hates Lawford, but he's in. Everybody's in, and I'm going to be out if things don't get patched up."

"Well, can't you have someone to talk to Frank for you? Maybe Dean—"

"Dean doesn't stick out his neck to shave it. Angie's got more spine than Lawford, but Frank doesn't care what a dame's got to say. Joey's lucky to be around . . ."

Real suddenly it was dawning on me what I was doing in the Hollywood Hills first thing in the morning.

"Sammy—"

"Please, Jackie . . ." Lifting himself up now but still too destitute to stand, Sammy did his pleading from where he sat. "There's no one else."

"Me? I'm supposed to go to Frank Sinatra and . . . I'm not—"

"He's soft for you. He likes you."

"Yeah, but I'm . . . I'm . . ." As much as I hated to say it, the reality was "I'm nobody."

"Jackie . . ." A lot was welling up inside Sammy. A lot of imploring and beseeching concerning the desperation of the situation. There was a lot of hurt and a lot of need, and there was a whole lot of fear of a man who was looking at everything he'd ever built up, everything he ever held dear . . . There was the fear of a man looking at his whole life about to come crumbling down around him, smashed to bits because of one moment's indiscretion. And all of that came crying from him in one single word: "Please."

I thought of that day in Chicago. I thought of me in the airport listening to Sammy on the radio and thinking: Oh, well. It's his business, not mine. If I'd known then what I know now . . .

I said: "All right."

———

SINATRA WAS IN PALM SPRINGS. He had a place out there. Sammy gave me the number and, later, after working up some courage, I called. Jilly answered, and I was glad for it. I told him I wanted to speak to Frank, hoping he wouldn't be around. I could tell Sammy I called, I tried, but Frank wasn't—

Jilly told me to hold on, went away from the phone, came back, said: "Frank says sure, c'mon out."

"But I—"

Jilly started feeding me directions.

A face-to-face wasn't what I had bargained for. But I knew well enough that once you got an invite from the Chairman there was no declining it. I wrote down Jilly's directions, got in my car, and headed for the desert.

Close to three hours of driving got me to Frank's place, which wasn't a place. It was a compound—a ranch house in the middle of a few acres on Wonder Palms Road just off the Tamarisk Country Club. Tennis court, pool, a couple of guest cabins ringed with cactus and ocotillo and prickly pear; it was the desert outpost of some swinging missionary.

I parked, went for what I thought was the front door. The welcome mat read: GO AWAY.

Nice.

I rang the bell.

The desert was hot, the air was baked sandpaper rubbing at you, rubbing at you.

A second ring of the doorbell made Jilly eventually appear.

"Hey, Jackie," he said but said flat, not happy to see me, but was, like a couple of months of winter, resigned to my being around. Jilly's sole occupation in life was being Frank's friend. I got the feeling he didn't much care for other people intruding on his work. "C'mon back and say hey to Frank."

Jilly led and I followed. The house was mostly decorated with memorabilia—posters of Frank's movies. Frank's gold records, pictures of Frank with this or that famous person. In fact, the overriding motif was Frank. If most men's homes were their castles, Frank's was a temple to himself. It was that, and it was orange. Frank loved his orange.

"Orange is the happiest color," he said as he welcomed me into his living room. "I never get tired of it."

I could tell. He was wearing an orange sport shirt with brown pants. I guess they went together. Sort of.

"What are you drinking?" Frank asked.

I said: "It's a little early for me."

Dismissing that: "It's never too early to be somebody. Jilly, put some Jack over ice for Charlie."

Jilly did as told.

I stepped to some glass panes that ran from ceiling to floor and looked out over the pool and off into the desert. "It's a beautiful place you've got."

"I dig the desert. Hot, dry, sun cooks it all day . . . Makes the land tough. Makes everything that lives out there tough. You know what lives in the desert?"

"What lives in the desert?"

"Stuff that won't die."

The three of us gave the thought a moment to marinate.

Jilly handed me my drink.

Frank wanted to know: "How the shows going?"

"Good. Good so far. In fact, I really shouldn't stay long. I've got to make the show tonight."

"Well, I'm glad you could come out and visit. This place is for my friends. You're a friend now. Friends are always welcome. Ain't that right, Jilly?"

Jilly made some kind of noise.

"I appreciate that. I appreciate your time, and you looking out for me. . . ." How did I go into what I had to get into? There was no smooth way. I just started talking and hoped I'd stumble to a point same as I stumbled into this situation. "Friendship is really, really important. I know you know that. A friend of yours is a friend forever. And the reason I bring that up is I saw . . . I was talking to Sammy—"

One word. One word out of my mouth and Frank went as red as the walls were orange. "That lousy son of a bitch! That crumb. Who the hell does he think he is, bad-mouthin' me?"

I sputtered but said nothing, just wanted to stay out of the way of the lava flow. Remembering *the party,* I moved away from the plate windows.

"Bad enough he's got to talk me down on the radio, but he does it in Chicago. Chicago!"

"You got friends in Chicago," Jilly piped in, tossing gas on the fire.

"I got a lot of friends in Chicago, and he gets on the air and humiliates me? And after what I done for him. That backstabbin' dirty nigger," he spat without regard to me.

I didn't think, I didn't believe, that Frank had suddenly gone Klan. In that moment that word was for Sammy alone. Frank just wanted to hurt and was willing to use all the weapons at hand.

"Thinks he's big? Thinks he's bigger than me? I'll crush him." He looked dead at me. "I'll smash any crumb that crosses me."

Jilly smiled.

The eruption was subsiding. If I was going to say anything, there was no better opportunity.

"Well, he asked for it."

That was a little left turn Frank wasn't expecting from me. "You think so?"

"Even if he did believe that nonsense"—I hit nonsense hard—"about him being a bigger act than you—and I know in his heart he doesn't believe it—no, he's got no business going on the radio and spilling his guts."

"No. No, he don't. See, you get it, Jackie." To Jilly: "See how Jackie gets it?"

Jilly made some kind of noise.

"That crumby kike screwed up, and now I got to teach him somethin'."

I said slowly, loading in a lot of doubt: ". . . I guess."

What I said, how I said it, it got Frank's attention. "What do you mean 'you guess'?"

"Oh, I'm agreeing with you. You could crush Sammy. I know

you could, he knows it. Everybody knows it. It's just too bad you'll give them ammunition."

Frank looked from me to Jilly and back to me. "Ammunition? What are you talkin' about? Who the hell is *them*?"

The way I figured it, there was no way to talk, argue, logic, or reason Frank into forgiveness. The only tool big enough to move a star Sinatra's size was ego.

"Them. The press, the gossip rags. Louella and Dorothy."

That struck bone. "Kilgallen? That goddamn chinless wonder."

"Well, that's what I'm saying. Day and night they're sharpening pencils for you. They're not going to write it up as Sammy getting what Sammy's asking for. The headline's going to read: Sinatra crushes guy for sport. Like I said, you're giving them ammunition."

"What's he supposed to do?" Jilly wanted to know.

"Well . . ." I took a pause, played as if the idea I was working toward was just then popping into my head. "You could do what nobody would expect you to do. You could forgive Sammy. I mean, after what he did, you forgive him, what are people going to say but 'Now, that Frank, there's a decent guy. There's a guy who's got some heart.' You do the right thing, and you look good doing it. Just let the chinless wonder try to write something bad about you then."

Frank wasted not a tick in saying: "You're shining me, kid."

He'd seen right through me. Maybe he had an ego that went with his stature, but it wasn't so big that it blinded him. Either that, or I was just too damn obvious.

I felt like the ax was starting to fall and it wasn't just Sammy's head that was going to roll.

I wound up my last pitch. "Then you want to know why you should forgive him? Because he's your friend. Because no matter what he said, he's the same guy you dropped everything for and drove out to sit with after his smash-up and he got his eye taken out.

You should forgive him because he loves and worships you. Yeah, *worships* you. He knows he owes you everything. He knows if it weren't for you, he'd be nothing, just another Negro kid out dancing for his lunch money. He's one of the most talented guys on the planet, and he's always—*always*—going to be living in your shadow. If things were flipped, if you had all that weight crushing down on you, don't you think just once you might go a little crazy, say something just a little stupid?"

Jesus.

Jesus Christ. If Sammy knew the things I was saying he'd probably take Frank's death sentence over the picture I was painting of him: a luckless no-talent who was only earning a living because someone else once took pity on him. But this wasn't just about saving Sammy anymore. He had put us in the same boat and I wasn't about to go down with him.

Following my little speech, nothing happened. Frank didn't react one way or another. He just stood where he was, looking out into the desert, every now and again taking in more of his drink.

Finally: "Have a good show tonight, Jackie."

And he was done with me. I set down my otherwise untouched glass of Jack Daniel's and headed for the door. Jilly made no move to show me out.

I got in my car and shy of three hours later arrived back in Los Angeles. With just enough time to shower and shave, I made it to Ciro's. Louis and Keely put on a hell of a show, but unlike the previous nights, it didn't feel like a party.

AT SOME POINT during the week I realized I was thinking about Liliah Davi. I was thinking about Liliah Davi more than most guys normally did. What started with me replaying our meeting evolved into me obsessing on it. I started breaking down our encounter, analyzing the event same as a pulp detective sifts through a crime scene: She came to meet me. She wanted to meet me. *Wanted,* Herman had said. She was alone when she came meet me, no guy escorting her. Her hand in my hand. She let her hand linger in my hand. Her dialogue: "I enjoyed watching you." Not *I enjoyed your show.* "I enjoyed watching you."

Enjoyed.

Enjoyed watching *you.*

She'd asked me how long I would be in L.A. Did she want to know because . . . Did she want to know . . . "I will see you," she had left me with, not . . .

Two minutes. Me and her talking in my dressing room amounted to two minutes' time. If even. But there wasn't a moment of those two minutes I didn't process second by second by second, first convincing myself of one thing, then telling me I was crazy for getting ideas in the first place. I didn't know what to make of the thoughts jumping around in my brain box. And I didn't know what to do about them. But no matter how the mental coins I flipped came up, the truth was, some opportunities come once in a lifetime. You do something about them or you watch them fade into the past.

"HALLO?" Liliah's voice was Bacallesque, and I swear I could feel the warmth of her breath even over the phone.

". . . Miss Davi, it's Jackie Mann."

Again, "Hallo." This time a statement, not a question.

"I'm sorry to . . . I hope you don't mind me calling you, but I wondered—and I got your number from Herman, by the way. Herman Hover."

Nothing was said to that.

"He said he didn't think . . . He thought it would be all right. To call. I wanted to know, uh, I'm sure you're very busy, but if you, maybe, wanted to have dinner som—"

"What time?"

"Tonight?"

"What time?"

I'd wished for it. Sure I had. Spent time fantasizing on it. But I never once figured Liliah'd really say yes, so I hadn't planned things beyond her giving me a no and hanging up. I picked a time.

"Seven o'clock? I hope that's not too early, but I have to make the show la—"

"Where?"

The first classy joint that popped into my head was "Chasen's."

"I will see you there, Jackie."

She hung up. No small talk, no chitchat. Just a ready okay to my request for a date.

I hung on her good-bye, on her speaking my name. Liliah's accent made Jackie come off as *Zhaqué*.

A good twenty seconds later I laid the phone back on the cradle.

CHASEN'S. SEVEN FORTY-THREE. Liliah and I at a table. All eyes on us. Actually, all eyes on her, and by default on me as well. About half the crowd wondering: Who's this lucky stiff sitting with Liliah Davi? The other half wanting to know: Why's Liliah Davi eating with a Negro?

She wore a gown, another gown—white with sparkles and a falle—that was two-thirds silk and one-third cleavage. Upon arriving at the restaurant, she had flowed through the room as effortlessly as wine from a bottle, her every movement executed with a certain ease. There was an economy to everything she did—her gestures, her expressions. She gave you very little, leaving you wanting so much more. She was style and grace and sophistication. She was the embodiment of allure. She was sexuality personified. So close to perfect, at times the woman seemed almost fabricated. Not an act of birth, a work of art—a living, breathing Vargas girl. But for all that made her artificial, Liliah had a way of engaging that made her more than human. When I talked to her, she looked at me, not over, around, or past me, trying to see and be seen by the rest of the Hollywood horde downing their dinners. She had a way of listening that made me feel as though I were being *listened to*. When I was with her she had a way of making me feel as though I should be with her, not that I was just fortunate to be near her.

Over our meal we talked. She told me about the picture she was doing at Columbia, this story or that about her director, her costar, one about Harry Cohn throwing a tantrum over some little thing that had to do more with getting attention than getting what he wanted. Liliah sounded bored with it all, bored with show business like the whole of it was a crazy children's game she was playing only for lack of anything better to do.

"Oh, well," she said, done talking about Hollywood, waving a hand once in the air, shooing away the subject. "So, tell me what it is you want, *Zhaqué*."

I must have been staring at her and wasn't sure if that had prompted the question. "From you?" I asked, pulling myself from her flame.

"From life."

"I don't know."

"Everyone wants something."

"What do you want?"

A slight shake of her head. "That is a question, not an answer. But I will tell you. I want to be happy."

"That's it?"

"What else is there? All the time, I want to be happy. If something makes me unhappy, I dismiss it from my life." With the back of her hand she pushed away her plate of cooling food, demonstrating the ease in application of her philosophy. "It is that simple." Elbows on the table, she wove a bridge with her fingers, rested her chin on it. "And you, *Zhaqué*? What is it you want?"

I tried to make my goal sound as simple as hers. "I want to be famous."

"And what does that mean, being famous? What does that mean to you?"

"It means you've made it. It means you're somebody, a star."

"Why do you want that?"

I laughed. "You're an international celebrity and you have to ask?"

Liliah didn't see the funny. "We are not discussing me. What does being famous mean to you?"

"It means . . . it means you don't have to just want things. You can get what you want."

"You cannot get the things you want now?"

"You kidding? When you're a Negro?"

"I don't know. I am not Negro."

"I'll tell you: When you're a Negro, there isn't much you can get except a shove to the ground and a kick to the gut."

Liliah's head lifted from her fingers. She angled it to one side as she tried to gain perspective on me.

She said: "You wanted to have dinner with me. You accomplished that."

"To be honest, I don't know how. Forget that I'm Negro. I'm sure there must be plenty of guys who want to go out with you."

"Many, many men want to be with me."

That sank me a little. ". . . So, I don't know, I mean, I'm thankful, but I don't know why you'd waste time with—"

"Because you made the phone call, *Zhaqué.* Many men want to be with me. Most are too frightened to try." Then, bluntly: "Being famous, fame: It is not something you can touch. It is nothing you can hold on to. It is not real. What does not exist cannot make you happy, *Zhaqué.* So I think you worry about the wrong things, which tells me you have nothing to worry about at all."

At first I thought she was trying to be rough on me, but then Liliah gave a smile. A rich, delicious smile that forced my lips into a matching one. This woman. This woman was the A-bomb of women—a force undeniable. I felt the dinner becoming more than a once-off episode to be recounted to "the boys" in the locker room like a fishing story. I felt as if I'd caught a ride on a runaway train moving too fast for me to jump off. More than that. I didn't want to.

The hour of the show was approaching and I secretly cussed it for killing the evening. But as we waited at the valet, Liliah asked if I would mind if she came with me to Ciro's.

Would I mind?

I yessed the idea. Fast. She told the valet to leave her car, that she would pick it up later.

I put Liliah into the passenger side of my rental, happy I'd sprung for a Caddy, then got myself behind the wheel. As I put the car in gear, she wrapped her arms around mine. There was nothing sexual in the way she held me, but at the same time her grasp was empty of innocence. Everything she did was a kaleidoscope. You saw what you wanted to see. You felt what you wanted to feel.

I felt desire.

AFTER THE SHOW. Liliah sat backstage in my dressing room as a few celebs came around to congratulate me. Maybe they truly wanted to wish me well. Probably they'd heard Liliah Davi was in the house and just wanted to ogle her.

Things slowed down. Joint empty except for staff, we had a couple of drinks at the bar before Herman closed up. Finally, Liliah said she was tired and I took that to mean the night was over. We got in my car and I started for Chasen's. Liliah told me not to bother. The restaurant would be closed by that hour. She'd send someone for her car in the morning. Per her directions, I headed on Beverly to Wilshire, then for Santa Monica. Her home.

Her home was near the beach. Nice. Not too big. Nothing about it screamed movie goddess. It just said, said quietly, Here's a woman who liked to be near the water, away from Hollywood, and able to watch the sun set.

I pulled into the driveway.

Liliah said: "Thank you for sharing your company."

"Are you kidding? I had a great time. Really."

"Do you have a girl?" She couldn't have been more plain about things if she was asking me if I owned a goldfish.

I couldn't have been more plain in my answer. "She's in Detroit. She wants to be a singer." I modified that. "She is a singer."

"And you have not seen her in some time?"

"We both . . . we work a lot. No."

"But you love her?"

"Yes."

With her precise motions that over the evening I had become accustomed to, Liliah took a platinum case from her purse. From the case she took a cigarette that she held before her. "Light me."

". . . I don't have matches."

A lighter, platinum like her case, was suddenly in her hand. And then it was in mine.

I flicked it hot, held it up, and through the cigarette Liliah sucked the flame. She blew smoke. And then she leaned to me. She gave me a lingering kiss, the dampness of which soaked through my lips, through my body, like an alcohol. The drunkening affect was the same.

She slipped from the car for her house.

Her lighter still in hand, I called to her. "Miss Davi . . ."

Without turning back she went inside.

I looked at the lighter I held. It wasn't a lighter. It was an invitation. It was a key that would open the door behind which Liliah Davi had just disappeared. All I had to do was use it.

I checked my watch. It was past two-thirty. It was past five-thirty in Detroit. Tammi would be sleeping.

I headed the Caddy east for the Sunset Colonial.

Along the drive I told myself how proud I was of me for doing right by Tammi. I congratulated myself on being honorable, which, even though Tammi would never know of my temptation, felt better and carried more satisfaction than I could ever get out of a couple of hours with another woman. Even if the other woman was one of the most sensational women alive. And all the while I was telling myself such things, I was squeezing Liliah's lighter so hard that the metal of it was tattooing the flesh of my palm.

I barely made West L.A. before turning around, heading again for Santa Monica.

When I arrived back at Liliah's house, before I could ring the bell, she opened the door—still wearing her gown. Hair and makeup still perfect, as if morning, noon, and night she remained at full glamour—in expectation of me, as if what was going on was inevitable. I resented her that, her knowing the power of her own sexuality. But I didn't resent it so much that I could do anything other than keep walking for her. When I reached Liliah I stopped. I tried to explain, to rationalize why I had returned as much for myself as for her.

I didn't even get a good start before she said: "What happens between the two of us has nothing to do with love. It has to do with a man and a woman, and what happens with a man and a woman when they are alone together."

Liliah had a near-fantastic ability to break everything down to its simplest elements. There was no fighting her. There was no refusing her. I didn't want to try.

"You could fool somebody with those looks," I said. "You are a thinker."

"And does that make me dangerous?"

"Very."

She smiled. "Sex without danger is just sex, and danger without sex is merely dangerous."

If I even began to understand that . . . "What?"

Liliah took me by the hand, led me inside her house. She explained all.

And then she explained it all again.

———

SAMMY CALLED. He told me that Jilly had called and told him to call Frank so he'd called Frank and the two talked. Talked about this and that and whatever else stars talk about. What they didn't talk about was the Jack Eigen show and Sammy's brutal excommunication from the church of Sinatra. But Sammy knew that the fact that they talked without talking about all that had happened was Frank's way of saying that all that had happened was over and through and in the past.

For whatever I'd done to smooth things, Sammy told me: "Thanks."

For whatever I'd done.

What had I done? I'd kept myself in good standing with the biggest celebrity on the planet. And all that was required was selling Sammy out.

part VI

*D*ale Buis and Chester Ovnand got killed.

When people die, when their lives are ended violently, it's sad and tragic. But as sad as it is, as tragic as it is, the reality of it is that in a world full of people, two of them dying really isn't any big thing.

Most times.

Except Dale Buis and Chester Ovnand were Americans. And Dale Buis and Chester Ovnand were in the military. And they were military advisers. And Major Dale Buis and Sergeant Chester Ovnand were killed by communist guerrillas in Bienhoa.

Bienhoa was in Vietnam.

The president didn't care for American military advisers getting killed, so he sent over more advisers same as the next president, who would send advisers and soldiers, and the next president, who would send more soldiers and some ships and planes and tanks after something that may or may not have happened in the Tonkin Gulf, and the next president, who would send more soldiers and more ships and more planes and more tanks and send them to a couple of other countries as well until the next president finally said: "There, that's it. That's enough. It's over."

And in between all that time the American public would go from not thinking about what was going on over there, to supporting what was going on over there, to disliking what was going on over there, to publicly hating what was going on over there. And what was going on over there—the Vietnam War— would rage in the papers, and then in the living rooms, and finally out on the American streets. And while the war got fought over there, its meaning and significance got fought out over here between the young and old, black and white, the establishment and the counterculture, vocal dissidents and the silent majority. This country would be torn apart. Vietnam would be rejoined. The North Vietnamese would lose some 600,000 soldiers. We lost 57,939.

And ourselves.

February of 1960 to December of 1961

I n early 1960 Eisenhower, Khrushchev, and de Gaulle had a summit conference in Paris. In the high heat of the cold war, after the U2 incident, the summit took on significant proportions. It was all anyone was talking about, all the news.

Frank Sinatra didn't dig not being the news even if the news that upstaged him was something as minorly important as world peace. So Frank decided he was going to have a summit of his own, a summit conference of cool. The ambassadors: Martin, Lawford, Bishop, and a reinstated Sammy Davis.

Then and now the uninitiated would call them the Rat Pack or the Clan. Frank hated both names—hated Rat Pack because Humphrey Bogart used to have a collection of friends who ran under that moniker. Frank loved Bogart. Frank wasn't trying to imitate Bogart. And race-tolerant Sinatra didn't care for the Clan for obvious reasons. To Frank, the group, like the event that gathered them, like the top of a mountain so few could climb, would be The Summit.

So Frank gathered his boys, a few broads, and headed out to Las Vegas to shoot a movie—*Ocean's Eleven*. But the movie just gave them something to do during the day. The Summit itself took place at night in the Copa Room at the Sands when all five would hit the stage. It wasn't just a show, it was a happening. With Bishop and Lawford thrown in out of pity, Frank, Sammy, and Dean, the biggest acts of their day in their element—a city of gin and sin—were enough to not only sell out the Copa but to sell out the entire burg. There wasn't a room to be had anywhere. Every casino was stuffed to capacity with people hoping, wishing, praying they might be among the lucky to catch the Lords of Cool. They had a better chance of sitting in with Eisenhower, Khrushchev, and de Gaulle.

The line formed behind the high rollers who got their way for dropping heavy at the tables, and even they were to the rear of the "special guests," showbiz buddies and Mafia cronies who came in daily chartered plane–style. At a mere $5.95 The Summit was the most priceless ticket in town. No one wanted to miss it.

I saw it all.

For the three weeks that The Summit was in session, I was the opening act, and for all my time in lousy little clubs, it was my toughest gig in years. I wasn't so much a comic as I was a delaying tactic. I would go up onstage and try to tell jokes while stragglers filed into the Copa Room, while the management hunted down one more chair to seat one more guest. I would kill time any way I could until the boys, who spent the day working—if you call doing one take of every scene work—and the evening napping, had roused themselves enough to grace the fans with their presence.

And eventually they would. Sort of. The shows were poor. Qualitywise, they wouldn't much hold up to a high school amateur night. Mostly they consisted of Frank and his crew—tired, hung over—mixing drinks from a cocktail cart, swapping jokes that only they seemed to get, talking about broads, dames, and dolls, and trampling to death any attempt by one of the others to actually do a serious number in its entirety . . . And the audience loved it. The stars, the thugs, the chosen few, were happy to pay their money to sit and swill and watch these icons get high on a mix of booze, fame, and the love of women. Who wouldn't want to drink up some of that? In a changing world, as the blitzkrieg of civil rights and Vietnam and the youth movement began raining their chaos across the American landscape, the sight of middle-aged men having frat-boy fun and saluting the martini and lounge music values that middle-brow USAville held dear was some-how reassuring. The Summit was counter-counterculture. It was the last party, the nightcap of a generation, and a good time to be had by all.

By almost all.

Sammy Davis, Jr. had come to Vegas to work. The man loved a good time as much as anyone—more than most—but while he was onstage he was strictly Mr. Entertainment. The horsing around was all right, but he actually wanted to perform, to sing or dance or do some impressions. He wanted to do something—anything—without having at least one of the others toss a pratfall into the middle of it. But all that clowning around was just injury to insult. The real nastiness were the jokes. The "smile so we can see you, Sammy" jokes. The "what's the matter, you got watermelon in your mouth?" jokes. And the big joke, the showstopper—Dino picking up Sammy, announcing: "I'd like to thank the N-double-A-C-P for this award." Oh, the howls that followed that one. Night after night, the same bits that were supposed to be funny because the guys who were telling them were "progressive." And night after night, upon hearing the punch lines, Sammy would grin and laugh and stomp his feet like he was just about to bust from the rib-splitting hilarity of a racial slur well told.

Onstage.

But while one of the other cats was trying, not hard but trying, to get through a solo, Sammy would go backstage and pour himself into a lonely folding chair. Out of the spotlight, away from the people, he would hunch and droop, all the energy and life that he carried for his audience wrung from his body. I would watch him as he sat, just sat, looking so very tired—beat down with a weariness that took a guy a lifetime to stockpile. A lifetime of trying to please and appease, of living in the shadow of a legend while day by day by year climbing a mountain and reaching the top, only to find out no matter how much *they* pay to see you, no matter how hard *they* clap for you, *they* are still going to want to know, in truth and in jest: "If I hug you, is that going to rub off on me?"

He was such a star. He had all that a person could want. What could it matter to him what *they* thought? But it did matter. To him it mattered more than any other thing in the world—the money or the fame or the lust of women of every color.

Looking at Sammy, I promised myself when I got to where he was I would stop trying to make people love me. I'd stop caring if they did.

And then there would come a cue and Sammy would bolt up, reinvigorated by an unquenchable desire to be before a crowd, and burst back onstage. And through the curtain I could hear a thunder of applause for any of the one thousand ways that only he knew how to entertain.

AFTER THE SHOWS the party went private, in one of the Sands suites that was strictly off-limits to anyone who wasn't FOF, or at least sixty percent legs and forty percent chest. It was a room filled with smoke and vacant smiles. It's where stars mingled with mobsters and politicians, and an election was bought and paid for in cash. One million, literally, in the bag. It's where the entertaining wasn't done by the entertainers but by starlets, and dolls who wanted to be starlets, and chorus girls who just wanted to get noticed and by plain old prostitutes lubed with liquor and ready for a little hey-hey.

I'd be lying if I said on occasions I wasn't part of all that. I was. But most times I wasn't. Not that I wasn't up for some ring-a-ding-ding, but I already had a girl. And I had a girl on the side. I had Liliah.

When I first called and invited her out to The Summit, she was an incalculable as ever. Maybe she'd come. Maybe she wouldn't. If she felt like it, she might. Or even if she didn't, perhaps she would.

I hated myself on the first day of the show when all I did was vex over her arrival or non-arrival, when I wouldn't leave the room for fear of missing the call from the lobby from her that never came. I hated myself for thinking that me and her could have anything more than a once-only fling. I despised myself for even letting Liliah get her hands in my head when I was truthfully so very much in love with Tammi.

Then, from up onstage, in the middle of wrestling a herd of people into an audience, I caught sight of her sitting front row and everything else I'd been feeling and thinking got shoved aside by desire.

Between pictures, Liliah had some free time and, despite her change-a-minute nature, decided on spending it with me. Nearly all of it. In that first week of shows she was front and center every night and the first face I saw every morning. In between, Liliah introduced me to the tables and got no trouble about it from the roughnecks who previously wanted to strong-arm me toward the nearest door. During the run of The Summit the color lines in Vegas got scratched out, even if just temporarily. There was too much dark-skinned talent in town for the show—Nat King Cole, Lena Horne, Harry Belafonte—for the management to be picky about who was spreading money around the pit. And with Frank on the premises, no one wanted to chance getting caught tossing around any Jim Crow jazz. I strolled the casino floor openly and freely, as I had always wanted, and better than I had ever dreamed. I strolled the casino floor with Liliah Davi wrapped around my arm.

The first thing I learned, the first thing she taught me, was the last and only game I had ever played: roulette.

"The simplest of games," Liliah said as I stared at the thirty-six numbers, the zero, and double zero, bordered with the outside bets. "*Zhust* play the action numbers."

"What are those?"

"Ten through fifteen, and thirty-three. They are spread evenly along the wheel."

"What difference does that make? I mean, the odds are still the same, right?"

The only answer my question got was Liliah discarding a couple of hundred bucks onto the table. "Black," she said, and the dealer swapped the bills for two hundred-dollar chips. Those got placed, by Liliah, on twenty-three, red.

"Black inside!" the dealer called.

"What about the action numbers?" I asked.

Liliah held up a cigarette before her. "Light me."

With her lighter, which I still had, I did as asked.

The dealer spun the ball.

A tap on my shoulder. I turned. Jack Entratter.

"Jackie!" His arm was around me long-lost-buddy-style. "How you been, kid?"

"Good. I've been real—"

The ball dropped.

The dealer called: "Seventeen, black."

Chips got scooped in. Some bets got paid out.

Liliah let another couple of hundred float down to the table.

Looking at me, Jack tilted his head a little toward her.

"Liliah, I'd like you to meet Jack Entratter. He runs the place."

Liliah smiled, nodded. "Hallo." Her attention got returned to her betting.

"Black inside!"

"Well, listen, Jackie, if there's anything you need, anything at all, you just let me know," Jack said to me but for Liliah's benefit. "I'll take care of it personally."

If Liliah heard him, it didn't show.

"You, uh, you enjoy yourself." Feelings hurt, Jack slipped back into the crowd of people who wandered the floor, clutching money, just looking for a good spot to lose it.

I looked back to the table as the ball dropped.

"Double zero, green."

Chips got scooped in. Some bets got paid out.

"In Europe, in the casinos, they have only one zero on the wheel," Liliah sighed. "That's all right, having one zero. Zero is a number. Everything begins at zero, yes? Not positive or negative, good or bad. It is *zhust* there.

"But Las Vegas is different, *Zhaqué*. Las Vegas has double zero. Why is that? Double zero is not a number. What is two times nothing? More nothing. You cannot have more nothing. To be zero is as nothing as something can be."

Liliah was in rare form, as far beyond my cognizability as ever.

Rushing to Lady Las Vegas's defense, I gave the only response I could come up with on the quick. "Double zero, that's just . . . that's the edge. You know, the house has got to have an edge. One more chance they've got to win and you've got to lose."

Liliah took herself a look around the casino, all the people scurrying from table to table, the hard count being dropped and racked in and on occasion paid out just to be dropped and raked in again.

She said: "It is the hole that this city was built upon."

I nodded to that. "I guess."

"And it is what fills it, a tribe of double nothings. What other kind of person would make this hell a home but twice the fool one would find anywhere else?"

She held up a fresh cigarette.

I lit it.

Well, let me tell you: When a woman talked the way Liliah did, all deep and philosophical, whether she's making sense or not, there's something in her lingo that makes you just want to sex her.

From somewhere in the casino came the call: "Money plays!"

I WAS IN MY ROOM, on the phone. On the other end, a good chunk of the country away, was Tammi.

"The guys are crazy," I was telling her. "Stand up onstage, drinking, telling jokes to themselves. They don't do a thing, and it's still a hell of a show. You should see it."

"I'd like to."

"Well . . . it's a spectacle, I mean. I don't think you'd much enjoy it."

"The show's not what I'd be coming out there to see."

"I know. I know, but, you know, now's not a real good time. Frank, he's like a . . . He likes to do a lot of boys' stuff, just the guys. Forty-something, and the cat's like a kid. And he . . . when he says do something, you've got to be there."

"So when do I get to see you?"

The phone was getting warm in my hand. "I've got another week here in Vegas, then . . . I was thinking of going back to L.A. for a little bit."

"You're starting to like L.A."

". . . I'm making some connections. But it's not like I have anything I can't skip," I offered with just a touch of reluctance.

"No. You should be there. I can meet you in New York after that."

"It's a date, baby."

Tammi gave a sigh. "I miss you, Jackie. I miss you, and I love you."

"I love you more."

We both hung up.

"That was very good of you," Liliah said.

I turned to her, her body naked under the sheets of the bed. "That was good of me? Lying to my girl was—"

"You did that for her. You did that so she would not hurt, told her that you miss her, you love her."

"It's the truth."

"Then you weren't lying. Even better."

"Better still if I wasn't cheating on her."

"It would be, yes, but it would be impossible."

Liliah stretched her arms above her, revealing her brown areolas and thumb-sized nipples. No, there was no dismissing those.

"So," she said in summation, "the second best thing to do is to lie. It's all right. It is her you love. Not me."

"That doesn't mean I—"

"It's good of you to worry about my feelings, but you said that you love her."

". . . I do. I'm going to marry her. I already have the ring."

"Then why have you not given it to her?"

"Because it wouldn't be fair. You should hear her sing. Her voice is like . . . I couldn't do that, you know. I couldn't take her away from people."

"That's wrong."

"That's . . . Lying to her is good, but allowing her to sing is bad?" I snapped.

Giving a broad yawn Liliah made her boredom with my outrage obvious. "You are *not* not marrying your girlfriend for her sake. It is for your sake; it is for your freedom so that you may do as you please, live as you please. . . ."

"You're wrong."

"I'm never wrong."

"Says your ego."

"No, it is not my ego. Not regarding men and their motivations. A woman chooses one of two things when she is beautiful: to be aware or to be stupid. A stupid woman is happy believing a man loves her for something more than her tits, and that the good things that come to her are not trailed by the hope of sex. And such a woman is very, very content in her convictions.

"But I am not such a woman. I am aware. I know that I am *zhust* time and sagging skin away from loneliness." Liliah drew a finger across her cheek. "I am *zhust* one horrid scar away from solitude. I know this. I know all of this, and sometimes the things I know make me want to . . . they make me . . ."

"You came to me," I reminded her. "In my dressing room, at Ciro's. It wasn't like I tried to pick you up. Never in a million years would I have thought I could. You came to me."

"Yes. I came to you. And you have a woman who you love. So, would you even be with me if it were not for these?" Her hands slid over her breasts. "Or this?" Her hands below her waist now.

"That doesn't make—"

"Do you even care for me as a person, *Zhaqué,* or am I to you *zhust* a . . . an object of sex?"

Did I care for her as a person? Beyond the cursory jazz we engaged in before and after we made hey, what did I know of Liliah? Where she was from, her family, what she dreamed of as a child, or what she would do in life if she weren't doing what she did.

Nothing.

Right then I became aware that all the disaffection and coolness I'd for so long read in Liliah was something besides the aloofness of a goddess. It was the sadness of her state of being.

Liliah *was* aware.

She was painfully aware. And right then I wanted to take her and hold her and kiss her, my motivation, for the first time, something more than lust. And the truth of that made me very ashamed.

Liliah got out of bed, dressed her naked body. I asked her not to go.

"It's all right," she said. Her voice calm and reassuring. "I will be back. You and I, we are not yet finished."

She gave me a light kiss and left.

I sat for a while.

With nothing better to do, I went down to the casino and let Las Vegas have a piece of me.

A BLURT. In one excited spasm it all came spilling out of Sid: "We got you television!"

"Sullivan?"

Might as well have punched Sid in the stomach for all the wind I took out of him. ". . . Fran's show."

I had mixed emotions on hearing that. Part of me thought: It's about time, not blaming Fran, knowing that CBS hadn't been excited about showcasing a relatively unknown black comic on their freshman program. My other feeling was of great disappointment. I wanted Sullivan. After the Copa, the Sands, Ciro's, I figured I rated Sullivan. Yeah, it'd be a boost to do Fran's show, but at the end of the day it was Sullivan that mattered.

"It's good exposure, Jackie."

"I know."

"Fran's show is doing good, and television, any television, is a good break."

"Sid, I know."

"Yeah, and I know you're disappointed—"

"How am I going to be disappointed about doing my best friend's show," I lied. If it took, it would be a miracle. Sid knew me like a brother. Even over the phone he could read the feelings in my voice.

"They've got you scheduled in three weeks," he said flatly. "I'm lining you up some dates in the city, let you work on your routine. You've got to have a sharp five."

"Sure. That's great." I put effort into sounding as if I meant it. "And keep a night open for dinner."

"At least one."

Sid hung up.

I hung up.

———

"ORGANIZATION. That's the key. Individual activity is righteous in a way. It shows whites that what's going on in the black community—the civil unrest—isn't confined to just one area, one region. But limited individual activity only has limited results. The key is organization."

Andre was talking. Andre was a black man, black besides just his skin. He wore a black leather coat, black pants, shades despite being indoors. And his lingo, delivered in cadence that was very dark. I'd never met him before. He was brought 'round to my New York apartment by Morris, the former Li'l Mo, who just sat off to one side, giving me a quizzical staring like it was him, not Andre, who was unfamiliar with me. Morris was different. More than just his hard attitude and his distant nature, he was physically different. Things besides the passing of years had made him so. His face was scarred, the most obvious defect being an indentation on his temple near his left eye that looked to have been molded by a policeman's billy club.

Andre: "The sit-ins we've had this year all across America have been effective. Woolworth's has had to open their lunch counters. Black Americans everywhere have been able to sit down and eat just like white folks. That's the power of organization. You don't appeal to their hearts, you attack their pocketbooks. They start losing money, you best believe they'll start opening their doors. And next May with the Freedom Rides—"

"What?" I asked.

"Integrated buses," Morris said from his corner. He said it very quietly so as not to disturb the careful staring he was doing at me.

"Blacks and whites riding together," Andre clarified. "We start in Washington, D.C., and ride down to Birmingham. Sit where we want, use whatever facilities we want, like the law says we're supposed to be able to. But all that takes organization, Jackie. That's what I'm talking about: organization."

"And what is it . . . I mean, why are you coming to me?"

"We're coming to you for support. We're coming to you to lend your name. Look, we have a protest or a march, it gets written up as:

Black agitators cause trouble. We get someone like you involved, all of a sudden it's Jackie Mann leads demonstration to end segregation."

"You talk like I'm a star."

"Star enough. Every time I turn around, I'm seeing your name somewhere."

"I'm not that . . . People don't know me that well." I could hear the squirm in my voice.

Andre looked to Morris as if for confirmation that the dodging he was witnessing was for real.

Morris screwed his lip.

Andre: "They know you a damn lot more than they know any of us."

"But it's not . . . I'm not Harry Belafonte. I'm just a comic."

Morris came at me with "So's Dick Gregory."

"But that's his thing. You know. He's more of a . . . Yeah, he's a comic, but he's more of an activist."

"And what you are, a non-activist?" The crack was sharp enough it could've come from a whip.

Andre tried to mediate. "We're not asking you to march on the front lines. We're just looking for help, at fund-raisers at least. You show up, a crowd comes along." A beat. "You can do that, can't you?"

Could I do *that?* Could I get involved with political groups whose politics I'd just been introduced to? Yeah. I could. Except it'd taken a good long time to get on Fran's show—my own friend's show—just as a black man. How long would it take me to get on the Sullivan show as a race agitator?

I hesitated with my answer to Andre's question. Just a second. That was a second too long for Morris.

"Damn, man." He was up out of his chair, swinging hands in my direction, swatting away the stink of me. To Andre: "Told you coming to him was a waste of time."

"How's it a w—"

Rolling right over me: "All he cares about is livin' on the easy. Don't want to do nothing to upset massa."

"You come around once every couple of years, telling me how I'm letting down the race, and then I'm supposed to throw away my career on your say-so?"

"Your career as a house nigger?"

"Yeah, I'm a house nigger. You know why I'm a house nigger? 'Cause I worked my ass off to have a house to be a nigger in. I'm a house nigger, I'm a big-Cadillac-driving nigger, I'm an expensive-watch-and-fine-clothes-wearing nigger. And the only thing worse than all that is being the I-ain't-got-nothing nigger who comes to me for favors."

Funny lines, but I hoped they hurt. From the you-make-me-want-to-spit look Morris sent me, I was sure they did.

What he said was: "If I'm an ain't-got-nothing nigger, it's 'cause of brothers like you. Instead of getting involved, you're too busy getting over. You're too busy staying in your white hotels and eating at your ofay restaurants to even know what time it is."

"It's called integrating. I'm doing exactly what you're protesting for—staying where I want, eating where I please."

Morris asked: "How many other blacks you see at your hotels and restaurants except the ones clearing the tables? When you're the only one getting in, that's not integration. That's selling out. If you ever once knew what it was like to be black"—he rubbed at the indentation on his temple—"you'd know the difference." To Andre he said: "There's nothing here," and was out.

Andre lingered, ready to go but not wanting to storm off, hoping, maybe, in the time it took him to get to the door I might change my mind about things.

My only offer was to make a donation, write a check. I wrote it. Andre took it and left.

To hell with him. Him and Morris both. Especially Morris and his stoved-in head, coming around acting like I was doing nothing besides living high. Acting like I didn't know how it was to be black.

I got hot right then. I filled up with anger I hadn't known in years. I remembered being on a lonely dark road in Florida. I remembered facing my own extinction. When you're solo in the night in the South, standing against three rednecks and their collected hate . . . that's when you find out what it means to be black. But all my indignation was wasted. I was alone in my apartment, and as usual had picked an impotent moment to be self-righteous.

So what? I had other concerns. I wasn't going to let Morris drag me down when there was so much else to lift me up.

⸺

I WAS LATE. The Broadway traffic that was snarled to a standstill was doing nothing but making me later. I told the cabbie to pull over, tossed money at him, and took off on foot without waiting for change. I traveled at a run/walk pace, wanting badly to get where I was going without working up a sweat while getting there. Couldn't afford to be sweaty. I was late for a date with my girl. Tammi was in town.

B'way and Fiftieth. I got to Lindy's. Moving quickly through the door, eyes rolling. Spotting Tammi, I swept past the maître d'. I moved for her, all light and smiles. As I went to kiss her, she turned her head so that I caught only cheek. Her eyes lowered. I followed them down to the tabletop, to what lay there: the *Amsterdam News*— a black newspaper. It was folded open to an article headlined: TOO FAMOUS TO BE NEGRO? It read:

> For the fortunate few who were able to secure tickets to the recent Summit event in Las Vegas, one of the highlights of the show was seeing both Sammy Davis, Jr. and comedian

Jackie Mann. Their performance with such luminaries as Frank Sinatra and Dean Martin before an audience that included the man most believe to be the next president was a source of pride for our community. Onstage. Offstage, however, their antics left much to be desired. While we're happy for the success of both Davis and Mann, it seems to have come at the expense of acknowledging their race. Instead of spending time in the Negro community, both remained entrenched in the brighter, whiter Strip casinos that, by and large, will not even permit lesser Negroes on their premises. And though the rumors of all-night all-white sexfests attended by Davis and Mann may be nothing more than rumors, there is little doubt that Davis's romance with Swedish actress Mai Britt has influenced the younger Mann to travel a similar path. While we regret having to be the ones to remind Davis and Mann of their obligation to the Negro community, what is of greater regret is the necessity to do so.

If the piece wasn't full of lies, then they were half-truths. Yeah, I didn't hang out in Westside, but the blacks in Westside wouldn't hang out in Westside—nobody would hang out in Westside—if they weren't forced to. And, yeah, there were some wild parties . . . more than some, but the paper didn't seem to have any problem with the white acts attending, didn't say anything about how they were bringing down the white race.

But there was one part of the story much more truth than lie. The part that said I was following in Sammy's white chick-sexing footsteps. The article only alleged it, but to give the allegation some teeth, the paper ran two pictures. One was of Sammy and his new girl, Mai Britt. The other was of me and Liliah, no doubt snapped by some scandal-rag photog while we were out to dinner.

I did a quick check of the byline. The piece was written by a woman. Figures. Hell hath no fury like a Negress eyeing a black man with a blonde.

It was the picture, the picture of me and some other girl—white or not, just some other girl—that had turned Tammi's head away from my approach. And that, the picture, is what I was going to have to do some serious explaining about.

It was time to get my lies straight.

I started things off with "Oh, baby, are you going to believe that?" I sat down, put a napkin in my lap, and looked at a menu as if the article weren't even worthy of my time. "You can't believe everything you read."

"I didn't just read it. I'm looking at it. I'm looking at the picture, Jackie. You and that . . . that . . ." Tammi's voice did all kinds of things with every word from her mouth. By turns it was accusatory and hurt. It was also desperate to find a truth in the things I was telling her.

"Yeah. A picture of me and that actress—" Not Liliah. *That actress.* By taking away her name, I hoped to reduce her from a female threat to a thing. "And about five other people." The picture the paper had chosen to run had, thankfully, some people leaning in around me and Liliah. Looked at with sympathetic eyes, you could almost believe that the two of us were part of a larger group. "You see how in the story they didn't mention any names. They didn't say I was dating the woman." *The woman.*

"But then—"

"They couldn't, 'cause I'm not. I'm not dating her."

"But then why put the picture with the article?"

"Well, they . . . It's not an article, first of all. That's the thing. It's not an article, it's an opin—"

"Why put the picture with it?"

Yeah. Why? "They have to put something."

"They had Sammy's picture, Sammy and his girl. Why did they need your picture?"

All my years onstage, all my years honing my comic timing, and I was having a helluvan effort quick-thinking my way out of this. I was slowed down by all the willpower I was burning to keep myself from breaking out in a liar's sweat. "You don't just go after a cat like Sammy Davis. They don't dig that he's dating—that he's going to marry, I heard they're getting married—the paper doesn't dig he's with this chick. But a star his size, he's too big to be writing cracks about. So they write a piece and they make it scattershot, make it look like they're throwing punches at any Negro who comes in ten feet of a white woman. What am I supposed to do?"

"Stay more than ten feet away from white women."

Tammi was softening some.

I said: "You going to stay more than ten feet away from all those wannabe crooners in Detroit?"

A beat.

"I guess I do sound a little jealous." The way she sounded was light and even in tone; some deadweight that had been crushing her for a day or so had been lifted.

I'd sweet-talked my way out of the corner I'd lusted myself into.

Tammi: "But you're the one who said the only people who call it jealousy are the ones who don't know passion."

"I guess I did, so I guess I'll let you off the hook. This time." I made it clear I was strictly giving her bits, but even as a joke, putting it all on her was the masterstroke. "Now, are you going to give me a proper kiss, or do I have to go out and find me a European starlet for real?"

Tammi gave me the kiss she'd held back when first I'd come to the table. It was deep and long and full of "I miss you" affection.

Later, back at the apartment, we buried my lies with sex. We buried our days apart and our differences with long hours spent rediscovering each other. What we found was that time and distance do not make love fade.

After the act, in the dark, in bed, as I held Tammi and guilt held me, I propped myself up with Liliah's words: It was not marrying Tammi, if anything, that was wrong. But the lies I was living were good.

⸺

IT WAS ALMOST like things used to be, going on four years prior. I was back on a Village club stage, but this time doing warm-up sets for my appearance on Fran's show. A small room, stale air choked with smoke and the heat of tightly pressed flesh. The audience no farther away than the length of my arm. My ears catching Tammi's laugh above all others. My set tight and funny. Great stuff, and not just by my own thinking.

"Great stuff, Jackie." A guy was coming toward me with a big smile and outstretched hand. "Chet Rosen," he reminded me. "William Morris. Heard you were doing a drop-in, thought I'd come by."

I gave him a hello, good to see you again, and introduced him to Tammi.

"Tammi Terrell. Sure. You're at Motown. Good place to be. That Berry Gordy is a sharp fellow. He's really going to break something big."

He knew Tammi. I was impressed.

To me: "Heard you're doing *The Fran Clark Show*."

"Next week."

"She's a friend of yours, isn't she?"

"Yeah. Yes."

"Same agent, the two of you. Sid . . ."

"Kindler."

Chet made a face as though there were a couple of things beyond his understanding. "Wonder why it's taken so long?" he asked, not to me in particular, but just out loud. "You've got the same agent, wonder why it took so long to get you on the show? I think someone's napping at the wheel."

Before I could jump in with any kind of reply, Chet streamrolled on with "Hey, heard you were sensational in Vegas."

"Sensational? Most of the people in the audience didn't pay attention to me, and the rest didn't even know who I was. It was like being vice president."

"They gave you more respect than they would most comics. You've got something up there"—directing a thumb at the stage beyond us. "You've got some good opportunities coming your way, Jackie. I hope you capitalize on them. What's Sid got lined up for you?"

". . . I'm doing Fran's show."

"And?"

And . . .

Out in the show room a singer worked her way through some Cole Porter while I came up answerless.

"Well, listen, Jackie, all the best on the show. I know you're going to be a smash. Miss Terrell."

Chet started away, stopped. "I hope you don't mind me saying so, but you two make a handsome couple." And he was gone.

"There's a man," Tammi said, "who knows how to say the right things."

He did. And he knew how to make them stick.

———

"THE THING ABOUT FRAN'S SHOW, there are always executives around. CBS guys. Do well, they talk. That's only going to help you later."

Sid was lying to me. I'd come 'round to get a pep talk before Fran's show; now all I was getting were lies. Sid wasn't lying with his words. Yeah, there'd be CBS execs at the broadcast, and, yeah, doing a solid set in front of them could only help me nail Sullivan. All that was truth. Sid was handing me other lies: his breath sweetened with mints to hide the fermented stink it carried, movements that worked at being precise and accurate to cover their being un-fixed and clumsy. Instead, his every action came off meticulously planned, then executed in slow motion, great concentration put into picking up a pen from his desk so as not to knock over a lamp in the trying. All the effort he put into appearing sober: Those were the lies. After so many years sitting front row to my pop's drunk show, I was not even slightly fooled, though Pop never did me the cour-tesy of trying to hide his binges.

"I don't mean to give you the heebie-jeebies, just want you to know . . . it's not Sullivan, but we're working toward it."

Sid talked at his desktop. Not looking at me, he wouldn't have to read the reflection of his deception in my eyes. Then we could go on with this little skit: him acting sober and me acting like I didn't know he was soused.

Man, how I hated drunks.

No.

I didn't hate Sid. What I hated, I hated a drunk's weakness, hated how they forced you to be an accomplice to their sin: I know you know what I'm doing, but please let me drink, or buy my booze when I can't buy it for myself, ignore my rants when I'm drunk and my blurry eyes when I'm lifted before noon. Please sympathize with my pain or problem, and if you don't, that's all right. Just don't say anything; go along like I'm fine even when I laugh too loud at something that's not funny, pass out in the middle of a sen-tence, or trip and fall down when I'm walking on a smooth, even surface. And when it gets that bad, just make a veiled comment about somebody else's "situation" that I can tsk-tsk at along with you, us both secretly knowing who you're really talking about. Then I'll go clean myself up. Dry out. For a little while. A couple of weeks. Maybe a month. Or the rest of the day. Then let's all pretend again.

Sid . . . How could he do this to me? He knew how I felt and what I'd been through, so how could he . . . And the day before my first TV shot!

And that was the thing: I didn't care about the *why* of what shoved Sid off the wagon. I only cared about the *why me*. I didn't need this, and it was so not good coming right on top of Chet already trying to poison me to Sid.

"You're going to do great, that's all I'm trying to say. This is . . . this is going to be big for you." Very slowly Sid's hand went to his brow, slid away beads of sweat.

"Yeah. Great." Then, pointed, hardly bothering with the veil: "Sorry my father's not around to see this."

—

IT WAS UNREAL. It was that way in a couple of meanings. It was unreal—surreal—the feeling: Is this happening? Is this truly, finally . . . And it was unreal—not real: Viewed not through the milky reception of a Zenith, but seen up close, the sets looked like what they were—painted plywood and decorated muslin. Lighting cables—giant black snakes lying dead to the world—zigzagged across the massive space. All around were union guys, beefy in size and in the volume of sweat and stink they produced despite the fact most of them seemed to draw a paycheck for standing around watching everybody else do something. But not even them, with their workman, day-laborer presence, could plane the luster from the moment. To me it was all some-kind-of magic. The moment remained unreal. Surreal. It was Oz. It was Shangri-la. It was the TV studio from where Fran's show was broadcast, and it was, right then, the place more than any other where I most wanted to be.

The lights, the cameras—big, four-eyed RCA monsters—the disarray, people shouting at each other, wanting this done or that changed, or wanting to know why in the hell they were just then finding out about something and all of them running around like ants in a fire. Chaos breeding confusion. And this was still twenty-four hours prior to broadcast. The insanity was contagious. My heart was a metronome that rapid-fired in time to the organized riot happening around me.

Fran was onstage. I'd seen Frances on television, sure, but it hadn't been since my pop's funeral that I'd seen Frances in the flesh. She'd changed. Or, rather, she'd been changed. She'd slimmed down some, and at the same time got blonded up and coiffed. She didn't wear clothes, she wore high fashion from designers all too happy to give her their best stuff on the off chance she might sport it on the air. These days Frances didn't look like a kid from Williamsburg. She'd been Doris Dayed into a suburban white chick at-a-moment's-notice-ready to head to a PTA meeting.

She was saying, as she would be saying in a day's time: "This next gentleman I'm so very glad to be welcoming to the stage not only because he's a dear friend, he's also the most sensational young comic around. Making his television debut, please welcome Jackie Mann."

From the wings I strutted myself onto the stage, getting a play-by-play from the floor manager every step of the way.

"You come right around here, Jackie," he directed. "Keep walking over to Fran . . ."

I did as told. Fran took my hands in hers, squeezed hard, gave me a kiss on the cheek for luck. Except that we were in a soundstage with all that broadcast equipment, dozens of technicians and suits watching the rehearsal, making sure everything ran smooth as silk, it was just like Fran and I were back on Fourteenth Street.

The floor manager: "Okay, Fran steps away . . ."

She did.

"Jackie, you hit your mark." He pointed down at a star painted on the floor. "Then you look right into the camera and be funny for twenty-two million Americans."

"But no pressure, right?"

"Hey, that's not the cocksure Jackie I remember." Fran had a re-assuring hand on my arm, a calming light in her eyes.

I corrected her. "The way I recall, it used to be us standing on a street corner, me scared as hell of tomorrow, and you going on about how everything's going to be okeydoke."

"We're a long way from a street corner, Jackie."

I nodded to that. We passed a smile back and forth.

Fran gave my arm a good grip, a shot of confidence.

"Frances." Across the stage, a couple of guys in suits calling for Fran.

Her expression went sour. With her head she made a couple of quick side-to-side shakes while her eyes did "oh, please" circles.

"Be right back." She crossed to the suits.

"Didn't mean to get you at all nervous," the stage manager was saying. "Fran's talked you up a lot. I'm sure you're going to do great."

"Can I ask you something? Twenty-two million people, that's really how many are going to be watching?"

"Well, a little more than half that live. The rest of the country gets it on the West Coast rebroadcast."

My heart found another gear and pumped out an exhaust of sweat over my palms. I had a bad case of the heebie-jeebies, and I knew they were going to be on me like a shadow for the next day.

I got myself over to the craft services table, tried to make a cup of tea but shook so badly, I couldn't get it to my mouth without scald-ing my hand. Food was out of the question. To my stomach—steely for the stage but new to television—the deli platter sitting out looked about as inviting as razors on rye.

A thought came to me, again: Maybe Sid was right. Maybe I wasn't ready for Sullivan yet. I wished he'd been there. Said he was feeling under the weather. Yeah. I took it for meaning he had to go and get himself clean.

I tried to never-mind my nerves, tried to focus on what Sammy had told me when I first met him back in Vegas: that I was strictly a star now. Stars don't get nervous. I went for a sip of my tea. My shirt took most of it.

"Jackie?"

There was a guy suddenly behind me. I hadn't heard him walk up, I hadn't caught any movement out of the corner of my eye. There was just a guy suddenly behind me like he had risen up from the ground. He was a kid-faced fellow. Well manicured. Clean-cut. Clean everything. He looked like he could slide headfirst through a cow pasture and come up wrinkle-free and sweet-smelling. And he had a smile. He wore a big old grin for no apparent reason except that maybe grinning was what he got paid to do. I sort of recognized him as one of the suits Fran was talking with not but a few minutes earlier.

"Jackie Mann? Les Elsner." He took my hand, shook it without giving me any choice in the matter. "Fatima cigarettes. We sponsor the program. Listen, Jackie, I was wondering if we could have a talk about a few things."

"YOU'RE CRAZY, do you know that? Both of you, you're both . . . you're . . ." Fran was red hot. Hot with anger and red from the hard-pumped blood surging her veins, making her fair skin flush. "You're just crazy!"

There were four of us in an office. Fran, me, Les—his grin had downgraded into a condescending smile—and right next to him some CBS guy, the other suit I'd seen Fran talking with. Just about as clean-cut as Les but on a budget. He wasn't smiling at all.

The CBS suit said: "Frances, it's just a kiss."

"That's right. It's just a kiss. So do you want to tell me why I can't kiss my friend—"

"Frances," Les started.

"*My* friend on *my* television show?"

"Frances, I can understand your fe—"

"It's *The Fran Clark Show*. And if I wan—"

"It's *The Fran Clark Show,* sponsored by Fatima cigarettes." Now it was Les who was doing the cutting-off. "And the fact of the matter is there are some people who are not going to be pleased by the sight of you kissing a colored."

"Colored?" Fran mocked. "Is it nineteen forty-eight where you live? The word is *Negro.*"

Actually, according to Mo and the militant fringe, it was *black*. But I just kept my mouth shut and did some quiet hoping that things would get worked out.

"Whatever you call him—"

"I call him Jackie." Fran turned away from Les like he was no longer worth conversing with and made her appeals to the network suit. "It took me this long to get you to *let me* have Jackie on the show, and now you're telling me I can't kiss him?"

All the suit had to say for himself was "Frances . . ."

"I kiss him all the time." To prove it, Fran crossed the office, came low, and gave me a kiss. No cheek this time. Mouth to mouth. Very firm. Very intense. Long, not short. Her anger equaled passion. I'd never before realized what a good kisser Fran was. Breaking from me, to the room: "How's that? You like that?"

"Quite provocative," Les said. "And what you do here in this office is your business. My business is selling Fatima cigarettes, and selling Fatima cigarettes is going to be difficult to do in a large part of the country if we are identified with race mixing."

Fran snapped back with "Well, I'll tell you what: I'll put on a white hood and do a couple of ads for you. Think that'll move a few packs?"

Les's smile remained constant.

The CBS guy weaseled his way back into the conversation. "Frances . . ."

"Stop saying my name!"

"Do you remember when Sammy Davis, Jr. was on the Eddie Cantor show? He shook his hand. That's all Eddie did was shake Sammy's hand. Do you know what kind of a hit Colgate sales took?"

"And that was how many years ago? It's almost nineteen sixty-one. Things are changing. Things *have* changed."

"Not enough," the suit said. "They'll never change that much. Fra—" He started to say her name but remembered Fran's edict. Getting right to his point: "Look, kiss Jackie, make babies with Jackie . . . I don't care what you do with Jackie as long as it's not Tuesday night at eight-thirty Eastern Standard Time on the Columbia Broadcasting System."

Les turned his smile toward me. "Speaking of Jackie, we haven't even asked him how he feels. After all, he is part of this."

He was sly bringing me into things. I'd tried to stay out of the discussion, and Les knew why. Like loaded dice, he knew which way I would tumble. And after I hesitated in answering, so did Frances.

Sid. If Sid were here, he could have found a way out of this for me.

There was a beat, one heartbreaking beat, then:

"Jackie . . ." Fran pleaded. "Oh, Jackie, don't. Is it that important to you?" Her voice was full with ache. Just having to ask me this question was causing her pain. "Is getting on TV more important than . . ." She crossed back over the room in a stride, took my arms in her hands, took them and squeezed them until her finger struck bone as if, by touch alone, she could give me an IV of inner strength. In a desperate beg she said: "Stand up for yourself! One time, just one time, would you please stand up for yourself!"

Was she saying that to me? Was she really saying . . . ?

I had. I had.

I'd stood up for myself years back when Sid said he wanted to rep a comic but not a singer. I'd stood up for myself and told Sid if he didn't take on Frances Kligman, he couldn't take on me. So he took on Frances. And Sid got Fran the record deal that got her the CBS audition that got her the CBS pilot that got her her own show. What had standing up for myself gotten me? It'd bought me a window seat to someone else's skyrocketing career. It'd gotten me into a tight spot in a back office squeezed between a couple of suits and Fran Clark, who was telling me to stand up for myself. Just one time, stand up for myself.

"Fran it . . . it's just a kiss. . . ." I looked away from her when I said it.

I shouldn't have said anything.

What I should have done was open up my hand, open it wide, and with the whole of it slap sweet Frances hard as I could across the face. The effect would have been the same. Maybe the hurt would have been a little less.

Fran moved away from me. She stood in the middle of the room, staring at me same as if she were trying, without success, to recognize someone she used to know. Her face was pure confusion. A thousand years of study wouldn't begin to help her understand the strange thing I'd become.

God, Sid, why aren't you . . . You could've handled this. You could've . . .

Fran turned to the other two men in the room.

Fran said: "It is my show, and if I want to, I will kiss him."

Him, she said. Him, like I didn't have a name anymore. Like I was no longer a person, just a symbolic object that's only purpose was for Fran to rally her convictions around.

A new volley of arguing started up. I left the room, unnoticed by the others, so that the chips could fall. I left the room feeling like a snake slithering its way through weeded grass.

I DIDN'T DO THE SHOW. Sid told me, later—feeling better—he tried talking to Fran, tried working out a compromise, but that she wouldn't back down and neither would the sponsor. And even though the Fatima guy and the CBS suit were pretty sure I'd play along, they figured Fran would kiss me out of spite, and as the show was broadcast live, that meant a good chunk of the country would see some real-time race mixing. So I didn't do the show.

It was just a kiss. I know to Frances it was a sign of friendship, and friendship wasn't anything that you tossed away just because some guy is afraid he isn't going to be able to push as many smokes next week as he did last week. But to me it was just a kiss, just a touch of lip to cheek that was standing in the way of myself and twenty-two million people. I tried to tell Fran that, tried to explain my thinking: It was just a kiss.

She wouldn't take my call.

I wrote her a letter.

Sid hand-delivered it.

He told me Frances tore it up without reading it. She tore it up; then she cried.

Fran had been my best friend, and twice I'd done her wrong. My jealousy over her making it, getting Sullivan when I didn't, she could forgive. My betrayal she couldn't.

In that office, her clutching arms, telling me to stand up for myself: It was the last time Frances and I ever spoke.

⚬⚬⚬

CHICAGO. Two weeks in St. Louis. Cleveland . . .

I was back on the road. I was paid well. I did well.

I was still just a club comic.

Maybe a little more well known than some others. Maybe I ran with a better crowd. But still nothing but a club comic.

Boston, Philly, Baltimore . . .

Los Angeles.

After Baltimore I had a hole in my schedule, so I headed back

West. I planed it. A train was cheaper, but it was also slower. I was in a hurry to be there.

"Hello, *Zhaqué.*"

Liliah was waiting for me in the terminal. She was dressed down, trying to avoid attracting attention. Her version of dressed down would've put some royalty to shame. I would've figured, a woman like Liliah, whatever it was that she found amusing in me would have long since gone dull. It hadn't. She came to me as I greeted her. We kissed, heavy and deep—Liliah physically placid even as her mouth searched mine—and I knew that the dysfunction that formed the core of our relationship remained.

Together again, me and Liliah made the Hollywood scene: a show at the Pantages. Dinner at Mocambo or Crescendo. Just that quick, not a stride missed, I was back riding that pony like I'd never been off. Only, this time around I was more careful. Liliah and I were clandestine, as private as we could be in public. There were whispers and there was talk, but we did our best to avoid cameras, avoid documentation that a man couldn't lie his best girl into disbelieving.

There's a line of thought that asks: How could I do that; how could I have a girl like Tammi—how could I say I loved a girl like Tammi—and still sly around on the side?

Fair question.

The answer comes in being caught up between two competing emotions: love and desire. If I were in a plane and it was crashing and I knew that in an instant I would be dead to the world, my final thought—my only thought—would have been of Tammi.

I loved Tammi.

But I was not in a plane and I wasn't crashing. My thoughts were not terminal but were of the moment. And sometimes, in the moment, love's got to accommodate desire.

I wanted Liliah.

THE WILLIAM MORRIS AGENCY was the most powerful talent agency in the world. If you didn't know that walking in the door, the pictures of its clients that lined the walls of its Beverly Hills digs told you so. Superstars. One-name stars: Berle, Monroe, Presley, Thomas, Sinatra, Davis, McQueen.

I was seated at a big table, an oak monolith laid to its side that the room seemed to be built around. Seated with me was Chet Rosen, whom I knew, two other agents I'd just met, and Abe Lastfogel, whom I hadn't met previously but had heard plenty about. Abe was head of the William Morris Agency, and as head of *the* agency, it was a call from his office that did what, up till then, Chet had been unable to do—break down my loyalties enough for me to take a meet-and-greet with WMA.

Looking like a four-eyed bulldog with wavy hair, J. Edgar Hoover in a blue suit, Abe was older by a good couple of decades than the other agents who themselves varied in age, shape, and size. What they had in common besides the blue suits that were apparently their combat gear was a certain quality of beguile. It was not readily apparent. Subtle, understated, but very much a part of them. A quiet callus developed over time that had come from playing angles for so long that their sharp edges had been worn round. The men, the agents, were all so very, very smooth. Smooth to the point of being slick.

The meeting started with small talk, the agents clattering among themselves for my benefit:

"See the overnights on Berle's special?"

"Great. Absolutely great."

"It's going to come up in the nationals."

"You know what I was thinking, that new comic we just signed—"

"Stunt him on Danny's show?"

"Great exposure. Could land him a series."

"I'll bring it up in the staff meeting."

When they finished up with all their agent jazz, Chet got to things with: "I'm really glad you could sit down with us, Jackie. We're all really big fans of yours, and we just wanted to have a chance to talk."

One of the other agents—Howie, I think his name was—said, not harsh, but with just a bit of barb attached: "We usually don't have this much trouble getting people to take meetings with us."

"Well, Jackie has an agent. A good one," Abe said. "And I don't want you to think for a second we're trying to poach you, Jackie. We don't do that. We don't take clients from small agents."

He was trying to show he was a stand-up fellow, but the way he said "small agents" made me think otherwise.

"Say, what happened with *The Fran Clark Show*?" Chet wanted to know. "Weren't you supposed do that a month or so ago?"

"That didn't . . . There was a problem."

"Have they got you re-booked?"

"I don't think . . ." I didn't much feel like explaining things, so I said again: "There was a problem," and hoped to leave it at that.

Chet didn't seem to get my meaning. "A problem? What did Sid do about it?"

"Everything he could. He said he did."

"Yes, however," Abe tolling in, "what exactly did he do on your behalf?"

"I don't . . . Everything he could."

The room got very still. It was as if there were a whole lot of lament going around and no one knew for sure how to put a stop to it.

"Jackie, we didn't ask you here to speak badly of your agent, but I think, for your own benefit, there are some things we should discuss." Abe sounded grave as a doctor about to outline radical surgery for a near-terminal patient. "As comedians go, you are one of the most popular club comics working. But you are a *club* comic and, honestly, Sid is partly to blame for that."

I started to protest.

Abe cut me off with "Yes, I know he's gotten you where you are, and I don't mean to imply that he's actively doing anything to hold you back. I just don't think he has the connections to move you any further ahead. And, being a Negro performer, you need special handling."

The other agent, the fourth one in the room, nodded and threw in a few affirmatives.

"I guess the question is: Are you happy being just a club comic?"

Abe left that line out there dangling for me.

"No."

"What are you looking for in your career?" Chet asked. "What is it you want?"

What did I want? Easy. Same thing I'd always wanted. Money, fame. Respect. And anyone who didn't give it to me? I wanted to be able to crush them Sinatra-style.

How did I get that?

"Sullivan," I said. "I want to do the Sullivan show."

Well, let me tell you: If I expected the heavens to open up and these four to hit the dirt before my grand plans, then I expected wrong. They just sort of sat and nodded same as if all I'd asked for was a stick of Wrigley's.

Chet wanted to know: "What else?"

I blank-faced.

"In terms of other television, your own show, getting some movie roles . . ."

"I don't know. I hadn't really—"

"You never talked it over with Sid?" Howie asked. "Never put together any long-term plans?"

"I figured . . . I thought, you know, once I got Sullivan . . ."

More quiet. More of that lament making its way around the room. The agent's non-responses saying: "Oh, Jackie, you poor, ignorant boy."

Abe: "*The Ed Sullivan Show* is a good thing. A very good thing. Honestly, for an act such as yourself, the Sullivan show is the kind of exposure that can truly set you right. But you have to look at it not as a be-all and end-all but rather as the beginning of the rest of your ascent."

Again the fourth agent nodded and yessed all that. A one-man, ten percent, Baptist congregation.

Chet: "Just curious. Why haven't you done Sullivan? The auditions didn't go well?"

"I haven't auditioned."

"You haven't even auditioned?" Chet offered that up with equal parts shock and disbelief.

"Sid wanted to make sure I was ready. He said I should be ready before I auditioned."

"How much more ready do you have to be than opening act for the Rat Pack?"

I gave a nervous sputter: "Actually, Frank doesn't like the term—"

"The Rat Pack at the Sands," Howie tagged.

Like I'd thought first off, these boys were slick. They said they weren't going talk down Sid. They were good to their word. They were letting me badmouth him for myself.

Abe to Chet: "Don't you know Bob Precht?" Abe to me: "Bob is Sullivan's producer."

Chet: "Sure. I see him almost every other week at Sardi's. Think he owes me a favor."

Abe looked to me, opened his hands palms up as if to say: Well, there it is.

Yeah. There it was. Sullivan. Sullivan, and all that came with it. Sullivan just sitting there for me. All I had to do was reach out and take it.

That was all I had to do.

But I couldn't.

Every word these men were saying connected straight to the

organ of aspiration that had driven me for the last half decade. The picture they had painted for me was sunlight bright, and clear as a Minnesota lake. And all they were offering—to simply get me where I most wanted to be—was only the shake of a hand away. But it was a gesture I could not make myself complete. Sid was in the way. I couldn't bring myself to shove aside all he'd done for me just for some guys who knew how to do alchemy with their tongues.

But all the loyalty I felt for Sid barely gave me the strength to say: "I really need to think about it."

"You take your time," Abe offered. Offered like it really didn't matter to him which way I jumped. "We want you to feel comfortable with whatever you decide."

That wasn't what I wanted to hear. What I wanted to hear was a little browbeating, some verbal pushing and shoving that would've gotten me over the border between devotion and urge. But all I got was some "thank yous," some "all the bests," and a "keep in touch" as I was walked to the elevator that took me to the lobby, to the street, to the California sunshine, and back to life as I knew it.

―――

"WHAT'S WRONG, JACKIE?"

Just hearing Tammi's voice, even over the phone, and all the craziness in my life seemed less so. It was as if her voice had a physicality, and its very touch was able to ease me calm.

She asked again: "What's wrong?"

"I met with some agents today. Some guys from William Morris."

"You're leaving Sid?" She wasn't accusatory. She wasn't judgmental. She just asked.

"No. No, I couldn't do it. All that he's done for me, all the times he's been there for me, I couldn't just cut him off. I don't think I ever could." I took a beat. "But sometimes I look at the way my life's gone: I do good at some club and get introduced to some guy who turns me on to some star who gets me somewhere . . . How much of that is Sid, and how much of that is luck? And if I'm just depending on luck, what happens when my luck runs out?"

"Then maybe you should leave Sid, sign with the Morris boys."

I didn't expect that kind of talk. Not from Tammi I didn't.

"It's that, or you spend the rest of your life resenting Sid because you think he's holding you back, and that's no good either."

"I could never . . . What would I—"

"You tell him the truth. He might hurt, but someone like Sid could never hate you for the truth."

She was like a rock. In my world, that had become mixed up as some kind of wild Droodle, Tammi was like . . . I fell back on the bed. Looking over at the nightstand through tear-blurred eyes: the box. The jewelry box with the little ring that should've been on Tammi's finger. I traveled with it always. Why, I . . .

Because.

Because one day I would get over myself and get on a plane or a train, or I would walk if I had to, but I would get myself to Tammi. I would get that ring on her finger. I would make her forever mine.

Through the phone, Tammi: "It's easier that way, Jackie. The truth is always easier."

The truth. I wanted to tell Tammi the truth. Right then, on the phone, I wanted to say: I've been with another woman. A very beautiful and charming woman. I have been with her, I have sexed her, I have cared for her, but what I feel for her is not what I feel for you. Do you understand that, Tammi? What I feel for her could never be what I feel for you.

And she would say: Yes, she understood. Or she might hang up the phone, only to call me in a year, or maybe just a day, or a decade. But she would call me and we would start the long, slow labor of building our relationship over. Or she might slam down the phone and never speak to me again. However it went, the lies would end. I would kill the sin I'd been building.

But the truth would only clean my conscience, I told myself. The lies were what kept Tammi from feeling any pain.

I looked at the clock. I needed to get ready for my show at Maxie's.

Tammi and I said our good-byes.

EARLY. The phone rang and I fumbled it up.

"Jackie Mann?"

"Yes."

"This is Harry Cohn's office," the woman on the other end said. "Mr. Cohn would like to set a meeting with you."

"With . . . ?" Jesus. Fuzzy-headed from sleep, from shock, I tried to pull down a mental calendar. "I could meet tomorrow fo—"

"Today. If possible, he would like to meet with you today." The woman talked quick, like she was on a deadline.

"Sure. Today would be—"

"Six o'clock. We'll send a car. You're staying at the Sunset Colonial, correct?"

"Yes."

"It will pick you up at five-thirty. We'll see you this evening."

She hung up.

I clutched the phone. Used it as an anchor to keep my mind from spinning off into the far end of sanity. Harry Cohn. The head of Columbia studios, stable to Rita Hayworth, Frank Capra, Gary Cooper, Montgomery Clift, Ava Gardner, and my own Liliah.

Harry Cohn, and he was sending a car for me.

Again: Jesus.

Excitement made me dial the phone. I tried to call Liliah, tell her the news. She wasn't around. I called Sid. I missed Sid. Batting oh-for-two, I calmed some, got rational. I talked myself into not making a big deal of Harry ringing me up. Shouldn't get crazy ideas.

Shouldn't let fantasies of movie deals and premiere nights take over. Shouldn't . . .

Jesus.

The day passed in a combination of too slowly and too quickly, eventually getting to five o'clock. I was first-date fickle about my clothes, finally picked a suit, and was in the Colonial's lobby at five-twenty. A Lincoln stretch was already waiting in the drive. The back door opened and a fellow came toward me. He was a razor of a man, sharp in every sense of the word. Sharp-dressed, sharply manicured. Sharp eyes. You would have thought the man foppish except his look said if you came at him wrong you were liable to cut yourself. His smile was opposite of all that, though. It was very, very pleasant.

"Jackie," he said rather than asked, obviously knowing who I was. "Neely Mordden. Very good to meet you." His handshake was firm. "Ready?"

I said yes, and he stepped back, allowing me into the car.

Once seated, once the driver was on his way: "Would you like something to drink?"

"No, thank you, Mr. Mordden."

"Neely. That's Dom, by the way."

Waaay up front, behind the wheel, the driver did his best to turn his girth back toward me. "How ya doin'?" His accent was Brooklyn particular.

"It's not far to the Gulch," Neely said.

"What's that?"

"Gower Gulch. The Columbia studios. Straight across Sunset to Gower. Not far at all." Neely settled back into the seat, the deep leather swallowing him with a soft crunch.

I kept on the edge of mine.

"Nervous?"

"I guess." No guessing about it. "Yes. I've met a lot of people, but the head of a studio just calling me up . . . What's he like?"

"Harry? He's a son of a bitch." Neely said that wearing the same pleasant smile he'd greeted me with. "And if you tell anyone I said that, I'll deny it to my grave. But truth is, old Harry is a son of a bitch."

"Hear he's cheap, too."

"Really? From whom?"

From Liliah, but the hell if I was going to drop her name. "Around," I said.

"Good man." Neely appreciated my confidentiality. "But from wherever you heard it, it's the truth. Harry's a son of a bitch, and a cheap son of a bitch. If he can Jew you out of a penny, he'll try for two. That said, as livings go, I make a good one."

"What do you, uh, I mean—"

"I'm Mr. Cohn's personal assistant. That's the title, anyway. What I do is whatever Mr. Cohn needs getting done."

"That sounds . . . interesting."

"Not a glamour job, but all of Hollywood can't be stardust and fairy tales. Some people get to pose for the cameras. The rest of us do work." He gave me a couple of pats to the knee. "Relax, Jackie. It's a short trip, but enjoy it."

I leaned back and was cuddled by the Lincoln's leather.

As Neely had promised, the ride wasn't long. We arrived at the Columbia gates and got waved through without a pause by a security guard who threw out the attitude of a man watching over Fort Knox. It was small. Small for a studio, not that I was studio familiar. But there was no backlot—that part of the grounds built up with false fronts of a Western town or New York street. And different from movie studios in the movies, there were no people milling around dressed as cowboys, or knights in armor, or gangsters like that was all they did all day, walk around in costume. There were just a bunch of soundstages, and a bunch more teamsters catching naps.

Still, it was the first movie lot I'd ever been on. Far as I cared, the place was built of gold.

We arrived at an office building. Dom stopped the car and Neely got out, held the door.

He said: "Take the elevator. Top floor. Someone will show you where to go from there. We'll be here when you're done." More of that smile of his.

I went inside, took the elevator up. Walked a long hall—walked it trying to beat down thoughts about offers of a screen test or a movie part that may or may not be lying ahead—to a secretary sitting just in front of some big double doors.

"Jackie Mann? One moment please and I'll see if Mr. Cohn is ready for you." It was that fast-talking gal who'd rung me up before. She hit a button on a black box, said: "Mr. Cohn, Jackie Mann is here."

The box said something back, but I couldn't make out what.

The secretary waved a hand at the doors like she was one of those game-show prize girls. Working on some kind of mechanical gizmo, the doors opened before me as I approached. They started to close up as I entered the office. I noticed: no handles. That hidden-majig was the only means of getting in or out.

Nutty.

Nutty, too, was the bank of lights on the ceiling—bright lights— that focused on your eyes, washing them out as you came into the room. It was like you were taking your mark in a police lineup. It was like this Cohn cat wanted to be able to get a couple of extra seconds to size you up before you ever got a look at him.

When I did get a look at him, there wasn't much to look at. Harry Cohn didn't come across as a mogul. Round-headed. Bald on top. Big ears, and a nose that oozed from his face. Sun-baked wax losing its form. He was a pint of a man. Shrewish. He sat behind a big desk. Guess he figured it'd make him look all the more imposing. Just made him look all the smaller.

He looked up. He said to me: "Quit fucking my star!" No preamble or pleasantries. Just down to business.

With that for a greeting, I knew what this whole meet was about. It wasn't a sit-down to back-and-forth on getting me into Hollywood. It was about getting me out of Liliah Davi. Sammy had caused Mai Britt a lot of problems with her career at Fox. Apparently I was in danger of doing the same for Liliah at Columbia.

Maybe the studio was beside itself over the situation, so much so they had to bring me in for instructions. But midgety Harry Cohn behind his too-big-for-him desk didn't cause me any panic, having had it made plain with his "quit fucking my star" I wasn't looking at any work anyway. In response to Harry's demand, I said: "Which star would that be?"

The crack turned Harry from white to red thermometer-style. "Do you know what you are doing!" From nowhere a riding crop got produced and slammed against the desktop. I'm guessing that desk was as close as the crop ever came to flogging a horse. Pure Hollywood: showmanship from a showman. "Do you have any idea what you are doing!"

"I haven't gotten any complaints from Liliah."

He just got redder. Red to the point I thought steam was going to shoot from his ears the way it does in a Three Stooges bit. But, maybe sensing that yelling and screaming wasn't going to buy him anything, Harry let himself calm down before going on.

"Jackie, I don't want you to think I'm some kind of a . . . a bigot. Nothing could be further from the truth." Harry came at me now same as a favorite uncle trying to wrangle a little extra turkey at Thanksgiving dinner. "I'm as progressive as the next fellow. If you and Liliah were two different people, I wouldn't have any problem with you . . . having a relationship. But you're not; you're not two different people. Liliah is a star, and the public will not tolerate a star being intimate with a *schva*—a Negro."

I noticed, behind Harry's desk, a shelf stocked with perfumes and nylons. A soldier bivouacked in war-torn Europe was not more supplied than Harry for his casting-couch conquests.

"I get the feeling Liliah doesn't much care what the public thinks."

"I do. I care." Harry was getting hot again. "The woman represents a significant investment of time and money."

"The woman is a person." Me, never previously having thought of Liliah as anything more than walking-talking sex, was suddenly, guiltily, rushing to defend her humanity. "You can't break her down into dollars and cents."

"The hell you can't!" From his desk Harry grabbed up a piece of paper and flung it at me. It caught air, fluttered, took the ground.

I wasn't about to pick it up, but from a distance I could make out most of its type: a list of itemized expenses for production costs, hair, makeup, publicity, travel . . . Harry had effectively bottom-lined Liliah to the penny.

"That's what the bitch cost me! That's what she's worth! Are you going to pay me back after you ruin her?"

". . . No."

"Then you're through with her. Right here, right now, you and the woman are done."

"That's it?"

"Should there be something else?"

Just then I decided I was plenty good and insulted, and that Harry the Horror should go screw himself.

I said: "Go screw yourself."

Harry went back to his old red-faced ways. His riding crop beat the living crap out of his desk. "You goddamn darkie bastard! I'm going to—"

"What? What are you going to do? Quit giving me parts in the movies you're not putting me in? You've got to flip to another chapter in your threat book. That one's no good for me. And I know you sure as hell aren't going to do anything to Liliah, so all you're going to do is keep on being the same little angry man you've always been. See you around, Harry. Don't get up. Or are you already standing?"

I went for the doors, the non-opening doors. Stood for a second, then shot some stink eye back at Harry.

He fingered a button on his desk.

The doors opened.

I eased my way out while Harry sent his voice hellhounding after me, barking ripe comments and dirty slurs.

The fast-talking secretary was at a loss for words as I passed.

"Think your boss needs help out of his high chair," I quipped.

I walked the long hall. I took the elevator down. Neely and Dom were waiting for me.

"Done?" Neely asked.

"Done," I said.

We got in the car. Dom drove us away from the Gulch.

"Well, how did you find Harry?"

"He was everything you said. Everything, and then some. You knew why he wanted to see me, didn't you?"

"Yes."

"And you didn't bother to hip me to things?"

"It's not my place. How did it end up, if you don't mind me asking?"

"It ended with him singing me a few variations on the word *black,* and me giving him a few screw-you bits on my way out the door."

"Like I said: He's a son of a bitch. You're taking it pretty well."

No. I wasn't taking it well at all. I was insulted. Not so much over the guy bringing me in and trying to strong-arm me into quitting Liliah. That was to be expected. If Hollywood couldn't stomach Sammy and Mai, could it ever tolerate Liliah and me? What cut me wrong was that Harry would try to get me to quit Liliah without offering me anything in return: no movie part, no audition. Not even a straight cash exchange. Was I so small-time I didn't even deserve an offer? I wouldn't've accepted any of that to get out of Liliah's life, I just wanted to know I rated.

I knew I wouldn't have accepted anything, I told myself again. And while I told myself that, my insides didn't feel very good.

"Don't take it bad," Neely said. "That's just the way this town is. What you've got to understand, Hollywood . . . it's . . . You got a minute? I want to show you something."

I mumbled an okay.

"Dom, head back to Beechwood, then up the hill."

Dom drove as told. We went up to Hollywood Boulevard, then piloted east.

Outside the car window passed Hollywood. The actual point-on-a-map part of Los Angeles that was Hollywood: the Chinese theater. The walk of fame. The Capitol records building. And people. Lots of people wandering the streets who'd come to Hollywood to be stars. Only, they weren't stars because they didn't know how to become a star, or they didn't have the talent to be a star, or they refused to give a little hey-hey to the producer who could make them a star, so they ended up wandering the streets of Hollywood, directionless, trying to find some reason to justify their lives while searching for a new plan to get where they wanted to be. In the meantime . . . set decoration is what they were. Tinseltown extras to be used or not used, moved here or there, or shredded up and thrown away at the whim of the self-important so that they might feel significant. Guys like Harry Cohn. Tiny, wretched, powerful Harry Cohn.

Very suddenly I was sick of Hollywood.

I was sick of the scene and the empty shells of flesh that took up space but didn't fill it. I was tired of their lying smiles and their air kisses and their cooing voices that told you "Dahling, but it's so good to see you" when all they cared about was being seen. It was all so phony. Phony as the peroxide blondes who slept their way into the good mother/strong woman roles. It was as fake as the matinee idols who spent their nights trolling the boys' clubs that poxed Santa Monica Boulevard.

I was mad at Hollywood.

I was jealous of Hollywood.

Most of all, I was bitter that Hollywood refused to do more to give me all that she had.

I was below the Hollywood sign. That's where Dom had driven us, a plateau maybe a football field south from the thirty-foot-tall letters. About as close as you could get without making the climb.

The sign. The shining beacon I'd sought in my youth, that had been calling me most of my life. This close, it was just cheap sheet metal and painted wood.

Dom and Neely got out of the car, and I did, too. From way up where we were you could look out over the Los Angeles basin, spread to the horizon, the lights of the city shimmering and popping.

Neely didn't so much look at all that as admire it. "You have to understand," he said, "guys like Harry, guys like Louis Mayer, David Selznick, Goldwyn, Zanuck, the Warners; you have to understand them. Little guys, ugly guys, sons of immigrants who had nothing but the dirt on their skin. Hated guys. Hated for the country they came from or their ignorant accents. Hated for the god they picked to worship. Just plain hated.

"Then one day those guys got it in their heads to come West—California, Los Angeles, a cow town that cows wouldn't be caught dead in. But they came out here and created something, those guys did. The movie business. They built the studios. MGM, Paramount, Fox, and Warners. They made stars, they told stories, they spoon-fed fantasies to the whole world."

Neely was so into his sermon, he was just about speaking in tongues.

Dom lit a smoke.

Neely: "And by the time they were done with all that, with their own bare hands they had torn an oasis up out of this useless land. They'd built a city. They'd made a dream. They'd given us Hollywood."

Hollywood. From my days in lumber I knew a couple of things. "Hollywood can't even grow out here. The soil's not right," I offered up, unimpressed. "Even the name of this place is just more of the bullshit the town uses for fertilizer."

I sucked a deep, raspy breath, pulling into my mouth and nose dirt from the ground where I lay. It mixed with stomach juice that burned like acid as it gushed up my throat, collecting in a greenish pool just before my face. My body rolled slightly with a spasm. My tear-blurred eyes looked up and saw Neely, hands clenched fists from the gut shot he'd just delivered me. He still had that smile.

Neely said at Dom: "Get him up."

Dom's hands—big slabs of beef—were all over me, hauling me from the ground by a combination of shirt and flesh.

I heard Neely say "Over there" but could not tell what direction he meant. Fear counseled me he was talking about the edge of the plateau.

"Oh, Jesus," I babbled. "Jesus, God, no!"

My back slammed onto the hood of the Lincoln, caught a piece of the hood ornament. The impact forced another spew of stomach juice from me. It gurgled over my chin and waterfalled down my chest.

"His pants," Neely said.

"Christ, oh, Christ . . ."

Dom tore down my pants as much as took them off.

Barely over my own wailing, I could make out the sound of metal scraping metal. A knife opening. The touch of it to my groin I felt through my entire body—the blade cold and hot at the same time.

I was in Florida. I could smell the humid air. I could feel the weathered wood of the gas-station wall trading its splinters for my blood.

"I'm going to give you a choice. Jackie? Jackie, you listening to me!" A couple of slaps to the face to catch my focus. "You got a choice. I can either cut off your little black balls . . ."

The tip of the blade slid over my testicles.

"Or I can chop off your big coon dick. I take your balls, you're the last nigger in your family, but at least you can fuck. I lob off your dick—"

"Please . . ."

"I cut your dick off, no more catting around when you're T-Birded, but maybe they can get some juice out and you can have a kid one day. It's up to you, Jackie."

"Please don't. Don't le—"

"Which is it going to be?"

"I'll do anything."

My slobbering only made him more insistent: "Dick, or balls? Dick—or—balls?" The blade shifted between the two.

I couldn't think. I could even begin to rationalize if one option was better than the other. Except for crying, I was useless. "I . . . mu-my . . ."

"Which?"

"Don't . . ."

"Dick, or—"

"Please don't!"

"Which?"

"I . . ."

"Which?"

I puked.

"Which!"

"My . . ."

"Goddamm it, pick one, or I swear to God I'll cut 'em both!"

"My balls! Oh, fuck, my balls"—slobbering and pathetic—"take them . . . take my . . ."

I made myself ready, if there was such a thing, for the violence that was an instant away.

The instant never came.

I felt the knife move not into me but away from my body.

Dom unhanded me.

With nothing else holding me up, I took to the ground.

"Can you hear me, Jackie?" Neely. Close. Whispering into my ear.

I sniveled a yes.

"You've got till morning, okay? I don't care who she is, I don't care where you find her, but you've got till morning to get yourself some little black monkey to marry, or I take your cock, your balls, and that's just for starters."

Neely didn't say any of that with anger or hate. He said it very calm, very cool, very matter-of-fact, and that made what he said all the more frightening.

He stood up from me, but I could still hear him clearly. "It's Harry's town, Jackie. He built it. And in Harry's town, niggers don't fuck white women. Not the white women he owns."

Dom started to pick me up, but Neely stopped him with "Leave him. Let him walk back. Maybe he'll find a jig along the way to make a Mrs."

From the ground my bleary eyes watched an odd-angled Dom and Neely get in the Lincoln and then the Lincoln drive away.

From the ground my bleary eyes looked up. The sign said: HOLLYWOOD.

≈

I LAY IN THE EARTH, in the dirt, my pants at my ankles but fully dressed in humiliation. I had been raped. My manhood, uncut, had been carved from me. I was a shameful sight. I was ashamed. I lay and I cried.

When I was tearless, I got up, fastened my pants around me the best I could, and began a shuffle from the hills, my body stooped as if clenched around the lingering force of Neely's blow.

Forty minutes worth of time got me to Franklin in Los Feliz.

Traffic—cars and pedestrians—all passed me without thought. Torn clothes, dirt-caked, I was a bum.

Worse.

I was a black bum, and bum that I was, I decided I needed some gas in order to complete the next leg of my journey. Booze had been good to me the last time I'd been threatened. I'd give it a chance to be good again.

I found a liquor store, the shopkeeper's face saying "you disgust me" all the while he was selling me my drink. The alcohol messed me up more and did nothing to even me out. Fear was an inhibitor. The phantom pain in my groin could not be drowned. Not by the first bottle. Not by bottle numero dos.

More walking. A drunken sway along Hollywood Boulevard, south to Sunset.

I must have been a sight by the time I somehow managed myself back to the Colonial. Rank, sweaty, drunk, and smelly. I must have been something like the missing link. A semblance of humanity but one step removed. I wanted only to hide in my room and welcome the new day by avoiding it. I felt my pocket for my room key. It wasn't there. Lost, probably, to the ground below the Hollywood sign. I could've just gone to the front desk, gotten a new key.

Could've.

But drunk from booze and a beating, I chose to have myself a little breakdown instead. I found a hidden chair in the back of the lobby and returned to my new pastime of bawling like a girl. I sat there in my own filthiness, my own foulness, in a dark corner that my own ego and lust had shoved me into: get married, or die. Where I was was a cell, and the feeling of being trapped with the walls closing in made me bawl all the harder.

Hands.

Hands on me. Gentle, loving black hands caressing me, holding me. And a voice as sweet and kind as the touch that went with it.

Doary. Dear, beautiful Doary. Kind, beautiful Doary. I never realized how beautiful. Her forgiving eyes. Her spun-silk skin. Her mouth, her kissable mouth . . . Doary, always with the sympathetic word no matter how late the hour, no matter I gave her the brushoff time and again. Doary. I never realized . . . I never . . . I loved Doary. It wasn't just the drink working me. In her touch, in her grasp, there was an affection and longing—a matching loneliness of a girl who toiled so close to success and excess, fame, and the love of the masses but always denied love herself—that the lonely boy, still very much a part of me, could not reject.

I took Doary in my arms, pulled her close, told her: "Doary, I love you."

She demurred, but I didn't allow her to protest. I kissed her quiet, I told her again and again how I needed her, how I had to be with her. I told her again "I love you."

Maybe she said something about me being a wreck, being drunk. I talked her past that. I convinced her of the absolute—we were meant to be together. We had to be together.

Probably Doary was the one who drove us to Vegas. My state wouldn't've gotten us out of L.A. alive.

Definitely what happened shouldn't have happened, but I kept myself drunk to get us a five-dollar license and a ten-dollar hitching.

Maybe I'd stayed liquored so I could say it wasn't the fear of threat that drove me to a wedding. A mistake of a wedding, yeah, but a mistake I'd made without the help of a knife to my balls. I had to believe I was still my own man. My ego needed to claim at least that. However it was, the deed was done. Miss Doary White had become Mrs. Doary Mann. And that was the punch line: When it was all over, I'd still married a White girl.

⹈⹈⹈

I CALLED TAMMI. By the time I'd figured out what I could possibly tell her, word was already on the street about my marriage, Harry's goons, no doubt, making sure that everyone knew the rumors of his starlet and Jackie Mann were just that.

Tammi, probably expecting me, didn't pick up the phone. Not the fifth time I called, not the fifteenth or the twenty-eighth. I called over to Motown, asked for her. I got Lamont Pearl.

"Let me talk to Tammi," I barked at him.

"I don't think—"

"What you think don't matter. Is she there?"

"It's not a—"

"Is she there!"

"Yes, she's he—"

"Put her on the phone!"

"Why? Why, Jackie? What are you going to tell her, huh? What the hell can you possibly say to her now?" With his voice, Lamont rode me calm. I swear, over the phone line, I could hear his thumb slipping across his fingers.

Weakly, I came back with "The truth."

"The truth, a pack of lies; does it matter? Does it change anything? You're married. You married a chambermaid spur of the moment after holding off Tammi for years. You can't soften that blow after it's already been thrown."

No. No, I couldn't. And would the truth have been any kinder—I had to marry Doary because I was about to get sliced for having an affair with Liliah?

"Just leave it alone," Lamont told me. "If you ever cared about the girl, then just leave it alone."

Right then it sunk very deep into me that I was losing Tammi. Tammi was lost to me. I don't know what we even were to each other. Boyfriend and girlfriend, yes, but I don't know what we gave to each other as different as we were. Opposites attract. But opposites also fight and bicker and can't see eye to eye, can't so much as agree on whether it's partly cloudy or mostly sunny. So, I don't know what it is that we brought to each other, but what Tammi took from me now that I was losing her was immense: a sense of purpose and a reason for being. She took with her the all that was decent in my life and left a space in me—a torn-out, wanting, needing, hurting hole, a self-inflicted wound—that would never conform itself to any other thing.

I asked of Lamont: "Would . . . Tell her that . . . Would you tell her—"

"No."

I NEVER TRIED TO CALL LILIAH. I was afraid. Not that she would be upset. I was terrified that she, in her disinterested way, wouldn't care that I was married. She would want to see me, I wouldn't be able to refuse her, and then my hunger would be paid for with a hillside castration. Rather than tempt that fate, I let myself just suddenly be out of her life.

In reality, she most likely never even noticed I was gone.

And then there was Doary. Doary, who probably had it worse than Tammi or Liliah. Doary was stuck with me. We made a go of things for a while, eight months or so, but there was no way it would stick. I think from the night we married, Doary knew I didn't love her. For whatever reason, she cared enough about me she was willing to take a gamble I'd learn to love her. What she got was me on the road every week so that every week I could avoid her—Doary, in my mind, having come to represent that which separated me from Tammi. I was never abusive to her, unless you count cold stares and distant silence. And I would never ask her for a divorce. No, not nice-guy Jackie Mann. I just drove her to beg one from me.

I gave her money.

She took less than I offered.

What I think she wanted, what she hoped to get out of the whole pantomime, she wanted a baby. Something to call her own. Some sign of love in an otherwise loveless and perfunctory affair. She didn't get that, and as far as I know, she never remarried.

Jack the Lady-killer, they should call me. Three with one blow.

There was this one time I'd gone out to dinner with Sid. We were eating pasta. The waiter came 'round, asked if I'd like Parmesan cheese or ground pepper.

I asked for the pepper.

The waiter, not hearing me, put the cheese on my food.

I didn't say anything about it, just let him put on the cheese and go.

Sid gave a laugh. "What was that? Why didn't you say something? You didn't get what you wanted, you got what you didn't ask for."

Yeah.

part VII

*N*o one thing changes everything else. No one person, no single occurrence alone makes for a world of difference. Black people didn't get civil rights just because Emmett Till was killed, or just because of the sit-ins and schoolkids in Little Rock. We didn't get out of Vietnam just because one soldier was killed or because one offensive went bad for our side.

Things change because they're building for a change, because a momentum of events takes them to a place of no going back. Change is without emotion and sentimentality. It doesn't care what else you've got planned. It works on its own schedule.

It's that way with history.

That way with people, too.

Want to kick your bad habits? A New Year's resolution might last you a couple of weeks, but it's when it builds up to it that real change happens.

From where I am now, I don't look on any one thing in my life—my mother dying, my father whooping me, Fran, Tammi, or Liliah; the people who were close to me, Frank and

Sammy; the giants in my life—I don't look on any one of those influences and say, yeah, that's why I did what I did.

I did what I did because of every moment of every day that I lived. I did what I did because that's where my life took me.

January of 1962 to June of 1963

Philly, Kansas City, Chicago was good for two weeks. Up to Milwaukee, over to Kansas City, Kansas, this time . . .

We were in Sid's office. We were going over my schedule.

St. Louis, Seattle, San Diego—

"Jesus, Sid."

"What? You don't want . . . ? San Diego's going to be good. It's this resort kind of—"

"It's not San Diego. It's all of it."

For a second Sid didn't say anything, not quite digging my problem. By way of trying to figure it out, like groping in the dark, he offered: "You're headlining almost every club. And for top dollar. You've got room, meals . . . travel."

"Yeah, I know. I've got all that, headlining every club, meals at every club . . . I'm still working clubs."

Sid sort of laughed a little, probably hoping it would lighten the mood. "Best clubs in the country."

"Clubs, Sid. Smoked-up dinner rooms trying to buy laughs between the salad and the steak."

"And most times getting nearly a thousand a stand for it." Sid was defensive with that. He caught himself, brought back the laugh, and added a smile. "You're all week at the Copa. Wasn't that long ago there was a kid who would've done anything for a grand at a joint like that."

"And it was too long ago I was opening for The Summit in

Vegas. I'm *back* to clubs, Sid. I'm not going forward, I'm moving back."

The smile dropped from Sid. This time it stayed off. "What do you want, Jackie?"

"If you've got to ask me what I want after all this time, that's not a good—"

"Jackie, what do you want?"

"Sullivan. You know I want Sullivan."

"And you don't think I'm working on that? In the meantime you're not hurting yourself any getting to be a better and better act. When you're ready—"

"I've opened for Frank, for Sammy, for Dino, Tony, Mel, Buddy G. . . . How much more ready do I have to be?" Again, it was my voice, but it was Chet Rosen doing the talking.

"I'm doing everything I can. It's not easy like you think."

"You got Fran on. You got her on a good long time ago"

"She's different. You can't compare yourself to Fran."

"Why? Because she's white, and I'm Negro?"

That threw Sid, truth or not, me bringing up race with him. Easing on: "It doesn't make things any simpler. And you sure didn't make fans at CBS, what happened with Fran's show."

Fran's show? Very nasty words nearly came hacking out of my mouth. Words about drunk Sid being on a bender when he should have been clean and dry and fighting my fights for me. But they were words that would hurt; and hurt Sid . . . ? Even in a hot moment they were words I could not bring myself to say. I bit them hard, gulped them whole. Instead, redirecting: "So it's all on me? It's my fault?"

"No, Jackie, it's my fault. Same as always. Whatever I land, it's never big enough. Whatever I get isn't good enough. I'm as tired of hearing it as you are of . . ." Sid held up right there. He'd been rushing toward the edge of a cliff but managed to make a hard, clean stop.

Outside the office, in the surrounding city, the people, the traffic, the noise of it all, was mostly beaten down by the sound of the labored, angry breathing that came from the two of us.

Sid looked down at his hands. They clutched at his desk. He stared at them . . . stared at them . . . then looked up full of disbelief that he could have reached such a pitch with me, that the two of us could ever come to angry words with each other.

He said haltingly, trying to find his verbal footing: "I guess I need to try harder."

A feeling came and passed inside me very quickly, remaining just long enough for me to recognize: disappointment. For a very real moment I wanted Sid to toss my words in my face and then I wanted him to throw the bundle of us out the door.

I wanted Sullivan, and I knew that Sid wasn't the man to get it for me. But the same as with Doary, I couldn't be the one to put him out of my life. The best I could do was try and get him to do the split for me. That weak maneuver I was well practiced in. But with Sid, my pushing didn't take. He was too much of a friend, and I was too much of a coward to do anything else but say, "So, you think San Diego's going to be good?"

⸺

THE BRONX HOUSE OF DETENTION. House. House was a funny thing to call it. A jail is what it was. A lockup for people awaiting trial. Not a homey thing about the joint, but . . . The Bronx House of Detention. The building was about as old as me, but it wore every year that had passed since its construction. The paint was faded where it wasn't chipped away altogether. Cracks raced each other along the plaster walls. The furniture in the waiting area was wood and cheap, and the chairs creaked in recognition of each and every shift of body weight. The tiles were broken, water leaked, there was a general mustiness from the lack of open windows and the warehoused men who sweat and stank together. The house lacked care. Of course it did. Four hundred ninety-six men locked up for one reason or another. Who cared about them? Maybe the few people who sat with me, marking time waiting for a husband or father or brother or lover to get cut loose for a few weeks before they went on trial, or a few months until they got pinched again and tossed back behind bars.

A lock got thrown on a heavy steel door and it squealed away from its frame. Li'l Mo, Morris, stepped through. He was getting out of jail.

"Goddamn it!" He wasn't happy about it. He took one look at me and got as hotheaded as a man could. "Goddamn it!"

"Mo—"

"You did this," he accused.

"Morris—"

"You did this to me!"

"Posted your bail? Yeah, I did that."

"Who asked you to?"

"What do you mean, who as—"

"I sure as hell didn't tell you to come down and get your nose in my business."

"Nobody . . . I read about the protest, or march, or whatever, in *The Times,* saw your name, saw how you got arrested. I'm getting you out of jail," I said strongly, trying to show him with my tone the good works I was doing that he seemed otherwise blind to.

"I don't want out of jail." Morris was back at the steel door, slapping at it with the flat of his hand. "Hey," he yelled to whoever was on the other side. "Hey!"

"Stop it."

"Open up!" Hand fisted, pounding now. "Open the door and let me back in!"

"Morris!" I went to him, grabbed him, pulled him from the door. He turned; our eyes got into a mum duel. The look he had melted mine, made me flinch. My eyes went to his coat I was clutching, torn at the shoulder. Torn on the sleeve. The shirt underneath torn, too. Below that were scrapes and cuts that hadn't been treated but allowed to dry and crust naturally.

I asked: "They do that to you in there?" my head nodding at "them," whoever was beyond the steel door.

"No." Mo's voice was quiet, tired of fighting for a minute. "Happened when I got arrested. And this." Mo lifted his shirt. Welts and bruises. A field of them. So bad, they were visible even against his black skin.

What do you say to that? I didn't know. I didn't say anything.

Mo lowered his shirt. The curtain coming down on the horror show.

"I didn't mean anything by getting you out. Read you got arrested. I read, and I figured . . . I thought—"

"You thought writing a check for my bail would make you down with the struggle."

"I thought you'd rather be outside than inside, so I came here to spring you."

"The point is to be inside. The point of our protest was to get arrested and stay in jail to be a reminder to the people of the inequity of the treatment of the so-called Negro by the white power structure."

"I'm not a reporter, so quit the lecturing. I'm trying to talk to you, and you're making speeches."

"I'm telling you what's what. The point is to demonstrate our suffering the way Dr. King demonstrates his suffering by staying in—"

"The point is to get beat up and tossed around so you can feel like you're super-Negro—"

"Black, Jackie. When you gonna get—"

"So you can look down your nose at anybody who isn't trying to integrate the same way you are."

"What kind of dumbass . . . You think I go out looking to take a beating from the pounders? You think catching their billy clubs makes me feel like the big nigger?"

"The word is black!"

"Then how about we integrate your way, Jackie? Should we shuffle over and get a room at the Plaza, or a suite at the Ritz? Or how about we just find us some white girls to fuck?"

Well, let me tell you: That was the straw. "Shut up!" I was grabbing Mo's jacket again, not caring about the rips and tears. "Shut the hell up! I'm sick of you talking me down!" My hand was a fist, my arm was cocked, ready to send it blindly into whatever part of Mo it could most quickly find: his temple. His jaw. His mouth . . . His mouth. His mouth was made up into a little bit of a smile, the corner of his right lip pulled up some, just some, toward his cheek.

Mo said: "How about that? I always knew you had some fire in you, Jackie."

My eyes took a sheepish trip around the room. With my yelling, with my hand ready to toss Mo a beat down, I figured people would be staring. They weren't. They had other things on their minds. A husband or father or brother or lover who was still on the other side of that steel door. I let go of Mo.

Mo moved across the room to one of the chairs and sat, the wood making noises as it took his weight. About half a minute later I sat in the chair next to him.

I said: "Know what I remember most about us?"

"The old woman."

I nodded. He knew.

"To this day I still got a picture of that ashy old battle cleaning herself out in the pond. Just about ruined me for women altogether."

Independently, we smiled some.

Another half a minute passed.

I said: "We were friends, Mo. How'd we wind up so different?"

"Don't know."

"Must be a reason. You don't like me, must be a reason why."

"I like you just fine, Jackie."

I got a little laugh from that. "Got a queer way of showing it: come around every two years to preach at me, let me know how I failed the Neg . . . black race."

"I preach at you because I'm trying to get through to you."

"Get what through? I don't have the pride you do?"

"Know what else I remember about us? I remember when people used to pick on you: kids at school, at that logging camp. I remember how you used to flip the situation, make jokes, make people listen to you. You're good with words, Jackie. You're good with your lingo. You always knew how to make people pay attention. And all you ever did with it was turn yourself into a comic, a nightclub Stepin Fetchit. Guess I just expected more from you."

"You see how wrong that is? You expected more from me, from my life. *My life,* Mo. You ever stop to think that this, what I'm doing, is what I want?"

Morris accepted that. "I didn't mean it as no dig."

"There's another way I should take *you* don't like *my* choices?"

"You should take it as meaning . . . to me, you're better than what you ended up doin' with yourself."

Another thirty seconds of sitting, the wood of the chairs doing the only conversing as we both fished around in them for an unfindable position of comfort.

Pretty soon I said: "Sorry for getting you out of jail."

"You were just trying to do right."

I know Mo was making an effort at being sincere, but even that little bit came off as stooping.

We left the House, left the other people to their waiting.

We did a little walking.

"Let me ask you something, being onstage, being in front of people. It's just you . . . you and nothing. That must be frightening as hell."

"Nah, it's not really . . ." I started my standard response, then quit it. The question Mo was asking was one I'd gotten a hundred times before. A hundred times before, I'd given the same answer. But this time, this time because I was talking to a guy I'd been familiar with all my life, but knew by the measure of distance we'd traveled apart, I was probably talking to for the last time, I thought about the question. I thought, I said: "There's this moment, this one quick tick that's always waiting right between when the audience stops clapping and you tell that first joke. When you're there, when you're facing that beat, it's like . . . Can you imagine what it's like to stand on the edge of a deep, dark hole, not knowing what's down inside it, but still you've got to jump in? Yeah. That's frightening as hell. But then you make the jump; you tell your first joke, you get your first laugh. After that, once you've got the audience, once you know you own them . . . Morris, can I tell you: It's the sweetest thing there is."

Mo nodded to that. Maybe he understood where I was coming from. Maybe he didn't and was just nodding to nod. Then he said: "I don't think I could make that jump." What he meant, what he'd never said to me before: He respected me.

We did a little bit of standing around.

I asked Mo where he was headed, if maybe we could head there together. He said he wasn't exactly sure, but that he figured he should go and try to get arrested again.

Trying not to make a joke of the moment, I wished him luck, then hailed a cab for Midtown.

Mo kept walking.

⚊

I WAS HOOFING BACK to my apartment after a set at the Copa. Walking, letting the night air clear out my gummed-up head. Doing a stand at the Copa had gone from being nearly all I could ever dream of to being *just* doing a stand at the Copa—going to work and doing my job. Nothing more. Nothing special.

As I approached my apartment, a voice called: "Jackie."

It stopped me shotgun dead. The voice, vivid as a bad scar. The accent, Southern.

WE SAT IN A BAR drinking. Dighton drank. I just watched as he liquored himself.

"Goddamn whore, Jackie. They all . . . She wanted tah leave me, she coulda goddamn well left. Ah don't give uh . . . World's fulla whores. But she ain't gotta make uh foola me." He was weepy and pitiful, the cracker version of my father, and every glass he downed only made him more so. Yelling at a waitress: "Sweetheart, yew see muh glass is empty!" To me: "She knows Ah'm tryin' tah get uh drink over heyah, an' she don't . . . Yew see how they all whores, don't yew?"

"Why don't you go home?"

"Don't yew tell me what tah do!" Me just opening my mouth swung Dighton's pendulum from pathetic to psychotic. It was a unbalancing made fertile by alcohol; its only growth would be twisted. "Ah don't need some black boy tellin' me . . ." That quick the pendulum swung back. "Jesus Christ. Tha principal. Tha grade-school principal she run off with." He was talking about his wife. I remembered her. Kind. Pleasant. A bruise to her eye. I wouldn't blame her for anything she did to this man. "Yew see how that makes me tha talka tha town, tha laughin'stock. That's what Ah'm sayin, Jackie—they're whores. Know sumthin': Ah thank she likely wanted tah do yew. That time we seen yew in Kansas City. Tha way she looked at yew up onstage, Ah think she . . ." Dighton gave me a good looking-at, his eyes x-raying my heart, trying to find truth or lie. The diagnosis: "Nah, yew wouldn'ta done that tah me, would yew, git all jungle with muh wife? But that no good . . . Run off with tha principal of tha grade school, an' took muh every last dime with her. Took muh money, Jackie! It was all Ah had left jus' tah get heyah. Knew you lived in New York. Big goddamn city. Didn't think Ah could find yew, excep' yew was playin' at tha Copacabana. Shit, yew play uh fancy place like that, it's all over tha papers."

My luck.

I knew where things were going, it was obvious, so I just went ahead and got there. "I'll give you some money, then you're through here. You're on your own."

For a moment Dighton looked ashamed. It was as if, even though his intentions were nothing but bad, it was still a disgrace to have arrived at a place in his life where he had to travel half the country to shake down a "nigger" just to get by.

He covered failure with rage. "Ah told yew: Don't yew tell me what ta do!" Dighton went to work on his freshly delivered drink, giving the waitress a sneer as she walked away. Anyway, the booze seemed to calm him. "Ah . . . Ah cain't go nowhere. Ah cain't leave yew, Jackie. Yer all Ah got left. Ah need yew, an' yew need me."

"How do I—"

"Yew jus' do! Yew jus' . . ." He took in a little more booze to help him grease his logic. "We tied together. Tha's tha queer parta it all. One wild night, an' now yew an' me arh like white an' niggrah blood brothers. Spilled blood bruthas."

I felt very ill and very cold.

"Nah," Dighton went on, "Ah don't think Ah'll much be movin' on from heyah. Ah ain't gonna be movin' nowheres 'cept tah maybe uh better hotel. Heyah that Waldorf place is real good. Yeah, Ah'm gonna want tah be real close tah yew. Jus' like Ah said, white an' niggrah blood bruthas."

I got his meaning. I'd always feared, in my heart I'd always figured, him putting the touch on me wasn't a one-time thing. But what he was talking about now was a state of permanence: me making money and handing a cut of it over to him like he was a Charlie on my payroll, a vig to be paid off, and if I didn't . . . The article, the incident, the police, the scandal rags.

Maybe.

Maybe there was all that. Maybe there was none of it. Maybe he'd send me to jail or kill my career, or maybe he'd just limp away a sick drunk too scared to risk doing time himself. Like old dynamite, he could've been harmless or deadly dangerous.

Sweat glued my clothes to my skin. I felt all bunched in, nervous and anxious, claustrophobic in my own body. I felt like I was being buried alive.

Drunk as he was, Dighton could see me going scared-white under my flesh. "What yew worried 'bout, Jackie?"

I hated the way he called me by my first name. Easy, I'd take "nigger" over him being familiar with me.

"Ah ain't gonna do nuthin' foolish." Some more of his drink, then Dighton followed that with a smile dimmed by his yellow and black teeth. "Lessin' yew arh."

Foolish?

Foolishness was thinking that a black man in the 1950s could walk alone at night from Miami Beach to Miami without encountering some craziness that would chase him for the rest of his life. Foolishness was thinking that once a guy got a taste of free money, his appetite for it would ever go away.

I wasn't going to be foolish anymore. From that moment forward, everything else I did were actions marked past due.

THE NEXT NIGHT AT THE COPA. I talked to Jules, told him I needed a favor. Told him I needed to speak with Frank. Frank C.

He asked what about.

I said it was a private matter.

Jules didn't ask anything else, just gave me an "I'll see what I can do."

The next day. Over the phone I got an earful of a raspy voice I hadn't heard in a good while.

"Jackie, what's doin'?"

"Hello, Mr. Costello."

"Frank. You know it's Frank with you."

"You well, Frank?"

"Ah, you know. Got some time on my hands now. Wife likes havin' me around. Drivin' me fuckin' crazy. Heard you got hitched."

". . . We took the cure a while back."

"Sorry for that. Sad thing when a marriage don't take."

I wondered how the table full of blondes Frank had when I first met him figured into his philosophy but was sure it did somehow. Anyway, I wanted to let the comment pass, all remembrances of my bogus wedding, and slide into another conversation.

Frank beat me to it. "Jules said you wanted to talk."

"Yes."

"Maybe we should have a sit-down."

"Yes."

Frank gave me the address of his place in Port Washington. I told him I'd be out in the afternoon. We swapped good-byes, hung up.

I took the LIRR out to the island, looking forward to seeing Frank. Most guys in life wouldn't be caught dead talking to a moolie. Frank had done everything he could to help me. He had always been a decent guy. Extremely so for a mob boss.

And being decent was the reason he was now an ex–mob boss.

When the other heads of New York's big five wanted to expand their trade to include hard narcotics, Frank nixed it. Not strictly because he was a thug with a heart of gold. He knew that drugs were as much trouble for the people who sold them as the people who took them. Cops might look the other way with prostitution, gambling—probably they were the best customers—but toss some heroin into the mix, all of a sudden all the greased palms in town can't keep the law off your back.

The other bosses didn't care. The other bosses thought Frank was getting old and should take a rest, and told him so Mafia-style—a bullet to the back of the head. Only, Frank had luck riding with him. The slug tore some flesh, chewed up his fedora, but otherwise didn't do much damage. Still, Frank didn't need things explained to him twice. He got the message just fine and took a retirement out on Long Island. He had a nice house, a nice quiet life, but, I hoped, not so quiet that he couldn't help me with a few things.

Forty minutes out of the city, and you were *out* of the city. Concrete and skyscrapers replaced with trees, grass, yards . . . suburban whites eyeballing the stray black who'd wandered into their neighborhood.

Real quick I got myself to Frank's.

"Jackie!" Frank's big hands swallowed mine as he welcomed me to his place. He guided me by the shoulder to his wife, Bobbie, did an introduction, and asked her to pour us some lemonade, then gave me a quick tour of the house—brick traditional down to the shuttered windows and front-yard birdbath. That, and huge—while we caught up some. He asked me how things were going, how the Copa was.

"Good," I told him. "Not like the old days."

"The old days, listen to you. Make it sound like you been in the business since the silents."

"You know, it's not even like a few years back. The room's not as jammed. Don't see people climbing all over each other to get in the door."

"Television," Frank lamented. "Television's gonna be the death of clubs. Sit at home, see whatever the hell you want just by changin' the channel. The box is the future," he prophesied.

Me, having zero television in my history and not seeing me with any in the days to come, was made nervous by the thought.

"But you didn't come all the way out here to talk about the Copa."

No, I hadn't. "Mr. Cos . . . Frank, you've always been decent to me. You helped me out early on with things for no good reason except you thought I was funny, and I appreciate that. . . . I could use some helping out now." I was very straightforward with my delivery. "And the kind of help I need, you're the only one I could think to turn to."

Frank nodded. He got my meaning.

He walked us over to some chairs out on the patio.

I sat. I said: "A few years back, when I was in Florida this one time—"

Brushing air with a hand: "I don't need the specifics. Don't want 'em."

"There's a guy causing me trouble. He can cause me—"

Bobbie came 'round with those lemonades. I thanked her, exchanged a few pleasantries.

When she was gone: "He can cause me a whole lot more trouble if he felt that way."

"And you want . . . ?"

"I would like . . . I want him to stop causing me trouble." I was not at all dramatic about that. Not dire, not desperate or weepy in my request. I was simply asking a favor. Could I borrow a cup of sugar? Would you pick up my newspapers while I'm out of town? Mind shaking up the guy who's trying to shake me down?

And that's how Frank took it, just one cat asking another for a favor. He made an offhanded gesture, said: "You gotta understand, Jackie, I'm sort of out of the life."

"I know."

"The thing you're asking—"

"What I'm asking—"

"You want things explained to this guy. Explained so they don't need explainin' again."

"I want him off my back."

A bird chose that moment to give a little whistle. Up the block I could hear some kids playing. Someone started a car. For a split second I had become hypersensitive to the whole world. Nothing escaped me.

Frank asked: "This guy, you know where to find him?"

I told Frank yes, told him Dighton's name and where he was staying, the Waldorf, courtesy of me.

Frank didn't follow that up with anything, didn't say he was going to help me or that he wasn't. We did talk on some, but completely off the subject and about nothing in particular. Movies. Frank S. What a bastard Kennedy was for making his no-good crumb of a headline-grabbing kid brother the AG.

Finally, from Frank: "Well, good of you to visit, Jackie." He said it without moving an inch from where he sat. I would be finding my own way out.

I thanked Frank for his time and asked that he give my good-bye to his wife. I started to go. As I made my way:

"Jackie . . ."

I turned back.

"You really don't look so good. You should take a vacation, get out of town for a week."

"I'm working the Copa. I don't think I ca—"

"You need to get out of town for a week."

Frank may have been mostly out of the life, but, by nature, his suggestions carried the weight of a command. Truth was, I could use a break. Things could wait. The clubs weren't going anywhere. I had a feeling Dighton wasn't going anywhere. Me, I sure wasn't going anywhere.

I used the train ride back to figure on where I should be getting myself to.

I DECIDED TO GET MYSELF TO HAWAII. I had never been, and, therefore, unlike most every other state in America, it held no memories for me.

The first thing I noticed changing planes in Honolulu was the air. Never in my life had I ever smelled anything so clean. Even in out-of-the-way burgs—Minneapolis, Lincoln—the air was good, but not like this. Hawaiian air was so sweet it was fragrant, a blend of tropical flowers, the ocean, rain, and sun. It was like a message to the senses: Forget the rest of the world. You're somewhere else now.

I took a hopper over to Maui, where I was going to make my stay for five days.

I dug Maui. Besides being beautiful and good-smelling and all that, I dug Maui because it was underdeveloped, quiet, and short on people. What people there were, the locals, *kamaainas* they called each other, were nothing but warm and friendly. Cousins you didn't know you had. They didn't care who you were. They didn't care what color you were. Treat them decent, they treated you decent right back.

Forget the rest of the world. You're somewhere else now.

By day number two, I was like Charlie Local, doing everything aloha-style: going barefoot, relaxing instead of rushing around. Not worrying. How are you going to worry when the sun's up, the breeze is cool? How are you going to have any concerns when your only concern is resting in the shade versus on the beach?

On the beach.

I was sitting out on the beach one evening, sitting, just watching the sun go down for no other reason than that's what I felt like doing just then, when I caught a man walking in my direction from up the shore. Walking. Taking his time. Not in any hurry. He was an Asian fellow, but very dark in skin. Very tan, as if he'd spent the last bunch of years doing nothing but walking along one beach or another. When he came upon me, he stood for a bit, looking out into the ocean, then he took up a seat in the sand. Not too close to me, but not so far off he wasn't trying to be in my presence.

He said to me: "Howzit?"

"Good," I said back.

He kept looking out at the water, looking at the falling sun bouncing off the Pacific. In a real low voice, like he didn't want to disturb nature's work: "Dat's sumtin', yah, bruddah?" His accent was strictly local. Pidgin.

"It's something," I agreed. "I could stare at that all day. Makes me feel like . . . you know, makes me feel not everything in the world is all that bad."

The man asked where I was from. I told him New York but that I traveled a lot. He wanted to know if I'd ever been to California, and I told him that I had.

Then he told me he used to live in California. Los Angeles. He had moved his family there decades ago, opened a small business— an antique shop—that had done fairly well. He never would have gotten rich off of it, he said, but they were nowhere near starving.

Then the war broke out.

He and his family were herded up with the rest of the Japanese-Americans, his business sold off for pennies on the dollar. They got shipped off to an internment camp—war relocation center, it was euphemized—in Manzanar. They were interned—relocated—no matter that his ancestors weren't strictly Japanese. They were from Okinawa. The government didn't know the difference. Didn't know, didn't care. And no matter that their own government locked them up, the man's two sons—one named Jeff, the other Tony—signed up for military service soon as they could to prove to every Jap hater out there that Japanese-Americans were good Americans. They fought with the 442nd Infantry in Europe—the Nisei Brigade.

Late in 1944, the man told me, he got a telegram at Manzanar telling him Tony had been KIA. Less than a week later he got another telegram. Jeff.

War over, the man was allowed to return to Los Angeles. There was nothing left there for him anymore, and he had no money to start over. He worked odd jobs, saved what he could, returned with what remained of his family to Hawaii. These days he worked as a handyman. He said he would never get rich doing it, but then, he added, he wasn't starving either.

At the horizon, the sun went down below the water, was doused.

The man picked himself up from the sand. "Take 'er easy, bruddah." He walked on down the beach.

I stayed in Hawaii three more days. I didn't enjoy it as much.

I RETURNED TO NEW YORK. The city was much the same as I'd left it, only now camouflaged with the unknown. I didn't know if—when—Dighton was going to come around sweating me for more cash. I didn't know if Frank had seen his way to making a call, arranging for someone to talk to my tormenting hick. Talk to him and talk to him until he got his pale behind back below the Mason/Dixon, never to come sniffing around for my green again.

So not knowing anything about anything, I tried to get on with the daily business of Jackie Mann, which I accomplished poorly at best. I couldn't ignore the redneck monkey on my back. So many times I'd reach for the phone to dial up Dighton, find out if he'd been paid a visit, if he'd gotten a message, but each time I stopped myself. If he was still around, what was the point of talking to him, reminding him that Jackie Mann, the human bank, was present and cash-ready anytime he needed? I was paralyzed. I couldn't move and wouldn't know which way to anyhow. All there was to do was sit and wait and hope that every day without hearing from Dighton would bring me one day closer to the time when I would never hear from him again.

I lived that way minute by minute.

There was a morning, routine like every morning: waking up too early from a bad night's sleep. Trying to write new bits but having no heart for it. Trying to watch television but having no stomach for it. An errant copy of *The Times* at my door the only part of my day that strayed from monotony.

I had to get out. I had to go into the city and lose myself. I had to go and shop and buy and spend money and slather myself with shiny items to distract me from my preoccupations.

Useless.

Everything I did seemed useless for getting me beyond . . .

Something wasn't right. Besides everything else that was wrong, something was shrewing at the flesh of my mind, dull and slow, but persistently demanding my attention. Something . . .

The Times at my door. Why was *The Times* at my door? I wasn't a subscriber. So why was the paper . . . It wasn't. It wasn't the whole paper . . .

My head whipped, looked for a newsstand. Found one. Went for it. Grabbed a *Times,* ignored the yelling newsy as I tore threw it looking . . . looking . . .

It wasn't the whole paper at my door, it was only—

I threw cash at the newsy, a wad of it, shut him up.

The Metro section: The MTA thinking about a fare hike. A man attacked by rats in the park. Suicide in Midtown. The borough president promising to devote a street crew to just fixing potholes. A string of muggings has ritzy Park Ave. all jittery. The library was opening—

The paper crunched. An involuntary jerk—realization delayed—crumbled it in my hands. I opened the paper again just ahead of a panic that was racing me down. The suicide in Midtown. My eyes bounced all over the article, unable to read it in a steady fashion: the Waldorf-Astoria. Tourist. Jumped. Miami man. Dighton Spooner.

The paper got crumbled up again; I strangled it against my body as I clutched at myself trying to hold in a sickness that was eating me from the inside out.

The newsy, not yelling at me now. Now he was asking me if I was all right. People touching me, grabbing at me: "You okay, mister?" "Mister, you need help?" A thousand shrill voices, ice picks to my head. I swung and swatted at them. I flailed my way free of the murmuring. I clawed through the avenue foot traffic madman-style.

A phone booth.

I stumbled into a phone booth. Shut the door. Shut them out. Couldn't breathe. Couldn't . . . I had to talk myself calm, had to talk myself into believing that maybe . . . that probably it was a suicide. Here was this Dighton cat, strictly a hick from Backwatersville, gets the heave by the Mrs., no prospects in the big city and the only dough he's got is out of my pocket. Sprinkle a little booze on top of all that, and it's a recipe for taking a fast trip to the sidewalk.

Wasn't it?

It was. I told myself it was.

I spent three minutes on the floor of a phone booth telling myself it was.

I didn't buy it.

One more minute of sitting.

I hauled myself up, got a coin from my pocket, and slotted it.

I dialed.

Bobbie answered. I gave her some hello, how are you, how's the house jazz, then fast as I could got around to asking if Frank was home. She told me he was and went off to get him.

Seemed like a year before he picked up the phone.

"Frank . . ."

"Jackie, what's do—"

"Did you kill him?"

"What?"

"Did you have some guys go over there and—"

"You fuckin' crazy?" His wheeze sounding like a bellows. "You out of your goddamn mind!"

Was I? I must've been to be talking to a man like Frank—a man like Frank, whose line could very possibly be cop- or FBI-tapped— about such things as murder.

I said for whatever ears might be listening: "I'm . . . I'm kidding around, Frank. I'm a comedian. I'm just . . . I'm a kidder."

"You had a problem."

"What's tha—"

"You had a problem, didn't you?"

"Yeah, I . . . I had one."

"Well, you ain't got one no more. That's what you wanted, you dumb-jig bastard. That's what you got. And don't be fuckin' callin' me up no more. Never! You goddamn—"

The exclamation was the slam of Frank's phone in my ear.

My phone just sort of fell out of my hand. In my head, Frank's words kept thrashing around. "That's what you wanted."

It's not what I wanted. I wanted Frank to send out a couple of guidos, I wanted them to take that bastard Dighton by the scruff of the neck, slap him around, slap him smart. Let him know—make him believe—that if he ever opened his mouth regarding what had happened on a back road in Florida, permanent trouble is what he'd get, but I didn't want . . . I didn't want . . .

I wanted this.

I did. I could claim things any way I pleased—dial up Frank and scream my innocence—but inside myself, within the dark that I owned, I knew the truth. I knew the kind of man Frank was. I knew with one phone call he could push the button that would pull a trigger. When I went to him with my vague self—I want you to talk to him, I want you to explain things to him—what was that but guinea-speak for rough business. An unpleasant chore. What was that but saying without saying "Make him dead for me."

And should that surprise me any? Really, when I thought

about it, should I be so shocked at what I'd done? Years prior I had killed a man. An accident. I hadn't meant to. But I had taken a pipe to his head. I had killed him to protect myself. Was this any different? A guy shows up out of my past, wanting from me, and to get what he wants he would tear down everything I'd built up over the years. Every single thing. What would that return me to? Being some poor black man with no prospects, no chances, right back on the unforgiving streets of Harlem? So was what I did *now* any different than what I'd done *then*? Wasn't it just protecting me one more time?

Yes.

At that moment I became fully aware of myself, that for the things I wanted, if it came to it, if it had to . . . if I had to, I could kill.

That was not the queer part. Honest: Back to the wall, knife at your throat, who wouldn't take a life in the name of self-preservation?

The queer part: I was fine with the concept. My breathing went regular. My heart slowed up. The knowledge of things, it didn't frighten me. I wasn't ill to my gut or scared of myself anymore. I felt very liberated in the knowledge of that which I could do.

LONGCHAMPS WAS ALL ABOUT FOOD. Hearty food. House-cut steak and potatoes heaped up high on your plate. Longchamps was a restaurant on Madison and Fifty-ninth where the tony people went to chow down and get greasy. Longchamps was where I invited Sid for some dinner. I had the New York strip, and Sid went back and forth on the prime rib. I encouraged him to go all out. It was my treat. He got the T-bone. Through our salads we talked some about a picture we'd both seen, whether or not we'd ever get to the moon, how much we hated bossa nova. We both talked a lot, desperate to fill what we sensed would otherwise be unnaturally dead air.

Done with his salad, Sid pushed his plate away. He took a look all around the joint, said: "Nice restaurant, good food. And you're paying. What's the occasion? What did I do to rate all this?"

"You've done a lot for me, Sid. You know that. If it weren't for you, I'd still be doing five minutes between strippers."

He shrugged. "I doubt it, but thank you."

Sid picked up his fork off his plate, twisted it around, gave it a good looking over, set it down again.

He said: "A condemned man eats a hearty meal."

"Sid—"

"I'm a big boy, Jackie. I've been in the game a lot of years. I appreciate it, but you don't have to be nice about things."

Okay. If he wanted it straight, no chaser, fine by me. "You know Chet Rosen?"

Sid nodded. "Took them longer than I figured to get to you."

"I want you to know if it—"

"Yeah. I do know: If it weren't for me . . . You'll always be grateful for all I've done . . . It's business, right? It would've happened sooner or later."

To my ears he was sounding snide. I didn't care for the way snide sounded. I laid things out. "He can get me Sullivan."

"And it's always been about that. You do the Sullivan show and you got no problems anymore. All the doors fly open, and you're king of Hollywood."

"I came to you, Sid. I came to you and you didn't want to do this for me."

"No! It's not that I didn't—"

"I came to you first, and you wouldn't do it."

"You're not ready."

"Jesus, please, not again with that."

Sid reached across the table, clamped me hard by the wrist, forced me to look at him. "You're still growing as an act, Jackie. Yeah, believe it or not, long as you've been at it, you're still growing.

You're good and you're only going to get better. Better, more confident . . . That set, the one you wrote in San Francisco—"

Yanking my arm back from him: "I'm sick of waiting. Every time I think I've got something good, I see it melt away. Every time I think I've got it made, it all falls to pieces. Not anymore. I'm not letting this get away from me. I'm not . . . Fran's got her own show, for Christ's sake!"

"Would you leave Fran? Quit comparing yourse—"

"When am I going to be ready? Huh? I have been ready since the first time I had to get down on hands and knees to clean up someone else's dirt for the nickels they gave me. I've been ready since the first time I got ridden to the floor by the back of someone's hand. I've been ready from the day I heard: 'Nigger, go' and 'Nigger, fetch' and 'Nigger, why can't you be a little bit smarter, nigger?' I have been ready all my life. Ready to get out, to go on, to move up—"

"Ready to do whatever it takes."

My mind real quick conjured up a picture of Dighton Spooner flattened on a sidewalk with a splatter of blood spiderwebbing from his body. "Yes. Yes. To be respected? To be treated like a somebody? I never had that, Sid. Not from my father, not from my so-called friends—"

"Not from Tammi? Fran? Not from me? All these years I haven't stood by you?"

And then I let fly what I'd held in so long: "When I was supposed to do Fran's show, when CBS was giving her grief about that kiss, where were you, Sid? Off drying out somewhere because you couldn't keep yourself sober. That what you call standing by me?"

My words came in a pack snarling and snapping. And you'd have thought, once said, no matter we were in public, match set to fuse, things would have exploded. Instead, they stayed real calm.

"You're right, Jackie." Sid was even in tone. Soft-spoken. The truth had always been with us. No denying it now, no fighting it. If anything, Sid was glad to have our shared secret finally spoken aloud. "I should have been there for you, and . . . I let myself fall off the wagon instead. I'm sorry for that, and I guess it doesn't matter that it was . . . or that I cleaned myself up. I never pretended to be a perfect person, so if that's what this is about—"

"It's about you not doing your job. Drunk or dry, you didn't . . . you know? So don't sit there now and act like . . . whatever."

Sure. Whatever.

Sid nodded. Just a little. He took up his napkin, wiped his hands. Not that they were messed with anything, it was just a way of saying he was all done.

Reaching for his wallet: "Think I'll take a pass on dinner. Let me leave you something."

"No. . . . It's on me."

"You don't have to buy me dinner to clear your guilt."

"It's business, Sid. I don't feel guilty."

He gave me a good looking-at. "No, I believe you don't."

Sid got up, started out. He stopped, turned, said: "If things don't work out at William Morris . . ." That was all the more good-bye I got from him.

Sid left.

The waiter brought around my steak. I ate it, then washed it down with a hunk of shortcake. When I was finished, all I felt was full.

Funny how freeing a murder can be.

THE PAPERS WERE IN FRONT OF ME. Papers. That's what they were called. Agency papers. They were contracts that signed me up to William Morris for two years. There was nothing queer about that. Not really. I'd been with Sid longer and at the same rate, ten percent. But with Sid, there were never any papers. No contracts. We just shook hands, and that was that. A shake of hands, then he was my agent, and I was his—

"Something wrong, Jackie?"

"What's that?"

Chet pulled me away from my thoughts. He was there in the conference room at the WMA New York offices. It was Chet, a woman who was a secretary or assistant or something, and that other agent I'd met back in Los Angeles who never had much to say for himself.

Chet said: "Bottom of page eight, that's where you want to sign. On all the copies."

I picked up the pack of papers, let them fall back down onto the table. "Pretty thick."

"Legal things." That came from the woman.

From the other agent: "All standard."

"It's for your protection," Chet offered.

I turned to the eighth page of the bundle of documents. At the bottom was a line just waiting for me to scrawl Jackie Mann across.

Just waiting.

Chet asked me again: "Something wrong?"

"No, there's nothing . . . I've never had to sign anything like this before."

Once more from the woman: "Just legal things."

"Really, it's all standard," the no-name agent said again.

"If you'd like us to get you a lawyer to look it over . . ."

"I know it's standard, agency papers an all that. It's just kinda weird for me. I've never had to sign—"

"And you're a little nervous?" Chet asked.

"This place is so big. You've got so many clients . . ."

"You're afraid you'll get lost in the shuffle. That's a legitimate concern. For any other act it is, but you're very unique: a Negro comedian who's acceptable to white audiences. Think of how many . . . how few, I should say; think of the Negro talent that is also popular with whites. You can list them on one hand. Davis, Belafonte, Cole, Poitier. That's an exclusive club. I'll be honest, you're no good to us unless we put you in it. All of us are here for you, Jackie. From me all the way up to Abe. So if you're afraid of getting lost, no; no you won't. You stand out too much."

Some smiles at Chet's double-meaning phrase.

Chet's little talk made me feel better, made me see he was right about things. Still, I just sat there.

"It's up to you, Jackie. I, we, don't want you doing anything you don't feel one hundred percent—"

"I don't have a pen."

Everybody did nothing for a second, then we all busted out laughing. Jackie didn't have a pen. Ain't that just the funniest thing?

Chet dug one out of his pocket, handed it to me.

Across the blank line went Jackie Mann. That was that.

There were handshakes and goodwill all around. We all chatted awhile, and when the talk fell flat, I excused myself, let them get back to work. Might as well. They were working for me now. I shook hands with the secretary, with the no-name agent, and Chet walked me to the elevators.

Chet told me he would be in touch shortly, that he was working up a game plan for me and wanted to get me started on it right away.

The elevator rang, and I began to get on.

"Jackie?"

I turned back.

"My pen?"

⸺

PHILLY, CLEVELAND, two weeks in Reno, Tahoe . . .

My life was in replay. My life was in clubs and show rooms and dinner theaters. I was where I had been, which was not on television. Not on the Sullivan show. I didn't expect—didn't allow myself to hope—that I would land the show straight off, even with all the might of WMA pushing me. I figured it would take time. I figured right. I just didn't figure how much time. Two months turned into four. Nineteen sixty-two turned into sixty-three. I remained Charlie Road-Comic. Maybe I was making a little more at each stop—seventy-five extra at this club, a hundred, hundred and fifty at that one—but other than that . . .

San Francisco, L.A., a week in Vegas . . .

And little by little, month into month, the crowds were getting smaller. The empty sections of the club were getting larger. People were staying home. Frank C's prophecy was coming true: The future was television.

Cats without television were dinosaurs heading for the tar pits.

I talked to Chet about it, me and Sullivan and me not being on Sullivan. He told me he was lining things up, that he was *this* close to landing an audition. It would all happen in time.

Time crawled on. As it did, gradually, seemingly, I found myself talking with Chet less and less. Just getting him on the phone was turning into a magic trick. And Abe? Forget it. More and more I was doing business with Marty, who used to be the no-name agent. Marty was turning into my day-to-day guy, the guy who would handle my bookings, make sure everything was okeydoke at all my shows. He made sure everything was okeydoke from New York or L.A. Not once did he ever make sure that everything was okeydoke from where I was actually playing.

I was being passed off. I was being handed over same as a baton in a relay race, only instead of rushing me forward, it felt to me like these guys were just standing around on the track. If not strolling backward. My fear was the next person to get their hands on me was going to be that secretary girl.

Marty told me not to worry about things. Marty told me that Chet had told him that he was very close to nailing down that audition for me. Very close. *This* close. In no time at all I was going to have my shot at Sullivan. Until then . . .

St. Louis, Minneapolis, Milwaukee, Chi—

Chicago. I was doing a week in Chicago. So was Tammi. Her

stand lapping over the tail end of mine. Had to happen sooner or later, us working the same city at the same time. I'd figured it would happen, but I never figured *what* would happen. What I hoped would happen was that she might call me. She might hear I was in town and call just to let me know that at the least she didn't hate me with every part of her there was to hate a person with.

But she didn't call. Days passed. My gig ended. Time for me to split town, and she hadn't rung up. Me call her? That took guts I didn't have.

All I could do: I went to see her show. I went to see *her*. I went but ended up standing around outside the club, unable to go in and sit and watch her.

But I was unable to do anything else.

I paid my money, got seated, waited for the show to begin. Short of breath and quick-hearted, I was a man waiting for his own execution. Same thing. Sort of. I knew seeing Tammi was going to kill me. It amounted to nothing more than penance, self-torture. I wanted to hurt me *for* her, the way I needed to be hurt for what I'd done *to* her.

The lights went down. The show started. She took the stage. Never mind the years that had passed. I saw Tammi and I was seeing her again for the very first time in that dingy, smoke-choked cellar of a joint back in the Village that she filled with light and beauty, the moment as fresh and as vivid but tinged with the knowledge . . . with the knowledge that I had fucked everything up. There is no other way to say it. The truth of it, the vulgarity of it, was that real. I had fucked up.

It wasn't but sixty full seconds of looking at Tammi, of listening to her, before I couldn't take any more. I pulled myself from the club and into a cab and back to my hotel.

My hotel.

I wasn't completely sad. I didn't feel as if I wanted to break down and bawl. As I lay on the bed, one hour into another, staring at the ceiling, I felt very little other than the rent in my soul that was as fresh as when Tammi first left me. On the radio: Ruby and the Romantics. "Our Day Will Come." The four walls of the room. Other than that, I was alone.

A knock at a door.

I lay still. Was it my door? Was it down the hallway? Was it even a knock or just a—

A knock again. A knock at *my* door.

I got up, walked for it, hesitant. I was scared. I was alone and I was scared, afraid a ghost had come calling. Hand on the doorknob, slipping under my sweat-slick palm.

I opened the door.

Oh, sweet Jesus . . .

Tammi. It was . . . it was my Thomasina.

I clutched at her. I clutched at her as I slid to the ground. I was on my knees before her, crying. Sobbing. Useless for anything but.

She took my head in her hands, pressed it to her stomach. From above me, in a whisper: "It's all right, Jackie. I'm here now. I'm here, and I love you. I will always love you. Nothing else matters."

Her love, love that I had been empty of my entire life, came raining down on me. It filled the want for any other thing required to survive. All that I needed to live and to be and to exist was Tammi.

She was there. She was there with me, *for* me, but why? Why should she give me her gift of grace when the only thing I'd done was carve across her heart with my deceptions? Why . . . ?

"Why me?"

Her hands lifted my face. My tears made her shimmer.

She said: "You're special, Jackie Mann. You're special, and don't ever let anyone—"

I jumped awake. My hands gripped the covers of the bed. My face was sheened with sweat.

I was alone.

The phone was ringing.

I looked over at the clock. The night had passed to forty after nine in the morning.

I answered. "Hello?"

"Jackie?"

"Chet?"

"We're going to have to pull you off the road a bit. We've got you the Sullivan audition for as soon as you get back. Call me when you hit the city."

Chet hung up.

≈

THE SINGERS DIDN'T HAVE TO DO IT. Neither did the rock and roll bands. Not the dog acts or the variety acts. Just the comics. The comics had to go over to the Delmonico Hotel, go up to the eleventh floor to a six-room suite where the Sullivans lived, and put on a show for Ed himself. Ed and Robert Precht, Sullivan's producer. Ed had to see the comics because Ed didn't trust the comics. Comedians by nature were freewheeling and unpredictable. Full of surprises. Ed didn't like surprises. Ed liked to get exactly what he paid for and nothing more. So comics had to do what singers and rock and roll bands and dog acts and all the rest didn't; they had to please the king before they were allowed to perform for the kingdom.

I went to the Delmonico. The eleventh floor. I did my set. I did my set for two people. I don't care how long you've been a performer, you take away the other hundred and ninety-eight people you're used to joking for and the deal becomes a whole new thing. No laughs to mark your rhythm, to let you know how you're doing. Just nods from Ed and Robert. Occasional smiles like they're digging your bits. Maybe they're digging your bits. Maybe they're just smiling not to let on how much they hate you. Hard to tell. Ed never had much of a smile to begin with, and had even less of one after a car smash-up bashed in most of his puss. Sunken-eyed and sullen-faced, he had the look of a professional pallbearer.

With the nodding and occasional smiling, my five-minute set got whittled down to four and change.

I finished.

I thanked Ed, Robert, and stepped outside the suite into the hallway. Chet was there, waiting for me, decked in his standard blue suit. He asked how I did.

How did I do? Two guys grinning and head-bobbing. How should I know how I did?

We hung around a couple of minutes.

Robert stepped from the suite. Bob, he asked me to call him. He was a youngish guy, groomed straight-arrow clean, but the way he talked—the quick edit he did of my act, taking out this joke and moving around that one—made me think he got to be the show's producer because he was sharp, not because he'd married the boss's daughter. Although, he'd iced things by doing that as well.

Chet led the Jackie Mann parade doing "Isn't he something" bits. "Didn't I tell you the kid is terrific. Good-looking, well spoken, presentable . . ."

"And funny," Bob added, almost as if reminding Chet of that.

"And funny. The funny goes without saying. What I am saying is that Jackie makes for a neat package, a real neat package. TV's going to like this kid, Bob. I'm telling you, TV's going to love him."

"A week from Sunday we've got an opening in the comedy slot. Ed wants to have you on then, Jackie."

"Perfect," Chet answered for me.

Bob just sort of smiled at Chet's enthusiasm. He was well used to agents. "So, you'll give me a call, work out the details."

"First thing in the morning."

"Jackie." Bob gave me his hand. "Great stuff. You're going to be sensational on the show." Back into the suite he went.

Chet said: "This is a really, really . . . You know, Sullivan pays better than any other variety show on the air."

"It's not about the money."

"It's not about the money. No. No, it's not. But the money don't hurt, it doesn't hurt a bit."

"Thank you."

Chet gave me a "for what?" look.

"For getting me Sullivan."

"You got the show. You're the one who was in there doing the bits."

"For getting me the audition, then, thanks."

"We told you we'd get you the audition. When we say something we . . . Unless, you thought maybe we weren't going to get it for you." Chet made a playful show of being offended. "Did you really think we weren't going to come through for you?"

Those days I was back on the road, those days I couldn't so much as get Chet anywhere near a telephone. Yes, that's what I thought. But all I said was, again: "Thank you."

Chet asked if maybe I wanted to go out and have a drink in celebration, but I declined. I just wanted to go home. I just wanted to walk home.

So I walked.

And let me tell you: As I walked, I felt real good. Real calm no matter that I was right up on the edge of everything I'd spent most of my life working toward. I'd heard about those fellows who'd flown supersonic test jets, how right before they hit the speed of sound the planes got kicked around and kicked around and then . . . nothing. They broke the sound barrier, and everything was lounge-act mellow. That's how I felt. I felt like all the head-banging and heartbreaking was in my past. I felt as if some cosmic court had handed down a vindication that every choice I'd ever made, no matter how it'd turned out, had been the right choice. For the first time I could ever recall, I felt that for the rest of my life the sailing was going to be nothing but smooth.

I REMEMBER IT BEING A WEDNESDAY. I remember it being a good day. I remember feeling rested, the five nights since my Sullivan audition being filled with deep sleep. I had the security of my television debut without being overly anxious about it. Things were happening as they should. When things happen as they should, what's there to be anxious about? I remember it being nice outside, the weather pleasant—sunny and warm without being too hot. I headed from my apartment over to a corner diner for a late breakfast, and I don't recall the normal crush of people packing the New York streets or the usual hectivity. All around, things were shaping up to make for a real good day. Maybe that's the way it was.

Or maybe it was a day like any other, but what the day revealed made the first part of the morning, in retrospect, seem so much better.

I got to the diner, a couple of guys in a booth trying to figure out Andy Warhol, and ordered food—French toast, two eggs scrambled. That was my favorite breakfast. French toast and eggs scrambled. The waitress wrote it up on a green ticket and put the order in the carousel at the kitchen counter for the cook.

Odd, I guess. Odd all of that commonplace stuff should stay so sharp in my mind. But all of that was part of the moment: what I ordered, the waitress taking it down and passing it off to the cook. Her going for coffee, and my eyes following her for no good reason but lack of anything else to do. As she crossed under a TV hung in the corner, I looked up at it and caught a face I'd only seen once, years before. There was no hesitation in my recognition. No matter how long it had been, I knew the face in an instant. Miami. That back road. The black man who saved my life was on television. His picture, anyway. His picture was on a news bulletin.

"What'd he do?" I asked for anyone to answer.

"What, hon?" the waitress asked back.

"That fellow, what did he—"

The waitress looked up at the television; the picture of the man was gone. Film was being shown of a house, the driveway with paint poured over part of it.

"I think they're talking about that man that got killed." She was as detached about the information as a phone operator dispensing a number.

I tried to say to her "What?" but could not generate the word.

"Last night or this morning. In front of his house. They shot him, I think. Well, here . . ." She went over to the TV, reached up, and, fingers tweezering the knob, gave it some volume.

The newsman droned about what was, apparently, the latest civil rights assassination. Mississippi. Long after dark. Medgar Evers was walking up the drive of his house, when he took a bullet to the back.

Just one.

But just one bullet from a rifle is all that's needed to punch a fist of a hole in one side of you and tear out the other, taking with it all the meat and bone it can gather. Taking all that, and not stopping until it passed through a window and a kitchen wall to end up resting on a counter like some kind of dark souvenir. All that, and still not enough to kill this man. Not kill him right off. The bullet had put Medgar down, but he managed, blood pumping from him, to crawl up the drive to his front porch . . .

Unaware of myself, my fingers bit at the counter, dragged me along it closer to the TV.

. . . Crawl to his wife and children, who rushed from the house to hold their dying man. He held on long enough to get loaded into a station wagon by friends and get raced to University of Mississippi Hospital, and just long enough to make it into the emergency room, where white doctors didn't exactly snap to operating on a shot black man. He held on that long, but no longer.

On the TV: another picture of the house. What I thought was paint on the drive was a slick of blood.

Medgar Evers. Husband. Father. My savior. Dead. Dead, because he thought black people should have the radical, unheard of, uninfringeable right to be able to sit where they wanted at lunch counters, ride where they wanted on a bus. Maybe even vote.

The news bulletin over, the broadcast went back to a soap.

Murmurs from the diner: The mayor's out of his mind, out of his damn mind if he thinks . . . The Yankees are nothing but bums, and what they need to do is . . . A guy telling another guy about some skirt at work—a looker, divorced—who was ready for a little . . .

Murmurers. Nothing about Medgar. No one was murmuring about him. For me, until that moment, he'd been a face without a name. For most of the rest of the world, he wouldn't even be a memory.

"Order up." Down the counter, the waitress with my food. "Your order's up."

I got up, went for the door, stopped, went back, and tossed over some money. I left.

THIS IS HOW IT WAS GOING TO BE: It was going to be the Moscow circus . . . actually, first it was going to be Ed. Ed would come out, do his "hello-we've-got-a-great shew" bits, then give hellos to any stars in the house. There were always stars in the house, because stars loved getting their mugs flashed coast-to-coast just for all the non-effort of showing up and sitting in Ed's audience. So it would be Ed and his hellos, and then the circus, and then me. It was all standard procedure. The gospel according to the man himself. Bob told me Ed's rule was "Open big, have a good comedy act, put in something for the children, keep the show clean." Kill, be entertaining, have a great set, but be clean. Clean, safe, pleasing to the people was what Ed Sullivan was all about.

As we walked through the rehearsal, I had an experience of déjà vu times déjà vu. I'd lived the moment so many times in my head, it was as familiar to me as any real-life event from my past. Despite the frenzied moil going on around me—the growing panic of the crew who, no matter how many times they'd done this before, were moving closer and closer to having to go out live to America—I was as I'd been since Bob shook my hand and told me I had the show, very calm. It was as if I were ghosting through a moment already completed, watching it specter-style. All there was for me was to play my part as scripted.

Except, the script didn't exactly read the way I always thought it would. It had changed severely in the days since Medgar Evers caught a bullet.

The stage manager called me over to what would be my mark, wanted me to run through my set right quick for the cameras. Like a gambler's ritual, one more time I pulled some papers from my pocket—yellowed, torn, but never thrown away. Stationery from the St. Regis in San Francisco. I looked quickly at a routine long dormant but never forgotten. I took my mark, looked into the camera, said: "Hello, my name is Jackie Mann. I'm a Negro."

<hr />

IT WAS ME AND CHET AND BOB in Bob's office. Bob was being sympathetic—as sympathetic as he could be, considering—but his compassion was being drowned under apprehension that, moment by moment, he was taking on through the hole I'd just blown in him. Chet was red-hot–volcano-style, but he held it in. Let Bob do the talking. Probably for fear of what would happen should he let his fury flow.

Bob said, delicate but to the point: "He's furious. Ed is absolutely . . . Your set was—"

"It was funny," I said.

"It was—"

"Funny. You heard those people at the rehearsal laughing. And the crew, they've heard, what, a thousand comics? Heard every possible joke? They were—"

"Nervous laughter."

"Laughter."

"Let him talk!" Chet barked at me. "Just let the man talk."

I didn't look at Chet. I didn't look at him or Bob. I didn't want to be hypnotized by whatever emotion came pouring out of their eyes. I just kept up a blank stare at a nonexistent spot somewhere in front of me.

Bob took a second, let everybody get calm. "You see the problem here, Jackie? You did a set for us at the Delmonico, a set we approved, then not only do you change it at the last minute, you do all that . . . going on about race, and Vietnam, for crying out loud."

"I'm talking about what's going on in the world."

"Half the people in the country couldn't point to Vietnam on a map. I mean, who in the heck cares what's go—"

"I'm talking about what's going on with Negroes. I'm telling jokes from my point of view. What's wrong with that?"

". . . Nothing. Nothing in particular—"

"It's not like I'm cursing. It's not like I'm going blue. I'm just talki—"

"In its place, nothing's wrong with any of that. But on national television on a Sunday night? That's not what we do. That's not what America wants to hear."

"How do you know if no one's ever talked about it before?"

"Jesus Christ," Chet spat.

Bob just looked exasperated. Still, he tried to get me to understand things. "Jackie, Ed Sullivan and this show are as committed to supporting Negro entertainers, Negroes period, as any television program on the air. Lincoln-Mercury gave Ed big trouble for hugging Ella Fitzgerald and Pearl Bailey. He didn't care. Ed has never once shied away from . . . Do you remember the heat he gave

Winchell for snubbing Josephine Baker at the Stork Club? But regardless of how Ed personally feels about Negroes, or civil rights, that doesn't mean you get to turn the eight P.M. time slot into a soapbox."

Bob stopped trying to sell me, and got very plain about the situation. "I think I can square things with Ed. I'll tell him . . . I'll tell him something, but I can keep you on the show only if you do the set you showed us at the Delmonico. I've got to have your word on that, Jackie. I've got to have your word you'll do the set we agreed on. Yes or no?"

I said nothing.

Chet said to Bob: "Let me talk to him a minute."

Bob nodded, got up. He started to go but first reduced the entire discussion to its essence: "Jackie, do not fuck with Ed Sullivan." He left his office to Chet and me.

Chet washed his face in the palms of his hands, then slid them up to his head, slicked back his hair. Little rituals for calming.

He said, asked: "What are you doing?"

"I'm doing my act."

"You're killing yourself, that's what you're doing. It's like . . . it's like you're taking a gun—God, I can't even believe you'd . . . It's like you're taking a gun and putting it to your head and spreading your brain all over a wall. It's suicide." Chet worked loose the knot of his blue spotted tie. "The Sullivan show! Why in the hell would you—"

"He saved my life."

". . . What?"

"Medgar Evers saved my life."

Chet didn't know what to say to that. He tried a couple of times to come up with something, but it didn't amount to much more than his mouth opening and closing.

"Years ago. Kept me from getting beat to death."

"So now you've got to . . . what? You gotta do a memorial to him?"

"No. Not for him. I think I have to do this for me."

"Okay. Okay, that right there is the problem: For you, you're doing this for you. You even thought about what you're doing to Bob? You're putting a fire to his ass! He went to bat for you! I—" Chet's hands clenched up, he rolled one of his fists on his forehead, made a couple of sharp, herky-jerky moves, working hard to check his anger.

After he rode it down: "I went to bat for you, Jackie. You come to the agency, you come to me, you say you want Sullivan. I get you Sullivan. I make the calls, I put on the pressure, I—GET—YOU—SULLIVAN! I put my neck out for you and now you're swinging the ax. Christ!" Chet did a little more anger-wrestling. Anger was getting the upper hand.

I did what I'd been trying to avoid. I looked Chet in the eye. No rage there, not like I'd thought. There was some hurt. There was a lot of pleading.

"Yeah, you know something, your set was funny. That stuff about race, civil rights . . . you can do things with that. Monday morning, you can do some serious damage with those jokes. Monday, after Sunday, after Sullivan, after you're a star. If you want to do something for yourself, make yourself a star, Jackie."

If I wanted to do something for myself . . . Was I doing this, doing my San Francisco set, for myself? Was I being selfish? Was I so desperate to soothe my grief over a man I hardly knew, my guilt that a man who worked for positive change was dead while I, working for nothing greater than more money and better fame, was still very much alive, that I was just putting all that ahead of the reality of the situation? Was I just trying to make me feel good about the shit of a human that I was?

I didn't know.

I didn't know. I'd been lying to myself so long, lying about what was right or wrong or okay to do for the sake of getting ahead that I didn't know what was truth anymore. Chet had put himself out for me. He had delivered as promised. He had gotten me Sullivan. How fair was it for me to turn around and do every unkind thing short of hitting him with a shovel so I could feel righteous about myself?

It wasn't fair at all. That much I knew to be truth.

Monday. Come Monday I could tell just about any joke I pleased just about anywhere I desired. Monday after Sunday there'd be plenty of chances for me to do things the way I wanted. But for now . . .

"Okay. Tell them I'll do the other jokes."

THE SMOOTH AND STEADY SWEEP of a bright-red second hand over the plain black-and-white face of the clock that was hung up on the wall. Minutes now. Minutes instead of years, days, hours. Minutes until eight o'clock P.M. Eastern Standard Time, until the start of the Sullivan show. From my dressing room I could hear a dull hum, the audience filling the house with their bodies and their swelling excitement. I didn't think anything of it. I remained relaxed.

At intervals a voice would come over a loudspeaker, staticky, giving instructions to the crew and counting down the time to air.

Minutes.

Chet was off somewhere else in the studio, shaking hands, greasing wheels, getting the world ready for Jackie Mann. Fine. I was glad for the time to think and be still. And I would be very glad when all of this was behind me. I was tired of the struggle. For as long as I could remember, the Sullivan show had been the focal point of my existence. It had been my Sunday nights, my escape, my dreams. In a way, in a very real way, it defined me. It had been my life. I wanted my life back.

I started to go through a mental checklist, give myself little reminders: Stand straight. When you walk out onstage, stand straight.

Smile. Make sure you smile for the people. Be confident. Own the moment. Why shouldn't I own it? I'd been paying for it on installment for years.

A knock at the door. It came as a gunshot, made me jump. I was more nervous than I would admit to myself. Even now, always lying.

It was Bob. "All set, Jackie?"

"Yes," I said.

"It's going to be a great show." He stuttered a bit. "I'm glad we could work things out."

"Sorry about all that. I owed you better for what you've done for me. I owed Chet, too."

"He's a good agent. I was glad to hear it when Sid told me you went with him. Nothing against Sid, mind you, but William Morris . . ."

Bob talked on, but I sat for a second, maybe it was a couple, not hearing him, not hearing what he was saying but processing what he'd just said. "Sid told you?"

"Yes."

"You talked to him?"

"When I called to tell him I wanted you to audition."

"You called Sid?"

"Yeah. He'd been working me for you a good long while. When I called him, told him I was ready to give you a look, he said you were with William Morris now, and I should—"

"And then *you* called Chet." Slow. Deliberate. "*You* called Chet and *you* told him you wanted me to audition?"

Bob couldn't quite figure what to make of my reaction. He couldn't figure why I looked so shocked, hurt. Why I looked as if a knife—long and jagged—had been slid, none too gently, deep inside me.

"Yeah. I called Chet. . . . He's your agent."

The god-voice came back over the speakers, told us it was three minutes to air.

"I've got some things to take care of, Jackie. A page will come get you about five minutes before your spot. Break a leg."

Bob left.

I'm not sure what I did.

I WAS STANDING IN THE WINGS.

Ed was before the cameras. ". . . Right here, on this stage . . . Sensational young . . . Television debut . . ."

Couldn't focus on the words, couldn't even . . .

Out of the corner of my eye, somebody giving me the thumbs-up.

From Ed, my name.

The orchestra. People clapping.

My legs begged to shake. My palms slicked up.

I walked out to center stage . . .

Stand straight. Make sure you walk out straight.

Walked out to a little star that was painted there . . .

Be confident. Own the moment.

My heart went supersonic, the sound of it pumping made me deaf to the world. I looked at the audience but couldn't see them with the electric white of the lights in my eyes. Just dark silhouettes—that living ink blot. Clapping shadows—and the television cameras. Three bulky beasts staring me down. The whole of America looking at me through them.

And smile. Make sure you . . .

Couldn't work up a smile.

Couldn't.

The applause died out.

It got quiet.

The quiet again. Same quiet I'd spent so many years facing down. The empty void.

Only . . .

This time the void wasn't empty. This time, as if I were watching a movie show of my life just prior to dying, pictures of the past jumped up before my face. Call it: Story of a Man. Me, years ago, seventy blocks and a world away, watching Ed Sullivan up at Grandma Mae's. Me working the burly-ques, the Village clubs, the Copa, Tahoe and Vegas, the stars I'd opened for, the shows I'd closed. I saw the road traveled and the mountain climbed. I saw all it took to get me to the very moment when I stood where I stood.

All it took.

I saw me shuckin' and jivin' so the crackers at a lumber camp wouldn't beat me. Dancing so rednecks wouldn't lynch me. Dodging while Frances put her career on the line just to kiss me. There's me getting chased from Liliah by Hollywood thugs. Me marrying a woman I didn't care for. Me letting the woman I'd loved more and longer than anything else slip further and further away.

And then there's me cutting Sid Kindler out of my life so some other guy could grab the credit for getting me where I was.

All it took.

All it took . . .

All it took from me.

In the void I saw Jackie Mann ducking and sliding and kowtowing and yawsuhing and bootlicking and cowering and truckling and groveling and chipping, and chipping, and chipping away at himself until what was left couldn't even occupy the space where he stood.

Jackie Mann.

Jackie Mann?

Jacking Nothing. Not one single thing. I was nothing.

Jackie Mann?

Jackie Mann.

I said to the audience, I said to the world: "Hello, I'm Jackie Mann . . . I'm a Negro. I have to tell you that because I wasn't always a Negro. Used to be colored. As I understand it, pretty soon we're going to be calling ourselves black. We keep changing what we call ourselves all the time. I think we're hoping we can confuse white people into liking us: 'I hate them.' 'Who?' 'Those col . . . Ne . . . bla . . . Never mind!'

"I think Negroes are finally starting to get respect. Used to be if you were a Negro you had to sit at the back of the bus, wait at the back of the line. Now they're sending soldiers over to Vietnam, everyone's like: 'Oh, no, please, you Negroes go first.' See, I think Negroes are going to make real good soldiers in Vietnam. We're going to get sent to a strange place where we're hated and people want to kill us for no good reason. For us, that's like another day in Birmingham, Alabama. I'm not even sure if there's any fighting going on over in Vietnam. I think Governor Wallace finally figured a way around integration: 'Now, yew Negroes jus' git on this heyah boat, 'n' sail away . . . we all come 'n' git ya later.'"

People didn't laugh. The hell they didn't. People screamed. People screamed and they screamed in waves. That hip, smart, New York audience had never seen, never heard, never conjured up anything like me, a young black man not talking about his mother-in-law or the last crazy date he went on—cooning with himself. I was taking the stage full of confidence, making a stand. Standing up for myself, my people. I was joking with a point of view. I had a perspective.

I had a voice.

I hit one bit—won't pick cotton from a bottle of aspirin—and I had to stop dead for all the cheering and clapping. I had to wait for the audience to clap themselves out.

In my mind I started cutting jokes, fearing I'd run three minutes long over my original five.

Five minutes.

And I filled them. I filled them until they burst. If there was a smoother comic, you tell me who. If there was a funnier man alive, you give me his name. For those five minutes I was fresh and sharp and dangerous. The best I'd ever been. As good as I would ever be.

And no one outside that studio would ever see or hear a word I said.

〰

I THINK THEY WERE READY FOR ME. After my little show at rehearsal, despite my promises otherwise, they were ready for Jackie Mann to go off the page. Or maybe, being live television, they were always ready for anything. But there must have been someone somewhere with his finger over the kill switch. As soon as I started my first bit, just as soon as I started talking about being black, the switch got thrown. I got cut off. Most of the country saw five minutes of PLEASE STAND BY.

For the West Coast rebroadcast a bike-riding bear from the Moscow circus got edited in to fill my time.

Then they really let me have it.

Ed Sullivan, pious, upstanding Ed Sullivan, cut into me with a buzz saw of language that would make drunken sailors bleed from the ears. Ed demanded to know what the "ef" I was thinking, let me know what an "effer" I was, how badly I'd "effed" up, and how badly I would be effed now that I had effed him. He was slightly more incoherent, very inconcise, ranting at a fever pitch, but that was basically what he said.

And Ed was a man of his word. I was plenty effed. He put the word out and put the word out good: Jackie Mann was a lunatic of a comic, liable to go off on a filth rant on live television. Book him at your own risk.

In the early 1960s that was a risk no one wanted to take.

Chet, feeling betrayed, feeling the heat from Abe Lastfogel, who was feeling the heat from Ed, threw the first shovelful of dirt on the rest of my career. I had a two-year contract with William Morris. William Morris wouldn't book me anywhere. Not in any of the good clubs. Dives, Village cellars, they let me work those. Let me. But for two years any joint that had more audience members than roaches crawling in the bathroom wasn't allowed to hire Jackie Mann to do their dishes.

I had nowhere to turn, no angels to save me. I'd burned my favors and my bridges with Frank C. He wouldn't lift a manicured finger to help me. Same with Frank S once our agency, William Morris, hipped him to their version of the truth of Jackie Mann. For a guy who always played so big in the gossip columns, Frank was incredibly ready to swallow the slime he was spoon-fed about other people. Smoky? Sammy made little efforts to set things straight, a phone call here and there. A promise to help me same as I'd helped him out a couple of years prior.

I'd helped him out by selling him out.

I hated to think how he would help me.

Frances called.

No doubt she'd heard the real deal concerning the Sullivan show. Around then her TV show was losing steam, but Frances still had juice and connections. Frances could still jump-start my career. So she called. She called and called. I dodged every one of them. Not for a second did I even consider letting her burn off what was left of her career by helping her best and dearest and oldest friend who'd shown his fidelity by giving her a slap to the face.

Sid tried getting in touch, too. He got about as close to talking to me as Frances did.

Tammi never tried to call. I don't think she did. Anyway, I never heard from her. Not directly. But she was heard from. Teaming up with Marvin Gaye, Tammi finally broke and broke big like I always knew she would. Hit records came pouring out of the pair. "Ain't No Mountain High Enough," "If I Could Build My Whole World Around You," "Ain't Nothing Like the Real Thing."

"You're All I Need."

I fell apart the first time I heard that song. Tammi never sounded more lovely, she had never expressed more passion and emotion. Her voice, always her gift, always able to make you feel what she felt, made me feel love. It made me feel, again, the hole in my soul that was beyond healing.

In 1967 during a concert at Hampden-Sydney College in Virginia, just as she was ending "Your Precious Love," Tammi collapsed onstage. They got her to a hospital. Diagnosis: brain tumor.

Three years.

Three years of wasting away, dropping nearly forty pounds from her tiny frame, loss of memory and muscle control. Three years with eight operations in eighteen months. Three years of trying to record again but being so busted up, another chick had to lay down Tammi's vocals on the last songs to bear her name.

March 16, 1970. Tammi Terrell, Thomasina Montgomery, died in Philadelphia. Three years of suffering ended that day.

After she was gone, my thoughts went to our arguments, those times, those many times, Tammi would clutch her head hurting from the nonsense I force-fed her. And then my thoughts went to my father and the way he worked my mother to her death. And then my thoughts said to me: The apple really doesn't fall very far from the tree, does it?

My years of loss had begun.

They began with me not being able to say good-bye to Tammi. By the time I found out about her illness, kept hidden from the public, which was all that I constituted to Tammi, she was already gone. I considered going to the funeral.

I figured, who'd want me there?

I didn't make the trip.

My loss of Frances as a friend remained constant. Though she tried, my shame kept us from ever speaking again. An interested but uninvolved observer, I watched Frances pass through her life. Eventually her TV show got tired, then canceled. Her records stopped selling. She had a couple of parts in some movies but never really took to the big screen. Her career went real cool, but it sort of didn't matter. Frances had made some good money over the years and had been smart with it. Smart as in banking most of it, and what she didn't bank she used to buy up land near Santa Barbara. A lot of land. By the time showbiz was through with her, she was equally through with showbiz, no longer needing the work. But Frances had always come across as sweet and sincere, as being a decent person. She'd come off that way because that's the way she was. So, naturally, big fat corporations wanted sweet, sincere Frances to peddle their wares. She did, did their commercials, and people loved her for just that, selling stuff. Some never knew her as anything but a pitchwoman, but that and her personality were enough to revive her some, get her a morning talk show that ran for another bunch of years, and when that folded Fran pretty much finally, officially retired. Other than the old-school Hollywood parties she occasions, once a year she makes an appearance at a golf tournament the big fat corporation she shilled for sponsors and named after her. I'm not even sure if Fran golfs.

Li'l Mo, Morris, was killed along with Fred Hampton in a police raid on a Black Panther house in Chicago in 1969. The cops, busting in in the middle of the night, fired over one hundred shots. Morris fired none. He was unarmed.

Frank Costello went in 1973. Unlike most mob bosses, he got to go unassisted. Bobbie buried him in a silk suit. Dapper to the end.

Liliah eventually got bored with movies and left Hollywood, left America, and ran off to marry some prince or sultan or emir or some kind of guy who was rich in that way. Eventually she got bored with him and ran off with a guy who sailed boats for a living. After that me and the rest of the world got tired of tracking her mood swings and allowed Liliah to fade away.

Sammy Davis went on being a big star, then not such a big star, then just a legend for sexing white chicks and hugging Nixon. He was a legend for being a hell of an entertainer, too, but somehow that became secondary to sexing white chicks and hugging Nixon. Ultimately all those years of smoking finally got Smoky. Throat cancer. Before Sammy Davis went Big Casino, when he was thin and ravaged and surgery had left him with just a whisper of his old, digable voice, Hollywood started in with the star-studded tributes and awards and honors they heap on their dying stars: "We're going to miss you, pal. Here's a plaque; thanks for the dances." After he was gone, there came a slew of testimonials from the new black Hollywood, the young black Hollywood on what a talent Sammy was, and how he was the Jackie Robinson of showbiz and if it weren't for Sammy hanging with white cats and staying in white hotels and dating up white starlets and doing whatever the hell he pleased, doing all those things he got nothing but heat for from the black community, where would "we" be now?

Funny . . . not really funny. Sad. It was sad. Sammy finally had the respect he'd spent his whole life chasing, and all he had to do to get it was die.

Finally, Sinatra. Eight plus decades he spent living, more than five of them as *the* celebrity among celebrities. We listened to his records, saw his movies, read every gossip piece—right or wrong, good or bad—ever planted about him. But I think if Frank had lived ten times ten decades more, we never would've known the guy. He moved with the same swinging style among princes, presidents, pimps, and mobsters. He would hug you one second and get just the same amount of joy from crushing you the very next. But with Frank you took that. You took it all, because if he were just one part of one percent any different, then he wouldn't be Sinatra. And at the end of the day being Sinatra was the only thing Frank was about. There may be better singers, it wouldn't take much to be a better actor, there are some cats who were bigger personalities, but I don't think, ever again, anyone will so comfortably and completely fulfill the occupation of star the way Francis Albert Sinatra did.

I returned from my exile by Ed Sullivan and the Morris agency, but I never recovered from it. The two years I was out of things might as well have been a hundred. Clubs, the big showcase clubs, were shutting down on a regular basis. Ciro's, the Copacabana, mighty as they once where, couldn't beat back eventual death. The crowds were gone. The living room was a much more convenient place to get your entertainment. The nightclub's crooner-and-cocktail style was self-parody in the new world.

The new world was a place were presidents got blown away and so did their brothers and so did civil rights leaders on a schedule. Wars got fought on the nightly news and in the streets and on college campuses and just about everywhere except in the war zones. There was protesting and race mixing and free love, quiet rage and generational discord.

And people talked about it. Comics joked about it. You were tired and corny and out of step if you didn't.

By the time I got back into things, the voice I'd found that night on the Sullivan show was no longer unique, just one more among many. Worse than a has-been, I was a never-was.

But I kept working, kept taking whatever stage time I could book because . . . I don't know why because. Because at first I had a glimmer of hope that I could still find a new voice, cut through the noise and get myself back to the top of the heap. But when that dream finally croaked, I took stage time just because I didn't know what else to do with myself. In the shrinking venues and diminishing crowds there were still, at least, some familiar faces, people who passed as acquaintances. It was a weak pantomime of life, without friends, family, or possibilities, as far from any existence I had ever wanted. And maybe very close to being what I deserved.

These days

ate nights again. Going onstage, trying to pry laughs from a handful of drunks. Again. No strippers. Not anymore. Just me and the drunks and thirty years' time separating where I started and where I ended up.

Thirty years.

In that time I'd collected age and wrinkles, an apartment that once was a symbol of my moving up and moving on but was now just rent-controlled and affordable. And late-night comedy spots. Those I had. Again.

One of those late nights/early mornings at a West Side club I ran into a comic I'd known for a long time in passing. Like me, he was a guy who was well past his prime. We got along okay. With all the new faces, the fresh faces, constantly popping up in comedy clubs, being a couple of older guys made friends of us.

After our sets, at a bar, we sat over some drinks, swapping old-days stories, traded information about this club booker or that who would still toss a maturing act some dates. Age didn't make it any easier to get work. Didn't matter what your act was like, it was the young who were hip. It was the young who got booked.

And then the other guy lamented that he'd been working with Sid for a while, but really had to scramble for work since he'd died.

I made a little noise, a little gasp as my breath choked out.

The other comic: "You didn't know?"

No. I didn't know. I'd figured. Sid wasn't a young man the day

I'd met him. It'd been nearly twenty years since I'd last talked to him. So, I didn't know, but I'd figured. But hearing it, hearing that Sid was gone . . .

The comic gave a couple of sketchy details. It was a few years back. Peaceful. He went in his sleep. The comic saw my expression to all that, asked me if I was okay.

No, but I said sure, I was fine. I begged off another drink, wishing the comic well.

I went back to my apartment.

I did some thinking.

What I came up with was that I had to do . . . something. Maybe it was too late to do anything, but Sid had died, and no matter the years, no matter how long it had been since we'd so much as spoken, I knew that I couldn't let him pass without doing . . . something.

His brother. Sid had a brother. I did some poking around, people who used to know Sid. Got a phone number. A retirement home. Made a call. No good. Sid's brother had died as well.

His brother's daughter. Sid had a niece. Some pleading. Some begging. Some rule breaking. Some woman at the retirement home gave me the niece's name and number.

I made a call.

"Hello?"

"May I speak with Allison Wallach?"

"This is Allison."

"I'm very sorry to bother you, and I don't mean . . . My name is Jackie Mann. I was a friend of your uncle's. We hadn't talked in a while. I guess it had been a long while. I just now heard of his passing, and I wanted to . . ." I took a beat. "Your uncle was a real fine man. He was . . . I just wanted to let someone know that he would be missed."

A pause.

"Jackie Mann?"

"Yes."

"Are you in the city?"

". . . Yes, I am."

"Would it be possible for us to meet sometime? I have something that I need to . . . that I would like to give to you."

Something . . .

Yes. I told Allison that, yes, it would be very possible for us to meet. That I would like that very much. I suggested the following day, but she thought the sooner the better. We set a time for that evening.

A coffee shop in the Village. Not like back in the day. Not a place for poets and artists and beats. A chain joint with fifty variations of Folgers, and wannabe actors hanging around complaining about the state of their non-lives.

I recognized Allison the moment she walked in. She was a handsome woman, maybe just shy of forty. Maturity looked good on her. But what made her recognizable was something in her eyes, some of Sid.

We traded hellos. We sat at a table, and for a moment we said nothing to each other. What was there to say? Two strangers who had only the dead in common. Then from the pocket of her coat Allison took a legal-sized envelope. Bent, discolored, it looked years old.

"Before Uncle Sid died, he gave this to my father, told him to keep it safe and told it to him in a way that made him know it was important. The same way my father told me before he died. I guess my uncle knew . . . at least he always hoped you would get in touch one day."

Allison held out the envelope. Written on it was one word in Sid's scrawl: Jackie.

I took it. I opened it. Inside, a letter:

Jackie,

My hope is that you will never read this letter, that the things I want to say to you I will be able to say face-to-face.

But, if that's not the case, then this letter will have to do my talking for me.

Jackie, I can't tell you how badly I wanted to be there for you the night of your Sullivan appearance. I know how important that show was to you, to your career, and after all we'd been through together, even from the shadows, I wanted to share your night with you. But it was *your* night. I thought better to just leave it alone. Instead, I watched the show from the apartment. When you were cut off, I was stunned and angry about the dumb luck that would bring about some technical problem at the top of your set after all you'd done to get where you were. Then I was kind of happy for you. I knew Sullivan would re-book you, and the glitch was sure to get you some press. Only, they didn't re-book you, and you didn't get any press, and I couldn't figure out what in the hell was going on.

I asked around. I found out.

I don't know what the circumstances were, I don't know why you picked that moment out of so many opportunities, but, Jackie, I can't tell you how proud I am of you for doing the "San Francisco" set. The way I hear it, you were terrific—poised, in control, and funny. You were the comic I always knew you could be. I see where comedy, where the country, has gone in the last decade or so, and I think: Where would Jackie be now if some guy hadn't pressed a button and erased his jokes from history? But if you ever wonder if you did the right thing or not, if it would've been better to do some other bits than get tossed aside, quit wondering. You stood up for yourself, Jackie. You did what you had every right to do. You were your own man, and at the end of the day they can take every other thing away from you, but they can't take from you who you are: a funny comic, and an exceptional person. Thank you, Jackie.

Thank you for having let me represent you. And thank you for having been my friend.

Sid.

By the time I'd gotten to the "my friend," and the signature, a steady leak of tears was running down my face, dripping on the paper. I tried to play my crying off, just sort of rub away the wetness. You can't rub away a river. I quit trying. I broke down. I buried my face in my hands and my hands on the tabletop; the whole of it shook with sobbing. Over my own sucked and heaved breaths I could hear the whisper of people who watched my remorse act. Let them whisper. I was saying good-bye to a friend.

I felt a hand on my back. Allison. I heard her voice in my ears. A mourner's Kaddish, a prayer of both strength and forgiveness. In Hebrew, I understood none of it. But her touch, her sound, it sent my crying into overdrive. She sat with me until I had emptied myself.

Allison asked me if I was all right.

Guilt, over time, had compounded in me. It crushed me with a weight I could hardly bear, but couldn't purge. Sid's letter freed me of all that. The load gone, I felt as if, for the first time in nearly twenty years, I could take a breath blameless, deep and clean.

I told Allison yes, I was fine.

"It was very good to have met you, Jackie. Take care."

Allison left me.

Very, very carefully folding Sid's letter, I put it back into the envelope and the envelope into my pocket.

After a time I flagged a waitress and ordered some cheesecake with strawberries. The waitress brought me cheesecake. No strawberries. Whipped cream. Politely, I sent it back and had her bring me what I'd asked for.

I WORK SOME, STILL. When there's work to be had. The comedy boom that started in the eighties—a club in every strip mall, a stand-up show on every cable channel—went bust by the early nineties. The art itself, and I'll call it an art, had gone full circle. Comedians had stopped setting fires and were almost to a man as uninhibited as store-bought mayonnaise, having have-you-ever-noticed themselves out of relevance. That, or they demonstrated an acute ability to slyly, deftly, comment on the state of society by swearing over and over and over again for no good reason except that they could.

Be real still. You can hear the gyrations coming from Lenny's grave.

Anyway.

The venues that are left have little to no use for an old man, his time long gone, cluttering up their stage.

. . . But there are casinos.

America is gamble crazy, and there are casinos everywhere now. Theme casinos, Indian casinos, riverboat casinos. And every casino has a lounge, and every lounge needs an act. A guy of my years who's got roots in Golden Age Vegas; I can pull a decent audience—most times my age or even a little older, trying to relive the past. Sometimes younger, kids who want to soak up the "Rat Pack" vibe wherever they can find it, any way they can find it: sipping highballs and martinis, smoking cigars, but not knowing those were just the extras that guys like Frank, Sammy, and Dino accessorized themselves with. For The Summit, cool was a state of being.

Whatever.

I work. I do my shows like always. Like always, but, post Sid's letter, different from before. Before, being onstage had always been about getting ahead, getting over, being famous. Being someone. It was a means to an end. Nothing more.

Now . . .

Now it's about the simplest of things, what it should have always been about but never was, using the little gift God gave me to give people a good time. Make people laugh.

So I do that now. Ten people, a hundred; I go up onstage and enjoy the moment. Most times the shows are good. Usually entertaining. And sometimes, for whatever reason, because I'm hitting a groove, or maybe the audience is on my wavelength, or maybe it's a combo of those and a thousand other things starting with a butterfly flapping a wing over in China, sometimes I'm on. I'm really on. The jokes are just as crisp and the laughs are coming just as strong as anytime I ever played the Sands, the Copa, or Ciro's. Sometimes I'll say a line, and like back in the day, I'll have to stop and stand and wait for the audience to finish wringing every last laugh they can out of themselves. And somewhere married up with their laughter and applause . . .

You can say I'm corny. You can say I'm just a sentimental old man. In my day I've been called everything there is, so you want to call me names, go on. See how much I care. But somewhere in the laughter and applause I hear my mother's voice saying to me like she was right there beside me: "You're a special one, Jackie Mann. Don't let nobody ever tell you otherwise."

Maybe age has just made me comfortable with myself, but after all these years, what that voice is telling me, I'm finally starting to believe.

In memory
of
Etta Jennings